QUEEN'S CRUSADE

THEIR VAMPIRE QUEEN RETURNS
BOOK 1

JOELY SUE BURKHART

QUEEN'S CRUSADE
THEIR VAMPIRE QUEEN RETURNS

Shara Isador's back for justice... and Blood.

Her first match with the queen of Rome might have temporarily ended in a draw, but she has plenty of other battles brewing. Taking her seat at the Triskeles Triune brings immense new power to House Isador.

And for a vampire queen, with great power comes great *hunger.*

To sustain and feed her new power, she needs more Blood. Desperately. Before the Dauphine can attack her nest again.

She already turned Shara's dead mother into a walking zombie to send a nasty message. Now it's her turn to send a message to the Dauphine—and anyone who messes with her family. In the brutal game of queens, Shara plays for love.

What this queen takes, she loves, and what she loves, she keeps for all time.

Don't mess with her loved ones. Because she will protect them. No matter the cost.

The Dauphine can't escape this time.

House Isador rides to war, and the last Templar knight

carries Shara Isador on the greatest crusade this world has ever known.

For my Beloved Sis.

Thank you to Sherri Meyer
for all your help and late night edits!

Special thanks to Sleep Token.
Your songs speak to my soul. Thank you for inspiring Vore's character!

Thank you to the following people for recommending songs for the
Their Vampire Queen playlist:

Cheyenne Boatman for "You've Created a Monster" by Bohnes

Stella Price for "Vivien" by Crosses

Miranda Vaughn for "Begging to Bleed" by 8 Graves and "Champion"
by Neoni, burnboy

1

SHARA

I 'm going to need bigger Blood.

Sitting behind me in our favorite chair, Rik didn't move so much as swell around me, muscles pumping up with blood so fast that his pants split open over his massive thighs. "Excuse me?"

I licked my bite in Mehen's throat and lifted my head. The king of the depths sagged against my knees and then slowly slipped to the floor with a sleepy draconic grumble. One of the oldest and most powerful living Aima kings—drained into a stupor.

"I don't mean a *singular* Blood but a larger group of Blood. Besides, no one's bigger than you, my alpha."

"Finally." Guillaume rolled Mehen aside so he could drop to his knees before me. "I didn't know how much longer I should wait before bringing the matter to your attention. My queen tends to ignore and suppress messages her own body sends."

With a wry smile, I reached out and took his hand in mine, stroking my fingers over his knuckles. When the last Templar knight had first come to my side in Kansas City, every single finger had been warped and twisted, broken countless times during the long torture he'd endured. Now well fed on my blood, his fingers were straight and strong, though his palm still bore the calluses from his sword. "You should always bring concerns to my attention. I kept telling myself that I only needed to rest."

I blew out a sigh. Ever since I came home nearly a month ago from helping Helayna save her nest, I hadn't felt... right. Thin and hollowed out—no matter how long and well I fed from each of my Blood.

My dragon wasn't the only Blood passed out around me. Ezra snored like a buzz saw on the couch. Curled around Rik's thick calf, Daire had his head on my right foot, sleeping so soundly that he didn't purr or budge, even though Mehen now lay on his long hair. Itztli and Tlacel slept back-to-back in front of the fireplace, and Nevarre used Itztli's thigh for a pillow.

Blood rarely slept. They didn't need that down time for their bodies to recover when well fed by their queen.

Unless she was draining them to the brink.

I didn't regret answering Helayna's request for assistance, but it'd been a close call. Closer than I cared to admit. By the time we traveled to her nest, everything except a few trees and her cabin had been destroyed by a massive hurricane of sunfires, driven by a Sepdet, one of Ra's descendants. I'd held them off until Karmen Sunna had returned with her own Blood and called the sunfires to her side. A difficult task for sure, but certainly not more than a Triune-level queen could handle. At least that's what I told myself, confident in the sheer raw power I'd gained by resurrecting the Triskeles Triune after hundreds of years. If Karmen could control the sunfires, then surely I could hold them off until she arrived. Right?

Wrong. I might as well have tried to hold a supermassive black hole in the palm of my hand. I wasn't called to handle solar magic. My greatest magic was accomplished in complete darkness, not the burning light of day. That mistake had almost cost House Ironheart their nest and might have irreparably damaged my own power.

It'd shaken me. For the first time since I stepped into my power as a vampire queen, I'd drawn hard on my own gifts, expecting power to flood me like a bottomless ocean. Instead, I'd barely managed to pull a trickle more beyond my normal power.

My arrogance made me fucking sick. I stood against the queen of Rome and played her games without bowing to her will. Yet a bunch of sunfires nearly burned me out. How could I even begin to hold my seat at the Triune?

Vivian's sunfire, Smoak, blazed in her bond. *:Even the god of light struggled to contain them, my queen, and he was the one who imprisoned them in the first place.:*

Guillaume lifted my hand to his mouth and rubbed his lips across my knuckles. "You know the answer to that question, Your Majesty."

He wasn't one to use formality lightly, not after everything we'd been through. Power flowed through me like a midnight ocean. Rippling rivers wrapped around each of my Blood, pulling them to me. Binding us together. Forever. They were still bound to me, as I was bound to them. But now I knew that seemingly infinite ocean had limits that I'd never encountered before.

His head cocked to the side, blue eyes surprisingly light and teasing. "Does it, though? Or do you simply need more Blood?"

"I pulled on my power until I strained, and there was nothing left," I whispered, inwardly cringing with shame. "It felt like an empty, bone-dry well. If Karmen hadn't come when she did, I might have ended up killing one of you."

Rik shrugged. "So be it. You would have resurrected us anyway."

I scrambled around in his lap so I could see his face, though I didn't let go of Guillaume's hand. "No. I would never forgive myself. And what if I'd burned myself out and destroyed my gift? Then I wouldn't have been able to bring you back. You would have been gone."

My voice cracked, my throat aching. I'd done it once already. Sometimes the guilt still bubbled up inside me like a giant vat of acid that I would never forgive. "I've made so many fucking mistakes."

"You haven't made a single mistake." Rik didn't raise his voice, but his tone deepened to an earth-rumbling quake. "Our queen is always right."

No. That wasn't true. Though I didn't have the heart to argue with him. Not with words.

Instead, I allowed scenes to play out in my mind. All the things I regretted. Like accepting Coatlicue's red snake to make the mighty god of light mortal—even when the goddess required one of my loved one's death. Chopping off my beloved Templar knight's head in Heliopolis to buy myself time to get closer to Ra. Yes, Guillaume was known as the headless knight for a reason. But that didn't mean I wanted to see his head severed from his body by my own hand.

Sure, we could argue until the end of time that I had no choice. I'd done what needed to be done to win—to protect us all. I didn't feel any better.

Even more frustrating were the "wins" that didn't feel like wins at all. The times my hands were tied behind my back by Triune law and custom.

Like having to sit across from Marne Ceresa and sip tea and pretend we weren't trapped like fat flies in her web. Or playing her against the Dauphine instead of razing the New Orleans queen's house to the ground myself. Settling for subtle, polite, legal jabs rather than all-out war for justice left a bitter taste in my mouth not even the taste of my beloved Blood could wipe away.

I want my fucking justice.

What good is all this power if I can't do anything with it but desperately try to protect the ones I love from even further harm?

"The game of queens is the hardest game of all," Guillaume said. "You may not think so, but you've played an impressive game so far."

My throat ached but the greater pain was in my heart. Shredded, sliced, and ground into hamburger at the thought of losing any of my Blood.

What this queen takes, she loves, and what she loves, she keeps for all time.

Those words echoed through my head. My words. When I'd been a new, naïve queen. When I didn't know everything I'd built could be destroyed in the blink of an eye.

"You felt this way before, remember?" Sliding his hand up beneath my hair, Rik cupped the back of my head in his big palm and kissed my forehead. "When you called Vivian, everyone was passed out and you still needed more. Okeanos bought you a little time, but then you ascended to Triskeles. It's no wonder you need more Blood."

"There's a reason powerful queens have dozens or even a hundred Blood," Guillaume said. "You leveled up. You need a broader base to support—and continue—that growth."

"But..." I burrowed deeper into Rik's arms, pressing my nose into his neck. Rock and iron, hot from the forge. His scent made hunger stab through me, even though I'd fed from him already this morning.

He rested his chin on the top of my head. "I know. I do. I don't want things to change either. It pains me to admit it, but you need more than we can currently provide."

I loved my Blood with my whole being. If anything ever happened to one of them that I couldn't heal, I'd never fully recover. I'd always feel their broken bond like a phantom limb's debilitating agony the rest of my life. It was more than the blood we shared. Even more than the pleasure.

Our souls mingled together, creating something bigger and more magical than anything this world had ever seen.

"Exactly as our goddesses intended." Llewellyn hovered over G's shoulder simply because there wasn't more room at my feet for him to crowd closer. "And your mother."

Once my mother's former Blood, Llewellyn was mated to House Isador. He knew Esetta Isador better than anyone. Yet even as her alpha, he didn't know everything. My mother had been very good at keeping secrets. She hadn't wanted anyone to know of my birth so I could grow into my power free and unrestrained.

Though deep inside me, there was still a little girl who longed to lay my head on her chest and feel her fingers stroking my hair as she told me how much she loved me.

"She loved you decades before she ever managed to conceive you." Llewellyn's red-gold eyes sparkled with falling stars, burning with his gift. "I can show you countless scenes where we planned for your future."

"Was it like this with her? The Blood bond, I mean. Did it feel so..." I couldn't even think of the appropriate words to describe it. Deeper than the deepest ocean. Higher than the highest mountain. More infinite than the farthest realm of space. Yet also so tight and close and perfect. Bringing another person—or people—into our special relationship might unravel everything. Drama, jealousy, fears...

"Yes and no," Llewellyn replied. "I loved her with my whole being, the same as I love you. I cared about her other Blood, but most of us were more distant. She used us as individual weapons and often sent us out into the world on secret assignments. We were only rarely all together, and even then, we weren't as connected. We couldn't be. We each held our queen's secrets, which kept us from ever forming bonds as deeply as yours."

I kept no secrets from my Blood. I didn't think I could even if I wanted or needed to. I barely had a thought cross my mind, and they leapt into action to complete the task before it even registered fully in my head. I certainly wouldn't send any of my Blood away for any length of time. The thought made my nerves itch and burn throughout my entire body. "What kind of assignments?"

"Mostly reconnaissance to other courts, carrying private messages to Isador's many allies. All of us were sent away in the end." His voice cracked ever so slightly, though his eyes burned red-hot.

The end. Before my mother broke her bonds so she could slip away and conceive me without anyone knowing. "I thought Blood went insane without their queen's bond and turned into thralls."

Thralls were the monsters that had hunted me my whole life. They'd killed my adoptive human father and Mom, Selena Isador, the woman who raised me. Though later I learned she was actually my aunt. Her former Blood, Greyson, had been determined to be Blood again—though he killed her when he tried to resurrect that bond.

Llewellyn gave me a small shrug, his lips quirked. "Weaker-willed Blood than those called by House Isador to serve. Thank the goddess, your mother didn't call her blood back before she sent us away. Knowing I still carried Isador blood helped me hold on until you came to the tower and set me free."

"What happened to the rest of her Blood?"

His head cocked, his eyes sharp like a hawk. "Keisha Skye told me they'd all turned thrall and died, but I never believed it. Your mother whispered orders to each of us before she broke the bonds. They may have died in the years since she passed but I believe they're still out there waiting."

"Where? Waiting for what?"

He blinked, the falling stars in his eyes burning out into complete darkness. "For you, my queen."

2

LLEWELLYN

I couldn't say her name. All I could do was bring up my former queen's face in my mind. Her image forever etched in countless memories held in my internal databases. *"I understand now."*

Fingertips ghosted over my nape like delicate spider webs, gone so quickly I could almost convince myself it hadn't happened at all. But I knew she was still here with the daughter she'd given up everything to have.

I'd loved her like the night loves the dawn. Admiring the way the sky lightened each morning, even as her glory destroyed me. Brief moments where we'd existed at the same time, bleeding away all too quickly into the harsh light of day. Duty and service to House Isador made up most of the hundreds of years of my existence, with only a precious few nights where she was wholly mine to hold. Even then, she'd never been so open with her affections. I knew she loved me. She loved all her Blood. But open, raw emotion would make her vulnerable, which was one word that could never be used to describe my former queen.

But Shara would burn down the world to save one of us.

To save *me*. Again.

"She sent them to the other powerful houses, didn't she." Shara's eyes flared wide, the deepest velvet midnight sky dotted with sparkling diamonds of starlight. "But the risk! Goddess. I can't see Marne Ceresa accepting an Isador Blood into her court."

"It's not uncommon for powerful queens to exchange Blood," Guillaume said.

She grimaced. "I don't want spies in my house, let alone my bed."

The knight shrugged slightly, and a short silver blade dropped into his palm. "Spies are also weapons, my queen."

Her jaw flexed, her eyes glittering with the cutting brilliance of diamonds. "I won't send you into another queen's court to kill them. I'm not her."

Rik grunted with agreement. "We definitely don't need any other queen's weapons in our court."

Though our alpha was massive enough I had no doubt he'd swat away any inside attempt to attack our queen like a puny gnat.

"What do you think?" Shara asked, gazing back at me evenly.

I tried to suppress my surprise, but I don't think I succeeded by the narrowing of her eyes. "Me? As our alpha already said—"

"I didn't ask what Rik thinks," she cut in, though she dropped a hand to soothingly pat his thick thigh. "I asked what my mother's former alpha thinks about Guillaume's suggestion."

I hadn't allowed myself to think as an alpha since coming to Shara's court. It wasn't my place. Rik did a passable job despite his youth, and when he hesitated, he had the last Templar knight's experience to draw upon. Guillaume never hesitated to contribute his wealth of wisdom gained after centuries of service to Desideria, who'd consolidated an immense amount of power during her long Triune reign.

Which was the point of contention here and now.

Rik thought like a young alpha in love with his even

younger, extremely powerful queen. He didn't think like a Triune queen's alpha. I didn't doubt he'd be brutal and merciless to anyone who dared threaten our queen's life, but in the game of queens...

"G's right," I replied softly, keeping my gaze lowered from Rik's so he didn't bristle with challenge. "He's only here because your mother freed him, and she never did anything without a very well-thought-out and deliberate reason. At great cost, I will add."

Shara's head cocked slightly. "What cost? I know she died to have me, but I don't think we've ever talked about her paying any kind of debt because she indirectly killed Desideria."

"I can't speak to the cost your mother might have paid, but it didn't matter whether Desideria's death was indirect or direct," Guillaume said. "Your mother poisoned my blood with her cobra queen, knowing Desideria would die as a result. When any queen dies, you risk stirring her goddess' wrath, but especially a Triune-level queen."

Shara leaned forward, searching my eyes. Her hand cupped my cheek. "Do you have a memory you can show me about what happened to my mother after she killed Desideria?"

Slowly, I shook my head, regret tightening my chest. "I do not, my queen. Her Blood weren't privy to the recompense put upon her by the goddesses, and I wasn't present when she freed G. I can only tell you what I suspect."

Even though she nodded encouragingly, I still hesitated. I loathed the thought I might cause harm to my young queen's tender, precious heart. "I would say for the most part, none of us noticed any change in our queen, other than a huge increase of power. Not unexpected since she killed one of the most powerful queens to ever walk this earth, and those powers came to her. At the time, I thought she was making a direct play for the Triune herself, but decades passed without her even speaking to Marne Ceresa or any other queen, for that matter.

Again, I thought keeping those new powers hidden was part of her long play for the Triune. No one could know she was the one who killed Desideria until she was ready.

"She retreated to her library in New York City for long periods of time. Researching her new powers, so I thought. Or learning how to manage Desideria's gifts she'd inherited. But no. She never used any new powers she gained from House Modron. I think..." I exhaled heavily. "I think she was trying to find a way around whatever agreement she'd come to with the goddesses, but in the end, even she couldn't find a way to bypass their decree."

A shattered look flickered through Shara's eyes. Cuts of lightning to rend and destroy.

Steeling myself, I continued. "She already planned to sacrifice herself in order to generate the kind of power it would take to conceive you. To break you free of the other queens and their plans. That didn't change. But I don't believe she expected to be lost from collective memory. For you, her beloved child she'd given up everything to have, would grow up never knowing her. Let alone what she'd done for you. There could be no guarantee you'd ever even know her true name, since no one living could say it aloud. That, I believe, was the ultimate cost she paid to Desideria's goddess."

"Goddesses, plural," Guillaume added. "She used Modron to honor the Celtic fertility goddess, which was only one aspect of her power. She was descended from the triple goddesses, the Matres and Matronae."

Shara didn't cry, but the pained look still crackled in her dark eyes as she turned to the knight. "Three goddesses? I didn't know that was possible."

"She was well blessed." Though the curl of G's lip indicated his disgust at the things his queen had forced him to do. "Modron and Her sisters definitely demanded justice for her death."

"But she killed dozens of other queens," Shara protested. "She forced you to go into nests and kill everyone inside. Hundreds of people. Right?"

The knight clenched scarred fingers around the slim blade in his hand. "Thousands, my queen. Desideria amassed such power that even if a goddess exacted retribution, it was negligible. She was so powerful no one could stand against her."

"No one but your mother," I whispered softly. "For you. No matter the cost."

$\sim$

SHARA

I'D KILLED A POWERFUL QUEEN—KEISHA SKYE IN NEW YORK City. I'd taken over her nest completely. What recompense had her goddess demanded of me? Wouldn't I know?

A tumultuous mix of regret and guilt rushed through me, making it hard to breathe. The memory of her death surged through my mind. Xin materializing behind her on the dais, pinning her in his arms. Holding her still for me. I'd struck hard with my cobra-like fangs, drinking her down.

I drank a powerful queen. To death. Her blood. Her power.

The thundering winds of a hurricane. A million volts of lightning, like the flash in her court earlier when she'd tried to strike me down.

In that moment, I'd made the deliberate choice to kill her, rather than pull her back from the grave. I could have made her my sibling and forced her to her knees in her own tower in front of her entire court. Instead, I'd chosen retribution. For all the alphas she'd killed. For the pain she'd caused Rik and Ezra to suffer in her daughter's tainted blood circle.

What cost did I pay for taking Scáthach's daughter's life?

The clang of metal on metal rattled through my head. Screams. War chants. Pounding drums. Heavy grunts of effort, sweaty bodies straining against each other. The dead littered the rocky ground, the sickly-sweet smell of rotten death thick in the air. Ravens cawed, hopping from body to body, eating the choicest bits.

:No cost, daughter of the Great One. Death and war go hand in hand for me.:

I blinked, focusing back on my Blood before me.

"Not all goddesses will be as forgiving," Guillaume warned. "The more powerful a queen, the more likely it is for her goddess to demand retribution for her death."

"So if I'd killed Marne instead of enduring that ridiculous tea party…"

He huffed out a sharp, grim laugh. "Without a doubt, Ceres would have stripped you of one of your greatest powers. The cobra queen, for example. The wyvern or winged jaguar. The life of one of your siblings. She'd have made the blow deep and personal to you."

"The child I've seen in your memories," Llewellyn added. "The young princess will be very strong one day with a jaguar god as her father, especially since you named her an Isador heir. What better way to strike a blow against your entire House than demanding the life of your first and currently only heir?"

My stomach churned on Mehen's spicy blood, and I suddenly regretted feeding so deeply without any food in my system. I'd thought the worst thing Marne could do to us would be to simply kill us all. Not leave me alive—with the knowledge I'd brought endless sorrow to Mayte with the loss of her child. Or dishonored my goddess by losing one of Her precious gifts She'd instilled in me.

"Killing us all would have been way too easy, and sometimes you won't have the choice." Guillaume paused, his gaze flick-

on his back, belly exposed. Beside him, Daire was quiet, not even purring or making a smart-ass comment in our bonds.

I didn't know what to say. Their bonds gleamed like hard, bright swords in my mind. Ready to kill. Ready to die.

Especially Rik.

I glided along his bond, listening to his thoughts and absorbing his feelings. He wasn't offended or upset or even jealous. Anger pumped through his veins with every beat of his heart, but he wasn't pissed at me. He was angry at himself. For holding me back.

:You don't—:

:I do,: he snarled before I could complete the thought. *:You're a Triune queen. You need a Triune-level alpha.:*

:You're the alpha I choose. I love you.: Aloud, I repeated the words so they all knew. "I love you, my Blood. Each and every one of you."

Rage pulsed through his bond, cutting deeply like a double-edged sword. "And that love weakens you."

I shrugged. "So be it. I love all of you. I won't ever stop loving you."

Slabs of granite crunched in my mind, crumbling to dust. Rik tipped his head back enough to glare up at me again. "You're destined to be the most powerful Aima queen to walk this earth. You can't—"

"If I can't walk with you by my side, then I don't want to be a queen at all," I broke in.

Guillaume strode back with a plate of all my favorite foods from the kitchen. He bowed low, set the plate on my knees, and backed up a step so he could drop to his knees. There wasn't room between the other Blood and my chair for him to prostrate himself like the others, but I felt his absolute willingness to do so in our bond.

I didn't really want to eat, but my stomach still felt queasy and unsettled. My head ached. Too much turmoil and emotion in a span of minutes. The realization I needed to call more Blood had put me into a tailspin.

"What would you do?" Guillaume asked.

I met his gaze, not sure what he meant.

"If you weren't a queen," he added. "If you walked away from it all."

It could be done. Selena had left everything in London, even her Blood, to be with the human she loved. Alan Dalton had been a father to me. They'd raised me in Kansas City without me knowing a thing about Aima courts or queens or Blood.

Though the monsters had continued to hunt me. I'd slept in a window-less, high room to keep them from getting me at night. Dad and Mom hadn't been able to escape.

I tried to imagine what our lives would be like if I gave up my power. We could keep the house...

But it'd just be a house. A mansion, for sure, but the thick velvety darkness beneath the house would leak away. I wouldn't need a place of darkness for my magic any longer—not that I'd used it yet. The trees. My heart panged at the thought of losing the heart tree, grove, and its grotto. Maybe they'd still be here—as regular, everyday trees. We wouldn't be able to travel anywhere in the world simply by stepping into my heart tree. I wouldn't be able to pass through the grotto to the Deep Blue with Okeanos again. He'd be trapped in a little puddle of water far from the oceans.

If I gave up my power, he wouldn't be able to control his shift. He'd return to the ocean, roaming wild and free, but alone. Always alone.

I'd lose Mehen too. He'd go back to his dragon form. Would he find himself trapped beneath the mountain again, locked outside of time and space? I wouldn't be able to free him again.

The rest of my Blood wouldn't be able to shift at all. They'd lose their beasts. Vivian might lose Smoak, her sunfire.

And they'd do it without question. Simply because I asked them.

Even more, I'd lose the never-ending hunger burning inside me. Despite the delicious smells of creamy scrambled eggs, fresh fruit, and warm, freshly baked bread, I could still smell Guillaume's skin. I stared at the strong column of his throat above the simple white shirt he wore. The beat of his heart on my tongue. My fangs buried deep in him. Taking him. Again. And again. And again.

He let out a warm chuckle, his eyes sparkling like sapphires. "That's what I fucking thought, Your Majesty."

3

RIK

R age crawled through my veins, turning my muscles to heavy stone. The rock troll surged inside me, aching to pound his fists against the floor. The walls. The Ozark mountains surrounding the nest. I'd turn them into a pile of rubble.

I've failed her.

Worse, the only way to correct the problem…

Would be for me to die. She'd never allow me to step down for another alpha of my own free will. She loved me too much.

"I don't need to call more Blood immediately."

The soft, gentle tone of her voice pissed me off even more. All the soothing little touches and the careful way the other Blood avoided prickling my alpha pride. As if I was a toddler who needed constant reassurance that I was needed and loved.

The sound of ripping cloth mocked me. Maybe I was a toddler. I couldn't control myself enough to hold the rock troll back.

"If you don't fill your reserves, you'll lose them." Guillaume picked up the fork on her plate, scooped up some of the eggs, and lifted it to her mouth. "Not to mention the message it sends to other queens. They expect you to call more Blood. If you don't, then you're not stronger. You're inviting an attack before you can build a larger power base. The Triskeles means nothing if you can't hold it."

Such a fucking legend. The last Templar knight, renowned Triune Executioner. Reduced to hand-feeding his queen on his knees. Explaining basic court etiquette to us all because I sure the fuck didn't know either.

"I quite enjoy it," he said lightly without looking over at me. "Believe me when I say I'd have cut my own head off before I'd ever lift a finger to feed Desideria."

Shara let out a long breath ending on a fragile little sigh that twisted my heart into knots. "I don't know what I'm doing, G."

"You know what you need to do. You just need time and space to adjust to the idea."

"The stakes are so fucking high. One wrong move, and we're all fucked."

He huffed out a low sound of amusement that managed to sound like his hell horse even though he was in his human form. "Which isn't necessarily a bad thing, my queen."

She rolled her eyes, but her lips twitched. "At least I feel better about not killing Marne, though I have to admit, I've been thinking about the Dauphine. I didn't have time to deal with her before we received the summons to Rome, and then I had to help Helayna with her nest. I haven't forgotten what that bitch did to Mom, though. The tricks Marne played on her are nothing like I wish I'd done. What if she finds out where Dad's body is buried? Or what if she goes after my human friends?"

"One problem at a time." He fed her another bite. "Let's get your reserves taken care of. Your excellent consiliarius can arrange to have any physical bodies that might have been buried cremated, which will prevent any further manipulation of passed loved ones."

She looked at Llewellyn and he immediately lifted his gaze up to hers, sadly shaking his head. "Forgive me, my queen, but I have no idea what happened to your mother's body. She wouldn't have left anything physical behind, even if she wasn't under a geas. She was too smart to leave so much as a single strand of hair behind."

Shara's head tipped slightly, her eyes flaring with interest. "Her hair. I see it gleaming in your mind like black velvet sprinkled with stardust."

His head tipped back, beams of light blazing from his eyes. An image of Esetta appeared above his head, so clear and perfect that it was like watching a movie. Only better because he was able to play all of his senses for us. Long, thick silken hair hung about her shoulders, down past her waist to the floor. My fingers remembered the sensation of burying into the thick, black mantle. The buzzing tingle of magic creeping up my arms just from touching it.

She smelled like her daughter—blowing desert sands beneath a glittering crescent moon. A secret oasis beside the goddess' pyramid. But Esetta also smelled like sandalwood and spicy incense. Something floral and exotic that I couldn't place.

Blue lotus. He didn't say the word in our Blood bond, but petals tumbled through the vision of Esetta like large, delicate snowflakes.

Worse, we felt the gut-wrenching, piercing agony of her beauty he'd felt every time he looked at her. Knowing what she intended to do.

"She carried her power in her hair," he said hoarsely. "No other queen had hair like her."

Huge silver shears lifted toward her shining hair. Flinching, he closed his eyes, ending the vision before we witnessed her chopping off each shining strand.

"So beautiful," Shara whispered softly. "I wonder how she did it. If I could do the same."

"You are your mother's daughter. Will it to be so."

She sighed again, prompting G to lift another bite to her

mouth. Before she opened her lips, she said ruefully, "I wish you would all rise. I don't like to see you so subservient."

I'd started the impromptu demonstration. No one moved a muscle, waiting on me to decide if I was done proving a point yet.

"Again, my queen, you know exactly what to do."

I waited, flat on my belly. I wanted her to command me to step down. I deserved the shame. The agony of watching another take my place. She needed so much more than me. Other than shutting down her bonds so she could get close to Ra in Heliopolis, she'd never truly forced me to do anything.

She's Triune. She needs to be able to force us into uncomfortable, even horrible situations, without hesitation. Even me.

Especially me.

:Don't you fucking dare wish to be forced from her side.: Llewellyn growled in my head, his gryphon screeching in the bond. *:Or I'll play that memory of my former queen hacking off her hair. What it felt like when she simply disappeared. That torture was worse than anything House Skye managed to do to me.:*

They'd put out his gryphon eyes. Chained, hooded, and bound, he'd been raped.

Yet losing his queen had been worse.

:I don't want to lose her, goddess forbid. But I can't be the reason she fails to step fully into who she's meant to be.:

:You're a fucking idiot,: Mehen retorted. *:Nothing can stop Shara fucking Isador. She's been doing Triune-level shit all along. No other queen managed to free me in thousands of years. I killed them all. Yet here I am, wishing she'd decide to seize my throat in her jaws and take me again.:*

"Rise." Her single word knitted my muscles into action before the word even registered in my head.

On my feet, not my stomach. Not my knees. She didn't say the words, but I felt the compulsion in my bones. Return to my seat. My place. At her back, with her tucked back against my chest between my thighs.

Guillaume fed her another bite once I had her settled again. "What are you afraid of, my queen?"

She swallowed hard, as if the creamy eggs had turned to dust in her mouth. "Failing. Watching you die because I screwed up."

"My queen never fucking fails." Mehen blew out a deep draconic snort of displeasure. "She merely finds another, even more bloodthirsty way to get what she wants. Leviathan hasn't feasted in months, my queen. Allow me to bring justice for House Isador."

"No." Xin stepped closer, his silver wolf flashing in his eyes. "Allow me to kill in your name, my queen. There could be no greater honor."

She allowed the back of her head to rest against my chest. Longing flooded me. The urge to pull her close, wrap her in my strength, and never let her step foot out of our safety. To shield her. Forever. Not just from external threats, but also the turmoil whirling in her mind.

"The only way you fail is to not try at all." Guillaume gave her another bite, a smile playing on his lips. "You have Blood who were bred to be well-honed, brutal weapons. We're meant to be used—and used well—in your service. We're all eager to kill for you. You decide where to point us, and when you're willing to pay the cost. Besides, if they fail to accomplish your goal, you always have the headless knight at your disposal."

Tension bled away from her shoulders, but she didn't melt into my embrace. Not like before. "Not yet. But soon, I may have need to send my assassin Blood to bring justice for House Isador."

Fierce joy burned like quicksilver in Xin's eyes. "I await your orders, my queen."

∾

SHARA

DREAD STILL THICKENED MY THROAT AT THE THOUGHT OF incurring another goddess's wrath for killing Her queen. But I couldn't deny the jolt of anticipation shooting through me, matching the wicked glee sparking in Xin's eyes.

When he'd first come to me in Kansas City, he'd almost decided not to answer my Call to become my Blood. Not because I was too young or not powerful enough. But because he feared I wouldn't be a queen who'd use him like the assassin he was.

He'd killed countless queens before he came into my service, rivaling Guillaume's kill count when he'd served Desideria. Between the two of them, they'd probably done more to wipe out Aima blood on this earth than Ra had accomplished despite his hatred. Add in all the queens who'd braved Leviathan's prison in the hope of gaining the dragon king's power, and it was no wonder there were precious few queens left.

I didn't intend to start killing the competition. Far from it.

But I would protect my nest and all my loved ones inside. Especially my vulnerable human friends like Gina and Frank. A seemingly unlikely couple, my regal, brutally efficient consiliarius and my head of human security had found a second chance at love. They were absolutely adorable together.

Let alone Winston, who kept my house in order. All of Frank's team who took such pride in wearing the Isador logo on their uniforms. Angela, Marissa, Kevin, and countless others who assisted Gina in keeping the massive Isador legacy in order. Dr. Borcht. Magnum at the New York City house.

Not to mention the sibling queens under my protection and their households. They all depended on me to protect them.

I'd found a way to protect my Blood when I'd made the

agreement with Coatlicue. I'd have to find a way to protect everyone again. Because I refused to sit around and wait for the Dauphine to send another zombie-like goule into my nest and harm my people.

Despite the food I'd just eaten—and what felt like gallons of blood I'd taken from my Blood—a gnawing sense of hunger ached in my bones. A feeling of being unsatisfied and uneasy in my own body, and it only got worse with every passing day. A gnawing black hole expanded inside me.

Need. A need for more. Always more.

I promised I wouldn't take a Blood I didn't love. When queens made oaths, those words melded with our power, enforcing the promise into our very being. I'd sooner give up my nest and my Blood than even begin to think of breaking my word.

I already have twelve Blood. How many more can I possibly need?

Daire let out a rumbling purr as he pressed against my knees. "As many as you want."

Stroking my fingers through his long tawny hair, I closed my eyes. The tapestry unfurled in my mind, showing me the map of the nest. My house, the sacred grove of ancient trees with the heart tree in the center. My grotto, steam rising from the ground.

My blood circle burned against the night, glittering red jewels casting fiery light up into the sky. I could feel the burning energy deep in the earth as well, protecting the house and grove. Strong, well defined, as deep and tall as I could possibly make it. Yet it hadn't been enough to keep the Dauphine out.

The trees rustled, whispers on the soft wind. They'd sensed the undead and had immediately circled the goule. They would do so again until I could arrive and take care of the threat.

Though next time, maybe the intruder would bring fire. Or axes. I'd rather lose a limb myself than feel steel hacking into the Morrigan's ancient trees. I'd felt Nevarre's pain when his mother had lost the grove. Devastating agony, much worse than when I'd grown the heart tree and nearly died. I'd been willing to sacrifice to grow the tree. I couldn't bear to lose one branch.

Scanning outside of the circle, I looked for anything that didn't belong. A sense of unease or danger. The twinkling city lights of human lives in and surrounding Eureka Springs dotted the nightscape. I felt animals in the forest. Birds and squirrels, foxes and hares, coyotes and yes, wolves. They slipped south to speak to Xin and then ran back to their home territories, carrying wolf business across the country.

:Not wolf business,: he whispered in my mind. *:They're noses and ears for House Isador.:*

:And the crows are your eyes,: Nevarre added, sending an image of flocks of birds streaking across the sky. *:We're on the watch for where the Dauphine settles.:*

Marne Ceresa had driven her out of New Orleans, but I wasn't sure where she might have gone. Our ancient, powerful Houses had ridiculously large fortunes, so she might have gone anywhere in the world without blinking an eye at the cost. For all I knew, she probably had massive houses in every major country in the world. But something told me she wouldn't have gone far.

She'd lived as an obscure little-known queen named Leonie Delafosse in New Orleans—on the off chance she'd find me. So she could eliminate me before I could even step into my power. She might have been forced to abandon House Delafosse, but she wouldn't hesitate to stamp my house out before I could take any more Blood or siblings.

So she had to be close. Maybe the west coast, where Xin's former queen had held court. Or Canada.

:Once we have her scent, we'll find her anywhere on earth,: Xin swore. *:No matter how hard she tries to hide.:*

I swept my attention outward, looking beyond the imme-diate city for any sign of Aima. Something pulled my attention southward to a large city dotted with millions of human lights. Geography was hard for me to estimate exactly where I was looking, but with the large body of water nearby, I guessed it to be near Houston. Where humans looked like tiny twinkling stars, there was a small group of steady white glowing balls.

Not red glowing streams of lava or fire like my Blood.

Queens. Plural.

I touched Gina's bond in my head. *:Do we have news of any queens gathering near Houston?:*

She couldn't answer directly, but I felt her immediately reach for a phone to call the team.

I let my focus wander across the land, lightly marking my siblings' locations. Mayte and House Zaniyah. The brilliant prism of little Xochitl's energy gleaming like a rainbow. Far to the east, Gwen in Isador Tower, overlooking New York City. She managed hundreds of siblings for me. She might only have four Blood, but the White Enchantress of Camelot blazed like a beacon of power.

House Ironheart lay to the north in Minnesota. Helayna wasn't my sibling, but I'd been welcomed to her nest. I didn't make my presence known to her, but merely flitted by the island in the middle of the lake she called home. On the shore, a giant black wolf sat staring across the water. Her brother, Eivind, the wolf king. His nose twitched as I passed, his wolf rising, ears perked. Not to attack—his hackles didn't rise, and he didn't growl.

His hind quarters slumped down, and he tipped his head back with a mournful howl.

Ah. He thought I might be Karmen Sunna, using my power to seek him out. Though why she'd even consider taking him as Blood when he'd left her alone and scared, I had no idea. I didn't sense her anywhere nearby, and her phenomenal, blazing power would be unmistakable, even when she wasn't my sibling.

A thought rippled across the quiet pool of power flowing

through my mind. I could take him. He was a powerful Aima, a wolf king descended from the goddess Hel and the infamous Fenrir line. If I decided to call him...

He wouldn't be able to resist me.

I could bend him to my will.

I quickly disregarded the thought. He hated queens so much he'd left Karmen and his newly freed sister with only three Blood to protect them against the might of Heliopolis. Every moment of his forced service to me would be misery—for us both, I'd met him several times and never felt a single pull of attraction.

I wouldn't love him. I wouldn't even come to care for him.

He'd be a thorn in my side, constantly chafing at the bond he'd feared all his life. I refused to be those chains he hated.

I turned away, scanning the horizons stretching in all directions. No random red fires caught my attention. No Aima charged toward me, eager and ready to swear their blood to me. If I'd dreamed the last few nights, they weren't based in power. I hadn't felt any special tugs, like Okeanos trapped in Marne's koi pond. Or Leviathan, my mighty dragon imprisoned in a mountain.

If I had unclaimed Blood out in the world, I needed to Call them to my side.

I gathered my power, spreading my arms wide, but something made me hesitate. My nape prickled, a sense of unease crawling down my spine. I had no idea who might be watching for a blaze of power. The last thing I wanted was to alert the Dauphine or Marne Ceresa that I was calling more Blood. If Esetta had truly sent some of her Blood to their houses, how would they manage to escape? They'd taken on new bonds to new queens. If I tried to pull them away, they might end up dead simply to prevent me from having them.

Instead of blasting a Call out into the world, I cupped my hands and lifted them to my mouth. I focused all my intent, my will and growing need, into a small energy sphere between my palms.

Blood that I'll love.

Blood who need me as much as I need them.

Powerful. Protective. Dedicated. To me alone.

All their love. All their blood. Mine to take. So I might give them mine in exchange.

The ball pulsed with molten moonlight, gleaming like a captured star. Too bright, I decided. I bit my lip, adding drops of blood to the spinning sphere, darkening it to deep, blood red. Deeper yet, threads of darkness and shadow blotting the light.

Blood who are as comfortable in the dark as me. Creatures of darkness and night. Monsters and nightmares.

Your queen Calls. Come to House Isador.

Then I blew a kiss onto the ball and sent it spinning away. Heart pounding, I watched it hover a moment and then it exploded. Dark comets streaked in a multitude of directions, quickly disappearing.

Fucking hell. How many Blood did I just call?

4

SHARA

I must have put more energy into the Call than I'd thought because I woke up hours later in bed. Or maybe I was just that tired again. When I'd first come into my power, I'd had a hard time staying awake any time I used it.

Silky hair wrapped around me like a black velvet cape, the scent of ancient magic thick in my nose. Nevarre. Daire's purr rumbled the bed like it had a vibrating mattress, the solid heat of his body draped around me.

But I didn't immediately feel Rik.

Not in bed with me, at least, though he was close. Without opening my eyes, I sensed him sitting in a chair off to the side. His bond was quiet, almost like he was sleeping, but when I opened my eyes, I met his gaze.

"I wanted to let you sleep as long as possible," he said before I could ask.

So he'd given me my most comforting Blood to ensure I slept like a baby. I combed my fingers through Nevarre's hair, hugging his head in my arms. Shining ebony, just like his raven's wings. His mouth pressed against my skin, his lips tasting my pulse.

That quickly, my blood burned like hot streams of lava, cracking the earth open with the force of my lust.

I arched against him, tightening my arm around his neck. Daire shifted behind me, cradling my body against his. His hair tickled my cheek, dark at the base but each strand was dipped in tawny gold, just like his warcat. His hair was longer than when I'd first met him, but nowhere near as long as Nevarre's. The only other Blood who could compete in the hair category was Vivian. Though Itztli and Tlacel's hair came down to their waists.

Nevarre's fangs scraped lightly over the top curve of my breast, making me tremble.

"Yes," I whispered, tightening my fingers in his hair. He didn't need my explicit permission to feed. I wasn't that kind of queen. I loved feeding my Blood. Their fangs in my flesh. My blood spurting into their mouths, feeding their pleasure and their power at the same time. Knowing a part of me was inside them. Satiating them like no other.

It was a hell of a rush. Adding sex at the same time only made it better.

He tipped his head back slightly, flicking his gaze up to mine. So he could watch my face as he slowly bit into my breast. Exquisite. Pressure building in sharp pricks against my skin, finally giving way beneath the ivory fangs. The white-hot searing cut like electricity through my nerves. The heat of his lips. He groaned deep in his throat, as if he'd never tasted me before. My blood surged into him, forcing him to gulp quickly. Though he left his fangs deep in my flesh, trying to slow the steady stream.

Blood dripped from the corner of his mouth. Even the scent of my own blood stirred my hunger to a fevered pitch.

Daire sank his fangs into my throat, and I shuddered with bliss. Pleasure sparked and hummed in my body.

I wanted more. More bites. More mouths.

Itztli didn't say a word, but his grim satisfaction glittered in the bond like his obsidian blade.

:I've always liked you,: I told him approvingly.

:Same. No offense.: And then his blade sliced across my chest. I could only laugh as she jammed her nails deep into me, even while she drained Mehen dry. At least her nails wouldn't make me climax immediately, but I wouldn't last long if she was feeding on me. Unless...

I tried to sit up, but bodies were in the way. I tore bites into the offending flesh until I could curl around her. I bit into the top of her shoulder, pinning her tight between dick and fangs.

Her body quivered and twisted in my arms, so sinuously that I thought she might slip into the cobra queen. No matter.

She could bite me in half, and I'd still take her for the ride of her life.

5

SHARA

I probably shouldn't drain Mehen to unconsciousness again so soon, but my hunger raged out of control. Maybe that's why I was so pissed at Rik. Or maybe my anger fed the hunger ravaging through me. I wasn't sure.

My veins felt shriveled and desiccated like the mummy we'd discovered in the basement of the tower. Nerves crackled up and down my spine and limbs, sharp lightning bolts of sensation making me twitch and moan. Also fed by the gigantic dick pressing up against my cervix. Guillaume was hung like his hell horse, so taking him to the hilt always made me frantic. It felt like he shifted my organs around, taking up every square inch of space inside my body.

Rich, powerful, ancient blood of two impressive Aima flowed into me like molten rivers. And it wasn't enough.

Leviathan, king of the depths, made a low, deep sigh in the bond. Not a growl. A snore. Deep in slumber, Mehen sagged heavily against me. I pushed him away with a wave of power and another Blood immediately took his place. Sleek, strong throat against my face, silken hair trailing over my cheek. He already bled from a tidy but deep cut, straight into his jugular.

His blood tasted like a deep, dark jungle, roasted coffee, and cacao. The warm fur of a dog against my face. A deep mournful howl in the night.

His darkness flooded me, a blazing sun darkened, eclipsed in shadow. Cutting like the sharpest obsidian blade.

I'd once held Itztli's heart in the palm of my hand. I remembered its weight, the hot blood streaming between my fingers. The heavy pulse pounding up my forearm, kicking like a powerful, sleek thoroughbred. I'd grown the Zaniyah heart tree with his eager, willing sacrifice.

"Yes, my queen," Itztli said. "My heart is yours."

Then he jammed the brutal blade into his chest. Slicing deep, opening up his ribcage like a beautiful, bloody flower.

Regret tightened my throat—though I couldn't look away. I hadn't meant to recreate his sacrifice. There was no need.

Blood spurted from his chest cavity with every steady thump of his heart. I slipped my fingers into his body, shuddering at the hot, eager grip of his flesh. I could have yanked his heart free, and it would have kept beating, but I didn't need to make that kind of statement tonight. He'd already given his heart to me.

Delicately, I cupped the bottom globe of his heart, feeling it jump against my fingers. Quickening with anticipation. He wasn't scared, even with my hand buried in his chest. My nails pierced the muscle, giving me direct access to the source of his blood. So hot, burning up my arm like a raging bonfire of lust and hunger. I tasted the ancient magic of his house. His mother, Citla Zaniyah, so beautiful the sun god Huitzilopochtli had called her his star. Itztli's goddess, Coatlicue, Mother of the Gods, who'd given me the power to make Ra mortal.

The darker, tongue-curling taste of his father, the Blood of House Tocatl descended from the Flayed One. The god who'd given him a taste for pain.

:Flay my skin from my bones. Command them both to dance for you, my queen, and it will be so.:

Shuddering, I pressed my face to the bleeding hole in his chest, smearing my face with his blood. *:I quite like your skin and bones together in one body, thank you very much.:*

Pulling my other hand free from Guillaume's chest, I wrapped my fingers around Itztli's straining dick. Delicately puncturing the tips of my nails into his most tender skin. Feeding from both his dick and his heart, gripped in vicious talons that could shred him beyond recognition. His heart pounded harder, climax roaring through him on a deep bellow. His pleasure sparkled in his blood like the finest champagne, fizzing on my tongue.

I drank until his heart slowed. His dick softened in my fingers. His blood thickened and cooled. *Enough.* I forced myself to release his heart and retract my nails. *Enough!*

Shuddering, I bared my aching fangs, still maddened with hunger.

Molten sunfire energy prickled my skin, and I struck hard, seizing Vivian's throat in my jaws. I jammed my fingers into hot bodies still pressed against me. Nevarre and Daire. They'd fed on me at the beginning of this sensual feast, but I'd used them both hard today already. They couldn't take being drained over and over again, no matter how well they fed from me.

:Bullshit,: Daire purred in my head, a delicious rumble that vibrated my spine. *:Feast, my queen.:*

:Drain us again and again.: Nevarre's bond swept through me on black, silent wings. *:You make us stronger every time you fill us back up again.:*

Someone jostled the bodies pressed to me, as if they were trying to force their way closer. Or pull me free of Guillaume. He snarled against my shoulder, grinding his fangs deeper, hauling my hips close. Jammed down on his dick, still as massive as ever, especially since I wasn't draining him as quickly as he fed.

Climax shattered through me, breaking the shell of my body wide open.

Scales poured out of me, endless coils undulating. Black as night.

And as cold as the grave.

~

XIN

I STARED IN AWE AS MY QUEEN'S FULL MAJESTY REVEALED ITSELF. Her coils undulated across the bed, knocking weakened and unconscious Blood away. Her hood spread wide, lifting her head toward the ceiling.

Toward her alpha, who hung poised above the bed, tangled in thick shadows he couldn't escape. I watched the emotions flickering across Rik's face. Regret. Resignation. Acceptance. Then shock when she turned away, ignoring him like he was simply an annoyance.

A fierce smile flashed over my face, gone in a heartbeat. But she saw.

She saw everything. As she should.

Shifting her attention to the Blood pressed against her, she flicked her tongue out, tasting Guillaume's cheek. Testing his courage. Not that she should ever doubt the Templar knight's will to do whatever she commanded. Still erect and buried up inside her, Guillaume strained to thrust deeper. Not appalled in the slightest by her changed appearance, let alone the threat of her poisonous fangs. He'd endured her mother's bite more than a hundred years ago and used that poison to kill everyone in House Modron. He couldn't know if Shara's poison would affect him again or not. But it didn't matter. He'd willingly swell up, turn black, and die from her venom. He'd gladly let her suck him dry to a brittle shell. Even if she couldn't resurrect him.

She waited, her ruby eyes glittering with lazy hunger, as he strained harder, thrusting until climax made him shudder and shout out her name. Rearing back, she opened her mouth, allowing long, gleaming fangs to descend. Thick and long enough to pierce a man clean through with plenty of room to spare.

Swift and silent, I struck, using my sharpest blade to cut cleanly through Guillaume's neck. Turning him into his namesake, the Dullahan, the headless knight.

Blood splattered her scales, making her hiss with both hunger and frustration as his body went limp in her coils. She pushed him away, letting his body fall to the floor beside the bed.

"Take me instead, my queen." I stepped closer, holding the blade out to the side. Letting her see it in my hand before I dropped it to clatter on the floor. I reached behind me over my shoulder, pulling another blade out of its sheath hidden beneath my hair. Metal clanged as I dropped it beside the other. "I come to you willingly. Unarmed and ready to die."

I took another step, and something wrapped around my ankles, binding my legs together. Not her coils, but a deep purple tentacle.

Man from the waist up but with kraken tentacles writhing across the floor, Okeanos yanked me off my feet and flung me back over his shoulder. "Take me, my queen."

Tucking my head, I hit the floor and rolled back to my feet. Already running back toward her, I paused only to snag a blade. Okeanos flicked one of his tentacles at me, surprisingly fast given it was as thick as his thigh. Slicing it aside with the same bloody blade I'd used to behead the knight, I leapt for his back, using his shoulder to vault myself up toward our queen's brutal fangs. Close enough to see the black venom dripping from the tip. The dark maw of her mouth. The red diamond crowning her hood above her glittering eyes.

I dropped the blade and closed my eyes, letting my head fall back.

Only for a wall of fur to slam into me like a linebacker. We crashed to the floor and skidded against the bed, splintering the wood frame.

:Enough!: Shara roared in our bonds.

Stilling every muscle in my body as if she'd injected me with a paralytic drug. Panting, Ezra stared down at me. *:Huh. I never expected the bear to move so fast.:*

:You're a motherfucking idiot,: he grumbled back but without any real fire.

With another crash, Rik dropped to the floor beside us. He immediately surged to his feet and moved closer to her, holding his hands up soothingly. "All is well, my queen."

:No.: She hissed with displeasure, rattling the tip of her tail against the wall hard enough chunks of plaster fell from the ceiling. *:No, it's not. My alpha failed to keep the Blood under his control. Guillaume is dead and out of commission until he heals. Okeanos and Xin would have been next. The rest of the Blood are incapacitated. Do we even have anyone other than Frank's team guarding the nest? What if the Dauphine is watching? Now would be a perfect time for her to attack while we're distracted and ill prepared. And I'm still so fucking hungry I'm afraid I'll kill you all.:*

Her bond simmered with fury and thirst, but when Rik reached out to touch her, she recoiled, withdrawing into the furthest corner of the room. Her eyes burned like red pits in the thick shadows.

"Llewellyn and Tlacel are in the air, still guarding the nest. You fed the others well, so they'll recover quickly."

True, but what he didn't admit was they hovered directly overhead. A heartbeat from crashing through the ceiling to join the fun.

:G,: She raked her fangs across the wooden floor, splintering the boards and leaving a thick trail of venom like an oil slick. *:Itztli. I almost took his heart again.:*

"They're both healing. Look at them, my queen. Itztli's grinning from ear to ear, and G's head is almost completely reattached. They're both stronger than ever thanks to you." Rik stepped closer, finally placing a hand on her black scales. "Feed from your alpha to slake your thirst until the new Blood arrive. Xin, Okeanos, and Ezra are also here, eager to feed you."

Ezra looked a little pale and sweaty at the thought of allowing the cobra to feed, but to his credit, he didn't object.

Her coils tightened, her head swaying. *:I don't want to kill you again.:*

"Then shift first, my queen. Though I've never minded your cobra, either."

I risked her wrath by rolling to my feet and moving to stand by Rik. "Nor I. You're the most glorious queen I've ever seen, Your Majesty."

:Agony.: Ruby eyes slitted, her tongue flickering the air. *:Death.:*

I shrugged. "I've fed from Rik so I should already have the antidote to your venom, but if not, I'll recover."

Her head lowered enough for her tongue to dance across my chest. Black venom still dripped from her three-foot-long fangs. I caught some in the palm of my hand, holding her gaze.

"Nothing you could ever do to me will make me afraid."

And I tipped her poison into my mouth.

∾

OKEANOS

As the newest Blood of House Isador, I was still carefully searching for my place among them. I didn't crave to be as solitary as the bear and the wolf, though I was often as alone. I couldn't coach our young queen on court etiquette, though after being trapped in Marne Ceresa's court for a century, I knew enough about the queen of Rome to get me killed.

Older than Daire and Rik—but since I was caged and abandoned by my mother when the kraken grew too powerful, I still felt young and green. Especially compared to Leviathan. The other Blood, I still didn't know very well. My need for water kept me in the grotto more often than not.

I hadn't even known I could partially shift until I was able to wrap Xin in a tentacle and give him a toss.

Watching him stand fearlessly before the gigantic cobra, a renewed sense of admiration for his courage flowed through me. Especially when she twisted her head to the side, sank her fangs through his abdomen, and lifted him off the ground so he hung from her mouth. He didn't struggle or shout. Instead, a peaceful smile softened his face. Without struggling, he dangled effortlessly in her grip while she pumped him with venom.

Something he'd said made me turn to Rik. "You carry the antivenom for her bite?"

He nodded and held out his forearm. "I do."

I hesitated, searching his gaze. "Will poisoning me make her stronger?"

His head tipped and he shrugged. "Her poison changes our blood when she feeds in this form, but having the antivenom won't affect her ability to feed on you."

I turned back to our queen. "I'll take my chances."

Xin draped across her coils, eyes glazed with pleasure but still very much alive. She lifted her head and swayed back and forth, allowing her poison to spread through his body. Blood and venom dripped from two punctures in his midsection.

I allowed one of my smaller tentacles to flit across the floor, dragging my suckers through the droplets of poison she'd spilled. It tasted... good, actually. Strong, dark molasses, thick with bitter minerals but still sweet. Like a lingering taint of rusted metal and the burn of oil from a shipwreck laying at the bottom of the ocean for decades, but still my queen.

Just as powerful as the beckoning siren call of her blood. One drop in the ocean would be enough for me to find her anywhere.

The tentacle suctioning up her venom numbed but I didn't care. I spread my tentacles wider, searching out every drop of poison and blood. Even Guillaume's and Xin's. I would have it ready for her when she fed on me next. I touched her scales, tentatively cleaning the streaks of poison from her coils. Then more confidently when she didn't object.

Inching closer, I entwined my tentacles with her coils. Offering myself to her. Lifting my chest up to her invitingly.

She moved so quickly I didn't see the strike. I didn't even feel the glide of her fangs through my flesh. Only the impact jarring the breath from my lungs. Spreading cold crept up my tentacles, radiating across my midsection.

"Fuuuuuck me," Ezra muttered beneath his breath.

I laughed, though it came out more like a strangled wheeze. Her fangs were still inside me, penetrating my flesh. Claiming me in a way few would allow. Let alone crave.

:Drag me to the depths of the Deep Blue, my queen.:

6

SHARA

As the cobra, I could think coldly and rationally. My emotions were still there but distant, pooled in a silvery cup at the base of my identity. Even my lingering rage dripped toward that cup, draining away quickly as an inferno of anticipation rippled through me.

I could watch the way my venom spread through my two Blood and not feel the overwhelming guilt and regret at what I'd done to them. Tilting my head, I studied the effects, noting the differences. Xin had fed on my envenomed alpha before, so he carried the antivenom that prevented him from dying immediately. Languidly, he blinked up at me, his chest rising and falling deeply despite the black fluid leaking from the two punctures in his stomach as big as his fist. I'd cut his liver in half and shredded his bowel. But he still grinned up at me as if I'd given him the greatest gift of his life.

Okeanos was not so lucky. His belly swelled and blackened, his veins standing out like violet worms beneath his clammy skin. Though he looked at me in the exact same way. As if I was the most wondrous, magical creature he'd ever beheld in his life, even as he struggled to breathe.

Tentacles entwined around my coils, an odd tangling that excited me. His suckers moved on my scales like tiny mouths, arousing me even more. Making me think of a nest of mating snakes. Even as my poison spread through his veins, he managed to penetrate the same opening Guillaume had used before.

Before Xin had cut off his head.

The cobra didn't care. Didn't feel stomach-churning horror as my beloved knight's eyes had flown wide, his spine severed. Though even in death, he'd smiled, one corner of his lip quirking with respect and admiration for the Blood who'd managed to surprise him.

The cobra didn't mind the rattling sound of one Blood's wheezing while she latched onto the other man and drank him down in long, powerful swallows, making his back arch. His heart stutter. His body went chilled and limp. Yet Xin cupped my serpentine face as long as he could keep his palms pressed to my scales.

His arms fell away. His head lolled like a broken doll, his hair spilling like shimmering satin against my coils. So pretty. I didn't set him aside or allow him to tumble to the floor. Not after what he'd given me.

Though he was only the appetizer.

Okeanos twitched against me, his eyes roiling like an angry sea. Though he still gripped me tightly, winding our bodies together. His lower tentacles blackened with my poison, no longer the kraken's lovely shades of purple and lavender. Virulent green leaked from his suckers, his swollen tentacles cracking open with the force of his grip.

Also pretty. And tasty, I decided, flicking my tongue along the dripping streams. My poison seasoned his blood with the power of the grave and the suffering of agonies. Rubbery bones and liquified organs and screaming nerves. So delicious. I opened my jaws wide and locked my mouth around him. Drinking from my original punctures.

The sea swelled in his eyes. Crashing waves and thunder tore through our bond, filling me with the wild rapture of a storm-tossed sea. He rose in my vision, taller and longer and wider, a true monster of the sea. Tentacles slamming into ocean liners and tossing them like toys. Cracking them open like kindling. His rancorous destruction a beautiful thing to behold. Glowing green leaked from his tentacles, a poisoned stream killing everything it touched. Whales, humans, Aima, nothing could withstand his poison.

Except me. His queen. Quivering with his final thrust, his body turned cold in my arms.

Arms.

I pressed my forearm to Okeanos' mouth, blood still dripping from Mehen's enthusiastic bite. Blindly, I felt for Xin. Seized his hair. Pulled him closer. Cradled his head against my breast. My blood burned on my skin, throbbing bites still bleeding all over my body. They'd be able to absorb enough energy just by touching me, until they recovered enough to feed.

My skin felt too tight. My bones shifted inside me, not in the right location. Part of my head was still in the cobra. The part that couldn't comprehend legs or walking. Or feeling anything other than euphoria and hunger, though the cutting edge of my hunger had been temporarily dulled.

Until I dared open my eyes and look at the carnage around me.

Rik made his way from one downed Blood to another, straightening their limbs and laying them out more comfortably. Except Mehen, who cracked open a slitted emerald eye and snarled, and Vivian, who wouldn't appreciate the help from any male. She lay near the edge of the bed, one arm and leg hanging off, her red braids so heavy they slowly pulled her off the mattress to slump on the floor.

The huge bed we'd waited for weeks to receive was covered in blood and slanted crazily in the middle. The foot of the mattress lay on the floor, the heavy frame smashed to smithereens. The bedding was slashed and sliced by claws and knives and goddess only knew what else. Blood dripped from the ceiling and sprayed the walls like a gruesome murder scene. Half the ceiling had fallen, clumps of plaster mixing with blood. Even the beautiful old hardwood floors were ruined. It looked like G had tried to write into the wood with his sword.

"I would never," he said, his words barely intelligible. "Bad for the sword."

Tears filled my eyes as I turned to see him, lying just a few feet away, facing me. Reaching for me, slowly inching his way closer. The cut on his throat pink and tender as his spine knitted back together.

"Winston's going to fucking kill us," Ezra grumbled.

I turned to look at my grumpy grizzly bear who was actually a giant cinnamon roll on the inside. His jeans rode low on his hips. No shoes, no shirt, his broad chest and thick, beefy shoulders bare except for a mat of hair sprinkled across his pectorals.

"Come here." I didn't recognize the tone of my voice. I don't think I'd ever used it before. The words hung in the air, vibrating with intensity.

His eyes flared wide, lifting to my gaze. Making sure I meant him. Then he lumbered toward me, moving faster the last steps to sweep me up in his arms. My back thumped into the wall, raining down more pieces of plaster on our heads. Not that I cared. I rubbed my face against his chest, breathing in his spicy cinnamon scent mixed with a hint of pine trees. The deep, hoary forest of ancient trees of his homeland.

"Fucking hurry." My words were garbled by my fangs, and it

took all my will not to strike hard and fast to slake this burning thirst. "Get inside me. Now."

Panting, he jerked at his jeans while I climbed up his body, using the wall for leverage. My mouth hovered over his thumping pulse. Torment, my fangs throbbing in time to my heart. But if I bit him now, it'd be over before I could feel his hook expanding inside me. Filling me up, locked tight. That's what I wanted. What I needed. Just as badly as his blood.

He sank into me, and my breath sobbed out with relief. Grinding me against the wall, he covered me with his entire body, giving me his weight and strength. Somehow wrapping me up in a giant bear hug even while fucking me.

I couldn't wait any longer.

I jammed my fangs deep into his throat, riding the vicious wave of climax rolling through his body. He roared with release, swelling inside me. Locked deep.

His blood rushed into me, an eager fountain from a pure glacier high above, sprinkled with pine needles and cinnamon. So good.

Part of my brain knew I needed to slow the flow, or he wouldn't be able to maintain an erection, let alone his hook. But he tasted too good. I couldn't stop gulping him down. With a deep, rumbling growl, he shoved me higher against the wall. I tipped my opposite shoulder down, baring as much of my throat as I could without releasing my own bite.

He started to lower his head, but Rik grabbed a handful of his shaggy hair and jerked his head back. "Don't feed on her, not until she stabilizes. You keep giving us too much, my queen."

I snarled against Ezra's throat. :*I want us all to feast and feed and fuck some more.*:

"I know," Rik whispered soothingly, despite the fierce grip he had on Ezra's hair. "Once your new Blood arrive, and your reserves are filled, we'll gladly do whatever you wish. Right now, I need you to heal the Blood who're down with the blood you've already spilled in this room."

Shaking my head, even though my fangs tore Ezra's skin open, I growled again. Out of control and so fucking desperate. A gnawing, empty pit of a black hole spun wider, wrecking as much devastation as Sepdet's sinkhole that had almost swallowed Helayna's nest.

Which told me more than anything else Rik was right.

I hated feeling like this.

Ezra wobbled against Rik, his eyelids fluttering, his heart slowing. His dick softened and slid out of me, making me whimper with the loss.

"There's enough blood spilled in this room already to heal them all," Rik continued softly. "Call it to you, my queen. You'll feel better too."

I had to suck on my punctures in Ezra's throat to keep the blood flowing into my mouth. My sign to stop. I didn't want to drain him too low, or he'd need healing too. My breaths were choppy and shallow, my nerves on fire. Panic crawled in my stomach, but I closed my eyes and focused on calming my breathing.

It sucked. Royally. But I'd felt this way before and survived.

I willed the blood in the room to flow back to me. Mine. Theirs. Mixed with venom and cum and saliva. Heat flared in my chest, lighting up my bonds. I allowed the energy to flow as it wanted, gliding to the ones who needed the most help. The most healing.

All too quickly, the surge of energy waned and the hunger returned, just as vicious as before. Worried, I opened my eyes and met Rik's gaze, my mouth still locked to Ezra's cool skin. Without my alpha holding him up, he would have already slid to the floor unconscious.

"Mehen and Vivian, take the sky. Itztli and Daire, you've got first watch on the ground. Everyone else, fuel up and be ready to swap in. G, give Winston the heads up in the kitchen and assign the next watch cycle."

The door slammed open and Llewellyn and Tlacel made a beeline straight toward us, while the other Blood filed out to their assignments without a word. Even Mehen—a feat indeed.

I could smell the blood in the air. Both Lew and Tlacel already bled from cuts on their throats. I would have laughed if I didn't feel so shitty. They had no intention of going as quickly as Ezra.

Releasing my mouth-lock on his clammy skin, I leaped for them both like a woman possessed.

7

RIK

I fucking hated making any mistake, but especially one that upset and offended my queen. She needed me to be right one hundred percent of the time—or she could end up unprotected and vulnerable.

One of her Blood dying because of my mistake would be bad enough. But for my queen to suffer even a second of discomfort and lack because of my actions was intolerable.

Especially Shara.

I would rip my own heart and throat out, allow her cobra to poison me a dozen times, ask Xin to chop off my head, and break every bone in my body before I'd fail her again.

:Rik.: Her bond shrieked in my head, a burning misery of endless hunger. One arm locked around Llewellyn's neck, she pressed her entire face to his bloody throat, while her fingers jammed into the wound on Tlacel's. :Don't let me hurt anyone else.:

:We've got you, my queen.: I strode to the door, mentally giving a tug on the other two Blood bonds for them to follow out to the hallway.

Across from the master suite, another wing stretched in the

opposite direction with guest rooms we'd never used. I opened the first door, relieved to find a clean and tidy room with a regular king-sized bed.

I touched Guillaume's bond. *:Tell Winston our queen has vacated her suite until it's cleaned.:*

:Done,: he replied immediately. *:He's apprised of the situation and has already arranged for a new bed to be delivered first thing in the morning.:*

:So quickly?: Shara asked. *:Tell him thank you.:*

Guillaume huffed out an amused chuckle. *:He says he learned to always have extra beds available and ready at a moment's notice, especially special orders.:*

Dropping to the guest mattress with Shara on top of him, Llewellyn laughed. *:Let's just say House Isador has always been hell on beds.:*

Tlacel lay beside the other Blood, curling on his side close so she could touch him at will. Lew smoothed his hands up and down her back, stroking her hair, keeping his touch gentle and comforting rather than sexual. He even rolled her toward the other Blood so they could both touch her, skin to skin, giving her the warmth and energy of their bodies. Slowly, the sharp urgency in her bond eased. Without Blood feeding on her at the same time, the gnawing hunger lessened from madness inducing to only starving as she fed from them both.

As the former Isador alpha, Llewellyn could take a deep, long feeding without losing consciousness as quickly, but Tlacel hadn't served a queen before Shara. He was older than me, yes, but not alpha, and as one of the lesser Blood, he simply didn't feed her as often or deeply as me.

Quietly, I eased onto the bed behind him and wrapped my forearm around to offer my wrist.

Surprised, he hesitated for a moment. *:You should feed her directly, alpha.:*

:I do, often and regularly. I will again. But for now, it pleases her to feed on you, and this allows her to enjoy you longer.:

He relaxed against me and sank his fangs into my wrist. *:Thank you, alpha. I'd give her my head like the knight if she needed it.:*

Shara turned her head so she could see us, though she still fed from Lew's throat. Her eyes gleamed like liquid starlight, shining with all the love in the universe. *:Thank you, alpha.:*

My throat ached, my heart weighing like a ton of crushed granite in my chest. I'd allowed the pressure of the Triune to get to me—and it wasn't even about me at all. The Triskeles had called Shara Isador to its table. Exactly as she is, and was, and always will be.

All I had to do was love her. Exactly as I do. Exactly as she needed.

"No more heads will be lost tonight," I said aloud, my voice gruff against the rawness in my throat.

~

SHARA

Even though I was exhausted, I could only sleep fleetingly. I felt Rik send Tlacel to the kitchen, his knees wobbly despite the kick of alpha blood he'd taken while I fed on him. I was aware of the silent communication flowing between Rik and Lew, questioning whether he needed to leave for food. I didn't hear his response to my alpha, but Lew stayed at my back.

I wanted to sleep deeply, hoping I'd dream about the Blood I'd called. Instead, I roamed my house. Searching restlessly, I walked the halls, opening every door, looking for... something. Someone. My manor house blurred into the house in Kansas

City where I'd grown up. The room in the attic, pitch dark and silent. Stifling. My parents' bedroom before they'd died. Mom's quiet yet piercing sorrow still hung in the air.

Down the stairs, remembering Rik and Daire laughing and teasing each other in those early days. Guillaume and Xin joining us. The pizza party in bed.

The smile slipped from my lips when I realized I stood before the heavy, thick door to the basement. I could already smell the musty, damp odor of the rock and cement foundation. Walls closed in, the door shut and locked behind me. The tiny window high up at the ground level. Blocked with iron bars. Rusted but too thick for me to bend with my bare hands.

Trust me, I'd tried. Screaming through the grate as the monsters closed around Mom. The bright red spray of her blood on the pavement, shining in the streetlight overhead. Pounding my fists on the door with desperate fury. Digging my nails into the loosened screws. Blood dripping from my torn hands but the hinge broke. Letting me out—too late to save her.

I must have whimpered in my sleep, or maybe the nightmare bled into Rik's bond. His arms tighten around me, his lips against my ear. His broad chest an impenetrable wall against my cheek.

"You're safe," he whispered. "All is well, my queen."

Still asleep enough to not be able to answer but awake enough to smell his skin. To feel the satiny heat against my lips. Hunger spiked so viciously I trembled, sucking in a harsh breath. An image filled my head. Tearing my way through his chest, cracking open ribs, so I could bite directly into his heart. The eager jump of the muscle on my tongue. His heart just meat in my mouth.

My eyes flew open. I jerked back from him, bumping back against Lew's chest. Shuddering, I stared up into Rik's steady gaze.

He wasn't appalled in the slightest. In fact, his slumberous eyes dropped to my lips. "Take what you need, Shara. However it pleases you."

My eyes fluttered, my pulse thumping so hard I could feel the veins moving beneath my skin. He hardly ever used my given name. In fact, I couldn't recall the last time, especially since I'd ascended to Triskeles.

Just miles away in a rundown motel where I'd worked cleaning rooms, he'd said my name the same way the first night we were together. Somehow reverently—but also dirty filthy good. Like my name alone turned him on.

"It does," he rumbled, stroking my hair back out of my face. "Everything about you turns me on, but especially your name. Shara fucking Isador, Last D—"

"Just Shara." I pressed my fingers to his lips. "I don't want or need to hear a litany of titles right now."

Lew tipped his head closer, his mouth on the top of my head. I felt him breathe in my scent as he rubbed his lips against my hair. The fierce surge of hunger in his bond. Not for my blood or power. Just... me. My scent, the feel of my body against his. "Shara, would you like for me to leave or stay?"

Rik's gaze didn't flicker, flinch, or narrow with concern or jealousy. His bond remained open in my mind, his feelings laid bare for me. He wasn't closed off like before, trying to pull himself away to be the perfect Triune alpha—that I didn't want or need. "You have two alphas in your bed, Shara. It'd be a fucking crime to send one of us away."

"I didn't think two alphas would play together very well."

He gave me a wry smile. "This alpha has been reminded of his ideal role for his queen and has no problem whatsoever with any of his queen's Blood, however you see fit to use them. In fact, I urge you to remember how many times Llewellyn must have fed on his former queen over the centuries. How much Isador blood he already carries. How much of her power may still reside in his body. Besides, you could use the extra kick his alpha blood will give you."

"Stay," I breathed out, letting my body relax between them.

A long, lean man behind me. A mountain of a man before me. So strange not to have Rik at my back, but I loved being able to rub my face on the impossibly wide expanse of his chest. Breathing in his scent stirred my hunger to a fevered pitch, but I couldn't bite him yet. Not until my body had a taste of his strength, every cell and fiber yearning for the feel of him moving inside me.

He cupped my knee, lifting my leg up over his hips so he could sink into me on one smooth, powerful lunge. My head fell back, my body singing with pleasure. His dick stretched me wide, filling up every inch without any fumbling or straining. Like his cock was perfectly made to fit the sheath of my body while maximizing my pleasure. A blazing red-hot sword freshly forged, blazing a path straight through me.

I dug my heel into his hamstring, locking my leg around him. His palm wrapped around the front of my throat, his thumb stroking over my pulse. He simply meant to remind himself physically not to feed on me, but the feel of his gigantic hand on my throat sent a heavy pulse of lust straight to my core. So fucking big and strong, my formidable rock. I felt like a tiny delicate bird in the palm of his hand, even though we both knew I had the power to blast him into nothing more than a black-ened smear of ash and charred bone.

"Just Shara likes that," he murmured, tightening his fingers slowly. Letting me feel the immense strength in his palm. How easy it would be for him to simply crack my spine in half.

Lew reached around to seize my hand, twisting my arm behind my back. Exquisite pressure, grinding the tendons and delicate bones in my wrist, tugging my hand higher so I felt the strain in my shoulder. "Then just Shara should like this too."

Something loosened inside me, a screaming tension I hadn't

even noticed until it started to wane. I loved being their queen. I loved our lives we were building here in my nest.

But here in this bed, in this moment, I realized how much strain I carried. Day in, day out, the royal weight of House Isador stacked another boulder on top of my shoulders. My chest. Making it harder and harder to breathe. The immense weight of power crushing me just a little more every single day.

So much fucking power.

It was a blessing from the goddess, and I wouldn't change a thing, but it was also fucking exhausting just to hold so much power inside the fragile confines of this physical body. To call it and allow magic to pour out of me—without destroying everything I loved or killing myself. To guard against my own strength, constantly aware of how many people depended on me to protect them. The weight of so many eyes looking to me for every fucking decision.

Here, now, I didn't have to do a goddess-damned thing but close my eyes and soak them in.

So that's exactly what I did.

Lew dragged my captured hand lower, raking my nails across his stomach. The scent of his blood made my fangs throb and my nostrils flare like a ravenous wolf finally scenting its prey. His gryphon screeched in the bond, pouring red-gold flames through my mind as his blood flowed into me. Tawny lion fur and gold-tipped wings rushed through me. Vicious talons ripping his kill into raw, bloody chunks. A furious protector, the magnificent, haughty guardian of House Isador. His blood carried alpha power, with something else even Rik couldn't give me. No one else could, actually. Unless I found more of Esetta's surviving Blood.

Through Lew, I could taste a hint of my mother. I could almost feel her hovering nearby, a ghostly visage I couldn't see with my physical eyes. Blowing sands swept through my mind, and I could almost hear her laughter. Just by feeding on her former alpha.

His blood dripped down my ass, smearing on my skin. The best lubrication for vampires.

He dragged his dick through the blood, making sure he was well coated before he nudged against my tight hole. Rik paused, and I felt the heavy thump of his dick inside me, an eager beast with a mind of its own. Then the pressure building as Lew pushed into me, his dick gliding deeper. Rubbing the thin flesh separating him from Rik. Heat flared through me, liquifying my bones, lighting up every nerve ending to a fevered pitch.

My thighs quaked, the muscles of my stomach quivering, and they weren't even moving inside me yet.

Lew pulled back slightly so he could push my wrist back up higher between us. My shoulder ached, but when he thrust deeper, grinding against me, all I could think about was my nails deep in his stomach. Every thrust impaled himself on my brutal straw-like nails, driving them deeper into him, even as he pushed deeper into me.

He groaned, a deep, guttural sound of pleasure that pushed me over the edge. I writhed and twitched between them, my veins on fire as every muscle clenched in release.

Panting, I blinked rapidly until I could finally focus on Rik. His thumb tipped my chin up so I could see his face, though his fingers were still firm on my throat. Not choking me but giving me the sensation of being controlled and held in place. They were both still rock hard inside me, which made fine tremors shudder from my head to my toes.

He gave me a lazy, slow grin. "The benefit of fucking alphas is our control."

Lew grunted heavily, grinding himself against my ass. My nails gouging deeper. "Even when you're feeding on us."

I was only feeding on one of them. Opening my mouth wide, I allowed my fangs to descend but I didn't move my head. I wanted to see what Rik would do. If he'd hold me back to try and make this last. Because once I sank my fangs into him…

Tightening his grip on my throat, he hauled me to him, bringing my mouth over his heart. He jammed my fangs into his chest himself.

His back arched, his body heaving on a deep bellow of release. His blood hit my tongue, a thick molten river of pure energy. The strength of granite and basalt, weathered but eternal, towering mountains and deep roots of precious minerals in the earth. Tumbling boulders, burying me in an avalanche but not crushing me. Because he cradled me in his arms and shielded me from all harm.

My rock.

While the gryphon dug in his talons and shrieked.

8

SHARA

"I'm surprised to see you so early this morning," Gina said with a smile as she sat down beside me.

Bleary eyed but upright, I set my cup of coffee aside as Daire brought me a plate of stacked pancakes. My stomach growled embarrassingly loudly, making my smile more of a grimace. I'd worked my way through all the Blood, some multiple times, and there was no end in sight to my hunger. Even with Rik refusing to allow anyone to feed on me. "Me too."

I picked up my fork and cut a bite but hesitated when I realized there were chunks in the batter that weren't fruit. I stabbed a chunk and lifted it up. "Is there sausage in the pancakes?"

"Yep." Daire dropped down to the floor beside my chair and curled around my knees. "It's my creation. Slathered with extra butter and maple syrup too."

I wasn't usually a fan of sweet things mixed with savory meat, but what the hell. I was too hungry to be picky today, and the extra protein might help stave off another bloody orgy.

:Not if we're lucky,: Daire purred.

I rolled my eyes but cut another bite of pancake. "What did you find out?"

"There wasn't much to go on, honestly. They were trying to keep it very quiet. If you hadn't asked me to look into Houston, we'd never have realized that Skolos is having an impromptu gathering near the Gulf of Mexico."

My eyes widened. "How many queens?"

"At least a Triune quorum. We know Houses Kijin and Gorgos are present because they have property in the area and the staff was activated. I suspect that House Ketea is also present, though Undina doesn't have property of record in Houston or Galveston. Marissa is checking a wider area to see if we can find other Ketea properties she might be using for the visit."

My nape prickled uncomfortably. At least two Triune-level queens were a few hundred miles away from me. Perhaps all three. "Shouldn't they have notified us? We were careful to let Mayte know when we were going to Venezuela, even before she was my sibling."

"It would have been polite, but not expressly required, unless you're claiming that Texas is part of your territory." Gina gave me a calculating look, her lips pursed. "Does all of the United States belong to House Isador?"

Shaking my head, I could only laugh. "All I really care about is my nest here."

"But you hold New York City, the largest city in the United States. You could also potentially claim ownership of Mexico City via your sibling relationship with House Zaniyah, which would give you claim to all of Mexico. There are other queens in Central and South America but they're not strong enough to dispute the matter. You certainly have grounds to make such a claim, but we'd need to file a formal petition with the Triune."

"I want as little to do with the Triune as possible." Just the thought of voluntarily reaching out to Byrnes, House Ceresa's primary consiliarius, made me want to hurl, even though he was Kevin's grandfather. "So two if not three of the Skolos Triune queens are meeting just a few hours away. Why? Are they planning some kind of attack?"

Gina grimaced and picked up her cup. "We have no idea why they're meeting, especially so close. House Gorgos came from the Mediterranean and Kijin from Japan. If they're meeting here to avoid Undina's notice, it's possible they're conspiring against her rather than you."

:My queen.: Okeanos' touch in my head was hesitant, a feather-light brush of his tentacle. *:Forgive me for accidentally eavesdropping. I felt my mother's name echoing in your mind.:*

:All my Blood are welcome in my mind any time,: I assured him. *:Especially ones who've faced my cobra. Are you able to join this conversation?:*

The door opened and seconds later he stepped into the breakfast nook. His dark hair was slicked to his shoulders and his jeans clung to his thighs, as if he'd pulled them on while soaking wet from the grotto. Since facing the cobra, his eyes had changed. Rather than the lovely blue green of a secret lagoon, his eyes burned with the neon-green acid of my venom.

Without hesitation, he came to stand between my chair and Gina's. "How can I help, my queen?"

"Do you know if Undina has any property she might use in the Houston area?"

"She doesn't have any human-type holdings in cities but uses reefs and islands cloaked by her magic. When we were in the Aegean, fishing ships could pass right by the nest without noticing anything amiss."

"If she doesn't have human property, then my team can't confirm she's present based on what we have access to," Gina said.

Okeanos' eyes flickered, the green giving way to inky black. Then he focused back on my face, blinking away the darkness. "She's much closer than before, due south of here." He pointed in the direction I'd felt the queens gathering. "I'm not skilled at estimating land distances though."

Oh shit. Of course. It hadn't dawned on me he'd always be able to feel where his mother was. He still carried her blood, even after she basically sold him to the queen of Rome.

My stomach clenched, and for a moment, I feared I might lose the pancakes. I set my fork down and leaned back in my chair, letting the whirling thoughts tumble through my head. Queens often placed their own Blood in other houses so they had eyes and ears inside. But also for situations like this, where Okeanos would have a sense of where his mother was at all times. I'd been so worried about being spied on, but it actually went both ways.

"Have I betrayed you?" He asked hoarsely.

I jerked my attention to his stricken eyes. "No. Not at all. In fact, you've helped me understand one benefit of having Blood from other houses here to share information with me. She's not trying to contact you, is she?"

His shoulders sagged with relief. "No, my queen."

"Though she could," I said slowly. "And you could contact her if you wished."

When Kendall had come to Kansas City to attempt to strong-arm me into submitting to House Skye, he'd tried to use his blood bond with Daire. My bond as his queen had been strong enough to block Kendall out, but even Rik had felt the man's attempt to communicate through that prior bond. Using those bonds, Kendall had known exactly where to find us.

Itztli and Tlacel still had a strong familial bond with Mayte, but then she was also my sibling and carried my blood. Guillaume's former queen and her entire house were dead. Vivian's parents were also dead, though she carried her sunfire, and Smoak shared a single consciousness with all the sunfires.

If I needed to reach Karmen, Smoak could make that connection, even though we didn't share blood. In a way, we each had a spy in our Blood. A link. Even though I had no idea where she was.

I touched Rik's bond. :*Do you, Daire, or Ezra still have any blood bonds strong enough to converse with House Devana?*:

His big palms gently kneaded my shoulders. :*My connection to House Devana was through Daire, but I do still have bonds with my mother and a few sibs in Hyrrokkin.*:

Daire rubbed his chin on my thigh. :*In addition to my mother's bond, I had several minor sibs throughout Devana, but only two or three that might be strong enough to tap for communication. Though right now, I can't even feel them beneath your bond.*:

I wrinkled my nose, resisting the urge to get huffy that they still had blood bonds with other Aima. They had family long before I called them. They'd had to survive for decades— centuries—before I could call them.

But I hadn't grown up in a nest, or even known what we were, for that matter. I'd never fed on blood until Rik and Daire found me. I'd had no idea how it was all supposed to work.

I certainly didn't carry any matriarchal bonds. My heart ached with an empty hollowness. I would never know such a connection.

:*I still carry Wu Tien blood,*: Xin admitted. :*My former queen dissolved her Blood bond, but I have living siblings who returned to China with her I could contact if you wished.*:

He'd been alive for much longer than Rik or Daire, so his bonds should be easier for me to visualize. I slipped deeper into his bond, closing my eyes. :*Show me what those bonds look like.*:

Cool fog parted in his mind, revealing the silent, silver wolf staring back over his shoulder at me. Eyes shining like quicksilver, he lifted his nose, scenting the air, and then he loped along a rocky path through a chill, wet forest of tall, ancient trees. Dripping with fog and moisture, the air was heavy and cold in my lungs. The path steepened, a rocky snake winding along a treacherous cliff on one side, and a sheer wall of icy gray stone shooting up into the clouds on the other.

We seemed to climb forever. My lungs and thighs burned. Usually weather temperatures didn't bother me in the slightest, but the fog crystalized into stinging ice particles.

:Almost there,: Xin whispered in my head.

Finally, he dropped to his haunches and waited for me to catch up with him. For a moment, I panted, head down, my hand braced on his shoulder. The air was so thin and cold I felt lightheaded, and my teeth started to chatter. I pressed closer to his fur, letting his body heat warm me. *:Where are we?:*

He gazed out over a chasm so deep I couldn't see the bottom. There were vague, hazy shapes in the distance, fading into the horizon and the cloaking fog. They might be mountains, but they were much lower in elevation. More like foothills.

:This peak is your bond. This is how high you stand, my queen.:

Oh shit. *:And those other mountains are your sibling bonds?:*

His ears twitched violently, and he gave me an affronted look. *:Hardly.:*

:Then where are they?:

He lowered his nose to the ground and rolled a dull, rough marble over to my foot. *:Here, my queen.:*

A pebble compared to Mount Everest.

:If you have need of these prior bonds, the hardest part will be finding them beneath the majesty of yours.:

I opened my eyes, blinking away the haze of Xin's bond. Goosebumps stood on my arms, and I shivered a little. Daire pressed closer, draping himself across my lap and wrapping his arms around my waist, while Rik rubbed his palms up and down my shoulders, solid against my back. Gina sipped her tea, watching the interaction with an amused quirk on her lips.

My cheeks heated. "Sorry. Xin showed me something and I got cold."

It sounded lame to my ears, even though it was the truth.

Though it wasn't in Gina's nature to question me. "Shall we assume that House Ketea is part of the Skolos quorum?"

I nodded, turning my attention back to Okeanos. "Remember when you took me to meet her? She asked if I'd be her ally against the Triune."

"She often said that Skolos stands alone," he replied.

"The division between the Triune and Skolos has definitely widened in the last few centuries," Gina said. "According to the archives, all three courts used to meet at least once a year to conduct Aima business for all houses. I assumed the practice ended once Triskeles was lost."

"Triskeles wasn't lost," Okeanos said slowly, his gaze flickering from me to Gina and back. His shoulders tensed, as if he was bracing for my reaction. "The queens were deliberately killed."

"By Desideria, right G?"

Standing guard at the door to the living room, Guillaume made a low sound of agreement that weighed heavily in the bond. "She did."

Though Okeanos shook his head, drawing my attention to him.

"What?" I whispered, gazing into his eyes. "Was someone else involved?"

Though I already knew the answer in my bones. Or perhaps his knowledge had already leaked into my thoughts from our bond.

"The queen of Rome."

9

SHARA

Okeanos wasn't braced for my reaction. Deep down, he feared retribution from Marne Ceresa.

In all the times we'd talked, I'd never heard him say her name aloud, as if he feared drawing a hint of her focus to him.

I held out my hand and he took it, coming close enough for me to wrap my arm around his waist and lean into his side. I didn't question him, trusting him to tell me what he could in his own way.

"I saw much in my long stay inside her nest."

His hushed whisper barely reached my ears, so he dropped down between my chair and Gina's. We both leaned closer, though he only touched me.

"She has many gifts. It's not wise to say her name or speak of such things where anything reflective can catch evidence for her."

The kitchen behind us was full of brand-new, very shiny, appliances. I stared straight ahead at the windows that spilled natural light over the table. The crystal glasses holding water and juice. White china plates. A silver serving tray holding all the tea and coffee accouterments that Winston had brought as soon as I sat down.

I swallowed hard. How many times had we sat around discussing Marne Ceresa out loud without a care in the world? Stupid, really. I knew she had mirror magic. I'd been lured into thinking if the mirror she'd sent me was put away safely in salt and coffee, we'd be safe.

:Another reason to work your best magic in darkness,: Llewellyn reminded me of my mother's words.

I nodded. "Gina, can you do a little research on this matter for me before we discuss it any further?"

"Of course," she replied a little too loudly, very much aware of the possibilities. "Dr. Borcht is at the gate. Is it alright for her to come up for your regular checkup?"

"Sure." I tipped my head closer to Okeanos, intending to give him a chaste kiss of thanks on the cheek. But the warm skin of his bare throat beckoned me like a deadly siren luring a ship to its destruction. His scent filled my nose, a salty wave of Deep Blue that pulled me under the tide, and I was lost.

The tender skin of his throat filled my mouth, his pulse a drum of thunder in my head. Quietly, Gina stood and moved away from the table, presumably to go meet her friend while also giving us a few moments of privacy.

After the trial he'd already endured with the cobra—

He leaned harder against me, twisting his head side to side so my fangs scratched and teased. *:Please, my queen.:*

I sank my fangs deep into his jugular and locked my mouth around his throat. Blood gushed down my throat, even with my fangs still penetrating him. I didn't even have to swallow.

He arched against me, coming so quietly Gina might not have even known if she'd still been sitting beside us. But I knew. I smelled the musk of sex mixing with his blood, and I could only think about his tentacles writhing with my coils again.

His blood didn't carry an alpha kick, but the extra power of my venom was addictive. A brutally enticing concoction that stirred my hunger even as it satisfied me.

I could drain him dry again and again and still not get enough.

Shuddering, I pressed my tongue against the punctures to seal them, though I couldn't release him immediately. His skin felt too good in my mouth. Velvety soft, still tasting of the sea, with a deadly punch of poison lingering just beneath the surface.

Gina called loudly from the front door, making sure I heard them approaching. "Dr. Borcht is here, Your Majesty."

Regretfully, I pulled back from Okeanos. His pupils were blown wide and dark like tidal whirlpools, sparking with acid-green lightning. "Thank you, my Blood."

He darted closer, swiping his tongue over my lips and chin to lick up the blood I'd dribbled. Daring to touch me, kiss me, without being so careful and reticent, which I absolutely loved. So I gave him a lingering kiss, even as he slowly stood as the humans came closer.

:My pleasure, my queen.:

10

SHARA

Having a needle in my arm wasn't nearly as good as fangs. It didn't hurt—but I still didn't like it.

Even though Rik stood behind my chair, I didn't have to see his face to know he was glowering at Dr. Mala Borcht as she slipped the vial into the black case for transport back to her lab. Not because of the small stick of the needle.

But because she took my blood when we were already rationing how much my Blood could take. She took what was *his*.

:Not mine,: he rumbled in my mind. *:Yours.:*

:I gave it to her gladly, the same as I give it to you.:

He sighed in the bond, though outwardly I didn't hear any difference in his breathing. *:She'd better not waste a single drop.:*

"All done, Your Majesty." Dr. Borcht quirked her lips, aware of my alpha's displeasure, even though her near-weekly blood draws had been a regular occurrence for months. "How have you been feeling?"

Ever since Heliopolis, we'd been working to get my hormones regulated to calm down my periods. They'd always been extremely regular—and extremely dangerous. Which was why the monsters had always been able to find me every couple of weeks. The scent of my period blood had been a tantalizing lure no matter what I did.

After taking my first Blood, my hormones had gone into overdrive. Miserably long and bloody periods with vicious cramps, draining my power and nearly incapacitating me for a fucking week.

Not that my Blood complained one bit. They loved every drop of my blood, but *period* blood contained goddess-level mind-blowing power, and for good reason. It was the only time a queen could get pregnant. Human men might be turned off by menses but for an Aima, nothing was hotter.

:*Not fair,*: Daire protested in the bond. :*I'll gladly lick every drop you'll give me, but I hate when you're miserable.*:

He'd walked behind me down the long procession during my formal presentation to House Skye, licking my period blood off the floor. My foot. My calf. He'd have been more than happy to slip beneath my dress and clean every inch of my body if I'd let him.

"A little better," I said aloud to Dr. Borcht. "I only bled for five days, and it wasn't as heavy this time." Though honestly, I wondered if it was my body adjusting for my growing hunger than any human medicine she'd given me. I couldn't afford to lose so much blood right now.

"And the cramping?"

I shrugged. "The same. Not debilitating but I'd definitely rather be in bed with a cup of tea or taking a long hot bath than actually doing anything."

Gina gave me a stern look. "Which you should do much more often. Let us take care of you as befitting a queen of your stature."

Now it was my turn to sigh. "I've got too much to do to take a week off every single month. Just look at that stack of papers you're dying to show me."

A stack of black folders sat on the table to her right, nearly a foot tall.

"All of this can wait indefinitely. Especially if your health is at stake." She picked up the entire stack and dropped it back into a leather satchel on the floor. "The Isador legacy was shut down for more than twenty years, and we lost you for five. All of this can certainly wait a few days or even years until you're ready to deal with it."

"Rome wasn't built in a day," Guillaume said over his shoulder, standing guard at the back door. "Especially not on twelve Blood."

"I'm fine." My voice rang with a little more volume than I intended, betraying exactly how not fine I really was. Under the table, Daire pressed closer to my legs, his purr like distant thunder. Rik kneaded my shoulders, trying to ease the tension straining in me.

"The results from the last blood draw were concerning," Dr. Borcht said. "Your red blood cell count was down significantly, and anemia will contribute to your feeling of weakness and tiredness. After your recent period, I'm afraid you're likely even more anemic. Are you feeding enough?"

My jaws tightened, and I bit back a retort. *Every day and night, every fucking Blood, and it's still not enough.*

Gina reached over and closed her fingers over my clenched fist. "Oh, Shara. What's wrong? How can we help?"

My shoulders slumped and my throat ached, but I forced myself to admit the truth. "No, I'm not feeding enough despite our best efforts. Rik has started rationing my blood until I manage to call more Blood to join us."

"It's no hardship on us, my queen," he said. "You've been more generous than any queen I've ever heard of. Cutting back on what you give us for a short time is the least we can do until you feel better."

"I could give you a high dose shot of iron," Dr. Borcht said.

"It's only a short-term solution but it might help for a day or two. Do you have a sense of how long it'll take before more Blood arrive?"

And here, at last, was the real source of my short temper and anxiety.

"No," I whispered hoarsely. "I can't feel them. I sent the Call out, but I don't feel even a hint of anyone approaching yet."

Meanwhile, every time I fed, the bodies of unconscious Blood littered the bed and every flat surface in the room.

"There was a line of at least ten people at the gate when I arrived," Dr. Borcht said slowly. "I assumed they were Blood candidates asking to swear to House Isador."

I shook my head. "It's not that easy. None of them are mine to call."

"Fucking Blood dropping like fucking flies," Ezra muttered. Then he grunted softly. I assumed one of the other Blood punched him, but then I caught the whiff of his blood.

My hands trembled, my fingers clenching so hard I tasted my own blood through my wicked nails. And Daire's. His warcat wound through my mind, sleek fur and muscle, rumbling, soothing purr. I was only half aware of my nails gouged into his throat, his head on my lap beneath the table.

"Go make yourself useful and drop like a fucking fly." Guillaume's low voice rang like steel. I turned my head, catching the glint of silver in his hand.

Blood poured from a surprisingly large stab wound on Ezra's side. Usually G's cuts were neat and tidy, not gaping punctures. Another illustration of how tightly wound we all were. They felt my need intensely, driven and desperate to satisfy me.

Even if it killed them again and again and again.

Tears burned my eyes, even as my stomach knotted desperately for the rich blood dripping down the front of Ezra's shirt.

"Our queen is going to need some privacy," Rik said, his words crashing inside me like an avalanche.

Gina stood immediately. "Of course, Your Majesty. Call me when you'd like to go through some Triune business."

On my other side, Dr. Borcht stood, but she didn't move away immediately. "I do have something else to discuss with you, Your Majesty. It's not urgent, not yet at least, but..."

Blinking away the haze of bloodlust filling me, I looked up at her, searching her face. "Of course. What is it?"

She flicked a quick glance up at Rik, wary of delaying my Blood's request. "We had an interesting blood sample come into the lab last week. I didn't disturb you since I knew I'd see you this week, but it was another queen. The other doctors didn't know what it was, but I recognized it immediately."

"Who?" I asked softly. "Do we know?"

"It came from a hospital in Chicago. The sample had been taken a few weeks prior at Northwestern Memorial from a woman who'd been found naked and presumably dead in a back alley by police."

Karmen. The wolf king had found her and sent human police to get her. When Soldiers of Light came for her, she fled the hospital, found Eivind, and he'd driven her to his sister's nest in Minnesota. "I know who she is."

Dr. Borcht nodded but her eyes tightened, her brow furrowed. "She's not human, so laws of privacy don't bind me in this case. Her blood sample was interesting in more ways than just yours, Your Majesty." She hesitated, her lips a tight, slashing frown. "It might affect your decisions, especially about your own cycle."

Vivian's bond flared inside me, her sunfire's agitation sending sparks through my body. At House Ironheart, she'd told me there was a secret that all sunfires knew about Karmen. Something she didn't wish to tell me unless I ordered it.

I could guess then, and by the tight, alert concern bracketing Dr. Borcht's mouth, I knew exactly what they feared.

They feared my reaction. My jealousy and rage. And yeah, I was furious enough to gouge my fingers deeper into Daire's throat, not that he minded in the slightest. But I was furious with *them*—not because of Karmen. They doubted me. *Me.*

I'd escaped the golden hellscape of Heliopolis, where I'd been subjected to the barest glimmer of Ra's lust before I killed him. I could all too easily imagine what Karmen must have endured in her centuries-long captivity as God's Wife. The term alone made my stomach heave with revulsion.

Harming her in any way was the absolute last thing I would ever do. Especially if she carried an heir. Even the sun god's.

By the dread paling Dr. Borcht's cheeks, she thought I'd move to eliminate another queen, simply because she might carry an heir that might someday be in competition with mine.

Rage flared higher in me, fueled by my hunger. My desperation.

"I am not Keisha Skye." My voice crackled with lightning. Ironic, since that was the former queen of Skye's power. "As long as Karmen doesn't fuck with my Blood or my human family, she's safe from me. No matter what she decides to do with her secret."

"Of course, Your Majesty." Dr. Borcht dropped into a deep curtsey and held it, her head bowed. "Please forgive me for offending you."

Rik reached down and pulled my arm away from Daire, lifting my fingers to his mouth so he could lick my nails clean. Slumped against my legs, Daire couldn't even purr any longer. My rage shifted to guilt so quickly that my throat closed off and my eyes filled with tears.

Vivian streaked toward me, her shame and guilt thickening my own. :*I'll give you the secret, my queen. Everything I have is yours.*:

I put up a mental hand, stalling her flight so hard that her phoenix jerked midair and started to tumble toward the ground. :As you said, the secret isn't yours to give.:

That poor woman. Tormented and tortured and raped for literally centuries, finally freed after an eternity. Only to find her nightmare continued. Even though her captor was now dead, she was forced to carry his memory. I couldn't imagine the horror and fear and dread she must be feeling. Not just fear at how other Aima queens might react, but the possibilities of what even a lingering drop of Ra's essence might do to her from the inside out.

"Keep her blood and her secret as secure as you keep mine."

Dr. Borcht straightened, pale and trembling, wringing her hands. "Of course, Your Majesty. Again, I'm so sorry. I don't doubt your integrity in the slightest, and I'm ashamed I've given you a reason to doubt mine."

Ezra came closer, brushing past the doctor to turn and face me. His plaid shirt clung to his flank, wet with blood. Dripping down his thigh. I pressed my tongue hard against one of the holes where my fangs throbbed, trying to keep them from dropping and terrifying the very human doctor even more. Which meant I couldn't talk.

With my free hand, I shoved Ezra back against the table hard enough dishes rattled, my eyes locked to the blood. My fingers dug into his waist, hooked in a belt loop of his jeans. So I didn't immediately jerk open his fly and take him on top of the fucking table while the humans watched in stunned horror like a gory car accident unfolded in slow motion before them.

"Her Majesty understands." An earthquake rumbled in Rik's voice. He pressed my other hand around his biceps, squeezing hard enough to drive my nails into the muscle. "She'll contact you if she needs any further advice on the matter."

Hot rock, smoking iron, the blood of my magnificent alpha, rolled through me. Though I still couldn't prevent myself from leaning toward Ezra. He gripped the shirt and tore the flannel open effortlessly, baring his chest and stomach for me. The puncture was below his ribs, carefully placed to give me blood and lots of it. So much gushed I had to wonder if G had nicked the aorta.

:*My queen hungers,*: he said in the bond. :*So the bear fountains for you.*:

"The helicopter is ready to take you back to Kansas City, Mala," Gina said loudly behind me.

Urgency shuddered through me.

"She can't spare Nevarre," Rik replied immediately. "Someone else will need to fly the doctor back to the city."

"Of course," Gina said quickly. "Angela obtained her pilot's license."

I hoped to goddess they were gone. Because I couldn't keep my face out of Ezra's blood any longer.

11

VIVIAN

My sunfire phoenix had never faltered before. Smoak had always been with me, my only companion for most of my miserable existence until I managed to leave Heliopolis.

But I'd never tried to keep a secret from my queen, either.

Smoak didn't send words to me. We didn't communicate that way. Images flickered through my mind in rapid succession. He was one of many sunfires, a single drop of molten solar energy compared to the full brilliance of the massive blazing sun of this solar system. All of them united in a way even I couldn't fully comprehend. One of many, united but also separate. Smoak had his own consciousness—even though he simultaneously knew and felt all things the other sunfires knew and felt.

All of their burning, magnificent energy belonged to Karmen Sunna, who'd called the sunfires to her side. Not my queen, Shara Isador.

Smoak felt the constant pull to be with the others of his kind. It wasn't his nature to swear to an Aima queen. To feast on her blood and live solely to protect the queen carrying our

oath. Though he was evolving to our new life, and he especially liked participating in our queen's love life. Our gender
had always been fluid, though he'd started feeling more male
lately.

The rest of the sunfires were also adapting to a life tied to
their new queen, but for now, they were simply reveling in their
newfound freedom from Ra and Sepdet. Imprisoned thousands
of years ago by the god of light, the sunfires had been warped by
the dark lusts of the god. Even Smoak's fire pulsing in my veins
had one purpose only for centuries.

To kill as many queens as possible for my evil sire.

Shame smothered the familiar flames of my gift, and I
dropped like a stone toward the ground. I didn't deserve Shara's
oath, let alone her forgiveness for holding anything back from
her. She'd freed me from the darkness of my past. She'd
conquered the cursed fire in my blood. And the first chance I
got, I betrayed her trust by keeping a potentially deadly secret
from her.

I started to shift back to my human form but something on
the ground caught my attention. A small hill of dirt and pebbles
shifted *up*. Something was coming up through the ground.

Flaring my wings out, I soared past and circled around for
another pass. I didn't see anything moving in the pile, but I was
sure it hadn't been there thirty minutes ago. We were inside the
queen's blood circle, so nothing should be able to get through,
but the hill was slowly growing and spreading. Now a foot tall.

I touched Rik's bond and sent him an image of the small hill.
*:I don't know what this is, but it wasn't here just a few minutes ago.
Might be an animal, but I've never seen anything like it before.:*

The alpha's will wrapped around me like a massive stone
fist, pulling me back around in a lower swoop so he could look
for himself through my own fucking eyes. Distantly, I felt him
calling the other Blood on patrol to come closer, especially the
dragon. *:We were attacked by ants once, sent by Keisha Skye before*

our queen killed her. Is there anything moving inside it? Even as small as an ant?:

I dropped to the ground but kept my phoenix so I was armed with my sharp beak and vicious claws. I swept a fiery talon through the hill, scattering the dirt. Looking for anything out of place. :Nothing. Wait. There's a small hole.:

:The trees aren't alarmed,: Nevarre said. :Neither are the crows.:

:I don't like it,: Rik growled. :Nothing should move in this nest that we don't understand and recognize as belonging to our queen.:

:Even fucking bugs?: Mehen retorted. :Wanna tag all the maggots and worms wriggling through the ground?:

I leaned in closer and dripped smoldering liquid flames into the hole. Seconds ticked by. The breeze of Leviathan's wings as he passed again rustled my braids. Nevarre's giant raven dropped down to face me opposite the hole. Head cocked, he pecked at the small grains himself, as if not trusting me to find the trap.

Xin's wolf materialized beside me, startling me so badly I twitched before catching myself. :Smells like thousand-year-old sand, not Arkansas dirt.:

:Something of Ra's?: I made myself ask, dread weighing like one of Rik's massive boulder thighs on my chest.

The wolf bristled, though he said, :I don't smell the gold of Heliopolis.:

I didn't realize gold had a smell, but then again, all I'd known for centuries was that garish hellscape. All I remembered was the smell of scorched flesh. Usually my own.

:Movement in the hole,: Nevarre said sharply.

The three of us on the ground leaned closer, crouching, ready to pounce. Above, Leviathan's lungs sucked in air like mighty bellows, preparing his dragon fire. Though the wolf and raven would be roasted alive, they didn't back away. A shiny piece of glass pushed up out of the sand. Blood red glass, translucent and opalescent, oval in shape. Maybe a jewel?

Though it didn't look like any precious stone I'd ever seen before.

The glass split down the back, opening into wings and revealing a black body and legs beneath. *:SCARAB!:*

Both Nevarre and I stabbed downward with our beaks at the same time, though I was slightly faster. Skewered between the sharp tips, the scarab scrambled and clawed helplessly, but we kept it pinned.

My phoenix flames flickered around me, protecting me from Ra's tricks, but I was worried about the other Blood. I'd seen what one of these nasty beetles could do. Once inside a body, they deposited solar energy to melt from the inside out. At least I would be immune to it. Hopefully. *:I've got it. Back away.:*

Nevarre only pinned the thing with his taloned foot and pecked it again. *:Tastes like a normal beetle.:*

:So it tastes like a puddle of still-warm shit.: The dragon dropped to the ground with a heavy thud and came closer. *:Send the hell horse out to stomp the shit out of this thing like he did the queen ant.:*

:No need.: Nevarre lifted his head, giving a little toss back. *:It's dead unless it doesn't need a head to survive.:*

:Ask the headless knight his opinion on that little matter,: Leviathan replied.

Hesitantly, I loosened my grip on the bug, fully prepared to skewer it again if it moved. A bit of black fluid leaked from its body, the wings outspread but not moving. Legs crumpled and curled up like a dead spider. Unlike the scarab that had torched the Skye consiliarius, this one didn't smell like Ra at all. There wasn't a telltale glimmer of molten light inside it. *:I don't think it's one of Ra's scarabs. The ones we saw in New York were blue and green. Not red.:*

:Only one?: Rik asked, his bond still cutting like a steel sword through us all. *:Be very sure.:*

A smaller, normal-sized crow dropped down beside Nevarre, hopping closer to the dead bug. :*She wants to eat it.*:

:*Ask her if she's ever seen a bug like this before,*: Rik ordered.

I didn't even try to follow the head bobs and short squawks between the two birds.

:*Never,*: Nevarre finally replied. :*The murders agree. They've never seen this particular bug with this coloring. It's very unique.*:

:*Don't let her eat it, then,*: Rik said. :*If they've never seen one before, it has to be something magical. Keep it guarded until our queen can examine it to be sure.*:

In the Blood bond, we all heard a heavy whomp and a deep, rumbling snore as Ezra slipped down to the floor with Daire. Both of them out cold.

:*Lucky bastards,*: Leviathan grumbled, though without any heat. How could he, when she'd drained him twice yesterday?

:*She wants to see it.*: Rik's bond rumbled with the crashing roar of a landslide, clearly not happy at the prospect of putting our queen anywhere near this unknown threat, even if it was dead. :*We're coming out. Everyone assemble, but if you're not already there, form a second ring around the site in case the first Blood are compromised.*:

In a few moments, I felt Shara draw closer, the invisible blackhole pull of gravity inexorably dragging us all toward her. Though Rik halted her ten feet away from the hole I'd discovered. Somehow, I was surprised to see her sitting on the hell horse's back. She'd never used the knight as a normal horse, at least that I'd seen, but if he'd been the one to stomp the ants in the last attack, it made sense Rik would want her off the ground.

:*Bring the scarab to me,*: Shara ordered. :*Away from the hole. Just to be safe.*:

Smart. I shifted back to my human form so I could pick up the bug and cradle it on my palm as I carried it to her. I smelled her blood, and an instant knife of hunger twisting in my guts, though I didn't see a wound. She'd started using her magic to keep her blood from spilling out when on her period, and now that she was stretched so thin, she didn't want to risk wasting a single drop. Though I missed seeing my queen clothed in nothing but blood. Hers. Ours. Mine especially.

The hell horse blew out a loud, rattling snort as I neared, so I let G smell the dead bug in my hand. Rik blocked my path too, silently holding his hand out to take the bug from me. Sure, his meaty fists could crush it in a heartbeat, but it still felt like a demotion.

Which I fully and rightfully deserved.

The scarab looked like a grain of rice against his gigantic palm. Shara studied it for a few moments. The smell of her blood intensified, making me shiver. Smoak rippled around me, a fiery cape of sunfire energy responding to her magic. Hairs prickled up and down my arms, though I didn't see her do anything with my eyes.

A soft sigh escaped her lips, ending in a choked sound that jerked my attention to her face. Tears pooled in her eyes and her chin trembled imperceptibly. "I hoped it was a new Blood answering my Call."

"They will come," Rik assured her, gently tipping his wrist so the dead bug dropped into her hand.

The ground rumbled beneath my feet, sending me staggering into Rik. G shifted his weight to keep Shara balanced on his back without tack.

Whirling around so fast my braids whipped G's flank, I watched as the ground suddenly fell away beneath the other two Bloods' feet. Nevarre leaped into the air, taking wing immediately. The wolf dropped from my sight as a crater opened in the ground.

Shara screamed. "Xin!"

12

SHARA

Nevarre's raven dived downward, out of my line of sight into the gaping hole. Sand and dirt blew up out of the crater as if a giant wind machine had been turned on, obscuring my vision. Closing my physical eyes, I focused on their bonds. I felt the sharp dig of talons in Xin's fur. The strain in my raven's wings, struggling against the hurricane-gale winds swooping up out of the ground. He surged up out of the sandstorm and tumbled to the side clutching my wolf, a blur of silver and black rolling free of the cavity.

Tlacel and Llewellyn circled overhead, skirting the winds but sending me images of what they saw. The hole was twenty feet across and at least ten feet deep. A perfect circle with smooth, symmetrical sides, quickly filling up with sand spiraling up out of the ground like a tornado.

Blowing sand. A hot desert wind in my face.

In my mind, I flashed to Isis' pyramid. Sands swirled around the base of Her pyramid like billowing clouds with the same dusty musk. Woody and warm, like cypress and amber, with a hint of floral. Not the night blooming jasmine this time, but something heavier and richer, like a velvety rose. I didn't feel any sense of alarm or danger from Her, though I didn't call out for Her attention. I switched to the tapestry, hope rising in my chest.

A new Blood, answering my Call. Quietly, secretly, just like I'd asked. Though I hadn't intended for one to penetrate my nest and push my Blood into full alert.

However, the tapestry remained unchanged. My glowing lava and golden flame bonds wound through my mind, illuminating the gently blowing fabric of space around me. Something new stood where the hole was, but sands still obscured it. It didn't glow like a bonfire or pull me to investigate. It was... blank.

Blinking away the vision, I focused on the crater, though now it was almost completely full of sand. Ocher and clay and sparks of glassy pearl, swirling up out of the ground. Glittering with red glass.

Like the dead scarab on my palm.

:*Beware,*: Rik bellowed down the bonds. :*More scarabs hide in the sand!*:

Wrapped up in a shield of my power, the beetle didn't move on my hand. It was still dead. Though the crater hadn't opened until I touched it.

Scarabs boiled up out of the ground, rising higher with the sand and wind. A shape started to coalesce in the storm, scarabs crawling and swarming together. Hardening, the plates of exoskeleton fusing together into glittering red armor plating.

The winds died, allowing the sand to settle around a giant statue of a sphinx, though it didn't look like the Great Sphinx of Giza. It cast a shadow as big as Leviathan's, but its head was a ram with thick curling horns spiraled on either side of its head. The rest of the body was the more familiar lion. It crouched in the middle of my nest like a mighty guardian, glittering with the red shells of the scarabs.

:*I need to get closer.*:

G's sides quivered between my thighs, automatically balking before Rik could even refuse. :*We still don't know what it is.*:

:*It's not attacking.*:

:*Yet,*: Rik growled. :*If you don't recognize it as Blood, I don't relish letting you get closer to it.*:

Though he would. If I ordered it.

Inwardly, I sighed. They were right to be concerned. My nerves still felt frayed and raw. Okeanos lay face down in the grotto, floating like a dead man, and Daire and Ezra were collapsed beneath the table. If this went badly and I tapped my power deeply, I'd only have nine to pull on.

A month ago, I would have laughed and shook my head. Of course nine Blood were plenty to sustain me.

Now, the thought made my hands tremble like a junkie desperate for another hit.

Which was exactly why I had to try and wake this sphinx statue. It was huge, rivaling the dragon. It had to carry a lot of blood—and a lot of power.

My fangs dropped so hard and fast that I shuddered, my whole jaw aching. My mouth filled with blood, my lower lip shredded. I swallowed it, my hunger shearing through me like a million volts of lightning. :*I have to try.*:

Positioned before me, Rik paced closer to the statue with G right beside him, slightly behind to allow my alpha to take the brunt of whatever might happen as we neared the sphinx. Leviathan, Tlacel, and Llewellyn spiraled above in slow circles, staggered so they wouldn't all be taken out at the same time if the statue exploded. Itztli, Vivian, Nevarre, and Xin—thankfully unharmed—circled the beast, claws and talons bared like brutal swords. G's ears flickered back and forth, listening to me, my bond, and the statue. He blew a rattling warning snort, arching his neck, his haunches coiled into tight springs. Fully prepared to whirl at full gallop to carry me to safety.

Every step of the rock troll made the ground groan and

protest beneath the force of his granite boulders. He laid a hand on the statue and gave it an experimental shove. Nothing moved. The scarabs didn't swarm around his hand. His alpha senses strained, wide open and alert for anything that didn't smell or feel right. But the sphinx smelled like sand and rock without a single sign of life.

Looking through my power with my blood dripping down my chin, I didn't see anything different either. Just a statue. Nothing magical, other than the scarabs forming the exterior plating. I could barely see the delicate seams where they all fit together. The one in my hand was still dead.

Expectation filled me, a coiling of anticipation. With my bloodline through the Great One, it made sense that a sphinx might answer my Call. My only hesitation was the scarab. Madeline Skye had melted before my very eyes after vomiting out one of these creatures, and I'd burned her queen's body to make sure I killed all the critters crawling in her dead flesh. Granted, everything Ra touched had been fouled and warped by his lust. Maybe he'd only gained the scarabs after absorbing a lesser god or goddess.

The only way to know for sure would be to give the sphinx some of my blood.

None of my Blood said a word, though I felt their intensity ratchet up another level toward explosion. If I woke this thing with my blood, it'd probably be pretty fucking hungry.

But so the fuck am I.

Carefully, I dabbed a drop of my blood onto the scarab on my palm.

The statue clicked, millions of tiny glittering wings unlocking. I braced for them to explode toward me in flight, but they melted deeper into the statue, leaving only the weathered tan color of stone behind. I sucked in a deep breath, and even from feet away, I could smell the musk of lion mixed with sand. Very similar to Llewellyn's scent, though his gryphon also smelled like leather. The sphinx didn't move or breathe, but I could almost feel its fur beneath my fingers. One step closer to waking it.

Rik hissed and grabbed my arm, locking his thick fingers around a faint tickle on the inside of my wrist. *:It's going for your blood.:*

The dead scarab wasn't in my palm any longer. Heart thudding heavily, I peeled back one of his fingers on my forearm. I'd used my nail to puncture my wrist before I stepped outside, though I hadn't allowed the blood to drip free of my body. If it'd crawled inside that small hole...

My stomach heaved. Power surged through me, a liquid wall of raging fire and lighting to expel the creature before it could dig deeper into my veins. I didn't feel it crawling through my body, or any dip in my reserves.

Rik lifted another finger cautiously, revealing the red glitter of the scarab's wing embedded in my flesh. Like the serpent, before I'd deployed it against Ra, it looked like a beautiful jewel against my skin. A glowing, bright tattoo of exquisite detail in ruby red, emerald, and black. Wings outstretched over its head, it framed the small puncture hole where my blood glowed. A red disc it carried like the sun.

Like Isis' crown.

Rik's fingers softened, though he remained at the highest alert. Giant slabs of rock moved beneath his broad, massive shoulders. His thighs like massive obelisks. His hands powerful enough to crush marble and granite into dust. Yet if I sank my fangs into him...

I licked my torn lip and chin, gathering up the drool mixed with my blood. I'd find hot blood waiting beneath that stone.

Now to see if hot blood pooled inside the sphinx.

:Even cobra fangs shatter against stone.: Leviathan dropped to the ground beside us. The dragon's eyes burned with emerald fire. Hunger, yes, drawn by my blood, but also jealousy.

I was his secret hoard. The thing he craved above all. Even his freedom. Not allowing him to drink as much as he wanted from me, whenever he wanted, had stirred dragon ire burning like acid through his veins.

I didn't dare risk letting him feed until I had this sphinx taken care of, but I also loathed denying any of them. Ignoring his bared teeth and smoke pluming from his nostrils, I reached up and pulled his head down closer so I could press a bloody kiss to his snout. :*My fangs penetrated your scales, so I think I'll be just fine, my dragon. But I might need your help in holding them still until I've had my fill.*:

He snarled, black smoke curling around me in a thick cloud, his tongue snaking out to swipe along my chin and mouth. Cleaning every drop. :*I'll fucking bite it in half for you, my queen.*:

13

SHARA

I stared up at the sphinx's stone exterior, letting ideas pop and flow in my mind. I still didn't have a sense of life or personality from the statue, so in that regard, Leviathan might be right. There wasn't anything here for me to feed on.

Yet.

The statue was big enough the rock troll and hell horse were both able to stand in its shadow with me. My mighty dragon draped himself over the sphinx's lion haunches, his jaws poised to sink into the ram's neck where it joined the lion body. The scarab buried in my wrist made me hesitate. I didn't want all of them to surge back up out of the sphinx and attack us.

But I didn't feel any threat from the scarab. In fact, its iconography resonated with me. It felt... right. Like it was meant to be a part of me.

The shadows lengthened as the sun began to set over the giant statue's shoulder. Leviathan's neck arched, lifting his head for a moment to shade my eyes against the setting sun. :*At least it'll be dark if this motherfucker's as feisty as I was once freed.*:

My cheeks burned at the thought of Winston or someone on Frank's team watching the equivalent of a bloody garden party orgy on the lawn. To be safe, I touched Gina's and Frank's bonds. *:I'm getting ready to do some queen shit in the grove. Please let Winston know.:*

I gave G a gentle nudge with my will, asking him to step closer to the sphinx. "I need to touch him."

Blowing out another deep breath making his sides rock beneath my calves, he stepped closer to the giant statue between its outstretched front paws. Using Rik for balance, I carefully stood up on G's broad back, swaying slightly as he sidled his hindquarters closer to the sphinx.

"Great One, Isis, please let this work," I whispered out loud, reaching up to smear some of my blood on the sphinx's snout.

It didn't move but the smell of lion intensified, feral and raw musk. My other furry Bloods' hackles rose on low snarls. My blood glistened wetly on the rock, almost black in the shadow. Then it was gone, soaked into the stone. I could feel it flowing through the statue in a hot rush of electricity, charging it up.

Bringing it to life.

I smelled its blood, calling to me as surely as a wolf will howl to the full moon. Though the sphinx still didn't move. No breath, no heartbeat. Just the pooling blood deep inside as if I'd turned a faucet on in the bathroom to fill up the gigantic tub.

Urgency pulsed through me. Sand swirled around G's hooves, draining away back into the ground. Disappearing back to wherever the sphinx had come from like an hourglass. Time was running out. The sun was setting. When it was dark...

Closing my eyes, I silently prayed, *Goddess, don't let the sun set on this Blood. I need them. Please.*

Then I stretched up to my tiptoes, carefully balancing on G's back, and sank my fangs into the sphinx's shoulder.

My brutal fangs cut through the exterior stone like a hot knife through butter. I tasted blood, but it didn't immediately spurt and surge into my mouth. Not like a living, breathing Blood. Of course. If the sphinx didn't have a heartbeat, there wasn't anything to pump the blood to me. I was going to have to work for it.

I retracted my fangs, though a pang of loss made me shudder. I loved being inside my Blood when I took them. Locking my mouth tight on the punctures, I sucked a swallow of blood into my mouth and held it on my tongue. Tasting.

Male. Powerful. Extremely old.

Midnight velvet skies sprinkled with millions of stars. Eerie green and blue flares of comets streaking to the horizon. Blazing sun, baking the earth until it cracked open. Howling, hot winds and stinging sands. Torrential rains pounding the earth, swelling the river until it overflowed its banks and poured around my feet.

His feet. This endless guardian, standing watch since the beginning of time. Or so it seemed. Always awake. Always guarding.

The sphinx never slept.

I swallowed his blood, shivering as flares of energy sparked through my veins. Oh yeah. He carried quite a kick.

His mind stretched toward me from an impossible distance, crossing thousands of years to find me. *:Your Majesty, we rise in answer to your Call.:*

I sucked another long swallow of his blood, drinking him like a cold, foamy draught straight from the tap. *:We? There are more than just you?:*

:If you can hold us.:

Pressing my palms to his chest, I groaned when I found only stone instead of the luxurious fur of his lion. *:How many?:*

An image filled my mind of a long, dark avenue lined with shadows. The sun peeked over the horizon, slowly illuminating the line of sentinels. Sphinxes lined the cobblestoned road. Pair after pair after pair into the distance as far as I could see. Stunned, I blinked, and another image filled my head. Columns of a palace, flickering from its grandeur thousands of years ago, to the ruin it was now. Broken obelisks, worn carvings, hieroglyphs wiped away by the endless passage of time. Blowing sands swallowing the city. Hiding the crumbled, chipped remains of sphinxes.

Still guarding.

Statues deep in the Nile, lost to floods centuries ago. Buried in mud, tangled in reeds.

Still awake. Always watching.

Waiting.

:Thousands,: he replied. *:Take me, Your Majesty, and call as many of your army as you can before the sun sets in your world. Though I must warn you. The more you drink of me, the more of them you claim, and consequently, the harder I am to hold. Lose me and lose your legion.:*

Thousands? Goddess above, why did She send me an entire army? Surely I wouldn't need a legion of sphinxes to bring justice to the Dauphine.

I hesitated for a moment, not willing to take a dozen new Blood at once, let alone thousands.

:They're your army, not your Blood. You bring me alone into your circle.: A deep cough vibrated through his chest. A lion's laughter. *:Besides, not even the Great One's daughter can hold three thousand sphinxes to her will.:*

I bit back a knee-jerk response, "Watch me." Had I learned nothing from taking on the sunfires? They'd nearly burned me out trying to hold them all.

But my ego insisted I could do it. Sphinxes were in my lineage. They were monsters.

While the sun sank lower in the sky.

:We've got him, my queen.: Rik sent me an image of him gripping one of the curled ram horns in his mighty biceps, twisting the sphinx's head into an armlock, while the dragon rode his back. *:Suck him fucking dry.:*

14

SHARA

How much blood could I physically hold?

I had a moment to laugh at myself, remembering how concerned I was when I'd first tasted Daire and Rik's blood. Terrified my fresh hunger would injure them. They'd told me my stomach couldn't hold enough to actually incapacitate a fully-grown Aima warrior, but they were wrong.

I could hold a fucking lot. So much it'd taken help from the Aztec sun god—who knew all things regarding blood—to help me understand how I managed to drink so deeply and not be in physical pain.

How sweetly dangerous would it be to simply feast—without fear of yet another mighty Blood dropping unconscious at my feet?

Surrendering to the thirst, I pulled hard on my punctures, wallowing in the bottomless pit inside the sphinx. So much blood. The cheese grater stopped flaying my tender nerves, easing the nagging, burning pain growing exponentially over the past few days. Until I couldn't smell or look at my Blood without wanting to tear them apart.

At first, I didn't even try to track where the blood flowed

into my reserves. I drank until the stone softened against my lips, heating with the flesh of a living, breathing lion. His heart pulsed once. Twice. Blood spurted—but not into my mouth. Away from my pull. His heart sent the blood pounding away from me. Not to his extremities—but to the other sphinxes.

Alertness flared through them. Stone heads grinding, turning toward me. Looking at me. But when I paused drinking, their heads started swinging back straight ahead.

Oh fuck no. I sucked harder on my punctures, drawing his blood. Swinging those heads back to me. More. *I want them all.*

Heavy grunts filled my ears. Muttered curses. Roars. Rik wrestled the ram's head downward, refusing to let the beast rear back and away from me. Leviathan gripped the sphinx's spine in his mighty jaws, his claws scraping deep gouges down the statue's sides. No blood, just stone.

The blood only came to me. If I could hold it.

Llewellyn's gryphon shrieked and he sent me an image of the sun starting to dip below the horizon. *:You're running out of time, Shara.:*

Rearing back, I jammed both hands deeply into the sphinx's chest, letting my nails join the fight. Because it was a war now. Stone heaved against me, struggling to break free of my Bloods' holds, trying to jostle my lips loose. Crashing boulders filled my ears, the screech of claws sliding down stone. Thuds as my smaller Blood threw themselves against the sphinx's legs and paws, trying to keep him down.

Swallow. Again. The sphinx bellowed with fury. Shaking his head, he reared up so hard Rik's feet dangled off the ground, but my alpha tightened his locked forearm. Twisting harder, granite muscles swelling with effort. Itztli and Xin couldn't bite the statue, but they sank their teeth into Rik's lower legs and added their weight to his, pulling him back down to the ground.

Taking a deep breath through my nose, I strained harder. Eyes closed, I pulled with not just the suction of my mouth but

my entire body. My will. I opened my throat, throwing the
floodgates of my body open wide.

Rivers of blood to rival the mighty Nile itself. Flow to me.

Gushes and torrents of blood filled me, sweeping my awareness into my Blood, a tiny stick tossed on angry floodwaters.
Lighting up their root chakras, energy flowing up their spines.
My energy made them stronger. Bigger. Badder than ever. I
strained harder, filling each of them up. All my reserves.
Stacking another layer of glowing power into them. My alpha, a
giant. His fists locked on the ram's horns. My dragon, his jaws
so big he gripped all the sphinx's throat. Squeezing, suffocating
him, bearing him down beneath the full weight of the king of
the depths.

Down. Down to me.

So I could feast until the end of time.

Too much. They were full. I couldn't lay any more bricks of
energy into their bones. Yet blood still raged, threatening to
sweep me away.

I poured energy into my closest sibling bonds. Mayte
Zaniyah. Every jungle in the world, hers to nurture and
command. Plagues that made the deadliest pandemic the world
had ever seen look like a common cold. Trees and ferns pushing
up out of the earth in her footsteps, crowned with the rarest
lilies and orchids long extinct.

Her jaguar Blood. I stacked their spines with my energy.
Their cats screamed a triumphant warning in the jungle, eyes
glowing like eerie lamps in the trees. They rivaled the jaguar
god's size now, and he was even bigger than Rik.

I tried to dump power to Tepeyollotl, her jaguar god, but his
channel was locked. He wasn't mine, and he was strong enough
to refuse my access. I didn't dare touch Xochitl. I didn't know
what this power would do to a child.

Gwenhwyfar Findabair Camelot, a true descendant of Guinevere, the Once and Future Queen. Her loyal knights had fought

to stay free of Elaine Shalott, who'd forced Gwen to swear to never take her own Blood for over four hundred years. Sir Lancelot du Lac, the famed Round Table knight, the prize alpha of Camelot. His manticore roared with pride, his thick scorpion tail dripping venom.

Her tattooed Blood, Bors, his giant stag's rack stretching out like the world tree, armed with barbed crossbow tips to protect her. Mordred's golden war eagle screeched with victory, leading the charge on his queen's next epic quest. The dark one, Merlin. Not Aima. Hungering for flesh rather than only blood. I wasn't sure what he was and hadn't met him yet. Though his creature soaked up my offering as eagerly as the knights.

The White Enchantress blazed with all the glory of Arthurian legends, and the clang of swords filled my head. The power of centuries of fables and lore passed down from generation to generation, becoming legend that time would never forget.

Carys Tylluan, lover of knowledge, who could see probabilities for any strategy I might devise. Her mind powered higher, driven with the ultrafast power of CERN's particle accelerator. Her archives and databases sparking with energy. All books, all knowledge, any computation, stacked within her like my dragon's priceless hoard.

Yet still the power surged higher, demanding release. Grunting with effort, Rik slipped backward, driven by the ram's broad head, his feet furrowing deeply into the earth. The hell horse reared high and slammed his front hooves into the ram's skull, knocking him back. Thudding again and again.

My trees. I shoved energy into the ground, letting their roots soak up the overage. My grotto, steaming hot enough I feared for Okeanos, though I didn't feel him swimming. Too much power blazed through me now to differentiate between Blood bonds.

My blood circle already gleamed like fiery rubies from the

ground, hundreds of feet into the air. Higher. I willed the circle to spread a dome of protection over my entire nest, using the sphinx's blood to power it.

Redline. The strain of holding so much power made my teeth vibrate. My skull throbbed, tender plates fracturing apart beneath the shearing torque. My blood hummed in my veins, sizzling too hot. My skin couldn't contain so much. My bones couldn't carry the weight.

I dumped more power into the New York City Tower. My blood circle encompassed all one-hundred floors already. A full city block. Thicker. Taller. Deeper. Reinforcing the concrete and glass with sheer energy gleaming with starlight. The bone-white branches of the tree in the basement, grown with pain and blood. It couldn't get taller, but its roots dug deeper into the soil, its trunk so thick Leviathan could curl inside.

My bones splintered. My spine burned, liquifying into molten, glowing steel. I jammed my silver nails deeper into lion flesh, hooking my fingers. Dangling against the flailing, surging beast by nothing but my nails stabbed into him.

I am Shara Isador, last daughter of She Who Is and Was and Always Will Be!

My mother is Esetta Isador! She died to have me. She gave up her name from all living memory so I could be free. So I could stand here in the shadow of a sphinx and claim my legion.

What this queen takes, she loves, and what she loves, she keeps for all time.

You will come to me.

All of you.

So let it be!

The sun slipped fully beneath the horizon.

A geyser ruptured through me. Sweeping me away in a crashing barrage of blood.

I lay on my back. Staring up at the sky, indigo streaked with purple and pink. So beautiful. The first star twinkled at me.

Make a wish. I tried to giggle but it didn't sound right. A choked, wheezing gasp.

A hard thrust of dick sheathing deep in my body made me blink. Trying to focus. Twitching. My arms flopped. Useless.

Gurgles when I tried to speak. His name. I still didn't know. Who?

But his teeth. Ripped my throat. Out.

~

SEKH

CHAOS ERUPTED AROUND US.

Wallowing in bloodlust, it slowly occurred to me that I might have made a critical error.

Rather than reveling in what our queen had wrought, her other Blood forcibly dragged me off her before I barely had a taste. The alpha had his arm around my neck so tight my spine popped, threatening to release my head. The dragon savagely ground deeper against my buttocks, his rage lashing me like flaming whips while he fucked me.

"G," the alpha boomed like thunder. "Get her to safety!"

The Blood who'd been pummeling me with his hooves just moments before grabbed her beneath her arms and dragged her a few feet away. Leaving a blood trail that gleamed like priceless jewels in the starlight. I strained against the alpha's chokehold, ignoring his ire. If they took her away from me, I'd at least lick her blood from the ground.

I only had a fucking taste. A drop in the ocean from what she'd taken from me. Fresh, hot blood dripped down my chin. Shuddering, I licked every drop. My infinite thirst, agonies. Thousands of years in the making.

The fragile scent of her skin in my jaws. The lush oasis of her body. Insanity to lose it. To not revel in her. A queen fucking called me from my goddess-given role, and they didn't want me to bask in her glory and pleasure?

"Shara." The horse—G, evidently—wrapped his palms around her throat, quelling the blood spray. "Close these wounds before you bleed out and waste all the power and blood you've gained."

Shara. Yes. Her name. Now it was engraved in my hide like a hieroglyph that would never weather away.

She made a ragged sound that tightened the alpha's head-lock, wrenching my head harder. Darkness threatened, making me struggle even more. Not because I feared oblivion. I hadn't slept or closed my all-seeing eyes in millennia. Unconsciousness would be a fucking relief, even for a moment. But why waste one fucking second, one sweet drop, of her exquisite blood?

The dragon rutted harder, stirring my bloodlust higher. Since I couldn't breathe, I used the newly forged bond gleaming in my head like a blistering sword wreathed in fire. Hopefully the alpha would hear it. *:When does she fuck new Blood?:*

A boulder slammed into the side of my head. Lightning crackled through my vision.

"You. Don't. Touch." He punctuated each word with another punishing punch, slamming my head to the ground. Though I still couldn't get my face in the pooled blood that was quickly soaking into the dirt. A fucking travesty. "One fucking hair. On her head. Not without permission."

No feast. No fuck. Not until she invited me. Fine. *:Then fucking bring her back so she can give permission.:*

"Motherfucker," the dragon snarled in my ear, leaning hard on my shoulders to hasten my head popping off sooner in his alpha's big hands. "Even I didn't try to fuck her without permission."

:Not that I mind in the slightest, but I don't recall giving you permission.:

He roared, raking my flank with his claws. "Exactly!"

:Bring it the fuck on, dragon. I'll fuck you all to get another taste of her.:

She made a choked sound again, and one of my vertebrae cracked, the alpha wrestling my chin past my shoulder.

"All better," she said in a bright voice. "Wait, where'd my clothes go?"

"She's fine," G said, amusement softening his voice. "She's blood drunk, not hurt."

"And that dick? I want it back."

:You fucking heard her!:

"Not so fast, motherfucker," the dragon snarled.

"Agreed," the alpha said, though he did at least allow me to draw breath. "How drunk are you, my queen?"

She giggled, lifting her hands up. "Help me up."

The horse pulled her to her feet, keeping an arm around her when she swayed. I smelled dog and wolf. Something fiery like burned spices. The alpha and dragon, of course.

So much power, even for a daughter of the Great One.

Such immense *hunger*. I'd seen her calling Blood after Blood, but still, I had no idea it would feel like this.

Un-fucking-believable. They had no idea what she'd done. Evidently, neither did she.

Staggering closer to us, she beamed up at her alpha. "I feel better. Everyone can feed now."

The dragon pulled back and thrust hard enough a grunt escaped my lips. "Not you."

"Oh." Her eyes went round, her mouth sagging open. "That's so fucking hot."

I couldn't help but groan again, a wordless plea. *Come closer. Touch me. Let me touch you.*

Her cheeks blazed bright red, and she covered her mouth. "Goddess, I'm so sorry. Are you okay with... with..." She gestured vaguely at the dragon humping me.

The alpha unlocked his forearm from my throat, though he

didn't move aside. "He gets what he deserves, my queen, and nothing less."

A test. The rational part of my brain recognized his actions for what it was. More like a trap, honestly, because now she stood before me, and it was madness not to touch her.

This queen. Who'd ended my eternal watch and called me to her side. Who'd made me a living, breathing being with the formidable strength of her will alone. She'd danced and bathed in my blood like the goddess who made me.

Goddess fucking incarnate, graced with beauty and strength. Thick, black hair gleamed down her back like a velvet cape. Her midnight eyes shone like the stars and moon above. Lush, sweet curves to drive any man to his knees, praising the goddess who'd made her. Begging for a chance to worship at her altar.

All I wanted to do was ignore her alpha's instruction—reinforced by his fists—and drag her back beneath me. Lust hammered through me, a vicious, brutal spike of desperation. Plan B. I rocked back against the dragon, rearing back against him so my erection was on display for her. I groaned roughly, taking him deeper, not afraid to let her hear my need. I'd fucking beg the alpha to let me suck him off too if that eventually brought her closer.

Though the dragon knew all too well what my motivation was. He and I were woven from the same fibers, though where he had scales, I had razor wire. He shoved me back down beneath him, with an extra hard elbow between my shoulder blades. Putting my face in the fucking ground where I couldn't even see her.

Plan C. Two could play this fucking game. At least now I was closer to her spilled blood on the ground. Cold, a little gritty, but after thousands of years, I'd eat the grass from the entire clearing like the fucking horse just to get another taste of her.

I dug my fingers into the ground, tearing up the earth. Inching my fingers perilously closer to her bare toes.

"Don't be so mean," she scolded.

"He fucking touched you!" The dragon gnashed his teeth, the fierce clang of swords. "When you were unaware. That's fucking unforgivable."

Those pretty little toes moved closer. She stood between my splayed hands. Closer. My outstretched arms trembled with the effort of not seizing her. Her scent filled my nose, and a strange pang seized my heart in a fist of granite to rival the alpha's.

Home. She smelled like home. Shining moonlight on crystal sands, holy incense softly wafting on a gentle breeze with a hint of pure, clear water sparkling in a deep, secret pool. Sprinkled with velvety petals of fragrant flowers.

The kind of place a goddess would bathe.

"I sucked him hard." She dropped her voice to a conspiratorial whisper, as if only the dragon could hear. "Like when I pulled your dragon out. Remember? I drained you to the point of death, so close to killing you. If either of us had been able to walk, I would have fucked you on the hillside then, my dragon."

The alpha grunted sourly. "Not with the broken arm he gave you."

Drool streamed from my mouth, my teeth throbbing as hard as my dick. I fought the urge to retort a smart comment. Better to remain silent—and not give her a reason to step away—than get another dig into the dragon. The last thought on my mind had been injuring her, though granted, I'd bitten her a little too enthusiastically in my eagerness to taste her. She'd only been injured when they ripped her away from me.

"The arm fucking healed," the dragon retorted. "He can't undo putting his dick in *our* queen."

She swayed, bumping my shoulder, her hand reaching out to steady herself. A red-hot branding iron on my flesh. "I decide whose dick goes where." Then she hiccupped.

Something broke inside me, a snapped rubber band sheared by the strain of holding myself firmly in place. But I only moved slightly, shifting my shoulder to provide a wider base for her to lean against.

Knees replaced her toes as she dropped down before me. Her fingers gentle on my cheek, tipping my face up to hers.

Before she could say anything, I said, "Forgive me, Your Majesty."

"There's nothing to forgive." She cupped my face in her hands. "What's your name?"

"Sekh."

Her brow wrinkled in a slight frown. "What's your house name? Your lineage?"

"I was created by Sekhmet to stand guard for all time."

Eyes like an endless night sky streaked with a million stars widened with shock. "You're not Aima? Like us?"

Even though he wasn't thrusting while she talked to us, the dragon's cock pulsed inside me like a second heartbeat, adding to the clamoring need that surged inside me. Pounding, brutal, savage. Fucking feral.

I almost wished the alpha had me in a headlock again, squeezing my windpipe into oblivion. At least I couldn't fuck this up if I passed out. I was quickly losing the ability to think in complete sentences.

Flesh. Blood. Feast. Fuck.

Not appropriate words to give her.

"Never mind." She draped her arm around my neck. "What are you waiting for?"

15

SHARA

He might not be Aima but he moved with the same lethal, inhuman speed as my other Blood. One arm shot up, his big hand palming the back of my head. His other arm snaked around my hips, jerking me off my knees and sweeping me beneath him so fast that a squeak escaped my lips.

Panting, he froze, cradling my head so it didn't thud against the ground.

"I'm okay," I said aloud, both for him and Rik, who'd already started to reach for me with a formidable glower on his face.

Still in his rock troll. I blinked rapidly, trying to make my fuzzy brain work. He must still be worried about the new Blood. That's why he was willing to let Mehen work some of the feistiness out of him. Like Rik had done to him.

Which only made another wave of heat flood my entire body. I moaned, my back arching involuntarily. I tightened my arm around Sekh's neck and opened my thighs wide. Welcoming him in. He sank into me with a deep, shaky sigh of bliss that brought tears to my eyes.

Though his sigh quickly turned to a rough, guttural wordless sound of hunger. He wanted my body, definitely, but thirst burned in his bond, a miserable, punishing need. No fucking wonder. I drank so much from him I still wasn't sure how he was able to function, let alone fuck.

Mehen's forearm wrenched the other man's throat back, pulling him away from me. Slitted green eyes glittered over Sekh's shoulder. "The new man feeds last."

Not a rule I'd ever given anyone. I glared up at him. "Remember what I did to you that first night."

When I'd bitten him again and again, forcing him to climax multiple times, while Rik fucked him.

Green flickered brighter in Mehen's eyes, and he practically chortled with glee. "Yes, my queen. Bite him a thousand times."

"Be my guest," Sekh said, his voice rough from the pressure of the forearm on his throat. "Even if you can't ever feed on me again."

Was I so buzzed on his blood I simply didn't understand what he meant? Sure, I'd taken a huge amount from him, but never feed again? He didn't know me yet, I got that, but goddess. What kind of queen did he expect?

Confused, I studied his face, noting bruises on the proud planes of his cheekbones. One eye swollen shut. Rik hadn't been too happy with him. His jawline was outlined by a trimmed, neat beard. Silky black spiraled curls hung in his eyes, burning like twin suns. The molten gold sent a shock through me.

Scarabs. Heliopolis. Ra.

Sekh's eyes narrowed, his fingers tightening on my nape. "Fuck Ra."

:*Fuck yeah,*: Vivian replied loudly in our bonds, so that I'm sure all of my Blood heard it. But then in a soft, targeted whisper to me, she said, :*I sense nothing of Heliopolis in him, my queen.*:

Relieved, I lifted my other arm toward my dragon, bypassing

Sekh for now. Of all my Blood, Mehen felt the lack of feeding whenever he wanted the most. Not for the blood and the power necessarily, though he reveled in that too. It was the connection and touch he wanted beyond even sex. He wanted the soul-to-soul communion of feeding from me, while he took care of me. Though he'd blast all the pyramids in Heliopolis into a misshapen golden puddle before he'd ever fucking admit he *needed* me.

Without loosening his grip around Sekh's throat, Mehen leaned harder on his back, giving us more of his weight so he could seize my hand and press my wrist to his mouth. Which drove Sekh deeper. My eyes rolled back in my head, pleasure humming through me as Mehen's fangs sank into me.

"Our queen doesn't lay on the ground when she can lay on top of Blood." Guillaume dropped down behind me, lifting my head and shoulders so he could scoot partially beneath me, bringing me onto his lap.

Which put his thick cock right there. Beside me, pressing against my side, a hot velvety rod to torment me. Though that wasn't why he'd joined us. He had a knife in his right hand. One of his bigger ones. A crystal-clear message to the new Blood.

Touch me in a way that Sir Guillaume de Payne didn't like, and his head was going to roll.

I squirmed between them, deliberately rubbing against G's dick. I even tugged on my arm, trying to pull my hand back down so I could further torment him, but Mehen growled and tightened his grip. While Sekh's thirst fanned my desire into a blistering inferno. I pushed my heels into the ground, rocking my hips up against him. Though with Mehen's weight on his back, there wasn't much thrusting that Sekh could do. Not until my dragon cooperated.

:*Bite him, and I'll fuck you both.*:

Sekh had told me to bite him, and he seemed game for

anything, though that might be his thirst talking more than his true desire.

:*Sorry,*: I warned him, tightening my arm on his neck. Lurching up, I sank my fangs into his throat, braced for all hell to break loose.

And it did, but not from Sekh. Mehen bellowed so loudly I wasn't entirely sure he hadn't shifted into his dragon. He convulsed on top of us, crushing Sekh against me. Startled, I released his throat so I could see. Rather than taking Guillaume's dick in his face, he'd twisted slightly to my left. On his elbow, braced on his forearm, head pressed against his hand. His shoulders shook, but not in climax despite my bite.

His bond was a convoluted mess of sensation. Too much need. Ravenous thirst bordering on madness. All mixed with random words. :*Test. Hold. Wait. Test! Don't. Fuck. Up.*:

Still a dead weight on top of us, Mehen twitched and groaned. I smelled his cum as if my bite had driven him to climax instead of Sekh.

The knife floated past my line of vision, a silver blur making my heart seize in my chest. Guillaume dug the brutal tip into the man's throat above my two gaping punctures, pressing deeper until he turned his head enough to look at him.

"Don't fucking rip her throat out again."

"He might need help," I started to say, but Sekh opened his mouth, baring all his teeth.

Not Aima. Not even human.

Despite the ram head of his sphinx, he had the brutal teeth of a lion with four gigantic fucking canines.

My pussy clenched so hard he squeezed his eyes shut, his face straining. But he nodded. Once. Pushing the knife deeper into his neck.

G lowered the blade, yet Sekh still waited, his face strained and tight. Sweat trickled down his face. His nostrils flared wide with each deep breath. Taking in my scent. And he was still rock hard inside me. My orgasmic bite hadn't affected him at all.

Turning my head back toward Guillaume, I bared the left side of my throat and shoulder for Sekh. I threw my arm around G's erection, gripping the base in my hand and hugging his dick closer to my body. He was too thick to get in my mouth without unhinging my jaws, so I simply licked everything I could reach.

I felt a hot gust of air on my skin as Sekh came closer. The delicate prick of his teeth despite the ravenous thirst hammering in his bond. He gripped my shoulder in his jaws rather than my more vulnerable throat. His blood dripped down on me, splattering over my chest. Adding to my pleasure. Stirring my hunger.

He hesitated, a jolt of shock flickering through him. *:You still hunger?:*

In answer, I leaned up and licked my way back to my bite on his throat. *:Always.:*

This time, I could simply enjoy his taste rather than strain to hold the sphinxes' attention on me. Honeyed sweetness flowed on my tongue, spiced with desert heat. Drinking him was like lying in the pleasant warmth of the sun and simply soaking in all that luxurious heat.

His entire body trembled against me as he fed. Frantic gulps at first, the same as me when I'd first tasted the wealth of his blood. Though he quickly settled in to enjoy a slow feast. His sandpaper tongue rasped over my skin, his teeth scraping without penetrating me again. Pleasure swelled inside me, a gentle wave slowly filling me. A cup shimmering with pure, sweet water, almost overflowing. Hovering right on the edge of too full. Too much. Only to take another drop. Another thrust and grind.

I still gripped G's dick against my body. His rock-hard thigh beneath me. Blindly, I reached out with my left hand.

Rik's fingers closed around mine. He dropped down to his knees beside us. I wanted to touch him. Needed to feel the hot granite of his need in my other hand. I didn't have to ask. He sensed my desire and wrapped my palm around his dick, gliding our hands up and down his length. Pushing me closer to spilling over.

Though it was a slow, long tumble over an endless waterfall, taking us all to crash in the rocks below.

Pleasure still eddied inside me as I came back to awareness. Two dicks still gripped in my hands. Sekh collapsed on top of me. Mehen a dead weight on top of us both, still mumbling and moaning incoherently.

Someone laughed. "Fuck me sideways." It took me a moment to recognize Ezra's voice. "That gives new meaning to double fisting."

My head didn't feel attached to the rest of my body. Maybe I was still blood drunk. "At least I didn't take them on top of the table."

Mehen heaved out a deep, rattling breath though his head still lolled over Sekh's shoulder. "What the fuck did you do to me?"

"Only what you deserved and nothing less." Sekh lay curled on my left side, his head pillowed on his elbow. His golden eyes still burned with slumberous heat as he looked at me. "One of my many powers is transference, Your Majesty. I can shift any sensation to a target of my choice and magnify its effect a hundredfold."

I grinned at him. "So you shifted the orgasm of my bite to him and basically blasted him to queendom come. Nice."

His lips quirked. "You have no idea what you've done, do you?"

I blinked, slowly shaking my head.

"You took us all," he answered softly. "Including me."

"And who the fuck are you?" Ezra retorted.

Sekh's eyelids weighed heavier, sleepier, though his bond stilled with the kind of deadly menace that usually rolled from Xin or Guillaume when they were hoping I'd send them into another queen's nest.

"Sekh." He said his name with a hard *kuh* on the end, giving it a second syllable. "General of the All Seeing, Never Sleeping Legion of She Who Dances In Blood."

16

SHARA

Calling a goddess' general to my Blood wasn't on my bingo card.

I couldn't quite wrap my head around it. Not that he was a powerful general. That part made absolute and complete sense. His controlled, confident stride and direct, penetrating gaze gave him the aura of a supremely confident, dangerous leader. Not just any leader, either, but someone with the mental and physical strength to command a legion of bloodthirsty killers.

No, what I struggled to comprehend was the fact we'd just fucked said confident, powerful general.

Though we were far from unscathed.

Rik carried me to the house because my legs still wobbled. My vision kept swimming in and out of focus. Plus, my blood circle had been penetrated yet again by an outside force. Mehen was slung between Guillaume and Ezra, head down, his steps more shuffled stumbles than walking. Of course neither of them were too careful with him, either, casually dumping him into a heap on the floor in front of the fireplace. Rik started to walk past his crumpled form.

"Wait, let me see if I can heal him."

Silent, Sekh stood off to the side, his shoulders relaxed, his arms loose at his side. Naked, of course, because we all were after the Blood had shifted. Evidently my clothes had been shredded off me without me even realizing it. He didn't have any weapons. He made no threats. Yet the hairs on my nape prickled with apprehension every time I looked at him.

So fucking dangerous. He may have answered my Call, but he wasn't the kind of man who'd bend his head easily to any queen. This went deeper than alpha or whose dick was bigger. He was a sacred guardian created by Sekhmet Herself.

Who was I to interfere in Her work for him?

Evidently, his queen. For now. If he deigned to stay. I wasn't one-hundred percent sure that my blood bond would be enough to hold him if and when he decided to leave.

Grudgingly, Rik squatted down by Mehen, who still mumbled incoherently. I smelled his blood, but I didn't remember biting him. Touching his bond was like sticking my arm into a fire ants' nest—with honey smeared to my elbow. Angry buzzing, stinging, a whirlwind of shrapnel that cut through our bond, making me wince.

I laid my hand on his shoulder, and he shuddered, moaning, his legs and arms twitching. Even more concerned, I lifted a nail toward my wrist, intending to call my blood so I could heal him, but Rik closed his fingers around my hand. "He's fine."

"But—"

Mehen moaned. "Don't let her touch me again."

Stricken, I bit back a choked gasp. I played back the scene in my mind, horrified I might have upset or injured him. If anyone had a right to be pissed, it'd be Sekh. I didn't think anyone had taken the time to interview the new Blood about his sexual preferences before we'd banged him.

"I know it's difficult for you but try not to be an asshole for once." With a fierce scowl, Guillaume nudged Mehen with his foot. "Tell her what's wrong with you before she wastes a single drop of her blood."

"Still." Mehen gritted his teeth, the ligaments standing out in his neck. "Coming."

Oh fuck. "Still?" I squeaked out.

He roared, rolling over on his back. "Yes!"

Blood dripped from his eyes, nose, and ears. Distended veins roped up and down the full length of his purple, swollen cock. Definitely still rock hard. Twitching, quivering with another wave of climax, though no cum spurted out.

"Next motherfucker. To touch. Me." He panted, eyes squeezed shut. "Gets roasted alive. Once I stop. Fucking. Coming!"

We all looked at Sekh with varying stages of admiration, consternation, and downright envy. One corner of his mouth quirked up and he inclined his head. "At your service, Your Majesty."

Guillaume stepped over and slapped him on the shoulder. "Someone get this man some clothes."

WITHIN A FEW MINUTES, WE HAD EVERYONE NOT ON DUTY—OR still coming or passed out—dressed and assembled around the dining room table. Nevarre had brought me a light, flowy sundress in simple white cotton. No underwear, because of course not. Hopefully the material was thick enough I wouldn't accidentally give poor Winston an eyeful. At least I wasn't on my period.

Winston had whisked away the tumbled dishes and soiled tablecloth while we were outside, though he was still thankfully absent from the kitchen when we'd all tromped in naked. Daire still slept underneath the table, though he was purring softly. I hadn't drained him badly enough that he needed healing.

None of the Blood sat down with me, taking up their normal positions around the room. Present—but not relaxed. Rik stood at my back, his hands on my shoulders. Ezra rummaged around in the fridge, pulling out food. His stomach growled like his grizzly after feeding me earlier.

Sekh watched us, taking in everything in that calm, casual manner that belied his experience. Dressed in black jeans and a simple black T-shirt, he looked like any other modern man I might see on the street. Not human for anyone who knew what we were, but he didn't move with stiff military formality. Despite being the new man in a room full of powerful Blood and their queen, he didn't appear to be self-conscious or concerned about his place. He just watched.

All seeing. Never sleeping. His nature. Taking it all in.

Softly, I asked, "How much can you see at once?"

"Everything not deliberately cloaked," he replied just as easily and quietly. "The entire world."

"What do you watch for?"

"Everything," he repeated. "I am Her eyes." His head tipped ever so slightly to the side. "Now, I'm yours."

I gestured to the chair beside me, inviting him to sit. His eyes flickered quickly to my alpha behind me and back to my face. Noting none of the other Blood sat with me, I'm sure. He stepped closer to stand behind the chair but didn't immediately sit.

I fought the urge to sigh. Blood could be very particular about formalities, let alone a general. I didn't want to start off by ordering him to do something as silly as sit with me. "Are you hungry?"

The skin around his eyes crinkled slightly. "I haven't had a physical body in over three thousand years."

Huffing out a low laugh, Guillaume dragged out a chair on my right and sat down. "So yeah, he's fucking hungry for all things, my queen."

All things… I touched Sekh's bond lightly, not wanting to be intrusive when he was so new to not just me but evidently this world.

Rending, tearing teeth, a deep rumbling growl rolling through his body. Blood on his jowls and paws. His muzzle buried in the carcass of his kill. Devoured. Still alive and kicking. Lust, as hot as the blood on his face.

Not a kill. He looked up at me, his face between my thighs, his gold eyes burning like the sun.

Cheeks scorched, I dragged my touch away from his bond.

One corner of his mouth lifted wryly, though he did at least pull out a chair and sit down on my left. "The world has changed a great deal since then."

"What happened three thousand years ago?"

"Queen Nefertiti called me." He watched my face for my reaction. "Though she could only call a fraction of the legion."

"Why did she want the sphinxes?"

"She and her pharaoh were determined to convert Upper and Lower Egypt to a monotheistic religion."

:Fuck Ra,: Vivian retorted in our bonds despite being on patrol.

Sekh nodded. "Though he was known as Aten, then, or at least that was the part he played in the world. It was his first attempt to eliminate all others—especially the goddesses—and be worshiped as the sole creator of the world. He only needed the right people in places of power to attempt the change, but they couldn't possess enough power to overshadow his own pompous radiance. Queen Nefertiti carried enough of Sekhmet's blood to bring me to her side." He laced his fingers together loosely on the table. "But she could not hold me."

As I suspected. I fought to keep my features as smooth and as easy as his without betraying any of my doubts and confusion. "Was she a vampire queen like me?"

"She was a vampire queen, but not like you. She didn't revel in her hunger or embrace her gifts. She hid what she was and lived as a human queen with her royal husband. Perhaps if she had more magical experience, she could have strengthened her gift and used me to guard their dynasty, as her goal. Instead, the sun god's influence soured the people's beliefs, and the Eighteenth Dynasty died with Tutankhamun, though he at least managed to return Egypt to our goddesses before he continued his journey beyond."

"If Ra was influencing them, it makes sense she had to hide what she was."

"The goddess' blood was thin even then." Sekh lifted his shoulders in a small shrug. "It took every drop of Sekhmet's sacred blood to bring me and twenty sphinxes to her Call. Queen Nefertiti only managed to hold us for three days and nights before we returned to our eternal watch."

Stunned, I leaned my head back against Rik. He kneaded my shoulders soothingly but didn't say anything. None of them did.

I had to let it all soak in. Even though my brain rebelled.

An Egyptian queen millennia ago—a direct descendant of the goddess who'd created the sphinxes—had only been able to call twenty of them. It'd taken every drop of Sekhmet's blood to hold them. For three fucking days.

I'd called three *thousand*, and I wasn't even descended from Her line.

Three days. Could I make arrangements to go after the Dauphine so quickly? But why did I need thousands of sphinxes to take care of one vampire queen? Sure, she was Triune, but I didn't think the legion cared whether I brought her to justice for what she'd done to Mom.

I shuffled the pieces of strategy and ideas around in my head, but nothing went together yet. I had too many pieces on the board, especially with an entire legion. I couldn't even voice a clear plan to Carys to get her probabilities.

I must need them, but for *what*? The storm Undina had

warned me about? I didn't even know what the Screaming Madness was yet.

I blew out a shaky breath. "What the fuck am I going to have to do to hold you for longer than three days?"

A harsh, rasping croak escaped his lips. Another. He leaned forward, dropping his head onto his forearms, his shoulders shaking.

I honestly thought he was crying. Though that made about as much sense as using a legion of sphinxes to tear New Orleans apart looking for the Dauphine.

So if he wasn't crying, he was fucking laughing at my very justifiable worry. Drumming my nails on the table, I waited for him to contain his mirth.

"Goddesses above and below." Wiping his eyes, he finally lifted his head. "Forgive me, Your Majesty."

A wide, warm smile and blazing golden eyes softened some of my frustrated wrath. It was impossible to stay mad at someone with such a generous smile. I didn't know him at all yet, but everything I'd seen so far told me his true smile was a rare and precious thing.

"Now that I'm here, you need do nothing to hold me. In fact, I dare you to try and make me leave."

17

SEKH

I could drown in the infinite expanse of her midnight eyes.
"But... You said..."

I shook my head in a slow, deliberate denial. "You have me in a headlock as surely as if your alpha was still choking me with his impressive biceps. I'm not fucking going anywhere."

Doubt still flickered in her eyes, streaks of confusion to cloud the stars, which I could not abide. "I Saw you. Not from the beginning, of course. Your mother must have worked some impressive magic to hide you as long as possible. Red brick house with a square tower in a little, abandoned town called Stuller. Your room was at the top. Always dark, no windows, to keep the monsters away. But I could still See you.

"I Saw you flee the house when your aunt was killed on the street. You got on a bus and left everything behind. I Saw you on the run, always looking back over your shoulder, terrified of the things hunting you. Because you were hunted, Your Majesty. Not just by the monsters you knew of but others. Blank spaces of evil always searching. Even after the first two Blood came to you, a blank space almost got you."

"The bar," she whispered, nodding. "In Kansas City. Something was there."

"It was close enough to see you. To almost touch you. Then you would not have been here, in this moment, no matter how strong you or your Blood were then. But for me, the most impressive thing I Saw you do was sit on a bench in Cairo as dawn broke the sky and allow an Aztec god to kill you."

The alpha's fingers tightened on her shoulder, reflexively pulling her back against him. Trying to protect her even now, when he'd been denied then. She'd had no one with her other than the god. No one to shield her.

What had happened on the other side... I could not See.

But I knew all too well the horrors spawned by millennia of Ra's unfettered arrogance and depravity. I could imagine what fate awaited the young, beautiful daughter of his most hated enemy.

She shivered with the memory. "Dawn waits for no queen."

"You could have stopped him, struck him down with your power, but you didn't. You had a purpose, and nothing could sway you from your goal. You allowed him to drag you through the obelisk portal to a place worse than any hell humanity has ever imagined, and I despaired. I grieved for this world and all it had lost. As my infinite days unfolded, I'd watched you grow stronger, and I'd allowed myself to hope. Not that you would call me, which hadn't even occurred to me as a possibility. I'd hoped the goddesses were at last reclaiming this world. So to lose you..."

I leaned forward, holding her gaze intently. "I am All Seeing, so hear me when I say that without you, all will be lost. This world is being devoured by madness. My watch will end, because there will be nothing else to See. The Great One walks the earth again through you, Your Majesty. Other goddesses awake from their long sleep. They see what Isis wrought in you, and they're regenerating their lines with fresh, new blood. Now, more than ever, this world needs you. It needs you alive and more powerful than ever. More vicious. Harder. Meaner. Bloodier. With all the teeth and claws and fury of creatures born to dance in blood like She who created us."

She stretched out her arm and took my hand in hers. I clasped both hands around her fingers, squeezing too hard, I knew, but unable to ease my fierce grip. "Your hunger matches mine. You revel and dance in blood. So use me, Your Majesty. Dance in mine."

∼

SHARA

HE KNEW WITHOUT ASKING THAT MOM HAD BEEN MY AUNT. HE could describe the home of my childhood as if he'd seen it with his own eyes.

He had. He saw everything.

"Did you see my mother? After she had me?"

His eyes unfocused, the gold darkening to bronze. Long moments passed, and my heart sank. She'd sacrificed so much to have me, yet I didn't even know what had happened to her after she left me with her sister. No one did.

She'd died alone. Without the child she'd given up everything to have.

Esetta Isador deserved so much more than ending up lost to all living memory.

"I See her," Sekh whispered hoarsely. "At least I think it's her. She looks like you. Or what I would imagine you to look like if..." He blew out a long breath and focused on my face. "Are you sure you want to know?"

Wordlessly, I nodded, clutching his fingers.

"She's pale, weak, and very thin in spirit, as if she's already stepped partially into her next life. Crying. Bleeding. She has no power remaining, and while her will is as strong as ever, her physical strength wanes."

His voice cracked with emotion, as if he felt what he was seeing. Or maybe he felt mine. Tears streamed down my face.

"She walks down an abandoned highway that's cracked and falling apart. Colorful graffiti's been painted on the remaining sections of asphalt. Steam rises from the broken road. It's hot beneath her bare feet, blistering her skin with burns. Yet she trudges on."

Lew's gryphon howled with agony. I tugged on his bond, willing him to come to me. So we could hold each other. The two of us who'd loved her, even though I had never seen her face outside of his memories or brief visions.

Pausing, Sekh waited for the other Blood to reach me. Lew dropped down beside me and buried his face in my lap, his arms locked around me.

"Gryphon, of course." Sekh nodded to himself. "The highway leads to Centralia, Pennsylvania, a mostly abandoned town still burning from a coal fire deep in the mines. She walks into darkness, disappearing beneath the ground. Smoke. Fumes. So hot. Smiling, she walks into the flames." Sekh exhaled heavily, his eyes refocusing on my face. Now back to gold. "And so she passed from this world."

I dripped tears on Lew's head, stroking my fingers through his hair with one hand. Still clutching Sekh's hands with my other. "She didn't leave. She's still here. Waiting, for us."

"I told you she would be sure to destroy her physical body," Lew ground out, his shoulders shaking. "At least we know how and where."

"She hid well," Sekh replied. "She was beyond my sight until the very end."

I swallowed the aching lump in my throat. "Because she used the last of her power to ensure she hid my birth. So Selena could get me to safety."

Ezra set a plate stacked high with cold fried chicken and potato salad in front of our newest edition. "Eat up, man. You're going to need it in this nest."

I released the death grip on Sekh's fingers so he could eat. "Hopefully not so much now. I feel a lot better."

Ezra blew out a huff. "That wasn't a complaint, my queen. Bring it the fuck on."

Lew climbed to his feet, though he bent down to press our foreheads together, his hands cupping my face in a gentle caress. Then he turned to Sekh and bowed at his waist while still holding his gaze. "I'm Llewellyn. Thank you for sharing my former queen's last moments with us."

Sekh inclined his head, and I could almost hear the grinding stone of the sphinx statues as they'd looked at me. "It's my great honor to be of service to our queen, Llewellyn."

Guillaume made himself a sandwich and sat back down. Ezra ate half a chocolate cake for dessert. Daire roused enough to lick his way up my calf, his purr deepening to a dull buzzsaw.

A deep, throaty growl rumbled the table, rising in intensity to a bone-shaking roar. My heart pounded. Fragments of the roar still vibrated in the room, strumming my nerves.

Daire scrambled out from beneath the table and leaped to his feet.

Gnawing on a chicken leg, Sekh stared levelly at him. He didn't roar again. He didn't say anything at all. Even in the bond.

But Daire stopped purring. Immediately.

I braced for some yowling and posturing, like two alley cats meeting for the first time. Lew was part lion, and he'd never had a problem with the warcat. At least not to my knowledge. Sekh wasn't all lion either. Not with the ram's head. But evidently it didn't matter.

Daire meekly turned and walked into the kitchen to get himself something to eat.

"Guess we know whose cat is bigger," Guillaume said mildly.

"Um, are you going to have a problem with Daire?"

Sekh dropped a completely cleaned bone back to his plate and picked up another leg. "No problem whatsoever, Your Majesty."

"Shara," I said firmly.

He gave me a slow, sleepy blink of those heavy-lidded golden eyes. "Shara, Your Majesty."

Ezra snorted. "Welcome to House Isador. I'm Ezra."

"I know you, grizzly. Thank you for the food. Who's the wolf?"

Silent as always, Xin glided closer to the table, not as his wolf, though. He'd pulled on soft gray pants but didn't wear a shirt or shoes. He circled behind my chair and started to step around Sekh's. Perhaps to test his reflexes, or to simply take the other seat, though he could have just as easily gone behind Ezra.

Sekh's left hand shot out and closed around Xin's throat. His hair whipped back, his body arching away as he tried to flip out of the man's grip. Silver flashed and Sekh leaned aside, easily tossing Xin away from him.

Still casually eating another chicken leg. With my Blood's knife buried in his shoulder.

Sekh pulled the blade out of his shoulder and tossed it toward Xin without even looking at him. "I Saw you holding the enemy queen for our queen's vengeance in New York City. Nice work."

Braced in a crouch to attack again, Xin snagged the wickedly sharp blade effortlessly. "Wu Tien Xin. You can see me?"

"I'm *All* Seeing," Sekh drawled. "Of course I can See you. However, I am *not* All Knowing, so I'm still connecting names to faces for each of you."

Though he turned his head and gave G a nod. "No introduction is required, Sir Guillaume de Payne. The knife earlier gave you away, combined with the scar on your throat and the hell horse."

G flicked his wrist and a blade dropped to his palm. He tapped the slim knife to his heart and then made it disappear back up his sleeve again.

The scent of blood stirred my hunger. Yes, I'd pulled an ocean of blood from him already. Enough to bring thousands of sphinxes to my side. I still wanted more. Though at least this wasn't the punishing, desperate hunger that made me want to gnaw my own arm off.

Slow, sultry heat pulsed through me.

I tried not to react in any way. The man deserved some food after millennia. But I felt the throb of Rik's erection against the back of my head. With the smell of blood in the air...

Sekh stood so fast the chair tumbled over and crashed against the wall. "You think I'd rather eat human food when I could have you?"

With a low, warning rumble, Rik swept me up in his arms. Rock hard everywhere, my mountain rising out of the flood threatening to carry me away.

"Are you going to have a problem with my alpha?" I asked breathlessly.

Sekh paused, his body loose and easy, his hands relaxed at his sides. But his eyes blazed brighter, and when he spoke, I heard the growl of his lion roughening each word. "Do you want him to fuck me first to prove exactly how few problems he'll have from me? Or would you rather watch me suck him off?"

Dismissing the man as a challenger, Rik turned toward the stairs. "I'd rather not fuck around with those lion teeth unless our queen promises to lick up the blood at the same time."

18

SHARA

Even though I'd already fucked him, welcoming a new man to my private bedroom probably should have been embarrassing. Especially when I had another man with me already, and so many others in my house.

Which was the side of my brain raised thinking I was human. Consuming human media in a capitalist, patriarchal society—tainted with Ra's kind of bullshit that believed women didn't even enjoy sex. And if they did, they were filthy witches who deserved what they got.

Fuck that shit.

Sekh, Guillaume, and Ezra followed us upstairs, though the latter two stayed outside the door, shutting it behind us. Winston had worked a miracle in bringing in the new bed to replace the one we'd broken, but the repairmen hadn't come out to fix the plaster or hardwood floors yet. Body-sized dents were outlined in the crumbled remains of the wall. I watched Sekh note the damage. The absolute monstrosity of a bed as my alpha set me on the edge of the mattress.

I wasn't surprised by the burning suns in his eyes when he met my gaze.

"Did you see what happened the last time I was in this room?"

"Your magic was too thick to reveal the event fully, even to me. But I can guess."

Regret still weighed heavily on my chest, tightening my throat. "I doubt it."

His head lowered slightly, his shoulders dropping. It reminded me of a lion going still in the tall grass, hiding as he sighted something tasty in the distance. "You hungered. Your Blood provided. It will be my great honor to provide whatever it is that you need, Your Majesty."

Rik pulled his shirt over his head, snagging my attention. I didn't care how many Blood I ended up calling, or how long we loved and fed each other. I would never get tired of looking at any of my Blood, but especially my alpha.

Cut slabs of sheer rock glided beneath his skin, and I could remember all too well the explosive strength in every inch of him. His massive hands grasping the sphinx's horns, twisting his head into submission. His strength, every bulge straining to bring the new Blood to my side. Even if he provided competition to his position. A five-thousand-some-year-old general of a goddess' legion.

If I hadn't been able to take so much of Sekh's blood... If my hunger hadn't been raging out of control...

Without my will pulling him to my side, he could have eaten anyone—all—of my Blood for lunch. Literally.

Rik knew it. Even as my alpha. Especially as my alpha.

Even Leviathan, who'd enjoyed being the oldest and biggest Blood in my nest, had not fared well in our first meeting with Sekh. That we were all still alive and mostly unharmed was more a testament to the man's willingness to come to my Call than our strength.

Though all I could think about was Rik's impressive weight drilling into me as he dropped his pants.

"How do you want us, my queen?" He leaned down, planting a hand on either side of me on the mattress. "Do you want either of the things he offered? Or something else entirely?"

My eyelids fluttered, my breath catching in my chest. Smoking iron filled my nose as I rubbed my face against his chest. Pain wasn't really his thing—that was Itztli's department. Rik wouldn't enjoy the threat of lion teeth on his dick, though he'd do it if I asked. Especially if I teased him by enjoying his blood at the same time. "You know I love every drop of your blood but I'd rather not watch you shred your dick when I could have you inside me."

His big hands slid under my armpits, and he lifted me to my feet on top of the bed. He was still fucking taller than me. His shoulders so wide he blocked out the other man waiting silently near the door. Until he dropped down to his knees, sitting back on his legs so his head was as low as possible. Lightly, he wrapped his hands around my ankles. "May I make a request, my queen?"

I looped my arms around his neck, leaning against him for support. "Of course, my alpha."

"I'd love to see how long the new Blood can fuck you before you drain him to unconsciousness."

~

SEKH

ALL THE TIMES I HAD SEEN HER FUCK HER BLOOD FLASHED through my head. Never dreaming that I would be here someday.

Now that I was here—in a man's body—I was not prepared for the reality.

The absolute blissful pain of her beauty in person. Of smelling her skin. Feeling its exquisite texture against mine. The heat and wetness of her body sucking me down to wallow in her pleasure. The punishing, addictive thirst of her need driving me higher.

The taste of her blood. Sheer magic. Explosive power. A living, breathing goddess walking this earth. Calling me to her side.

"I will eagerly do anything you ask of me." The rough timbre of my voice echoed with my lion's roar. "Though I must warn you that unconsciousness will be impossible. Sphinxes do not sleep. Ever."

Her alpha laughed. "I used to think Blood never slept too. But she's drained multiple Blood to unconsciousness in one sitting, including me and the dragon."

Lust pulsed through me, a roaring, insatiable beast of hunger. "As the bear said, bring it the fuck on."

Though she hesitated, her brow furrowed with concern. Not for herself.

For me.

She actually thought she could hurt me in some way, when her immense hunger was what made me crave her the most.

"You've not seen me at my worst." Ruefully, she shook her head. "I poisoned two of my Blood in this very room and drained everyone but Rik to the point they couldn't walk. Just last night."

Searing heat blistered from the crown of my head to my feet. The borrowed clothes felt like they were strangling me. A caging prison far worse than anything her Blood had been able to do while her Call sank into my bones. I shredded the shirt off my body and kicked off the jeans so I could drop down beside her other man on my knees. "What kind of poison?"

Her sultry gaze locked on the still-bleeding knife wound in my shoulder. "Cobra."

"So you poisoned them with your venom, sucked all the

souped-up blood out of them, and then basically resurrected them. Nice."

Her eyes flared, a startled laugh escaping her lips. "Yeah, I guess so."

Though my surprise far exceeded hers when the alpha crawled onto the bed, giving us a respectable space.

To do whatever the fuck she wanted with me.

A sign of his trust. Not in me—but his queen. The strength of her hold on me. The power of her bond. And yeah, she had my balls in her gloriously vicious teeth, even if she didn't touch me. "I fucking love cobras."

She laughed again, tension bleeding away from her tight shoulders. "You're the first Blood to say that, though you might change your mind when you see me transform the next time."

Her arms looped around my neck, bringing me closer.

The invitation for which I'd been waiting.

I locked my arms around her hips and pressed my wounded shoulder against her. Rubbing back and forth, marking her with my blood. Dragging the stab wound lower on her body, down the flimsy gown she wore. So thin my blood made it cling to her skin. Delicate white fabric. Wet with my blood. The shadow of her dusky skin beneath. Exquisite.

Her breath caught, her head falling back. Through her bond, I could feel my blood soaking into her skin, spreading heat almost like a burn. Stoking her thirst ever higher. Even after drinking enough from me to pull the entire legion to her command. How the fuck was that possible?

I could only marvel and press my lips to the tops of her feet. "I wish I could coat you head to toe in my blood."

"Sounds good to me. Just mind the claws—don't shred the bedding—and try not to break the frame again. I don't know how many more spares Winston has handy."

I whipped my head up, eyes searching hers. She was fucking serious.

In a blur, I switched places with her, scooping her off her feet, laying her back on the mattress, and standing on the mattress over her. One foot on either side of her hips, I tore open my wrist, laying the flesh open to the bone. Too deep, but I didn't fucking care. Holding my arm out, I dripped blood onto her chest. Splattering the lush curves of her breasts. Rivulets and streams tracking down her stomach and throat to puddle in the sweet secret hollows of her body.

Moaning, she writhed on the mattress. Spreading my blood with her hands. Rubbing me into her skin. Eyes smoldering with desire, she stared up at me and opened her mouth wide. Her long, white fangs a brutal promise I couldn't wait to feel again. This time, I'd be keeping that orgasmic blast for myself. I'd blow us both to smithereens with the force of my climax.

Teasing her, I dribbled blood on her chin, deliberately missing her mouth. Her tongue swept down over her lips. Her fingers glided up her throat, scraping blood to spill into her mouth. Her eyes rolled back in her head, her back arching. Lifting her breasts toward me.

Small pains jabbed into my calves. It took me a moment to register it. To look down and note her other hand gripping my lower leg. Long tipped silver nails dug into my skin. Not to shred me open. Not for the enjoyment of flesh beneath her fingertips.

For blood.

Her hunger was so immense her goddess had given her numerous ways to feed. *Praises be to the Great One and the Mother of All for creating such a daughter of blood. Let her sink her teeth into me for all eternity.*

Her bond rippled with flames, slicing through my body like the knight's sword. Shifting to one side so she could keep her nails in me, I knelt beside her and swept my bleeding arm in an arc over her legs. I snagged the hem of the gown and dragged it up in a slow, torturous reveal. Watching the way my blood seeped through the thin cotton to smear her skin. Teasing myself with each inch of her body. I kneaded her calves and knees, rubbing my blood deeper. Her thighs spread wide, a siren call, though that meant I lost her nails in my calf. I rubbed my wounded shoulder against her inner thigh, fighting the urge to seize her hand and gouge a vicious tear in my throat so I could bleed directly into her pussy.

"Bite me," she whispered. "Make me bleed."

A tremor rocked through me. Such delicate flesh to have near my canines. Delicious torture for us both, especially after I'd accidentally ripped her throat out earlier.

Trust indeed.

I scraped my teeth along her inner thigh, licking her soft skin. Tissue paper thin, so delicate, blood pounding just beneath the surface. An invitation I couldn't refuse. I sank my canines into her femoral artery.

Hot blood sprayed directly into my face. Molten, liquid passion, blazing with the heat of her body. The fire of her hunger. Stirring my own to a fevered pitch.

Her alpha rumbled a low warning, not liking the waste of such precious blood.

:I'll pay her back every drop a hundred fold.:

I gripped her thigh in my jaws, capturing the spurting fountain on my tongue. I didn't have to swallow. I just opened my throat and let her pour into me. I tugged on her leg, sharp, small jerks. Letting her feel the power in my jaws. I could rip her joint apart with a hard jerk of my head. I could shred her flesh from her bones and feast like the lion roaring deep inside me. Though it wasn't the lion who wanted to pound her with all the force in my body. The ram pawed the ground, head lowered, ready to crash into her. Two beasts, wrestling for supremacy inside me. Bite and rend, or slam into her with all my strength.

She decided the war by jamming her nails into my throat

and pulling me up her body. I shredded the fragile fabric from her body, desperate to feel every inch of her against me.

Her pussy was just as hungry as she was for my blood. Swallowing me up, sucking me deeper. Locking me tight.

I ground against her, trying to imprint myself on her. She had so many Blood already, though I hadn't met them all yet.

None of them were guardians created by a goddess. None of them brought her a legion. Though I wanted to be more than her general.

:You are,: she whispered in my mind, hugging me closer. Her body wrapped around me, dragging me down to the depths like an anchor. *:I only call Blood I love.:*

I thrust again, feeling the surge of her hunger. Her body coiled tighter, her fangs glistening, though she waited, denying herself. Giving me as long as possible.

I strained harder, a raft breaking itself apart on a treacherous reef. My spine burned, my muscles quivering with effort. I sank my teeth into her shoulder, pinning her. Feeding on her.

Hunger spiraled higher, blending with her pleasure. Her climax a crystal pure spring bubbling up from the earth. She quivered beneath me, her hips arching up to take me deeper. Slammed to the hilt, I couldn't pull back for another thrust. My bones liquified, dissolving. Sinking. Into her.

She jammed her glorious fangs into the other side of my throat and my spine bowed. A million volts of electricity shot through my nerves, lighting up my entire body. Winds howled through me. Sand blasting me from the inside out, scouring my bones to blistering white, cleaned of every speck of flesh.

A dark shadow rose in my mind, swaying back and forth, a sinuous wave that hypnotized me. Red glinted at the top, a priceless, glittering jewel. White glistened against the black, brutal swords to hack and slice through my flesh. Coils squeezed around my lungs, suffocating me.

Choke. Hold. Never. Letting me go.

I fell into the dark maw of the cobra's gaping mouth, and the real feast began.

19

SHARA

My hunger rose in a brutal wave, fueled by his. Surging with our pleasure, a dangerous spiral ever higher.

I sucked him harder, guzzling his blood as deeply as I had from the sphinx statue, and there was no dipping wane in his strength. Especially when he was also feeding on me. Our bodies entwined, locked together as surely as Leviathan and my wyvern in a death spiral.

When we crashed toward the ground...

:I'll catch you,: Rik swore. :Though I won't allow it to go that far.:

I felt my alpha's concern, perched like a hawk beside us, watching intently. Calculating how far and high my hunger might soar before he needed to intervene. An image flashed in my head: his mighty fists pummeling Sekh. Trying to get him off me. While Sekh glared at him and bit me ever harder.

Another throbbing clench pulsed through my pussy, making me groan. My fingers dug in harder, one set of nails in his throat and the other raking his back. Shredding his skin. Not that he cared in the slightest.

So much fucking power it was terrifying. Bringing him to my side had increased my base exponentially. I wasn't great at estimating queens' power, but I'd felt the blaze of sunfires like a molten sun crashing against my shields. I'd stood in the storm of Marne Ceresa's locusts as she tried to bait me into defending myself.

Neither of which matched the feel of Sekh pouring into me, while he fed from me. There was no end in sight. No easing ebb to the cresting wave blasting through me. Feeding on each other, clutched together, skyrocketing beyond anything this world had ever known.

And he was only one of the multiple new Blood I had called.

Gripping his throat in my jaws, I fought the urge to bite him again. Just to force him to climax inside me again and again.

Still gripping my shoulder in his jaws, he tugged his head backward enough for me to feel the power in his bite. The knowledge he could crunch through bone. Shear off my entire arm with a casual shake of his head. A lion bringing down his kill. :*Fucking do it.*:

Which only threw gasoline on my inferno. I released his throat. My fangs shot down so fast and hard I cried out, a guttural gasp as if Guillaume had buried his sword in my belly. But no, it was me, sinking twin blades into Sekh. His throat again. His shoulder. Messy, hard, deep bites, each one sending a brutal cataclysmic climax through his body.

He roared around my flesh in his mouth and sleek fur sprouted beneath my hands. So massive, his sphinx swelled up out of the man. Giant paws folded me close, and he rolled toward the edge of the bed.

Away from Rik.

We crashed onto the floor, but I fell on top of the sphinx. His huge chest billowed beneath me, lifting me up and down like ocean swells. His heart a timpani drum slamming a rapid, frantic rhythm. I felt a surge of fury from Rik, his concern when I disappeared from his sight.

:*I'm fine.*:

Some of his rage eased, though he touched my back, checking on me for himself. I lifted my head, swiping lion mane and thick wooly curls out of my eyes.

Golden eyes blinked up at me, deceptively sleepy and relaxed as the sphinx licked vicious lion teeth. On his back without a care. Cleaning up my blood dampening the wool and fur around his mouth. *:You said not to damage the bed frame.:*

So I did. "Brace yourself."

His eyes narrowed, his forelegs tightening around me. Letting my head droop down against him, I closed my eyes and called all the blood in the room to me.

All the droplets that had splattered from his torn wrist. The wild spray from my thigh. The gushing wounds I'd made in his throat. Even the stab wound that Xin had given him.

But a bottomless ocean already rippled inside me. I barely felt the gentle plops of all the blood we'd spilled settling back into me.

:For what?:

I touched his bond, intending to heal his wounds, but they'd healed already when he shifted. A deep, resonating gong echoed through him, rolling me under. I sank like a stone. Not concerned—not when I still felt him with me, his fur soft and thick beneath my skin. The gentle prick of his claws on my back, along with the heavy weight of Rik's hand. They were both still with me, even as I fell deeper through Sekh's bond until I bumped into something like solid ground. A jolt caught me, shifting the world upside down and around in a crazy tilt.

A square cobblestoned plaza firmed under my feet, but it was only a few paces wide with a drop-off so steep I couldn't see anything below. The sphinx stood above me, his front paws on either side of my body. His muzzle lowered to touch the top of my head. The air was thin and dry, oddly empty of any scents. Clouds billowed far below, as if we stood on a mountain. I looked above us into nothing. Emptiness like space though it wasn't black. Devoid of any color. No sun or stars or moon. Just endless silence.

"Where are we?"

:Here stands the guardian,: the sphinx replied. *:All Seeing. Never Sleeping.:*

The complete and utter silence was deafening and more than a little maddening. I reached over my shoulder to twine my fingers in the shaggy ram curls beneath his chin and leaned against his leg, seeking his touch. The warmth of his body. "This is where you've been for five thousand years?"

:Longer. What would you like to See, Your Majesty? Direct your All Seeing eyes.:

My heart clenched at the thought of him being alone for thousands of years. No one to talk to. No one to touch. Nothing to smell or hear or taste.

Only seeing everything.

"Can you show me where the Dauphine is? She lived as Leonie Delafosse in New Orleans."

He breathed deeply, ruffling my hair. *:While I know place names on signs and maps, I don't recognize people by their names unless they show it to me in their daily lives. However, I See her face in your bond. Let us look for her together.:*

The cobblestone platform swung in a slow circle. Clouds thinned to reveal landscape flying beneath us as if spinning a globe toward a set of coordinates. Or perhaps we were the ones moving, though I didn't feel any sensation of air around us. The landscape sharpened with detail, as if he zoomed in the lens. I saw a peach stucco three-story building with green shutters and immediately recognized it as the place where the Dauphine had been living in New Orleans as Leonie.

I'd seen this place through Nightwing Starlight's eyes when she gave me the scrap of scarf and letter her kin had intercepted.

The sphinx's vision sharpened, lifting to a window on the

third floor of the building. Zooming inside to a woman sitting at an old-fashioned writing secretary. Short, curly brown hair, the same youthful face and warm brown eyes. Such a nice smile for a woman who'd trapped Mom's soul in a rotting corpse and sent her shuffling like a fucking zombie on foot hundreds of miles to make a fucking point.

"That's her. Can you see where she is now?"

The image went blurry, losing its focus while the platform slowly spun. Seeking her face anywhere in the world.

:Forgive me, Your Majesty. She is not to be Seen at this time.:

I blew out a sigh, though I wasn't surprised at all. "She's very good at hiding."

His chest vibrated with a low rumble that rattled my bones. *:Nothing can hide from me forever. I will See her again.:*

20

MEHEN

*I*f *motherfucker knows what's good for him, he'll keep right on walking.*

With a silent glare, I watched the new man hit the kitchen for another meal. In the dark, I lay curled before the fireplace with only a few low embers still glowing in the ashes. I didn't move a muscle or make a sound. Just watching through slitted eyes burning with hatred.

Motherfucker touched her.

Motherfucker hurt her.

Motherfucker was fucking big, too. Bigger than even Leviathan, though I'd die before I'd admit it out loud. Older, too. He'd seen the rise of the first Egyptian dynasties when I'd been nothing but a glint in my fucking mother's baleful eyes.

Fuck that fucking transference bullshit that had me fucking coming until I fucking whimpered like a fucking baby.

Fuck me for wanting him to do it again.

:*You're next,*: Guillaume said in my bond. :*If you're up to it.*:

I sent him a vicious snarl. :*Nobody's fucking taking my turn.*:

:*Then quit fucking around with the sphinx and go already,*: the knight said, clearly up to his neck stump with me.

Motherfucker turned with a loaded plate and looked straight at me. Gave me a sardonic wink that made bile burn up my throat with dragon fire. Then he sat down at the table and tucked into the food like the fucking cat he was. Though I did a double take when I realized he was gnawing on a huge, raw chunk of prime rib roast weighing at least ten pounds. Blood dripped down his chin and smeared his face, and he grinned, clearly having the time of his life.

Fuck. I could only curse my own fucking self for not thinking to be the first to tear into a hunk of beef just for the fun of eating something raw. Even better if we could hunt something alive.

She'd let us. Maybe.

Or maybe we'd go after that fucking bitch soon, and we could all feast until our bellies hurt.

I made my way upstairs to our queen's bedroom, surprised to see it was still relatively intact after she'd taken motherfucker again. Eyes closed, she curled against Rik, her head on his chest. No surprise there. A fucking pleased and satisfied smile on her face even I couldn't begrudge. Because my fucking queen deserved every fucking thing she could ever desire.

Though she slept. Which meant no feeding. Certainly no fucking. Not that I needed her to touch me again since all my nerves still echoed with a million volts of climax juice.

I slunk up onto the bed and eased against her back, just enough so she'd feel my body heat and know she had another Blood protecting her blind side.

With a low, contented hum, she rolled toward me and snuggled up like I was the fucking purr machine.

"You can feed if you want," she mumbled, her words thick and heavy with sleep.

Emotions sprouted inside me. Mostly ugly ones. Jealousy. Doubt. Rage.

She didn't fucking know it was me. Not really.

An image popped into my head. Soaring up through a dark, tight tunnel. Exploding out into open air for the first time in over a thousand years. Feeling the wind catch my wings, lifting me higher.

Even as she drained me dry, her small arms clinging to me with her fangs buried in my throat.

"Oh, I don't? That's funny." Though she didn't laugh, and she sounded more awake. "I could have sworn the destroyer of beds was here with me. Though I beg you not to destroy *this* bed until I make sure Winston has a few more spares."

I grunted a grudging acknowledgement. At least that explained why motherfucker hadn't torn shit up like I would have the first time I fucked our queen in a bed. If Rik hadn't practically choked me to unconsciousness.

Opening her eyes, she cupped my cheeks in her hands and dipped through my bond, making me shiver. Scales shimmered beneath my skin. Leviathan blew out a plume of smoke winding inside me like a black river of poisonous fumes.

"I need you," she whispered, her voice solemn. "Always. I love you. I wouldn't have been able to hold the legion without your help."

The smoke burned my fucking eyes. Choking me. Roughening my voice like a fucking gravel pit. "Then can I ask for a boon, my queen?"

Her lips quirked, her fingers softly tracing over my jawline. Her thumb stroked over my bottom lip. "Of course, my dragon."

"Can I kill something and eat it? I'd prefer to start with that fucking bitch but if you plan to delay your strike on her, then a deer will do. Or even a cow."

Startled, she laughed. "I can't go after the Dauphine until I know where she is, so I guess you'll have to settle on option two. As long as you don't hunt anything that's mine."

My lips curled with disgust. "Like I'd eat fucking rats and crows if I could have a cow."

"No wolves, either."

I rolled my eyes. "Fine." Though of course I didn't want to eat fucking wolves either. "Only me, though. Motherfucker doesn't get to hunt unless he begs on his belly and kisses your feet."

:Fucking bet, asshole,: motherfucker retorted in my head.

:Bring it the fuck on, motherfucker,: I snarled back.

Though what I really wanted to say was…

Me first.

"Fucking great." Rik heaved out a sigh like a fucking earthquake. "Give me a fucking reason to bash your heads together and fuck you both to unconsciousness."

:Bet,: echoed again in our bonds.

From both of us.

21

SHARA

What a difference a few days of rest—and one big sphinx—could make.

Sitting at the table with Gina, I braced as she patted the huge stack of files between us. "Are you sure?"

"I'm as ready as I'll ever be. Do we know anything else about the Skolos queens?"

"They're still in the Galveston area as far as we know. We have a Talbott Agency team on the ground, but we don't know anything new yet. They haven't even spotted any of the queens in person, and no one's coming or going from the houses." She opened the top file. "First up, House Zaniyah is asking permission to take a sibling queen for House Isador."

I resisted the urge to seize Mayte's bond and ask why she hadn't asked me herself. Plus, I wanted to know all the juicy details. Was this queen someone she had a personal relationship with? Or was it purely business?

Gina slipped a stack of papers in front of me, all in legalize that made zero sense. "The new consiliarius we sent to House Zaniyah did an excellent job writing up the agreement, and Her Majesty has been quite pleased with Deborah's work as well.

House Vitória is located in São Paulo, Brazil, and Queen Jacinta has ruled for nearly six hundred years." She flipped the legal documents aside to a typed page on House Isador stationary. "Here's their offer."

The page read like a tip sheet, neat and tidy and easy to read.

Queen Jacinta Vitória will swear fealty to Her Majesty Mayte Zaniyah, as well as Her Majesty Shara Isador, both by proxy through Zaniyah's sibling agreement and in person if requested by House Isador.

Princess Xochitl is named as House Vitória's heir unless Queen Jacinta produces an heir of her own. Then Xochitl receives an equal share of their legacy.

Princess Xochitl will claim at least one Blood from House Vitória once she comes of age, and as many additional Aima as she wishes to take as Blood, excluding Queen Jacinta's alpha.

I had to huff out a laugh at that one, though it also gave me an uneasy twinge. I didn't like the thought of anyone dictating any queen had to claim a Blood from their house. Marne Ceresa had tried that trick with me, and while I'd gained Okeanos and wouldn't change a thing, the thought of taking one of her personal Blood made me want to hurl.

I hadn't been raised in a court, and Aima customs were foreign to me. Mayte agreed, and she was Xochitl's mother. Besides, unless House Vitória had a unicorn, I didn't see the little girl being too pleased with any of them.

I picked up my coffee cup while I scanned the rest of the page.

House Vitória retains their nest in São Paulo, including one-hundred acres and a one-hundred-thousand-square-foot mansion, and all peoples living within.

Followed by detailed accounting of how many humans and Aima siblings lived under the House Vitória umbrella. Nearly triple Zaniyah's, from what I remembered, and their nest seemed to be much more lavish than the simple yet comfortable manor house where Mayte had grown up. Plus several other properties listed in South and Central America. On paper, House Vitória appeared to be the larger, wealthier house. Queen Jacinta might not be very powerful, but if she commanded such a large base, she had to be at least as powerful as Mayte.

Then I read the last line and promptly choked, spitting a mouthful of coffee back into the cup.

House Vitória will pay House Zaniyah one hundred thousand United States dollars and House Isador one million United States dollars annually until this contract is terminated and recorded as null and void in the Triune archive. Advance sums are already paid in full and non-refundable if House Isador refuses the contract.

"It's quite a triumphant coup for Zaniyah," Gina said. "And of course, Isador."

"Wait, wait, wait. Didn't we agree to pay out House Skye's sibling contracts when they left? They didn't pay Keisha. It was the other way around."

"They're the ones asking to be your sibling. They want your protection."

My mouth sagged open, and I sat back in the chair more than a little stunned. "That's like highway robbery, isn't it?"

Shrugging, Gina flashed a smug grin. "It's the sum they're willing to pay, and quite honestly, we could easily ask for more. Vitória can afford it."

"But that's crazy! A million dollars a *year*? It's like vampire mafia shit."

"More like Triune mafia shit." She laughed and offered me a heavy gold pen. "It's a very good offer, but it's entirely up to you."

I took the pen but didn't press the tip to paper yet. "Are there any downsides to taking them on?"

Her eyebrows raised and she breathed deeply, staring off into space. I loved that she didn't immediately give me a careless platitude for an answer. When she met my gaze, she gave a little nod. "The only downside I can think of is drawing the attention of the rest of the Triune. If M—"

Her eyes flared and she quickly changed her wording to avoid saying Marne Ceresa out loud since Okeanos' warning. "If the queen of Rome is worried about how quickly Isador is gaining allies, this agreement could draw unfavorable attention to you. Vitória is a very rich house, but they've had few dealings with the Triune in the past. Queen Jacinta isn't well known or extremely powerful as far as I'm aware of. I can't even say what her powers are known to be."

Nodding, I signed the contract page with a flourish. "It sounds like a good deal for Xochitl especially."

"It's a very good deal for her. Our little unicorn princess is gaining quite the entourage even though she's only four."

She pulled out the next folder with a wry smile more of a grimace. "This is everything I was able to pull together about the Dauphine."

It was one fucking page.

"Historically, the Dauphin was the heir apparent to the throne of France, beginning back in Sir Guillaume's time. The Dauphine was the title given to the heir's wife. Before that, Dauphiné of Viennois was a province in southeastern France. According to the human historical record, it was ruled by a man with a dolphin in his crest, which is how the province and title came to be. Of course the records fail to recognize that he gained this land and the title from his mother, Matilda, who just so happened to be the great-granddaughter of Jeanne Viennois, *the* Dauphine."

I nodded, remembering the crow queen's letter. Guillaume had immediately recognized the blue and red fish crest on the page as the Dauphine's symbol.

"Little else is known about Jeanne, unfortunately. Even then, she preferred obscurity, which makes sense given her bloodline from Despoina, who was worshiped by the Eleusinian Mysteries. Honestly, Jeanne Viennois may not be her true name either, though House Viennois, or House Dauphine as it's more widely known as now, is formally recorded with the Triune. We don't even know how old she is, though she's old enough to have a living queen granddaughter who's over five hundred years old. She doesn't have any siblings recorded in the archive, not directly to House Viennois, at least."

Rosalind Valois, the queen of Paris, was Jeanne's grand-daughter, who had both a romantic and strategic alliance with Keisha Skye. When I killed Keisha and took over Skye Tower, Rosalind had so kindly offered to take House Skye—and me— under her wing. No fucking chance, thank you very much.

House Valois had numerous siblings listed, including House Delafosse in New Orleans. Which we knew now to be one of the Dauphine's secret identities.

"Let's check out each of these other siblings listed for House Valois and see if they're legit. I'm especially interested in any that might be in Quebec. The Dauphine was writing someone there about me when we were in Kansas City, but I didn't see the name. Maybe she went north to Canada after leaving New Orleans."

By the glint of excitement in her eyes, Gina was thinking the same thing. "Some of these names I recognize immediately as having other business before the Triune, but many are obscure. They could be fronts for her to hide in plain sight again. I'll get Kevin started on them immediately."

We worked through paperwork for another couple of hours through late afternoon into the evening, mostly contract amendments that Gwen and Kevin had worked up for the siblings in Isador Tower. Then there was a final listing of all the properties I'd inherited from House Skye, including an entire island off the coast of Scotland near the Isle of Skye.

Winston brought a fresh tray of chocolate chip cookies to

the table and paused beside the table, waiting until Gina paused. "Your Majesty—"

"Shara," I said firmly. Though he'd only slipped up once and called me by my given name.

Dressed in a sleek navy-blue pinstriped suit with a soft pink tie and mirrored black shoes, he inclined his head with a slight smile. "Shara, my queen, there's a small matter I wished to run by you when it's convenient."

"Of course. What is it?"

"It seems as though a large quantity of fresh beef disappeared from the refrigerator over the last few days."

"Ah, yeah. I'm sorry about that. My newest Blood has a taste for... uh... meat." I could feel my cheeks heating—because that wasn't the only thing he had a taste for. Though that went for all my Blood.

Sekh's bond rumbled with the heavy panting grunt of his lion. *:Bring it the fuck on, Your Majesty.:*

"Not a problem at all, my queen, though may I suggest we add a larger commercial refrigerator built to store sides of beef, whole hogs, or whatever other kinds of meat he may prefer."

:All the above,: Sekh said.

:Lamb too,: Mehen added, not to be left out. *:I fucking love roasting mutton with dragon fire.:*

I bit back laughter. "That's an excellent idea, Winston. Though we may also want to add some livestock if we have the pasture for them. How many acres do we have here?"

"Just over two-hundred acres, but most of the land is wooded," Gina replied. "Let me see if I can get a local rancher to come out and inspect the property to make a recommendation. What kind of livestock were you thinking? Cows? Worst case, we'll just buy a local farm."

"Sure. Maybe some sheep."

:Pigs,: Sekh added.

:Mmm, bacon,: Mehen agreed. Then I felt a surge of irritation from him because they'd actually agreed on something.

Maybe they could bond over hunting and eating their kills.

"Pigs," I said out loud, trying not to laugh.

Gina wrinkled her nose. "Are you sure? They're smelly. Also, if we're going to add livestock, we'll need to hire some caretakers."

:Not if we fucking eat them all,: Mehen retorted.

"Let's start with a couple of cows, assuming we have enough pasture space. In the meantime, a larger fridge for fresh beef will be great."

Nodding, she jotted some notes. Winston started to turn away but paused, his hand slipping inside his pocket to pull out a quietly vibrating cell phone. He gave me a quick look. "It's Magnum."

She managed the New York City house. I hadn't been back to the city since I'd grown the tree in the basement at Isador Tower. I'd intended to stay the night with Magnum, but then the Dauphine had attacked my nest, and I'd come home as quickly as possible.

Winston answered the call, listened for a few moments, and then put the phone on speaker so we could all hear. "Say that again, please."

"There's a man here asking to see the queen," Magnum said. "He looks familiar, but I'm not sure it's him. He's not... right. There's something very wrong with him. I didn't think Aima could be ill like this."

"Familiar how?" I asked slowly.

"Your Majesty." Magnum inhaled sharply and her voice vibrated with intensity. "I think he might have belonged to your mother."

22

SHARA

Heart pounding, I started to reach for Llewellyn's bond, but he was already sprinting toward me across the lawn, in the back door, and to my side in seconds.

"Who?" I asked hoarsely. "Did he give you a name?"

"Not that I can understand, Your Majesty," Magnum replied. "He's only mumbling nonsense for the most part. I was only able to understand 'queen' and 'please.' Hold on a second and I'll switch to video."

Winston turned the phone around toward me so we could see the screen better. A thin man swayed back and forth slightly, his arms shaking in uncontrollable twitches. His head jerked every few seconds, and his complexion was pale, almost greenish. No wonder Magnum thought he was sick. Rail thin and raggedy, almost like a skeleton, with a dirty shirt hanging on his shoulders, I'd say he looked more...

Dead.

The pit of my stomach weighed heavy like cold, hard lead.

He wasn't sick. He looked like Greyson, Mom's former alpha who'd turned thrall after she dissolved the nest and his bond. The man who'd killed her and hunted me relentlessly. Thralls damned themselves by feeding on humans after they lost their queen.

Goddess. Magnum didn't have anyone to protect her other than a few human security guards. The house didn't have a blood circle to keep him out.

"Thierry," Llewellyn whispered hoarsely. "He's turned thrall."

Wavering, the man shook his head so vigorously he lost his balance and staggered. "Thrall." Then he said another string of words, looking at the phone intently. He could understand us and wasn't mindlessly attacking like a vicious animal. Though Greyson had been perfectly cordial.

Until the truth of what I offered began to burn him alive.

Thierry said a word again, straining so hard tendons stood out on his neck, his jaw working back and forth. Again. I could tell it was a word, but the syllables were all jumbled together. Plus it sounded like he had a mouthful of cotton preventing his tongue from forming the sounds correctly.

"Queen." He said very clearly. Then the jumbled word.

"He's spelled by someone." Certainty tinged in my head like a silver bell. Softly, I whispered, "the Dauphine."

Nodding hard, he squeezed his eyes shut and bloody tears tracked down his wan cheeks. "Help."

Lew blew out a slow, controlled breath, but the gryphon rended his bond with sorrow and rage. Thierry had been his closest friend in Esetta's Blood, as close as Rik and Daire. But like the prime fucking alpha he was, Lew said, "By your leave, I'll go to dispatch him, my queen."

My heart wrenched, even though I didn't know this man. If he'd been Esetta's Blood, she loved him. Lew cared for him like a brother, and he carried her blood. She must have sent him to the Dauphine, like she'd sent Lew to Keisha Skye. So they'd be there if and when I needed them. Even knowing the risk and likely torture awaiting them, they'd gone.

Simply because she'd asked.

Hoping for a chance to serve me and House Isador again.

If I'd acted quicker and taken steps against the Dauphine rather than going to help Helayna, maybe I could have gotten to Thierry before she'd hurt him. Though he looked like he'd been wasting away for years, not a few months.

"Is there any way I can heal him? Maybe I can break the spell like the geas on Mayte's nest."

Rik's hands squeezed reflexively on my shoulder, his instinct to keep me safe curling his fingers hard. "We can't risk you. If she boobytrapped him like the saleswoman in Kansas City, we're all doomed."

"Plus you can't risk bringing him into your blood circle," Guillaume added. "She might have embedded a curse in him that will only flare when he's inside so he can bring the whole circle down around our ears."

"That's possible?"

:I can absolutely bring down blood circles.: Sekh responded in the bond. *:I came in like a lamb with the scarab, but I could have decimated your nest and dissolved the entire blood circle like it was nothing but cobwebs. It takes time, depending on the queen's power, but it's certainly possible.:*

"There's no blood circle at the Park Avenue house."

"Doesn't fucking matter," Rik retorted. "You can't risk yourself trying to save one former Blood. Any one of us would rather die than compromise you."

Lew nodded. "I assure you, Thierry would want the same thing if he was in his right mind."

"Help," Thierry said again, harder with more force. Not plaintive. He wasn't begging for mercy.

"What if he has information that might help us?"

"It's not fucking worth it," Guillaume said. "Even looking at him on video could be compromising you this very moment. She might be looking at you through his eyes. Maybe she's trying to see how many Blood you have now. She might have even given him a nugget of something important just to lure you in for the kill."

"I don't care what he might know," Rik agreed. "It's not worth exposing yourself."

But there was something in Thierry's blue eyes that reached into me and touched my heart. Burning with intelligence, his emotions flickered rapidly from desperation and frustration to rage and resignation. And then growing hope as I delayed the order.

Not hope that I would save him.

Hope he could help *me* before the end.

I remembered looking at Mom's horrified eyes in her dead corpse. The knowledge and awareness of her soul trapped in a dead, decaying body. The horror of feeling death wrapped around her spirit, holding her captive, forcing her painstakingly to me on foot, mile by mile, while her corpse literally fell apart.

How much worse would it have been if her body had still been alive even as it rotted around her? Nerve endings still carrying messages of urgent pain to the brain. Failing organs still trying to work. Starved, wasting muscles forced to move. Bones crumbling even while carrying his weight.

So much fucking pain.

Yet his only thought was to serve Isador even while his body rotted around him.

One last time.

"I have to try," I said softly.

Guillaume dropped to one knee beside me, gently taking my left hand in both of his. "Shara."

I met his gaze, knowing what he would say, but I would hear it. Even when it wounded me.

"She knows exactly how best to twist the knife in your heart. She knows how much you must miss your mother. How a lost, young queen would cling to anything containing even a hint of her dear mother she'd never been allowed to know. I can see no greater trap to bring Shara fucking Isador down than deliberately manipulating the tenderness of your magnificent heart."

"I know." Tears spilled from my eyes. I gave him a tremulous smile, squeezing his hand. "But I like knowing I'm the kind of queen who'd burn down the world to save someone she loves. Even if I die in the process."

Bowing his head, he lifted my hand to his mouth and kissed my knuckles. "Then I'm eager to burn with you, Your Majesty."

"Magnum, if you're concerned for your safety, go into the room where I was born and lock the door. I'll be there within the hour."

Keeping our clasped hands off screen, I curled my thumb against my palm and pierced my skin. Power swelled inside me as I looked at Thierry. Even on the small screen, the taint of death billowed around him. Something black seemed to crawl beneath his skin that only my power could sense. Worms? Some kind of bug?

I clenched my teeth, steeling my nerves and focusing my intent. "Thierry Isador, you will harm no one in my house, or Llewellyn will seal your fate as soon as we arrive."

Thierry dropped to his knees, head bowed, his arms curled around himself. His shoulders heaved with ragged, groaning sobs.

I looked up at Winston. "Hang up, please."

I waited while he tucked the phone away. Then he pulled out a handkerchief and lightly dabbed at his eyes. "How can we help, Your Majesty?"

"Does Frank have a security team at the house?"

Nodding with a wry smile, Gina held her phone up. "I got an immediate text from Frank that we had an intruder. I told them to hold while I discuss with you."

"Good. I'd like to minimize the human casualties if Thierry loses control, so tell them to head over to the tower. Call Gwen and Kevin and let them know we're coming to the city but don't tell them the specifics of our visit. Only it's urgent and discretion is required. We'll probably need a couple of cars to get everyone to the house."

Gina immediately stepped into the other room, phone to her ear. Closing my eyes, I touched my Blood bonds, feeling where everyone was. Sekh, Ezra, and Xin were all in the woods outside of the nest, each alone, already returning as quickly as possible. Mehen and Vivian were in the sky, slowly circling the nest. Everyone else had drawn closer to me in case I had an order for them.

I opened my eyes and Winston offered me a steaming cup of tea. With a grateful smile, I took the cup. "Thank you so much for always knowing exactly what I need. Do you still have that gun?"

My dapper British butler gave me a sinister smile. "I do indeed, Your Majesty."

23

RIK

I *don't fucking like it. Not one fucking bit.*

But I didn't say a word as my queen prepared to spring the Dauphine's trap. Because that's exactly what it had to be.

A fucking death trap.

No queen would ever take a thrall into her Blood. Aima didn't believe in heaven and hell, but once a Blood was contaminated, there was no going back. If his contamination touched her...

We'd all be damned.

I touched Guillaume's bond, trying to keep from distracting her with my worry. *:Bring your biggest sword. Just in case you need to start dispatching us.:*

:Trust me when I say I don't need my finest Templar blade to kill any of you, even the sphinx. But it will be done, alpha.:

Even though there'd be no one left to dispatch the headless knight. Hopefully it wouldn't come to that.

I thought I was holding my shit together extremely well for the most part. I hadn't dragged her up in my arms or torn any of my clothes by partially shifting to my rock troll. A sure sign of my protective urges taking over. Until she reached up and laid her hand over mine on her shoulder, and I realized I was squeezing her far too hard. I'd probably bruised her.

"I'm open to everyone's recommendations on the best way to approach this problem with the least amount of risk."

A dozen responses rapid-fired through my head but I didn't voice any of them.

Don't fucking go.

Don't fucking touch him.

Let Lew finish him. Or Guillaume. Or Xin. Fuck, let the sphinx and dragon play tug of war with him. Though even the two most bloodthirsty meat eaters of the bunch wouldn't want to eat a thrall.

"He's not a thrall," she said. "He shook his head in denial."

"Semantics." Guillaume grunted with disgust. "He's contaminated like a thrall, whether that's what he is or not. Worse, even, because he's not just tainted, he's tainted with the Dauphine's magic."

She swallowed hard. "He's definitely tainted. It looked like he had black wriggling worms under his skin."

"Fuck that shit." Ezra said, still panting from the run back to the nest.

I sent him a hard, narrowed look of warning. Not that he fucking cared in the slightest. None of the Blood should be so far away from her they were winded when she called them to her side.

"What is it specifically about thralls that taints them when they feed on humans?"

I kept my mouth shut, trusting the eldest Aima to have better, more accurate information than me.

"It's an abomination," G replied. "Our queens carry goddess-level magic in their blood, so we shouldn't even think about feeding on anything else."

"We're built different," Xin added. "Human blood can't sustain us at all. In fact, it begins to destroy from the inside out, killing cells until we're tortured by our thirst which can never be quenched."

"Like an addict," she mused. "I wonder if I can separate out the contamination in his blood."

"It's never been done before," G said. "But if anyone can, it'll be you, my queen."

She breathed deeply, her forehead creased with worry. "I'm afraid I don't have that level of conviction, but I feel obligated to at least try. I wouldn't have gone to Mayte's nest if I'd known about Keisha's geas. We wouldn't have gone to the tower if we'd known about Tanza's blood circle trap in the basement."

Ezra shuddered and moved closer to us. I didn't blame him in the slightest. I couldn't have been in that circle more than an hour, but it felt like an eternity. Remembering the feeling of being trapped, subjected to her torture, was enough to break me out in a cold sweat of dread.

"What do you think, Lew?" She asked, reaching out to wrap her arm around his waist.

"I think it's a lost cause. Thierry's dead. He just doesn't know it yet. I love you all the more for being willing to try, though I'll never forgive myself if he manages to harm you in any way."

Carrying a stack of books, Carys came into the room looking vaguely lost and disheveled, as if she'd woken up and realized she'd lost a hundred years. The owl on her shoulder blinked at the new Blood, and then jumped off her shoulder, flapping in the opposite direction as fast as it could go.

"Me too, bird," Daire muttered.

"Relax, warcat." Sekh gave him a sleepy yet wide, bloodthirsty smile. "I don't eat anything that belongs to our queen. Except her, of course."

"You called, Your Majesty?" Carys asked.

"What's the probability I could heal a Blood of thrall contamination?"

Tipping her head back, Carys guffawed as if she'd heard the best joke of her life.

"Okaaaaaay," Shara replied, her voice dripping with irritation. "Let me phrase it differently. What's the probability I can spring a trap the Dauphine planted in one of my mother's former Blood?"

Jerking her head back, Carys gaped at her. Then paled. "Zeros. All around."

"Even if you don't know what kind of trap it is?"

"Doesn't matter," Carys replied hoarsely. "What's done is done. All the blood in the world can't change it. Not even yours, Your Majesty."

She turned her attention to Sekh. "What do you see of him?"

"Nothing, Your Majesty," he replied softly. "He's blank."

Nodding, she didn't seem surprised. "So we have to assume he might be one of the blanks that has followed me since I left Kansas City."

Rather than clamping my hands back around her shoulders, I dropped my head down toward her so I could press my mouth to her hair. "He might even be the thing you sensed in the bar. Even more reason not to go."

She leaned back against me but didn't agree to avoid this threat. Not that I expected Shara fucking Isador to avoid any danger if she could help someone she loved. Thierry had belonged to her mother. Of course she loved him, no matter the fucking cost.

"Is there anything else my Templar knight or General of the All Seeing can recommend before we go to war? Because once I take direct action involving the Dauphine, that's exactly what it is."

"War." Carys nodded vigorously though she fanned herself like she was about to faint.

"Don't tell me our odds yet," Shara replied wryly. "I still don't have a plan of attack."

"Assume the worst of her in all things," Guillaume said. "She hides in plain sight and wears different faces and identities to blur the truth."

Gina stepped back into the room, phone pressed to her ear. "Is there anything else you want me to tell Gwen?"

"Have her bring all the queens currently in the tower where she can personally see them. Weak, strong, it doesn't matter. Make sure none of them leave, and if anyone acts suspicious…" Her chin inched up and she stiffened against me, her shoulders straight and proud. "Order her to see that queen dead at all cost."

She normally kept her sibling bonds so muted I didn't even feel them, but the White Enchantress of Camelot blazed inside my queen, and I heard Gwen's voice echoing through our bonds.

:It will be done immediately, Your Majesty.:

No questions asking why. No protests or doubt. Just the fierce determination of the Once and Future Queen and her legendary knights of the Round Table.

:Touch my bond,: Shara replied. *:I'll pump you with enough power to level the entire city if you need it.:*

Aloud, she asked, "Has Mayte formally taken Queen Jacinta's blood yet?"

"Not yet," Gina replied. "The ink is barely dry, and it'll take some time for them to arrange to meet."

"Tell Mayte to delay until I'm sure who the Dauphine is."

Nodding, Gina started to step back into the living room, but Shara asked, "Do you want to go with us? Or would it be smarter for you to stay here?"

She flashed a broad smile and stepped over to the front door. No one knocked, but Frank stood there carrying a massive weapon slung over his shoulder. "It's safe to say we're both planning to go with you, Your Majesty."

Shara huffed out a laugh. "What kind of gun is that?"

"Flamethrower, Your Majesty. Winston recommended it after the last attack."

She glanced back toward the kitchen as Winston came out of his private quarters. Still impeccably dressed in a suit but loaded with guns that he started depositing at every door and window.

"I've also got a team of twenty security guards at the gate," Frank added. "With your permission, we'll bring a squad up to the house and into the grove."

"Perfect. Thank you." She glanced around at each of the people gathered around her. "A queen couldn't ask for a better army."

Guillaume bowed low and then headed for the stairs at a trot.

"Where are you going?" She called after him.

"Templar knights always carry their best sword on crusade."

She leaned back against me, and I wrapped my arms around her, determined not to crush her to my heart.

"Let's go to fucking war."

24

SHARA

The trip through the heart tree into the basement of Isador Tower and then a short drive to my mother's house only took a few minutes, including elevator and drive time.

I sat in the back of our car between Rik and Guillaume, waiting while the rest of my Blood deployed into and around the house. Gina and Carys sat across from me with Winnifred smashed against the tinted window so she could see the house. I had a suspicion that the owl didn't care about where we were or what waited inside. She was terrified of the sphinx and didn't want Sekh to sneak up on her.

Mehen and Vivian took up positions on the roof, while Nevarre and Tlacel flew overhead, scanning for any threats that might approach externally. Thankfully it was dark and none of the streetlights appeared to be working in front of the house. Bless whatever pull Magnum had with the city.

Lew led the rest of my Blood inside. I watched through his eyes as he went straight to my mother's library. The darkest room in the house, other than where she birthed me. She'd often locked herself inside the library alone, researching and strategizing how she'd keep me alive and hidden as long as possible.

Thierry was still in the same position, curled over his knees, his arms wrapped around himself. Unharmed, Magnum waited near the door as Lew passed, though she held a powerful-looking handgun in her right hand, her arm flat against her side but ready to shoot. It might slow him down, but I didn't think any Aima would die from a gunshot, even a direct hit to the skull or heart.

Once he heard footsteps, Thierry sat back on his heels, his hands gripping his knees. Head back, eyes closed, he bared his throat. Waiting for the stroke that would take his life. Lew didn't carry a weapon but shifted his hands enough to bare his gryphon's razor-sharp talons. One swipe, and Thierry would be put out of misery.

Because that was exactly what his existence had become. Absolute, horrendous misery. I didn't need a blood bond to see pain wracking his body. Shriveled muscles twitched uncontrollably, stretched like rubber bands to the point of snapping. Dark, swollen veins stood out against his thin, pale skin. Filled with goddess only knew what kind of contamination.

Itztli's black dog sniffed a hundred-thousand scents—all reeking of death. There wasn't anything remaining that smelled like the man Thierry had once been.

:Can you smell where he might have been before this?:

Itztli sniffed the ground, following the invisible footprints where Thierry had walked. :A variety of ground samples, as though he's walked a very long way. But the stench of death is too thick for me to tell any specific location.:

:I can follow his trail back to the source,: Xin whispered, gliding through my mind like a cool, still fog.

I hesitated for only a moment. :Go. She probably isn't there. It'd be too easy. But it's worth a shot.:

The silver wolf immediately raced out of the house and down the street. He didn't look back at me, but I felt the surge of excitement in his bond. He loved nothing more than a good, long hunt with the promise of a kill at the end.

:*I love you more, my queen.*:

I pressed a kiss to his head in the bond. :*Keep our bond open so I know where you are, my Blood. If anything changes, I'll call you back.*:

Offering a hand to my Blood on either side of me, I took a few deep, steadying breaths. "Any last-minute advice?"

Guillaume flicked his left wrist and a silver blade dropped into his palm. "Feed as deeply as possible before you see him. The last thing you want is to feel tempted to feed on him."

Rik added, "Don't even touch him unless you're absolutely sure he's clean. Remember the scarab."

It'd been dead on his palm—until it touched me. Now it was embedded in my wrist. If the Dauphine had planted something similar in Thierry, just waiting for me to touch him…

I shuddered at the thought. Before I got close, I'd bring up my power and shield my entire body just to be one-hundred percent sure.

With Sekh anchoring the legion of sphinxes to me, I hadn't felt the punishing thirst again, but I would never tire of tasting any of my Blood. My knight sliced a small, tidy cut on my alpha's throat. Rik lifted me onto his lap, his big hand wrapping around my nape. Holding me close. Slabs of granite gliding beneath me. He didn't ask me to allow my gryphon to do the deed without intervention. Not in words. He didn't have to, not with the siren song of his blood burning through me.

Stay safe. Here. In my arms. Forever.

While I fed, I was aware of the car door opening. Frank helped Gina out, then Carys. I felt Ezra and Daire hovering nearby, covering our approach to the house. Guillaume got out of the car and waited for me to lick Rik's throat clean before offering me a hand. Though with Rik plastered to my back, he basically just lifted me out to G, who set me on my feet.

When he turned toward the house, I blew out a low whistle. He'd buckled on his sword, and the sight of my Templar knight stopped me dead in my tracks.

Guillaume always wore at least a dozen blades on his body. Some visible, but mostly hidden beneath his clothes. Tonight, he wore jeans and a simple long-sleeved baby blue button-down shirt like usual. Over the top of his clothes, a long sheath was strapped to his back by a chest halter. The hilt rose over his right shoulder so he could easily grab it. Another strap steadied the heavy blade around his waist like a belt.

Pausing, he looked back over his shoulder, eyebrow arched. "You've seen me carry a sword before, my queen."

"Not that one." I didn't know one sword from the other, honestly, but his stance was different. I could hear the faint jingle of chainmail. The clang of swords, the screaming neigh of his warhorse. The way he carried this sword revealed the true core of his knight's honor, honed to a brilliantly sharp edge. The former Triune Executioner, assumed dead and lost after his former queen's death. Now fully healed and leading the charge to war once more.

Turning back to me, he drew the long, heavy blade in an effortless glide of steel that made me shiver. He lay the sword across his other hand and dropped down to his knees on the sidewalk, holding it up to me. "This sword was never used in Desideria's service. Now, Your Majesty, this blade is yours."

I traced one of the channels in the shining blade. "Is it real? I mean, the one you carried to other crusades?"

"Absolutely. I carried it for centuries before I was imprisoned by King Philip. It only ever knew the honor of a Templar knight. In fact, I only re-acquired the blade recently and restored it. That's why I was so close when you called me to Kansas City."

Deliberately, I nicked my thumb on the blade and smeared a long line of my blood down the steel.

His eyes flared and he pressed his forehead to the leather-wrapped hilt. "This knight is at your undying service for all time, Your Majesty."

"Then I have a request to make of you, Sir Guillaume de Payne Isador."

He lifted his head, his eyes clear, hard, and cold. Ready to kill. "Anything, Your Majesty."

"When you first came to me in Kansas City, I asked you to swear an oath to never kill any of my Blood. If any of us are contaminated by Thierry, I release you from that oath. I ask that you dispatch us with this beautiful sword."

His brow furrowed ever so slightly. "Of course, Your Majesty. Rik already asked me to bring the sword for that reason."

There was almost always a loophole with blood oaths if you were clever enough. It all came down to what you believed, wholly and deeply with your entire will.

He'd sworn to never kill any of my Blood, current or future, directly or indirectly with *intent to harm*. A mercy killing to avoid any of us suffering like Thierry would be a blessing, not harm. We'd already had discussions like this, hence his confusion.

Here, then, was my real command. I cupped his cheeks in my palms and stared deeply into his eyes. Imprinting my will on him, powered by my blood. "If a single drop of the Dauphine's power gets inside me, I ask you to kill me so she has no claim on any part of me. Once that's done, carry me to Centralia, Pennsylvania and walk into the fire like my mother did so we can all be together once more."

"You honor me beyond all reckoning, Your Majesty." He swallowed hard as I pressed a kiss to his forehead. Tears of blood dripped from his eyes. Tears I captured on my fingertips and tasted with a delicate shudder. "I will carry you safely to the other side of the Veil."

25

SHARA

I paused outside the open library door, waiting for Rik to settle the Blood where he wanted them. I couldn't even see Thierry between Sekh and Guillaume facing off across from Lew.

"The items you asked for are on a tray just inside the door, Your Majesty," Magnum called softly.

She stood with Gina, Carys, and Frank a few feet behind us in the hallway. Close enough to offer suggestions—but hopefully out of the danger zone. Itztli and Ezra prowled back and forth behind Rik, shifted to their beasts, ready to protect our backs just in case something managed to sneak through the four aerial Blood.

"Thank you. Did he threaten you at all before you called?"

"No. I heard a scuffle when the security guard tried to stop him, but he didn't hurt anyone. He just wouldn't leave."

I pierced my skin above the scarab marking on my wrist. As before, I held the blood inside my body, but instead of just covering the small puncture with a plug of power, I wrapped my entire body with a protective layer. Pulling it tighter against my skin, covered head to toe. Maybe too securely, since it dulled my senses. I couldn't even feel the heat of Rik's body behind me, and he burned like a furnace.

I didn't want to deaden sensation. Only protect myself from the taint.

Letting some of the magic sink into my skin helped, making the shield thinner. I'd have to play around with it until I honed the right amount of shielding.

:Whatever you're doing, I approve,: Rik said in the bond. :It feels like you have a layer of flexible armor over the top of your clothes.:

:Good. I don't want any openings in case anything crawls out of him.:

Sekh and G took a step apart, allowing me to see the man on the floor in front of them.

Thierry Isador slumped on his knees, his head sagged forward. His hands and arms were covered in festering welts, scabs, and bruises, though he didn't have any fresh wounds. My stomach churned at the thick, rotten smell in the air. More than death and decomposition. I imagined it smelled like a hospital ICU plus the morgue. Cancer and C-diff and tuberculosis and thick blood clots. Dying cells and virulent infection. Dissolving lungs and disintegrating muscles mixed with vomit and shit and curdled blood, poured into decades of fermenting sewage.

Horrible. I wasn't sure I'd ever get the smell completely out of my nose.

He wore tattered clothes that might have been jeans and a T-shirt once upon a time, but now they looked like the rags worn by someone shipwrecked on a deserted island a lifetime ago. His hair was a shaggy dirt-colored mess of matted clumps, and a filthy, scraggly beard covered most of his lower face.

But when he lifted his head, his eyes were the piercing sky blue of a bright summer day. Shimmering with tears at the sight of me.

Not the Dauphine's golden-brown eyes I'd seen in Mom's corpse.

His neck corded, his shoulders bunched up with effort. His mouth opened, his tongue flopping inside his mouth, coated with a thick white layer of scum. He croaked out sounds but not words. I wasn't sure if that was part of the geas the Dauphine had put on him, a visible element like a wad of cloth shoved into his mouth to silence him. Or if it was a side effect of his sickness. His head jerked, one side of his face tensing and pulling upward, while the other side sagged. Could Aima have strokes? Or brain damage from lack of blood and oxygen?

He didn't lunge toward me or otherwise move. Which was good, because Lew vibrated with tension, his arms poised around Thierry's head, ready to tear his head off his body.

I took a step closer, shadowed closely by Rik. He didn't block me from my goal or try to shield me with his body. Not when he had three of my most dangerous Blood between me and the threat.

Looking at Thierry in person didn't yield any new insight I hadn't already gleaned from Magnum's video. There was something black working its way through his veins, but I wasn't sure what it was. Not without examining it closer.

I either needed to touch him—which wasn't happening—or I needed to get my blood inside him so I could see what the hell was going on.

He could understand me, and I didn't want to cause him any more trauma than he'd already endured. "I'm going to take a sample of your blood—"

Recoiling backward in an awkward flop to the ground, he tried to crab crawl away from me, though Lew blocked him with his legs. Leaving dark smears on his jeans that made me shudder. Thierry's skin was literally falling off in thick, gummy layers, and there wasn't anything underneath but black goo.

I surged through Lew's bond, searching for any taint or curse sliding into his body, but his blood remained untouched. If Thierry was carrying a boobytrap activated by touch, it'd be waiting for me to touch him. Not one of my Blood. Though I still wanted them to have as little contact with him as possible.

"Okay," I said shakily. "Plan B. I'm going to give you my blood first, but I'm not going to touch you, alright? Okeanos, please bring the tray to me."

My Blood grabbed the silver tray Magnum had placed by the door and carried it to me. I'd asked her to have several clear glasses available to capture blood, and something we could use to send a sample to Dr. Borcht for further testing. If I couldn't do anything with my power, hopefully she might be able to help. Though again, I had little faith in human medicine.

I opened the shield just enough to allow my blood to drip into one of the crystal goblets. I had the feeling Thierry would need a whole lot of blood to even begin putting a dent in healing him, but I'd start with a few swallows. That should give me enough of a foothold in his body to see what we were dealing with.

"Daire, could you give this cup to him and help him drink it if needed?"

"Of course, my queen." Daire took the cup to Thierry, and I didn't miss the fact that he stepped around Guillaume's side—as far away from Sekh as possible.

Maybe it wasn't Sekh and Mehen who needed to bond, but my two felines.

:With all due respect, Your Majesty, that's not fucking happening,: Sekh said in the bond. :I will honor your bonds but I will not ever consider him friend.:

:Why not?:

:I Saw what he tried to do to your cobra queen.:

Ohhhh. I thought it was a cat thing. Not a Blood issue. :He—:

:There's no excuse,: Sekh broke in before I could explain. :Not for Blood sworn to honor his goddess through his queen. Your alpha was far too easy on him. I never forget and only rarely forgive. I'd have made you an attractive fur rug to place before your fireplace.:

Grimacing, Daire squatted down beside Thierry. I was worried he might have heard Sekh's comments in the bond, but Daire was only responding to the stench rolling up from the still flailing, flopping man on the floor. Thierry struggled to coordinate his body enough to leap up and reach for the cup of my blood. Daire had to help, tipping it up to his mouth and controlling the pour into his scabbed lips, torn by jagged, broken teeth.

He moaned so loudly I thought he might burst into flame without me even intending to burn him up like Greyson.

I touched my blood in Thierry's mouth, intending to slide through his body as my blood soaked into him.

Rotting meat engulfed my senses, crawling with maggots and filth.

I flinched, twisting my awareness away. Bile surged up my throat. I didn't want to throw up, especially not inside the shield. Whirling around, I pressed my face against Rik, clinging to him. Wishing I could smell the smoking iron and rock in his scent. Feel the heat of his body against me. He crushed me against him, lifting me off my feet, already turning to carry me away.

:*Not yet,:* I whispered in his bond, trying not to weep. :*I just need a moment to gather myself.:*

"He's not able to swallow, my queen," Daire said. "It's not even soaking into him."

"It's the contamination," Guillaume added softly. "His dying body repels your blood. It doesn't understand how to absorb the power any longer."

If I couldn't get him to ingest my blood…

How the fuck could I even begin to heal him?

26

LLEWELLYN

I'd never seen such an abomination.

He wasn't a thrall. In that much, he was absolutely correct. But he was so much worse. The very sacred gift that made us Aima had been twisted and corrupted beyond anything the Great Mother had ever intended.

Even thralls would be able to take a queen's blood, not that it would save them in the end. But Thierry couldn't swallow one drop of our queen's blood. And the agony. Goddess.

Not because he couldn't take her blood. Not directly.

Because she was Isador. She was our former queen's daughter. Everything she'd worked for, dedicating her life—and thus ours—to the single driving force of her will to make possible. She'd been successful, and a powerful, living, glorious daughter of Isis stood before us.

And there was nothing he could do to taste her one final time.

Thierry threw himself forward, impaling my six-inch wicked sharp eagle talons into his throat. Not to harm our queen. Not even to put himself out of misery.

But to end hers. Because she couldn't help him.

Thierry didn't have a bond to hear the desperate tumult in her mind, but he still had eyes and enough remaining mental capacity to understand what he was seeing. She clung to her alpha, gathering her courage. He could see the way we all looked at him with revulsion and pity and horror. Now more than ever.

Unable to feed on our queen. The absolute worst thing you could do to a Blood.

My stomach clenched at the black filth pouring out of him. Oily sludge, reeking of all the most revolting smells of this world. How Itztli could stay in the room with his sensitive nose, I had no idea. It was almost too much for me, and I didn't have a hound's olfactory glands.

I tightened my talons inside my old friend, ready to yank out a hunk of whatever flesh might remain.

"Wait," Shara rasped out.

Her voice quivered, fainter than any order she'd ever given, but I paused. Even though that meant I still had my fingers buried in his decomposing body.

"I have an idea. If blood can't heal him, maybe my darkness can. Carys, is that possible?"

Still in the hall, the other queen leaned against the wall opposite the door, pale and sweaty, weak enough her owl hopped down to the floor beside her rather than riding on her shoulder. "I need more information. What darkness?"

"I wish I dared take him to the tower's basement. Maybe I can pull it here…" Her voice trailed off, ideas flaring in her mind too rapidly for me to follow. "I need all the windows of this house covered. I don't even want starlight shining inside."

Immediately Daire and Okeanos ran out of the room with the humans, moving room to room to draw blinds and curtains. Sliding furniture in the way. Whatever it took to cover the glass.

Releasing her grip on Rik, she stepped deeper into the room. Eyes closed, her hands held out in front of her.

"What are you looking for, my queen?" I asked. "I've been in this house many times."

"Is there a basement? A crawl space? Anything below the house?"

"Not that I'm aware of, though given how old the original structure is, it's certainly likely."

"My mother was a fucking genius." She stopped in the middle of the room, nodding with a sad, fond smile. "Rik, I need this opened."

He squatted and gripped handfuls of a circular wool rug, large enough it covered most of the room. Muscles bulged in his shoulders, tearing his shirt down his back, but the fibers in the rug pulled apart just as easily in his bare hands. "There's a seam in the floor but I don't see a handle."

Guillaume looked over at the massive black dog and jerked his head toward Thierry. Itztli immediately took up position beside Sekh so Guillaume could step over to help.

"Oh, no, G," Shara cried, laying a hand on his arm. "Not your Templar blade."

Shaking his head, the knight huffed out a laugh. "I wouldn't care to test one-thousand-year-old steel on its ability to pry up a wood floor when there are so many other tools at my disposal made to hack through anything."

Dropping to one knee, he rolled up his jeans, revealing a leather sheath buckled over his boot, long enough to reach from knee to ankle. He pulled out a curved blade with a heavy, tapered point perfect for chopping.

Rik blew out a low whistle of appreciation. "You just happened to have a kukri on you today?"

With a wink, G wedged the tip into the seam. "You never know which weapons I'm carrying any given day, but a kukri's a good bet for just about anything."

Alternatively prying and chopping through a few stubborn

pieces of wood, the knight pulled up a hole in the floor roughly a foot wide.

"That's plenty," Shara said. "I just need access to the darkness below."

Maybe it was my imagination, but the room already seemed darker. Even though it was nighttime and there weren't any windows in the library, there was still an element of increasingly intense, heavy energy I couldn't see. Hairs prickled all over my body, and even Thierry stilled his twitching.

Straddling the hole in the floor, Shara held her arms loose at her sides with her palms up. Closing her eyes, she... pulled. That's the only way I could describe it. Through her bond, I felt the tug deep in her core. The same way she'd pulled the sphinx to her, only this wasn't blood she called.

"Ahhh, yes." Smiling, she nodded. When she opened her eyes, they gleamed with ultraviolet shadow rather than her normal midnight sky. "This darkness, Carys."

The other queen didn't answer, so Shara turned to look over her shoulder, repeating her name.

Carys stared at her, slumped on the floor, her mouth gaping open. Closed. Open. Like a fish. "Incalculable," she finally managed to say. "Unknown."

"What does that mean?"

Stepping back into the room with the others, Daire laughed. "I'm guessing it's like dividing by zero."

Carys nodded jerkily. "Exactly. It might work. It might not. I have no way of knowing."

I refused to get my hopes up. Not for my sake, or Thierry's.

For hers.

SHARA

Thick shadows poured into the room, curling like Okeanos' tentacles around my limbs. Swirling over the floor, billowing gently like clouds.

Black, deep purple fading to dark gray shadows—but not evil. Not tainted. The epitome of darkness—that had never been touched by the sun.

My domain—thanks to my father, Typhon.

I'd never tried to wield darkness before, so I wasn't sure what to try. I could push shadows into Thierry and try to force the taint out, filling him up like the tendrils filling this room. If it would cleanse him, somehow...

Experimenting, I lifted my right hand, willing shadows to rise around him. Winding up his body like slithering snakes. Flowing into his mouth and nostrils. The torn skin on his throat. Lew's talons were still buried in him, slicing deeper every time either of them moved. Only a few threads of something that might have once been tendon or muscle still clung to his spine. Everything else was... loose. Liquified.

Shadows moved through him, but the goo was still there. Like oil and water, it didn't mix.

Sighing, I pulled the shadows back out and stilled my mind. Letting the tides of darkness lap gently as they willed around the room. Tasting everything.

Ugh. My stomach rolled.

Closing my eyes, I exhaled hard, pushing the taste of taint away from me. From all of us. Darkness carried the taint away, soaking into the ground deep below the house. Dirt absorbed the decaying particles of contaminated blood and flesh like any other dead body.

The Mother accepted those dead, rotten things. Just like She accepted human bodies buried in a cemetery. A fallen tree slowly crumbling into the rich loam of the forest. A deer dragged down by wolves. Death was always used for rebirth, fueling the new growth in the spring. She created—and She destroyed.

Maybe I need to destroy him—before I heal him.

The idea made me uncomfortable. I didn't like the idea of deliberately hurting him when he was already suffering so much. Wouldn't it be better to put him out of his misery? Allow him to continue his journey to Esetta? Didn't he deserve an easy end after all that he'd suffered already?

I opened my eyes and met Lew's hard, unswerving gaze. "Do you have any memory of my mother with Thierry that might help me decide?"

He shook his head. "Nothing specific with her, though if you question whether he'd rather die now and join her, or stay and fight with you, then I know his answer would be to stay."

Thierry made those horrible, desperate sounds again, made even worse by Lew's grip inside him.

"Even if I fail?" I whispered, blinking back tears.

Thierry nodded, not caring it destroyed his throat even more.

"Even if I have to kill you to save you?"

He closed his eyes for a moment, and when he met my gaze again, I saw the same steely reserve I always saw reflected in Guillaume's eyes. Lew's. Rik's.

Use me. As you will.

No matter the fucking cost.

27

SHARA

"I need to drain all the taint out of his body."

I waited for my Bloods' reactions. Their shock or horror at what lengths I was prepared to go. Even to save one of them.

Lew started to raise his arm, trying to lift Thierry off the floor, but he grimaced and lowered him back to his knees. "If I apply any more pressure to what's left of his throat, he'll lose his head. I'm assuming that would take you longer to heal unless you can use the knight's ability to regenerate and fuse his spine back together."

Behind me, Rik suggested, "Someone could hold him up by his ankles."

Sekh looked around the room and up at the ceiling. "I think I'll fit."

The sphinx swelled up out of him. Giant haunches, his rear legs tucked underneath him. His mighty paws folded up rather than stretched out before him. He kept his ram head low, almost on the floor. With a careless toss of his mighty head, he'd take out the whole ceiling. *:Someone grab a rope and string him up. I'm not putting my teeth in him.:*

Daire ran out of the room. "I saw an electric cord in the utility room."

In a few minutes, he ran back in and tossed the thick orange cord to Guillaume.

G said, "Stand him up if you can."

Lurching upright, Thierry heaved to his feet with Lew's help. My knight looped the cord around his ankles several times, whipped a quick knot, and then tossed the remainder up to the sphinx, who easily snatched it in his mouth.

Slowly, Sekh began to lift his head, taking up the slack, testing how much room he had between the ceiling. *:Ready?:*

Lew gave a nod. "I'll help you flip him around but then I'm getting out of the fallout zone."

"Everybody else back," Rik said. "There's no sense in any of us risking contamination."

Hopefully the shadows would catch most of the taint. I thickened the blanket of darkness around Thierry, layer upon layer of shadow to capture the bulk of whatever came out of him.

Guillaume and Daire backed up toward me, and Rik wrapped his arms around me, ready to pull me out of the way if something worse than sludge crawled out.

With a silent coordinated countdown, Lew jerked Thierry backward off his feet at the same time as Sekh lifted his head up to the ceiling. Black rain splattered the floor beneath Thierry, quickly absorbed by the darkness flowing around him. Toward me—and the hole.

I stepped aside, not wanting to risk an accidental touch of taint even through my blood shield. Clots and chunks streamed out of him but nothing alive. Disintegrated organs and curdled blood. Shredded muscles and dissolved tissue. His skin shifted on his body, loose and wet as all his insides drained through the holes in his throat.

"Goddess," Lew whispered, slinging gunk off his hand as he backed away.

:*Back up more and I'll hold him over the hole,*: Sekh said. :*Less to clean later.*:

Rik swept me up against him and moved back toward Carys, who still sat on the floor. Though she'd pulled herself together and actually looked intrigued rather than horrified. Winnifred stood beside her, hunched down so I couldn't see her legs, while the queen absently stroked her.

Slowly, Sekh turned his head toward the hole in the floor, trying not to sling chunks everywhere. But it was a losing battle. Thierry began to twitch and swing back and forth, moaning. Screaming. Garbled words I couldn't understand between his ruined throat and whatever geas the Dauphine might have put on him.

Aima were fucking hard to kill. His body didn't want to die and fought. Hard. Even as liquified insides dripped out of his body.

His screams rose to a high, continuous wail. Long snaky streams of glistening black slithered out of him. Definitely alive.

With a thought, I lit them on fire. Sizzling and popping, the stench took on the distinctive odor of charred flesh.

Another thick, black eel began to slide out of his mouth, making his whole body convulse. I had a feeling it was the oldest, the first one. The root of whatever spell the Dauphine had cursed into him.

The sphinx lifted him higher, giving him a hard shake. Trying to jar the thing out of Thierry's throat. It finally slid out in a wet, black gush. Slithering with surprising speed straight at me.

Not today, motherfucker. Not this queen.

I wrapped it in a giant fist of fire, banded with darkness. Tightening my will around it to ensure nothing else escaped. A deep, dark river flowed around the charred ash, sweeping it below into the depths of darkness.

Taking a shaky breath, I pulled the streams of darkness up over the sphinx, absorbing the gunk splattered on his front legs and chest. The floor. The stains on Lew's jeans. The remains beneath his fingernails. Cleansed with darkness first—and then I flooded them both with power, bathing them head to toe in my energy.

"Do you feel anything else remaining on you?" I asked.

Lew grimaced, wiping his palm on his pants. "I still feel disgusting."

:*Same,*: Sekh replied.

"Do you know what the black eel-things were?"

Everyone shook their heads, even Sekh, All Seeing, Never Sleeping. :*I've never Seen anything like that before.*:

Slowly twirling above the hole, Thierry's body twitched. His eyes flickered.

"He's still alive," I whispered hoarsely, swiping tears out of my eyes. "Even after all that shit came out of him. How's that even possible? There's hardly anything left in him but his skeleton."

Guillaume shook his head. "We're hard to kill, but not that hard. Even me. If all I had left was some saggy skin and bones, I wouldn't still be reaching for my sword."

I wasn't so sure. I'd seen him trying to get to me even after Xin chopped off his head.

Closing my eyes, I sank my awareness into the darkness and flowed into Thierry's body. Well, what remained of it. Gray, rubbery bones, pitted and soft like they'd been soaked in acid. A shell of sinew and flappy skin. Seeing the inside of his hollowed body made my stomach heave, but I pushed deeper. His spirit must be stuck inside, trapped. Like Mom's had been.

I almost missed it, assuming it was a small, last remaining chunk of his heart. But the threads of darkness flowed over it, around it, pulling my attention back. It didn't move or flutter like Mom's spirit. It couldn't. It was drenched in black goo coating it like tar and glue. Keeping it stuck against his spine.

Grasping it with my power, I pulled the small chunk out of his body, straight out of his ribcage. I opened my eyes, watching the lump gliding on a thick stream of darkness toward me. It still didn't flutter or show any sign of life, but at least Thierry's body stopped twitching.

I stepped closer and allowed my blood to seep slowly through the shield on my wrist. Drop after drop, burning through the black gunk. Washing it clean with the Great One's blood flowing in my veins. Until its wings opened, wet with my blood rather than taint. A bird hopped upright, shaking its feathers out, revealing its coloring. White head with a blue body and long red tail feathers.

His head cocked, eyes bright blue, just like Thierry's.

"Goddess of Death and Resurrection," Carys whispered. "I've never seen your magic in action before, Your Majesty."

"What's the percentage now?" I whispered.

"Of what?"

Confused, I turned my head to search her face, surprised she didn't immediately say one hundred percent. "He's clean of the taint, now. Right?"

She gave herself a little shake and sat up straighter. "Right now, yes. He's clean. But if you put him back in that corpse, I still see zeroes."

"No," I whispered. Pain squeezed my chest, banding my heart as surely as his spirit had been trapped. "No! It can't end like this. I can heal him. I must."

"I'm sorry, Shara." Carys said in a gentle voice so unlike her normal snappy tone that a sob broke free from my throat. "You've done all you can for him. If you'd burned his body before you freed his spirit, he would have been burned alive."

Tears streamed down my face as I stared at the bird. I'd

fucking tortured him. I'd strung him up by his ankles like a side of meat and drained his entire body until only a shell remained while he fucking screamed, even with melted vocal cords.

And for fucking what?

Zeroes. All zeroes.

I couldn't bring him back. Well, I could, but I couldn't heal him.

He'd never be Blood again. I couldn't risk touching him, even so much as a hug.

I'd never taste my mother in his blood. Only black rotten taint.

Why? I silently wailed in my head. My heart. *Why send him to me if I can't save him?*

"You did save him," Lew said hoarsely. "You freed him from the Dauphine. You saved him when all else failed. Now he can fly to sit on your mother's shoulder, waiting for us to join them."

The sphinx gently lowered the body to the floor and allowed the cord to slip from his mouth. Lew straightened his head, tucking his chin closer to his chest to hide the gaping holes in his throat.

"He'll have to be burned." My voice echoed, hollowed out and empty. My throat ached. "I don't know if I can. Not so soon."

"We'll take care of him," Lew replied as he adjusted Thierry's arms and legs so he looked almost asleep. Peaceful. Not twitching and flopping and screaming with agony. "I know him better than anyone, Shara, and he's grateful. He wouldn't want you to feel a moment of regret or sadness for him."

But I do. My throat squeezed harder. Choked sobs swelled inside my chest until my ribs hurt.

Chirping softly, the bird hopped toward the body. He perched on the ridge of bone stabbing out of the mutilated chest and made another gentle sound. A soothing coo that wrecked my heart into shreds.

"No." I shook my head, swiping my tears away. "Go, Thierry. She's waiting for you."

He chirped again and hopped down into the cavity of his own corpse, popping his head back out to look at me.

"No! I can't make you live through that again. I'm fine. I'll be okay. I'll dream about you with her, safe and happy and whole."

But the bird chirped insistently. I stepped closer and squatted down, holding my hand out to him. "She needs you more than I do, Thierry. She's all alone."

I didn't know for sure, but all the times I'd felt my mother's ghostly presence, I'd sensed only her. I didn't know if that was part of her penance for killing Desideria, or if the rest of her Blood were still alive in this world. Waiting for me.

Or fucking trapped like Thierry.

Trapped by their honor and love for my mother, and their hope for a future Isador queen.

Coo, coo. The bird ducked down into the darkness of his ribcage. *Chirp, chirp, coo.*

I didn't need Nevarre to translate.

Stay. Help. Love.

No matter the fucking cost.

28

NEVARRE

"What was it like?" Shara asked, her voice slurred and heavy. "When I brought you back to life?"

She lay in my arms, her head on my heart that only beat because she'd resurrected me.

Together, we lay between the sphinx's front paws. One of her arms draped over his foreleg. A slash in her wrist steadily dripped blood onto the dead man she was trying to knit back together from nothing but a skeleton, a few scraps of skin, her own formidable will, the fierce love of her heart.

And an ocean of blood.

Goddess, I'd never seen her bleed so much. For so long. If she hadn't called Sekh to join us, I feared she would have lost more of us than just her mother's former Blood. Not even Shara fucking Isador could raise a thrall from the dead and keep a dozen severely drained Blood alive.

She had her other hand buried in the sphinx's chest, feeding from him constantly. Then one of us while he fed from her. Rinse and repeat. While her precious blood dripped into the shell that had once been Thierry Isador.

"I don't really remember much," I murmured against her

temple. "It was dark. I knew I was dead, and time passed, but nothing really mattered. Not until you called my name."

"I didn't have to heal you. You were already whole except for your spirit. You could talk and shift into your raven. Isn't that strange?"

I huffed out a laugh. "I suppose all magic is strange to humans."

"You tasted like Celtic magic, not blood in the beginning." She breathed deeply and let out a long sigh. "I won't ever know what Thierry tastes like. Do you think he'll remember what I did to him?"

"Remember," the corpse croaked. "Everything."

She jerked upright, scrambling to lean over the sphinx's leg. I sat up beneath her, keeping her in my lap, fully prepared to sling us both the opposite direction. Rik moved closer, ready to drop like a landslide and crush the man she'd worked so hard to heal.

"Thierry," she whispered, her voice thick with tears. "I'm so fucking sorry."

"Miracle."

His voice didn't sound right, more like the crackle of dried leaves and sticks underfoot, but his words were intelligible. His eyes were clear sky blue, fully aware. His chest rose and fell, too deeply still, but he had a heartbeat. His lungs worked. He started to lift his hand up toward hers.

I jerked us backward against the sphinx's chest, while Rik swatted Thierry's arm aside. Lew crouched, talons ready. Behind him, Guillaume stood completely still, on the surface relaxed and casual. Though the Templar blade was in his hand, the tip resting lightly on the floor at his feet.

"Sorry," Thierry rasped, nodding. His throat still gaped open, baring tendon and cartilage glistening with blood. "Forgot. No touch. You."

"What can you tell us about where you were? What did she do to you?"

"Geas." He closed his eyes, a faint shudder rocking his body. "Leeches out?"

"Yes," she replied faintly.

Goddess, those giant eels had started like a normal leech. How long must they have been in his body feasting to be so large?

"Esetta," he whispered, giving Lew a beseeching look. "Didn't know. Who."

Lew's face twisted with emotion, a flash of jealous rage that took me a moment to understand. Then I realized why.

Even as a cursed thrall creature our queen had brought back to some semblance of life, Thierry could remember and say their queen's name. Because he'd died.

Lew still couldn't remember or say her name.

"Why did she send you?" Shara asked.

Thierry rolled his head back toward her. "Close. Queen."

"So she sent you to New Orleans simply because there was a queen there. Not because of the Dauphine."

He opened his mouth, croaking again. Shaking his head, he worked his jaws back and forth, his eyes blinking as he tried to come up with a way to say what he wanted that didn't violate the spell put upon him. "Time. You need. Time."

She looked over at Lew. "What does that mean? Do you know?"

"Thierry's gift is stopping time. He had to physically touch her to make it work, and it would only last a few minutes before it knocked him out cold."

"Time," Thierry rasped. "Help. You need. Time."

"Oh, Thierry." Closing her eyes, she swallowed hard, letting tears stream down her cheeks again. "I'd rather lose time and die than watch you suffer."

"You," he repeated adamantly. "Need."

"But you can't touch me anyway," she whispered, shaking her

head. "There might still be some part of the spell that I can't see until it's too late."

"Miracle." He gave her a crooked, bloody smile. "Worth it."

Her shoulders slumped, her heart aching with such pain I wrapped her in my arms. Trying to ease her sorrow any way I could. She reached up and fisted her fingers in my hair, turning her face into the fallen strands sliding over my shoulder. Breathing in my scent. The only way she could breathe through the pain.

"Saw you," he whispered. "Failed."

She turned her head, opening her eyes. "You were there. That was you in Kansas City."

"Close. Warn." He coughed, a wet, ugly sound like his lung was coming up his esophagus. "Lost you. Came home."

Goddess. I couldn't even comprehend the pain. The tenacity. He could barely walk but had shuffled along on foot over a thousand miles from Kansas City to New York just to find our queen. Falling apart and rotting from the inside out.

"Where were you before Kansas City?"

"Swamp."

New Orleans was below sea level, but I wouldn't call it a swamp. Unless a hurricane flooded the city again.

"Was it a peach-colored house with green shutters?"

He shook his head. "Swamp."

I felt her reach out toward Xin, tracking his location as he followed the reeking trail of death due west. The silver wolf ran at a steady, ground-eating lope, his tongue hanging out in a wolfy grin. :Thierry was in Kansas City at Christmas, but he said he came from a swamp. Can you still pick up his trail from months ago?:

:I could follow his scent for years if I had to,: Xin replied. :Though to save time, I'll drop south toward Louisiana and pick up his trail closer to the source.:

"Enough," Thierry said. "Blood."

She shook her head. "You're not healed. I can bring you back—"

"Enough," he said again, as gently as his ruined throat would allow. "Rest." His face tensed, his eyes narrowing with intent. "War."

Black wings swept through my bond. The beat of drums quickening my heart.

A vision filled my mind. Shara. Standing in a dark, cold river. Dressed in the white sundress. Covered in blood. Something dark in her hands. Bending at the waist, she dunked her hands into the water, holding it down beneath the icy stream. She lifted her gaze to mine, locking eyes. Stealing my breath.

Black, empty eyes of shadow stared back at me.

"Let it begin."

29

SHARA

I showered and bathed and showered again. Standing under the spray until the water ran cold, scrubbing my skin. But I couldn't get the smell of death and rot off me.

Even washing myself with power didn't help. I could still smell the black chunks of slime and decomposed flesh. I tried to sleep, but when I closed my eyes, I saw giant black eels slithering across the floor. Or Thierry swinging back and forth from his ankles. His screams ringing in my ears.

Reliving the horror at what I'd done to him, trying to save him. I'd tortured him like Ra tortured Huitzilopochtli. Though Thierry didn't have enough heart remaining for me to pull out and wear on a necklace around my neck.

Shoulders slumped, I finally sat up on the edge of the bed and looked around the room. Wondering how many times Esetta or one of her Blood had slept in this room. If she'd made love to Thierry on this bed before sending him to the Dauphine.

"You need to rest," Rik murmured, shifting closer so he could rub my back.

"I know." My eyes burned, hot and dry, my thoughts

whirling in a jumbled mess. Too many questions tangled in my mind. Too heartsick. Too...

Angry.

I knew Esetta loved me. More than anything. More than her Blood. Her alpha. Her own life.

But I couldn't reconcile her love against the horrors she'd knowingly sent her Blood to face.

She'd sent Lew to House Skye, and they'd put out his fucking eyes and chained him up like an animal. Even if she hadn't known Leonie Delafosse was the Dauphine, she had to have known something similar might happen to Thierry. Maybe not the depths of the evilness she'd do to him, but the risk was there.

She'd sent him. And he'd fucking gone. Without question.

Rik kissed my shoulder. "So would I."

"I wouldn't send you in the first place."

Braced on his elbow beside me, he rubbed his palm up and down my back in long, slow, soothing strokes. "I went into Tanza's circle to save Ezra. To buy you time to deal with Keisha. I'd do it again, even if you couldn't get me out. Even if Guillaume had to behead me to prevent that darkness from touching you."

My chest ached, too tight for me to breathe. I felt like I was drowning. "That was a fucking awful thing I made you do."

"You never made me do a single fucking thing."

"I just... I can't..." My voice cracked with strain. I balled my hands into fists, even though my nails dug into my palms. The sharp pricks in my flesh sharpened my anger. Pitchforks and razors. Shining steel and brutal edges.

But that only made me think of my Templar knight.

All the horrible things he'd been forced to do by his former queen.

Would I someday do the very same thing? Would I be willing to send him into a nest and execute everyone inside?

If one of my Blood were trapped inside... Or Gina. Frank. Winston. Magnum. Kevin. Xochitl. Mayte or Gwen or Carys.

My family.

Absolutely.

:And I would fucking go without question.: Guillaume's bond vibrated with the sound of cold steel drawn from its sheath. *:I would gallop back to you covered in the blood of your enemies and rejoice that I had completed your task. I would kneel at your feet and offer you my bloody sword and beg you to send me again.:*

:Send me next.: Itztli's bond rang with the thunderous bay of his black dog. *:Your obsidian blade hungers. Let me flay them alive and make their skins dance for you.:*

The General of the All Seeing, Never Sleeping roared with the might of three-thousand sphinxes. *:The legion awaits your command, Your Majesty. We're ready to feast and revel in blood like the goddess who made us.:*

Xin's wolf howled, not the mournful moon song but sharp, excited yips. Calling the pack in for the kill. *:If I find the Dauphine at the end of this reeking trail of filth, I will rip her throat out with my teeth and crack her ribcage open so I can bring her heart back to you.:*

Goddess. I surged up to my feet and paced back and forth beside the bed. "You're all missing the fucking point."

"You point. We go." Rik didn't get up or reach for me. As if he knew I'd punch him for no fucking reason. "That's what we do."

Torn between guilt and pride, horror and glee, anger and all-consuming love. I wanted to rage at my mother and accuse her of failing to protect the ones she should have saved at all cost, while simultaneously doing the exact same thing.

Sending one of my Blood on a trail that might very well lead to his death. Or something much, much worse. My stomach heaved at the thought of Xin swinging from his ankles, vomiting out his insides and howling in agony.

:She's welcome to try.: His wolf bared his teeth, a snarl rumbling from his chest. *:Though my queen will resurrect me so I can hunt her again and again until she's fucking dead.:*

A storm rose inside me, roiling with emotions, tearing me apart. I wanted to slash and burn. Punch and kick. Wail and scream and rage. Keep my Blood safe. While simultaneously demanding justice. Rage at my mother for putting us all in danger—while stewing with impatience for my chance to strike the Dauphine at the first clue to her location.

Putting every single one of us into horrible danger. Not just from arguably the strongest living Triune queen, but her goddess as well.

Kill the Dauphine to protect my family…

And simultaneously put everything I fucking loved in this world on the line.

Esetta had been moving me into position before I'd even been born. Clearing the board before I even knew the game had started. Bringing in the pieces she thought I needed, even if that meant sending people she loved into nightmares I didn't want to even begin to comprehend.

The fucking scope of her game. At least a century in the making.

The fucking audacity.

She didn't know me. She couldn't have known what kind of daughter I would be. What kind of queen.

What if I was fucking insane like Tanza? Tainted by something dark and twisted? What if all I'd wanted to do was torture the Blood she'd sent to other courts once I found them? The people she'd loved. Lew. Thierry. Who else was suffering this very moment, wondering where the fuck I was? Why their queen had abandoned them to endless torment?

"Maybe you should ask her," Rik suggested, his voice a low, gentle rumble. "Make her tell you where the rest are. At least then we can go get them."

My throat felt like Lew's talons were shredding me from the inside out. "It's not that easy. I can't talk to her whenever I want."

"Why not? You're Shara fucking Isador. We're in the house Esetta Isador built. Where she planned every step of your birth in the shadow of the former Skye Tower."

I was born in this house. If there was any place in the world where I could talk to my mother, it'd be here.

Pulling on a robe, I nodded and turned toward the door. "You're right."

I didn't have to tell him to stay. Even—especially—my alpha who was always at my back.

$\sim$

SHARA

Pausing to gather myself, I traced my fingers over the carvings on the door. A large tyet, the Knot of Isis, framed by two hooded cobras with more snakes winding over the dark wood.

Irrationally, it made me even more angry.

Even before I was born, she'd known I'd carry the cobra queen inside me. Had she seen me kill Rik and Okeanos, the same way she'd killed Guillaume?

Holding my breath, I lay my fingers on the doorknob, not sure it would open. Magnum had used an old-fashioned iron key to open it the first time I stepped inside this house. I hadn't asked her to lock the room again, so the doorknob turned, the door cracking open easily. Letting out a sigh, I entered the small room and shut the door behind me.

Nothing happened in this house until its queen commanded.

Automatic lights flickered on overhead, softly illuminating

the beautiful panels of murals on the walls and ceilings. Esetta hand painted papyrus herself in painstaking detail and then wallpapered the entire room. It must have taken her years.

Years she'd spent planning every moment of my life. Bringing me into this world. Sending her Blood to wait for me. Tortured. Trapped. Wondering where the hell their queen was. If I'd ever come to end their misery.

I could have died a thousand different ways. I could have been stillborn. I could have been killed by thralls dozens of times before I ever fled Kansas City. Looking back over the past few months, I couldn't even list all the ways I might have died. All the tiny, seemingly insignificant decisions I'd made where things could have gone wrong so easily. Over and over and over.

If I'd cleaned that honeymoon whirlpool tub in Eureka Springs a little quicker, I might have ended up killing myself to avoid being eaten alive by the thralls—before Rik and Daire could reach me.

I might have refused Guillaume's bond, too afraid he would kill my alpha.

Ra's priests almost pulled me through the portal in my bedroom, which would have allowed the Soldiers of Light to slaughter my Blood while they lay spelled in the very bed where we'd just made love.

I'd almost lost Xin because he wasn't sure I'd be willing to use him like the blade he is.

I'd hesitated before taking the twins after Mayte had kept the geas on her nest hidden. What if I'd been too intimidated by court life to even attempt to arrange a sibling arrangement with her? I'd never have found Keisha's geas in the first place.

If I hadn't found a way out of the blood petition she'd put before the Triune. If I'd failed to reach Rik in that demon circle. If Rik died…

I didn't want to be here any longer.

If at the last moment, I'd been unable to let Huitzilopochtli drain me to the point of death. Or if I'd deployed the red serpent too early. Forced to endure whatever horrors Ra had subjected Karmen to for centuries.

If I'd twitched one single finger toward my power while the queen of Rome blasted me...

"There were never any guarantees," Esetta whispered behind me.

Whirling around, I gazed into my mother's eyes, so like my own but closer to brilliant indigo than midnight blue. She stood in front of the "Blood of Isis" painting, a crescent moon hanging low over the tip of a golden pyramid. *Upon this house, She builds Her future.*

Even though I'd never seen her outside of dreams or Lew's recordings, her beloved face was familiar, perfected and polished through centuries of power. High, proud cheekbones, an elegant nose a bit sharper than my own. Creamy mocha skin, flawless like a da Vinci painting without a single wrinkle or blemish. Glowing as if lit from within by the full moon—and our goddess' magic.

Her expression revealed nothing. Keeping her secrets. Even from me.

Her thick, black hair fell about her shoulders and down to the floor, streams and rivers of black silk dotted with jewels, crystals, pearls, and golden wire. Coiled tendrils flared out wide around her head and shoulders like the cobra's hood. Floating gently on the invisible breath of our goddess.

She wore a simple white sheath gown. Chunky gold around her waist and neck like armor. Thick segmented golden snakes twined up her forearms. No crown, but Esetta didn't need to proclaim her royalty in such a way. Especially for her daughter. The heir she'd died to produce.

So beautiful, even dead. It hurt me to look at her.

I would never feel her arms around me. My head on her breast, her heart beating against my ear. I would never smell the scent of her skin or feel her hair against my cheek. Now that I knew what we were, I felt the loss of her blood keenly. G's sharpest sword, slicing and dicing my heart to ribbons. She'd never whisper her secrets to me. Teach me about our magic and all the things she could have prepared me for in this brutal game of queens.

Which ones I should take as siblings. How to manage my Blood without any hurt feelings. When I should risk a goddess' wrath by killing one of Her daughters.

How I could possibly survive the kind of loss she'd endured.

The fucking pain she'd caused. Or at least allowed to happen.

"How could you?" My voice rang in the small room, bouncing off the black marble and painted papyrus.

She didn't wince or flinch away from my rage. "I didn't know."

"Bullshit," I retorted. "You knew everything. You planned everything. Don't stand here and lie to me. Did you see them put Lew's eyes out before you sent him to House Skye?"

An explosion of stars flared in her eyes, but her face remained smooth and unchanged. "Yes."

"And you fucking sent him anyway." My voice cracked with strain.

So he would be there when I needed him.

"He could keep you alive longer," she replied in a gentle, sing-song voice meant to soothe the tumult tearing me apart.

But I didn't want to be soothed. I wanted to rage and scream and destroy. It'd be so easy. Throw my head back and bellow boiling flames to darken the sky. A hurricane laced with teeth and claws to tear New York City apart. Skyscrapers turned to rubble like the ancient cities of Egypt. My wrath a blazing, blistering sun to rival the worst of Ra. Punishing the very earth with my fury, only to water it with the blood of anyone in my path.

Which told me more than anything how close I was to losing everything I cared about in this world. No one should have this much power. One slip. One moment where I lost control of my emotions and tore open the earth...

Too many innocents would die.

Vibrating with the strain of holding myself in check, I snapped, "And Thierry?"

She closed her eyes for a moment. "I couldn't see his fate. Only that he's necessary. When you need a miracle, he can buy you a few extra seconds."

"Exactly. You, the grand strategist, who made plans to free Guillaume de Payne a hundred years before I needed him, couldn't see what would happen to one of your own Blood. You didn't stop and think, 'Wow, if even I can't see something, it has to be terrible?'"

I lowered my voice to rumble with the rock troll's weight. "Maybe the Triune queen who's hidden herself for hundreds of years might be involved? You didn't see he'd be turned into a zombie, worse than a thrall. Rotting and falling apart for years. Decades. Stumbling, crawling hundreds of miles to find me, and for what?"

My voice, my heart, cracked like a crystal chalice. I sucked in a rasping breath and forced myself to say the words. "Even if you had seen his fate, you still would have sent him to New Orleans."

It wasn't a question, but she answered anyway.

"Yes."

And he would have fucking gone. Even if he'd known what he must endure.

I turned away. I didn't want her to see me crying. She didn't deserve the right. She died. She left us all to suffer without her. *She's dead and gone forever.*

The black-marbled pool in the center of the room mocked me. She'd suffered in that bloody pool of water. Straining to push me out of her failing, weak body. Her power gone. Her lover, my father, the god of monsters, gone. Her Blood sent away months before. Alone, except for her sister. Knowing exactly what happened next.

Knowing she would hold me for a few minutes. An hour or two. Then she would put me into her sister's arms and send me away. Never to see me again. Never to hold me when I wailed with loss, without even knowing why I cried.

She, more than anyone, deserved to see her daughter's tears. I only still lived because of her. Even though it hurt. So much. I couldn't breathe.

She didn't make excuses. She didn't plead for forgiveness. She didn't beg me to understand her choices. I knew the answer, but I still couldn't stop myself from choking out, "Why?"

"A queen must make terrible choices to continue her lineage and protect her house. To keep her goddess' sacred blood alive in this filthy, sacrilegious, undeserving world. But a queen mother…" She let out a ragged, unpleasant laugh that had me turning back to see her face.

She smiled, a fierce, sharp baring of glistening cobra fangs. "I'm the kind of mother who'll destroy the entire fucking world to make sure you stay alive another day. My death. My Bloods'. Your Bloods'. Whatever it takes. If it's within my power, you will stay alive until a time of your own choosing. If you choose now, this very moment, to end your life, it was always worth it. Every. Fucking. Move."

Her shoulders fell, the regal visage of her face softening. Crumpling. Just for a moment. Allowing me to see her pain. Her own rage at all she'd lost.

"I did my best for you, whether you believe me or not. I'm

not perfect. I made mistakes. I doubted myself. I even doubted Her. I see infinite possibilities in my dreams, but I'm not All Seeing like your general. My greatest strength turned against me in the end. My dreams began to torment me, twisted and warped by my own fears. Holding you for the first and last time…"

Closing her eyes, she shuddered, and something pinged onto the marble floor. Rubies and diamonds, falling from her eyes.

"I almost threw it all away just to keep you in my arms, Shara. We would have been happy for a time. You would have had Lew and Thierry whole and safe in our house, though they would be mine, not yours, at least until my death. By then, it would be too late. I could see Alrik, Daire, and Ezra with you for a time, but not Sir Guillaume. Without him, you wouldn't have called the other killers, either. They were too dangerous, too strong without him carrying the load like a cornerstone, supporting your power. Without him, nothing could have kept you out of House Skye, and once Keisha had you…"

Her mouth firmed into a harsh slant. "You would have lost your alpha. I couldn't see a single way for you to keep him if you ended up her sibling."

Stricken, I could only stare at her. My heart stuttered in my chest. Keisha's sibling… Giving her my alpha. Knowing the fate that awaited Rik in Tanza's circle. "No. I would rather have never Called him at all than allow her to have him. But…"

She nodded as the realization hit me.

Then he would have always been at the mercy of House Skye. Nothing would have kept Keisha from torturing him. He was only still alive because I Called him to my side.

A vicious circle of what ifs and possibilities tangled in my mind. How she'd ever kept so many threads straight in her strategic planning, I had no idea.

"I dreamed every single possibility, following the path of your life forward as far as I could see. Infinite possibilities narrowed to what *could* be. What might be. If I was willing to pay the cost. Some paths were hidden, cloaked in shadows and streaked with pain and misery that could only be the Dauphine. Some were happy for the most part, but you wouldn't have the loves you have now. Certainly General Sekh would not have answered your Call, and even if he did, you wouldn't have been able to hold him. You never would have found the king kraken because your other king would have happily devoured you if you went to free him with only Alrik and Daire to sustain you.

"Over and over. Death, misery, pain, death, agony, loss, death, death, defeat, death. That's all I could see. Unless..."

Her chin tipped up imperceptibly, her eyes flashing with spinning galaxies. Every inch the queen of queens, daughter of the Great One, She Who Is and Was and Always Will Be.

"Everything pinned from Sir Guillaume de Payne. He was the first and most important play to establish your path to staying alive long enough to reach the Triune. He was the first domino, with the rest of your pieces carefully lined up and positioned behind him. Maximize your power base. Bring the strongest killers to your Call. One by one by one. Trapped kings, assassin and monster Blood, even ones belonging to other queens, the General of She Who Dances In Blood. Call them, and they will answer. You need them all to stay alive as long as possible."

Two perfect tear-drop rubies gleamed on her cheek, slowly slipping down to the side of her throat beneath her jaw. Glinting like two pin pricks of blood just above the golden collar around her neck.

"Every single move was always your choice, Shara. It still is. I executed the queen's sacrifice to put the Templar knight on your board, available for the taking. I didn't know you would take him, only if you did, you might one day ride him on the greatest crusade this world has ever known. Take more Blood, or take none. Love them as you choose. When you're ready to leave this world, you'll find me standing on the other side of the Veil with arms open wide to enfold you in the Great One's embrace forever and ever."

Sobs ripped my throat. "But I want to be in your arms now."

Crying too, she opened her arms, and I ran into my mother's embrace.

30

SHARA

Her arms closed around me. Real and physical, strong and fierce with the depth of her love. I clung to her, not sure how it was possible but determined to hold her as long as I could while I breathed in her scent. Sultry, smoky incense of blue lotus and pure magic. The sweet oil in her hair, falling like silken velvet around me. Shelter from the coldest, stormiest night.

Her steady, fearless heart drummed against my ear. "Is it really you?"

"My baby." She squeezed me harder, her voice trembling with emotion. "So precious to hold you again."

Laughing. Crying. As my mother's spirit flowed into me, smoothing all the sharp, cracked edges. Melting the shattered chalice of my heart back to pure, strong crystal without a single inclusion.

She cupped my cheeks and tipped my face up to hers. "I have much to tell you and very little time."

"How is this possible?"

"All things are possible for daughters of She Who Was and Is and Always Will Be." She leaned closer, eye to eye, her whispered words a breath blending with mine, swallowed so they were a part of me forever. "This house mirrors Her pyramid in many ways. This room, where you were born, exists in both places. You were born in Her sacred space, not just my daughter, but Hers. Discover Her secrets hidden in this house, daughter of Isis."

Her lips curved, a secret, knowing smile of pride. "Plus you screamed my name with all the power of the universe and proclaimed yourself not just my daughter but Hers. The more who hear, remember, and the more they remember..."

I couldn't help but laugh. "There's always a way around a blood oath."

"With enough time—or enough blood—yes." Her smile faded, her eyes darkening as if a dark blanket covered the sky, hiding the stars. "As long as you're willing to endure the pain and loss until paid in full."

Like not holding her baby girl for twenty-two years.

"Five former Isador Blood are now sibs in House Ceresa, and the other two went to House Valois, hoping they might find a clue through Rosalind to the Dauphine's location. I wanted to give you plenty of options of Isador Blood to pick from in the queen of Rome's house in case something went wrong with the king kraken. They'll be quite willing to pass information to you if an opportunity arises. Marne, of course, will be more than pleased to give them back to you, but know they carry her blood into your nest. I saw no great danger for them and to my knowledge, they're happy and in no need of rescue."

"Did you see me kill the Dauphine?"

"It's risky but possible." Holding my gaze, her eyes narrowed with intent. "Bring justice to that fucking bitch, daughter of mine. Make her suffer as much as she hurt my Thierry and beloved sister. Make her soul rot in the rankest filth for all time."

Startled, I laughed again, relieved but also a little shaken. My mother wasn't someone you wanted to fuck with.

And neither am I.

"What will it cost me?"

Her breath sighed out against my cheek. "One of your greatest gifts will be stripped from you."

"But not one of my Blood or my human family?"

She kissed my forehead. "Few goddesses will be willing to dare lay claim to one of your loves when you've already sworn to keep them for all time. Due to the bargain you made with the Mother of the Gods, to take one of your loves is to take all, especially you, and our goddess would not be well pleased at such a loss. Though of course there are many others who'd leap at the chance to destroy the Great One's royal line in one fell swoop. You will find, as I did, that sometimes you won't have any other choice to reach the outcome of your desire than to eliminate another queen. There's always a way to work within and around the constraints They may put upon you, given enough time and blood."

Keeping her head tipped close, she released me but only to slide the golden snakes off her arms, slipping them on mine. "Plus, take note from Desideria, with moderation, of course. The more queens you kill, the more powers you gain through their legacies. So when a goddess demands payment, it's of no consequence to give up something from your arsenal, and honestly, some goddesses will be jubilant to have their gifts transferred to you as you change the face of the world."

"I don't need more jewelry," I protested. "I hardly ever wear what's in the legacy anyway."

Hurriedly, she reached around her throat and removed the heavy golden necklace. "You will want these. I kept them safe for a reason."

Safer than the locked Isis chest Gina kept in the Talbott safe?

Fashioned of long golden rectangles carved with symbols I

didn't immediately recognize, the necklace was heavy and cold around my throat. The belt was made from serpentine-looking scales that overlapped like chainmail.

"They're a part of you now. No need to remember putting them on."

"But—"

"You'll know when it's time," she cut me off. "You must find the Dauphine before she fully cloaks again, or all will be lost. Sands slip through the hourglass, even with Thierry as your ace in the hole. Now let me give you the pièce de résistance before you wake."

"But I'm not asleep," I started to say, but my words were slurred. The room had darkened, though I could still see her. Feel her. The walls were tighter, making the space close and dark. Almost like a coffin. Though if my mother was here with me, I would stay beside her, even buried alive, as long as she could hug me again.

Lifting her hands to the top of my head, she smoothed my hair in long, heavy strokes. Almost like she was brushing my hair, only with her hands. Mom had brushed my hair for me when I was a child, sitting on the bed upstairs in my attic. My eyes fluttered, sinking into the sensation. The simple joy.

As Esetta brushed undying love into every single stroke.

Her mouth pressed to my ear, her hair falling over my face like a thick velvety curtain. "I've always been with you, but here, in this room, this house, you can always find me waiting to answer your questions. There's no need to worry about dropping a blood circle around the house. If someone were to stumble into one of Her inner sanctums hidden within, they'd only find their worst nightmares and will never walk out again.

"I cut my hair off in this house for a reason, daughter of mine. A symbolic act, of course, as I surrendered my power and Blood, but also to keep it safe for the day I could give it to you. My power is an insignificant drop in the ocean compared to yours, but you'll find all my secrets woven into these strands. All my magic. Small yet precious treasures hidden within just for you."

In the darkness, the two ruby tears glowed in her throat, and I could suddenly smell her blood. Flowing over me, filling my mouth. Liquid moonlight. Pure, clear water glistening like crystal ice. Warming to thick honey, sprinkled with velvety petals of blue lotus.

"Carry my hair, my power, and know my blood already flows in your veins. You've tasted me because you've tasted Her. We're in every drop of your sweet blood. Generations of Isador queens, living on in you."

Her voice softened though her hands still stroked my hair. Her cheek pressed to mine. "Most of all, I am so proud of you, Shara Isador, only beloved daughter of Esetta, daughter of the Great One but not the last. Nothing you could ever do will disappoint Her—or me. I knew exactly what kind of queen you would be, and She is well pleased in our daughter."

RIK

MY QUEEN DIDN'T REACH FOR ME IN THE BOND, BUT I FELT AN urge deep in my bones to go to her. Her bond dipped into the quiet stillness of heavy sleep, and my queen always slept better wrapped in Blood.

I found her curled on her side in the sunken pool beneath a heavy black blanket that cascaded across the marble floor. Only when I touched her, I realized the blanket was her hair. Thick and heavy, several feet longer than when she'd left the bedroom. Like Esetta's hair in Lew's memory.

Reverently, I lifted her from the tub, trying not to disturb her. Her hair dragged the floor, but I was afraid I would tangle it if I tried to gather it up. Or worse, wake her, after she'd struggled to find any peace after Thierry's ordeal. Nevarre generally claimed hair duty for our queen, but I had a feeling he'd be challenged by everyone wanting to get their hands in our queen's new display of power.

:Dibs,: Vivian said in the bond, at the same time that Daire said, :Bet.:

Nevarre only laughed softly. :Anyone who wishes to assist with our queen's hair can challenge me for the opportunity on the green.:

:No fair,: Daire retorted. He'd already faced—and lost—Nevarre's caber toss. :You can't dress her and claim her hair too.:

Before the discussion escalated from Blood teasing Blood to a full-blown argument, I sent a firm alpha push through everyone's bond to quiet them. :As always, she'll decide who goes where when she's awake. Until then, Lew, keep Thierry under your watchful eyes at all times. Daire, Guillaume, with me. Sekh, take charge of the shift changes.:

Her first three Blood. Her closest in many ways—though Daire would object right now. With the addition of Sekh, Daire was feeling a little lost and overlooked. He didn't have the military and warfare background of Guillaume and Sekh. He wasn't an assassin like Xin. He wasn't a king or a renowned warrior. After seeing me killed by her venom, he couldn't deal with her cobra queen.

He was the brattiest brat there ever was, always good for a laugh and a cuddle. Not that she'd had time lately for much relaxing in bed while he purred for her. Now, he feared losing even that, since Sekh was also feline. Though I had no idea if the sphinx could purr.

:Can a sphinx stand in a blasting sandstorm beneath the blistering sun while raging floodwaters close over his head and still guard for all time?: Sekh made a low grunt of disgust in his bond. :Of fucking *course I can fucking purr the stripes right off the warcat. Let the little fucker purr, alpha, and I'll hold my peace. As long as he doesn't fuck up again.:*

:*He's young,:* I replied, feeling the need to defend him.

I am too. Too young compared to these ancient, powerful, legendary Blood she'd called to her side. I hadn't even hit one-hundred years on this earth, yet I was supposed to command a five-thousand-year-old sphinx and the last Templar knight while wrestling Leviathan, the king of the depths, into submission. Praying I didn't fuck up myself as my queen rose in stature on the Triune.

Daire hopped onto the bed with the lithe ability of his cat to land on any surface without jostling her sleep. Already purring, he made a nest for himself in the silken tumble of her hair, draped across her legs. Leaving room for Guillaume on her other side opposite me.

Sekh didn't challenge me. In fact, he seemed perfectly willing to do whatever I said, even after I'd tried to pound him into the ground. *Tried.* Because if he'd wanted to pull on his sphinx, he'd have ripped us all apart while she was unaware and drunk on his blood, and he wouldn't have needed the legion to help. My rock troll's formidable strength had barely put a dent in him.

:*So are you, alpha. Yet you never once thought to cause a single moment of harm to our queen to protect yourself. My sphinx will crumble to dust and blow away on the winds of time before I'll ever cause her a moment's sadness by harming someone she loves. Unless they fail in their sacred duty to protect her.:*

In the bond, Sekh yawned, head back, lion teeth glistening. :*Even the motherfucking dragon.:*

31

GUILLAUME

I didn't sleep so much as drift, soaking in Shara's presence. Wallowing in her scent of smoldering magic. Power rolled from her, even while she slept so heavily I couldn't feel her mind wandering the bond at all.

A luxury I'd never been allowed in all my years of service to my former queen. *May she suffer for all time in the worst hell imaginable.*

My queen's lips touched my throat, directly over my pulse, and my body zinged to full awareness.

Though she'd only been asleep a few hours, she felt alert and well, especially in her spirit. A feat indeed after the long healing session she'd endured to bring her mother's Blood back from a rotten shell of a thrall.

"We didn't die today," she whispered.

"The day isn't over yet," I replied lightly. It was, if we counted the sun rising since we'd left the nest, but she knew what I meant.

Until the Dauphine was eliminated...

Our days were numbered.

Her fingers curled in the short hairs at my nape, urging me

closer. Tipping her head back, baring her naked throat for me in silent invitation to feed deep and well and long. Before the battle came for us all.

I bared my fangs and started to sink them into her throat.

Gold flashed up out of her flesh, a protective, impregnable shield. One I recognized all too well.

I flung myself backward, sliding out of the bed. Chest heaving, knives in both hands before I even realized I was on my feet.

Startled, she sat up, or tried to. Her hair was tangled beneath Daire's weight, and the warcat didn't budge, even though I panted like a freight train. Wary, Rik narrowed a hard look on me, ready to pull her to safety.

Away from me.

The door opened behind me, Itztli with his obsidian blade glittering in his hand. Vivian, her short swords burning with sunfire flames. The general charged for the stairs. Not that any of them had a hope of stopping me if harming our queen was ever my goal.

"G? What's wrong? Guillaume. Answer me."

Her bond hummed with intensity, compelling the words out of me. "That fucking choker. Where did you get it?"

"What choker?" Rik asked.

He couldn't see it. I couldn't see it now that I wasn't trying to sink fangs into her.

Her fingers reached up to her throat, and as soon as she touched the choker, it gleamed against her skin. A high, tall collar as wide as my palm, golden armor around her throat. "My mother gave it to me."

Esetta. Of fucking course. "The rest, too?"

"Some bracelets and a belt. Why?"

Cold sweat dripped down my back. "Allow me to demonstrate."

I raised my right hand, saluting with the knife, and the

Bloods' attention sharpened to full alert. Rik surged up over her like a mountain. Itztli and Vivian both leaped at my back, blades flashing. I didn't have to turn around to feel the glide of red-hot steel as I stepped aside, twisted, catching Vivian's sword with the shorter blade in my left hand and shoving her aside. Ducked beneath the slashing obsidian meant to flay me open like a fish. My knife easily slipped beneath the rock troll's granite even as his fist wrapped around my throat.

A ringing tap echoed in the room. The tip of my blade against the golden belt wrapped around Shara's waist.

Midnight eyes spiraled with galaxies inches away. Her hand buried in my chest, her nails in my heart.

"As you can see." I coughed around the pressure of the alpha's grip. Blood dripped from my mouth. "Our queen is well protected. Even from me."

"G," she breathed out shakily.

Though she didn't pull her nails out now that she had a taste of me.

"Next time, may I recommend you yank the heart out completely, my queen. Though that wouldn't stop me, either."

The general bounded into the room with a roar that rattled the windows. "What the actual fuck?"

Rik eased his grip on my throat but didn't fully release me. "Someone check on Daire." At Sekh's low hiss, Rik added, "Not you."

Scowling fiercely at me, Vivian stepped closer to the bed by a Daire-sized lump. She reached under a pile of Shara's hair and gave him a shake. "He's breathing. I think he's asleep, but he's not waking up."

:He's spelled by your hair,: Lew said in our bonds. :The magic wraps around us like a heavy, silent blanket that cuts us off from everything except you. It's how your mother gave each of us secret instructions without any other Blood hearing or knowing the details.

Reach for his bond and pull him up out of the spell, or he'll dream as long as your hair is touching him.:

"My hair?" Shara asked. Then realized how long it'd grown seemingly overnight. "Holy fuck. She really did save it for me."

Easing her fingers out of my flesh, though she kept her nails deep enough to feed, she closed her eyes. The long tendrils of hair parted like the Red Sea, sweeping away from the warcat curled on her legs.

Rumbling loudly, Daire lifted his head with a sleepy stretch. Startled to see us all staring at him. Then he clamped the purr down to silence as soon as he saw Sekh. "What'd I miss?"

"Oh nothing," Vivian drawled. "Just Guillaume freaking out, falling out of bed, and then attacking our queen with a blade."

"Did the bed try to eat you or what?"

"I did not fall out of bed," I grumbled. "And no bed would dare try to eat me. I'm far too pointy and sharp. I'd lodge in any throat, even Leviathan's, assuming he ever managed to swallow me."

Rik finally released me. "You could have simply told us the belt would shield her rather than touch her with a blade."

"I didn't touch her, though," I said softly, sheathing both blades. "No steel, fang, or claw can penetrate her core now. Her wrists are secure up to her elbows. And goddess help the Blood who prefers to feed only from her throat, because she's protected from her collarbone to just beneath her jaws."

"I can take it off though."

When I didn't immediately agree, she pulled her hand out of my flesh and reached up to the necklace, gliding her fingers around front to back, looking for a clasp. "She took them off easily. Why won't they come off for me now?"

Her hands trembled, her breathing coming more rapidly. Panic flared in her bond. The same as mine when I realized what she wore.

She clawed at the gold. "Get it the fuck off me!"

Rik tried to slide one of his thick fingers beneath the edge, but it only tightened on her, increasing her panic. No blade would ever slip beneath the edge either.

Kneeling by the bed, I reached out and closed my hands around hers, pulling her hands gently down to her lap. "Desideria was extremely paranoid. I doubt they'll come off easily."

Panting, Shara swallowed hard, her heart thundering in our bond. "They were hers?"

"She never worried about fangs in her throat or steel in her vital organs because she wore golden armor that kept anything from touching her, though without my oath, I still would have found a way to kill her. Her triple goddesses blessed her well. Esetta must have inherited them as part of Modron's legacy, though she couldn't have claimed them formally before the Triune without revealing her secrets."

"She said she kept them safe for me." Shara closed her eyes, shivering. "I know I should probably be grateful, but it makes my skin crawl knowing *she* used to wear these. Especially after the look on your face."

"Such armor will definitely benefit you against the Dauphine," Sekh said.

I lifted her hands to my mouth and kissed her knuckles on each hand. "My deepest apologies, my queen. They're truly not a problem for me now I'm aware of them, and General Sekh is one-hundred percent correct. These pieces may even protect you from another queen's magic, say if Thierry touched your wrist. If they save your life and buy you time for one of us to finally kill that bitch, then they're worth it."

Daire peeked up at her, giving her the kitty-cat eyes she usually couldn't resist. "It's no hardship for us to feed elsewhere."

"It's a hardship for me. I don't want anything to keep you from feeding anywhere, at any time. I like having your teeth in my throat. I like being able to pierce my wrist with my nails without having to lift my hands up to my mouth."

Lightly, I squeezed her hands. "Then let's get them off of you, though I would ask you to consider wearing them when you know we're heading into battle."

She nodded, tightening her grip on mine. "Now that I'm not so freaked out, I'll try again."

"I never saw Desideria try to remove them, but I assume your blood would unlock just about anything."

Taking a deep, centering breath, she released my hands and pressed the pad of her index finger against one of her brutal nails. A single drop of her blood welled up on her finger.

And five Blood went rock hard, staring intently at our queen's power.

She drew her bleeding finger along her opposite wrist, and the serpentine bracelet fell off onto the bed. Her shoulders relaxed, and she quickly removed the other pieces the same way. Now that they were off her body, they looked like regular— though tacky, in my opinion—gold jewelry.

"Daire, can you put these in a closet or drawer for safekeeping? I'd ask you to give them to Gina to put in the safe, but..." She heaved out a sigh. "I don't think we'll be here that long. Esetta warned me to hurry and find the Dauphine before she manages to slip away again. Hopefully Xin will find something useful in Louisiana."

Daire immediately slid off the bed, scooped up the jewelry, and headed for the door, giving Sekh a wide berth.

"You dance the blades well, knight," Itztli said grudgingly.

"I should." Shrugging, I kept my voice light and easy. "I trained with and fought the best swordsmen for centuries before serving as the Triune Executioner, where I exterminated entire nests of skilled and powerful Blood."

"When I was in Heliopolis, one of the Soldiers of Light

sparred with me a time or two," Vivian said. "Have you heard of the Voivode of Wallachia?"

"Indeed." I huffed out a laugh. "The Impaler loved to watch people twitch on his spear. He was skilled in all weapons, but had a perverse, twisted sense of honor. Tens of thousands of men, women, and children were impaled under his command. Figures he'd end up getting resurrected by Ra to kill forever, until our queen put an end to that."

"He used to joke that he loved to gut a man just to see how quickly he'd get tangled up in his own intestines. He's still alive. I don't think it's a betrayal of trust to admit he's one of Karmen's Blood."

That I did not know, and didn't like much at all. The only time I'd come close to failing in our queen's defense was when the Soldiers of Light had attacked her in Kansas City. In close quarters with only two furry shifters and the rock troll for backup, they'd kept me busy with six skilled fighters while the rest tried to drag her through the portal.

The Impaler alone wouldn't be a problem for me to dispatch. But a dozen or more infamous warriors armed with sharp steel and centuries of warfare could do some serious damage.

:My jaws shatter steel still wet with the blood of my kill,: Sekh said. *:While the legion scatters their bones in the deepest ocean.:*

:If they have flesh, I'll fucking roast them alive,: Mehen retorted. *:If they don't, I'll toast their fucking skeletons until they explode like fucking popcorn. No motherfucking sword is getting through my scales.:*

"No one else would teach me." Letting out a harsh laugh, Vivian shook her head, tossing her red braids back over her shoulder. "So I fucking taught myself."

Her bond told another story, roiling with frustration, helplessness, and a choking sense of shame of what she'd endured in Heliopolis. I could only fucking imagine what a child raised to adulthood in the punishing wrath of the god of light might have seen. "Then perhaps we'd better start regular drills so we can give the still-living Soldiers of Light some entertainment."

Flames flickered around her. "Really? Yeah, that'd be fucking phenomenal."

I looked over at Rik. "Alpha?"

He nodded. "We shouldn't depend on only our beasts if we have to fight our way out. Remember Rome."

"What the fuck happened in Rome?" Sekh asked with a scowl.

:*I thought you were the mighty All Seeing,*: Mehen sneered.

:*Even I can't see through the queen of Rome's power, let alone the Dauphine's. If I could, do you think we'd be sitting around here with nothing better to do then pretend to hunt human pedestrians on the street, jerk off?*:

"Do I get to watch?" Shara asked.

"You shouldn't miss it for the world, my queen." Chuckling, I climbed to my feet and bowed low. "This is going to be amusing as hell."

32

SHARA

Discover Her secrets hidden in this house, daughter of Isis.
Looking around at the third floor, I realized I'd seen very little of this house. I'd only stayed in New York City briefly, much preferring my own nest in Eureka Springs. But in many ways, my mother had made the perfect home away from home.

This entire floor was open and airy with soaring twenty-foot ceilings. No walls to impede even my largest Blood, and only a few support pillars gave even Leviathan plenty of room to maneuver despite his massive wingspan. A giant retractable skylight provided quick and easy access to the roof for all the winged Blood.

Concrete floor, presumably to make the blood splatter easier to clean, though that didn't matter to a vampire queen. Well, it did matter to me. A great deal. I wanted to see their blood. Smell it. Wallow in it.

Blood didn't fuck around with dull swords even when they were only practicing.

Even Guillaume was pleased because the back wall provided ample storage for racks and shelves of weapons, ranging from swords and throwing stars to modern assault rifles and flamethrowers. Magnum had brought in some deep, comfortable chairs, plenty big enough for Rik to hold me while I watched my Blood. She even had staff bring up several trays of food for the Blood to wolf down in between sparring rounds.

Though of course once the humans left, I'd be more than happy to let my Blood wolf on me.

:No fair.: Xin's wolf touched his nose to my forehead in the bond. *:No one gets to wolf on you if I'm not there.:*

Touching his bond only made my heart pang with loss. *:You're so far away.:*

Hundreds of miles away, he ran a seemingly random back and forth swerving path along the edge of a river, nose tipped into the breeze. *:I should pick up his scent soon if he came anywhere out of Louisiana. If not, I'll cut back toward Florida.:*

:Touch my bond as soon as you have his trail.:

His wolf yipped agreement.

Guillaume squared off with Vivian after selecting two short blades similar to hers off the wall. I didn't know anything about swordsmanship, though it was impossible to not recognize greatness in every move my knight made. Even standing still, his body loose and relaxed, the swords lowered at his sides, he radiated the extreme confidence of someone who knew he'd win any battle.

At first, he allowed Vivian to attack and strike as long and hard as she wanted. Then he began to test her. Pushing her to respond. Testing her reflexes and speed. Driving her backward with seemingly careless flicks of his wrist. He didn't even need both swords to keep her from getting a single touch on him.

Breathing hard, she dropped to the floor and jabbed up at his groin with the pommel. Leaping backward as gracefully as a dancer, G avoided the blow meant to double him over in pain and left a bleeding cut on her shoulder.

"That's a good move," he said in the same easy, casual voice.

"Though you lost time and momentum by rotating your wrist, while also telegraphing your intent well ahead of the strike."

"I thought," she panted, bent over. "Our queen might object. If I gelded. You."

Lowering his blades, he laughed as if she'd told him the joke of the century. "You're wicked fast and the blades suit you. Though you should focus more on street fighting rather than trying for anything more formal. Be brutal and unexpected. Fight dirty. Make every blow count."

Straightening, she nodded. "That's what the Impaler recommended too. That move is one he taught me, and he promised to show me more. But when I had the opportunity to leave Heliopolis, I got the fuck out and didn't look back."

"As well you should. Take a breather. Who's next?"

The door opened, pulling my attention away from Itztli as he stepped out to meet my knight. Lew walked in with a Blood beside him.

Thierry. Though I wouldn't have recognized him if I hadn't known it had to be him. Lew had worked a miracle in cleaning him up, even trimming his shaggy hair and shaving off the raggedy beard. Thierry's natural hair color was sandy blond, set off by his startling blue eyes. Dressed in a long-sleeved shirt and jeans with a clean shave, he looked almost normal.

As long as I didn't linger on the darker patches on his throat. The purplish splotches on the backs of his hands. Or breathe too deeply and notice the ever-present reek of decay.

How long did he have before his insides started to rot again? Would he still turn into liquid mush if I'd gotten rid of all the leeches? If it took my wolf another few days to find the Dauphine, would I have to drain him again and bring him back with my blood? I'd do it. Though that was a fucking lot of blood.

:He has right now,: Lew whispered gently in our bond. :Which is all any of us has anyway.:

Thierry jerked to a halt and bent low, his voice still raspy like crumpling paper. "Your Majesty."

Lew patted him on the back. "I know."

I wasn't sure what was going on just from their words. Muscles flexed across Lew's jaws, his lips a grim slash.

"Hair." Thierry straightened and smiled, though black fluid leaked from his eyes. "Beautiful."

Oh. Of course. Lew had shown us the memory of all of them stroking and brushing Esetta's hair. Gathered around her. One last time.

Sitting here supported completely by Rik, my head against his chest, I'd forgotten the immense weight of all my mother's hair. The way it dragged and caught on everything, tangling beneath me and the Blood anytime they were close. It'd taken Nevarre, Vivian, and Daire to wrestle all this hair into submission enough for me get up and walk. Even though all I'd done was come upstairs to watch their practice, my neck still ached with strain. I'd only pulled a robe on for clothes, so I didn't have to drag something over it. "I have no idea how she carried all of this hair without needing a neck splint."

Both of my mother's Blood smiled.

"She didn't," Lew admitted. "Not all the time, at least. In formal processions, of course. But when it was just us, she allowed us to take turns gathering up her hair and helping her carry the load. It was always an honor." His face locked down even more, but he didn't say anything else.

He didn't have to. In his bond, I saw Esetta wrapping some of her shorn hair around his throat. Her final gift to him before she sent him to House Skye. One last piece of her.

If Thierry couldn't touch me, the least I could do was give him something to carry—both from me and from her.

"G," I called. "I need a knife."

Immediately, the clashing sounds ended, and my knight jogged to my side. Sweat glistened on his arms, his shirt damp, clinging to his chest. His eyes bright, his smile eager. Smelling of his hell horse, warfare, and a good sweat that I'd love to make him earn in my bed.

My knight was in his perfect element, training and sparring with other warriors. I hadn't realized how much he'd missed being a soldier. Which made me remember our first night together. How he'd laughed at Rik and Daire bickering over who'd have to pay for the pizza.

It's good to be Blood again.

How much more had Thierry missed being a part of Esetta's Blood? Especially knowing his fate?

As if sensing my intent, some of my hair had worked its way out of the thick, heavy mass my Blood had attempted to tame with smaller braids to bind it together. I lifted the tendrils up away from me and Guillaume solemnly sliced it free. The shorter pieces fell back against the rest, already blending in. For all I knew, they were already regenerating. I wasn't sure what magic Esetta had worked into her hair like spelling the Blood. Hopefully it wouldn't spell Thierry too just from touching it. Though maybe drifting forgotten in a dream would be a blessing.

Lew took the long hank and reverently lifted his hands to his face. Breathing deeply, eyes closed, his face relaxing as peace rolled down over his expression. "It still smells like her but better."

"Better how?"

Opening his eyes, he flashed a smile, his eyes flickering with red-gold stars. "It smells like you now too, my queen."

He turned to Thierry but my mother's former Blood recoiled a step, wavering, almost falling. "Taint."

Lew shook his head. "You can't cause any of the taint to spread to her by carrying her hair."

Thierry's jaw tightened, his lips moving, his throat working, as if there was so much he wanted to say but couldn't. He didn't fear giving me the taint. He didn't want to sully my—her—hair with that foulness. Especially since it carried our power and scent.

My throat ached but I blinked away the tears. I wanted this to be a fun, light memory for everyone. Not something sad.

Especially for Thierry.

Lew dropped a hand on his shoulder, squeezing firmly. "You deserve the honor of carrying our queen's hair into battle."

Closing his eyes, Thierry groaned deep in his throat. But he didn't pull away as Lew looped my hair around his throat and tied it into a necklace. Hand trembling, he lightly stroked his fingers over my hair. "Honor. Serve."

It's an honor to serve.

I made my lips curve into a smile even though I wanted to fucking cry. "Thank you, Thierry. You honor House Isador with your service."

My knight started to turn back to the sparring.

"Death." Thierry's tongue stumbling over the word. "Rides."

Pausing, Guillaume slowly turned his head, his eyes narrowed as he searched Thierry's face. "Death rides again."

Thierry nodded.

"You were there," Guillaume whispered. In his bond, a dark shape swayed back and forth and then struck. Swords in his chest.

No. My mother's fangs. The night she'd poisoned him so he could kill Desideria.

"That was you."

"Honor," Thierry said again. "Serve."

Lew nodded. "She was only allowed to take one Blood to Constantinople, and she chose Thierry to accompany her."

"That's why no one saw us in the courtyard. You stopped time for her." Guillaume let out a long, slow breath and stepped closer to my mother's former Blood. Flipping the blade in his hand so he gripped the tip, he offered it hilt first. "It's an honor to serve with you, Thierry Isador."

33

DAIRE

I was as nervous as a long-tailed cat in a room full of rocking chairs. Though the only one I worried about was Sekh.

And I had one long fucking tail.

I didn't give a shit about sparring with the knight, though I'd do it if Rik ordered it. My warcat could usually hold its own, and if that failed, then my charm and smiles smoothed any edges away.

Not with the general.

His sphinx would happily snack on my warcat and still go looking for more. I'd tried to be polite and respectful to the much older Blood, but that didn't smooth things between us either. He flat out didn't like me.

I knew why, and there was nothing I could fucking do about it.

I fucked up. I fucking got it. I hated that my queen had witnessed my failure, as well as Rik, Guillaume, and Xin. I hadn't realized an All Seeing general was also watching and judging my failures, who'd then show up in our queen's nest. Still hating me. Still judging me.

If any other Blood was pissed at me—other than Vivian—I'd

flirt and offer to entertain our queen by letting them fuck me. As hard as they wanted. I'd love every fucking minute.

But one, I didn't think Sekh felt anything like desire when he looked at me, and two, if he did, he'd probably fucking kill me. I liked pain and blood, sure. But I didn't like pain to the point of needing our queen to heal me when he was done.

The Blood were separated primarily into two camps—the ones who wanted Guillaume to make them look foolish, and the observers. Even Mehen lounged on a chaise like a dragon curled up on a ledge, silently betting on which one would die first.

I'd press up around Shara's legs like usual, but her mother's former Blood sat with her. Thierry, the poor bastard, deserved as much time with her as he could get. Not that Rik would even think about letting the thrall zombie get close enough to touch her, but sitting near her. Basking in her presence. Watching her smile. Fuck yeah.

Tlacel, Ezra, and Nevarre sat on her other side. I could go harass Ezra, but he'd pulled his chair up closer to Lew and Thierry, forming an arc around our queen. They were telling old Blood war stories and roaring with laughter.

Then there was me and Sekh. Standing in between the two groups.

Awkward as fuck. If I walked away, I'd look like a chicken shit. If I went closer to try and talk to him… I'd have to slink. I couldn't help it. Fucking embarrassing to be so intimidated by a fellow Blood, and Rik was no fucking help.

:Figure your shit out,: he rumbled in the bond. :She needs you to get along with him.:

:I know,: I sniped back.

I didn't need my alpha to hold my fucking hand. Fuck me, sure, but not protect me from one of our queen's Blood. No matter how fucking intimidating the general was. Though I couldn't make myself take a step closer to him.

I shifted slightly closer to the group, pretending like I

wanted to hear Lew's story. I didn't know the gryphon all that well but sitting with his old friend, telling a story about some Blood escapade, he showed a new side of him. Looser, smiling, and funny as hell.

"Thierry's a Greek siren, so even when he's shifted, he's still part man on the bottom with wings on the top. We were fucking around on the roof—"

"Moon." Thierry let out a gurgling laugh. "Skye."

"Yeah, we were mooning Skye Tower," Lew admitted with a sheepish grin. "Mallac shifted into his cyclops and used his glowing eye to spotlight the roof. Thierry dropped his pants. Then some humans started shrieking on the street."

"Mothman," Thierry said.

"Word spread about the strange bird man with glowing red eyes. People kept coming by the house at all hours of the night, looking for another sign of the infamous Mothman."

Gurgling, Thierry said something. A word. I could almost hear it. Almost understand it. But then it was gone, as if my mind couldn't translate it.

"Yeah," Lew said, his smile slipping and becoming more forced. "Our queen was pissed."

I lost track of the rest of the story because Sekh stepped closer, standing shoulder to shoulder with me, though he faced the sparring group. Not touching me. Not even looking at me. But I could feel the buzz of his energy hammering against me. The heat of his body. The power curled inside him. His lion musk made every hair on my body stand up with sheer terror.

More power than even our alpha. More nastiness than Leviathan. More deadly skill than the last Templar knight. Basically one step removed from a feline god who was disgusted by what he saw in me.

"Rik told me to talk to you." Sekh's dry, bored tone proclaimed his opinion of our alpha's command. "You're young. You made a fucking mistake. Fine. I still don't have to fucking like you. At least acknowledge I have enough honor to respect our queen's bonds and leave you the fuck alone."

My instincts insisted I needed to roll over on my back and show him my belly. Rub my head on his legs. Take on his scent to mask my own. My knees quivered with the need to drop down at his feet and plead for forgiveness.

Sekh snarled beneath his breath. "Don't you fucking dare. Besides, I'm not the one you should beg for forgiveness."

"I did," I replied faintly. "Rik punished me. I apologized. It won't happen again."

"Look, lie to yourself all you want, but don't fucking lie to me. I know you better than you know yourself."

Ouch. "You don't know me. You said yourself you're not All Knowing."

"I See you, warcat. That's all I need to know."

Now I was starting to get pissed. I turned to face him, keeping my shoulders stiff, my head up. "It'll never happen again. I learned my lesson. That's enough for Rik and for her."

"But not for me," Sekh drawled, his eyes burning molten gold. "Do you honestly want me to believe if you're forced to choose between her or Rik, you'll actually choose her? No matter what it is?"

"Yes! How dare you question my loyalty to our queen?"

Sekh nodded, his mouth quirked in a smug little grimace that made my blood boil. "You agree I'm stronger than Rik. I'm older. I'm bigger. I've been the fucking General of the All Seeing, Never Sleeping for thousands of years. Yet I'm expected to take orders from a young Blood not even triple digits old. I'm as hard and unyielding as the sphinx statue when she first Called me. No mercy. No forgiveness. If it was within my power, all her enemies would die before she had to lift her pinkie finger.

"Even better, I can feed her continuously. I carry the blood of three-thousand sphinxes for our queen, and her hunger is fucking immense as you well know.

"So let's say she decides she wants me to sit behind her instead of Rik. She wants to feed on me all fucking day and night, always keeping her power revved up for anything. Her nails planted deep in my thighs. My heart. Like I fed her while she healed Thierry. Do you think Rik's stepping down voluntarily from his position as alpha? Giving up his spot at her back? Or am I going to kill him to accomplish her goal?"

I opened my mouth. Closed it.

Rik would never give up his position at Shara's back. Not voluntarily.

"He's alpha because she wants him to be." Sekh shrugged casually. "Now she's changed her mind. She wants me. What the fuck are you going to do about it, warcat? Are you going to fly at me with your puny little claws and rumbly purr to protect your alpha? Or are you going to shut your fucking mouth while I feast and then take my seat at our queen's back?"

I tried to think of something to say. Something witty. Flippant.

Rik would choke him. He'd stick in his craw. He'd rip his way out of the sphinx's stomach. He'd crush him like a landslide and pound him to smithereens.

Something. Anything. To disguise the sick quake in the pit of my stomach.

Because the truth fucking sucked.

"Like I said, lie to yourself if that's what makes you feel better," Sekh said. "But don't lie to me, and never fucking lie to her."

"I love her," I whispered, my voice quivering.

"Of course you love her. We all do. But you loved *him* first. For some, that's the way it is. They don't have the capacity to love like our queen. I wouldn't fault you for loving him if you'd at least admit the truth to yourself."

A hard hand dropped onto my nape, tightening with a punishing grip. I hadn't even noticed Mehen walking closer. "You thinking about fucking the purr machine, motherfucker?"

Sekh let out a short, harsh laugh. "Be my guest, dragon. I'll fuck anyone our queen wants me to, but if given the choice, I like my partners with a little more fight in them."

"Me too." Mehen smiled but I could feel the snarl building in his chest. "But then again, I fucked you already."

As if this fucking conversation couldn't get any worse, now I was caught in a pissing contest between two dicks who both thought his monster was bigger.

Sekh only smiled. "If that's what you want to call it."

Mehen shoved me reeling to the side, out of the line of fire. "Pretty fucking sure I had my cock drilled in your ass, motherfucker."

"Pretty fucking sure I *let* you, motherfucker." Sekh didn't move or make any threatening sounds but his body loosened, the boneless stance of a feline locked in on his kill. "Pretty sure you fucking paid the price, too."

"Sounds to me like someone wants me to fuck him up again."

Sekh's smile widened, a lazy, slow grin that chilled my blood. "You're welcome to try."

~

MEHEN

I DIDN'T KNOW WHICH PISSED ME OFF MORE.

The fact that he didn't want to fuck Daire—taking away my excuse for wanting to break his fucking jaw.

Or the fact the motherfucker didn't think I'd break his fucking jaw. And that was just the fucking foreplay.

I didn't give a shit who Daire fucked. I just wanted to give the motherfucker as much shit as possible.

Rik's bond thumped inside my skull like when he'd fucking slammed his fists into motherfucker for touching our queen. *:I told you to work it out, not start a fight.:*

Blistering indignation surged through my veins, though he wasn't talking to me.

:I didn't start shit,: motherfucker retorted. *:Tell the dragon to shut the fuck up, or I'll stuff his fucking mouth for him.:*

:You want a piece of me?: I glared at him with murderous rage the way only a dragon can. *:Come at me, motherfucker, and I'll rip your fucking arm off and beat you with your own goddess-damned limb.:*

Rik heaved a sigh like a giant-ass landslide. *:Now you've done it. Our queen has taken notice.:*

Malicious glee and anticipation sweetened the fire burning in my veins. *About fucking time.*

"Is there a problem?" Shara asked.

"No," motherfucker said at the same time I growled, "Fuck yeah."

"Are you fighting over Daire?"

Motherfucker laughed like she'd taken a bite out of his funny bone. "Not at all, Your Majesty. In fact, I think the dragon's more offended about my lack of interest in the warcat than Daire is himself."

"Mehen? What's wrong?"

I didn't want to look away from motherfucker in case he took it as a sign of capitulation, but her bond tugged deep inside of me. Swinging my head toward the chairs where she sat.

Eyes fucking shining like she swallowed the fucking moon. Her color high. Her lips parted, giving me a peek of her tongue. Her fangs. Not all the way distended but very interested in whatever the fuck was going on between us.

Which only stirred my lust to a fevered pitch.

"Do you have a problem with Sekh?"

"I fucking hate him," I retorted with all the dragon fire burning in my gut.

"The feeling is mutual." Though motherfucker sounded fucking bored out of his skull.

Her shoulders fell, and I felt like fucking shit for putting that look of disappointment on her face. Because she thought our mutual hatred meant we wouldn't fuck for her entertainment.

When that was exactly my fucking goal. Luckily, mother-fucker was on the same fucking page.

"Someone's feeling grumpy today," he said in a mocking kindergarten-teacher tone that grated my teeth together. "We should play nice while our queen is watching, dragon."

"Or maybe you should start fucking bleeding all over the fucking floor."

"You first."

Guillaume stepped over like a fucking referee. I gave him my meanest sneer. "Hope you brought your biggest sword, knight. Not that it'll fucking help keep your fucking head attached."

His lips twitched. "I won't need my biggest sword to shut you up, dragon. But for some unfathomable reason, our queen actually likes you in one piece, so I won't make a dragon-hide saddle today."

He jerked his head toward the chairs, and the rest of the sweaty sword-and-knife wielders went to join our queen.

"We're going to set some rules—"

"Fuck your rules," I retorted. "Though I promise I won't kill anyone." I paused for dramatic effect. "Today."

Ignoring me, Guillaume continued. "To protect this conve-nient training area, if you shift, you automatically lose. Claws and teeth are fine but no full beasts. The support pillars can't take a hit from your tail or the general's horns."

"Fine," I muttered. Not that I intended to shift, though as a king, I couldn't guarantee my control would keep the dragon contained. If they thought I was feisty in the fucking bedroom, they definitely didn't need Leviathan trying to fuck our queen.

"What does he need to say to tap out?" Motherfucker asked. "Uncle?"

"I'll fuck you and your uncle."

Guillaume rolled his eyes. "No maiming. No one gets injured badly enough our queen has to heal you to save you. Otherwise, anything's game. You're Blood, so fucking act like it."

"So fucking bleed, motherfucker," I growled.

Motherfucker dipped his head but didn't lower his burning gold eyes. "As I said, you first."

Shara's bond was still tight with worry and upset, not fucking wet and roaring hot. "How cute. Our queen's actually worried about your wellbeing." To make our intent very clear for her, I pulled my T-shirt over my head and threw it on the floor. Then moved my hands to my fly. "Let's go, motherfucker. Someone's about to fucking beg."

Even if it ends up being me.

34

SEKH

A little payback time. A fucking violent fuck. A whole lot of blood. Fuck yeah.

I bent down to untie my combat boots so I could kick them off. Pants and shirt next.

"Only thing better than a hatefuck is fucking our queen," the dragon drawled as he shucked his pants.

"On that we can both agree."

And if we were extremely lucky, we'd get to fuck her again too.

Not that I was complaining but she had a lot of Blood, and a whole hell of a lot on her mind right now. They didn't realize how fucking crazy it was for her to be up and functioning after bleeding so much to heal the thrall back to some semblance of life. She'd fed on me deeply enough even I'd needed to feed. Un-fucking-believable.

He sauntered closer, eyes glittering with malice despite the quirk of his lips. Hands loose at his side, no claws yet. Green scales sprinkled across his shoulders and chest. His prison had been outside of this world, so I hadn't Seen his suffering, but I could measure the time he'd been out of my sight. I'd also noted how many queens went to free Leviathan—only to never return.

Only Shara fucking Isador had been able to free him and live to break him to her will.

He'd lived as a dragon for so long the beast never completely left him. After thousands of years of solitary confinement, he was lucky to still be sane. Mostly. "Should we pretend to play nice first?"

Our young queen's bond still vibrated with concern about our little demonstration. She feared I was about to rip his head off—rather than rip him a new asshole.

I locked my palm around his nape and hauled him against me, sealing my mouth over his. Grinding his lips against his own fucking teeth until I could taste his blood. A punishing, brutal kiss, sucking on his mouth to steal his very breath from his lungs.

Not to be outdone, he jammed his tongue into my mouth and opened his jaws wide, grinding back on me just as hard. He grabbed handfuls of my hair and jerked, trying to get leverage by twisting my head to suit him. Not that I'd fucking budge an inch.

So he settled for chowing down on my bottom lip instead. Though he'd never taste a drop of my blood unless our queen allowed it.

I shoved him back a step and looked directly at Shara, letting my eyes blaze with heat as his blood dripped down my chin. "This is all for you, Your Majesty."

Eyes wide and dark, she stared at the blood and flames licked over my skin. Then her eyes flared, her mouth starting to open, mouthing a warning, though I didn't need it.

I allowed him the opening to take his best shot before I took the upper hand. I wasn't into humiliation. Though if he wanted me to wipe the floor with his ass before fucking him, I would. Gladly.

His closed fist slammed into my lower jaw, turning my head with the force of the blow. His breath grunted out with effort. He really had put his fucking back into the punch.

Shaking my head—in amusement, rather than pain—I turned back to face him. "You should've taken note of the effect our alpha's fists had on me, dragon."

Mehen shook his hand, trying to get feeling back in his busted knuckles. "I saw him pound your face into the fucking dirt."

"Which I allowed because I wanted our queen's blood on the ground. Punch me all you want but know you'll break every bone in your hands on the sphinx who stands guard for all time."

Behind us, Rik grunted in agreement. "I punched him as the rock troll and didn't manage to do more than give him a black eye for an hour."

"Fine," Mehen growled out. "Let's see how much you'll bleed."

Scales shifted under his skin in a sinuous wave as his claws shot out. He paced around me, shoulders wide, arms cocked at the elbows, claws ready to swipe and rend. I didn't bring mine out yet.

Feinting toward my abdomen with his right hand like he intended to eviscerate me, he threw his left hand around in an arc, slashing at my face.

Not moving a muscle, I stared him in the eye. His claws screeched across my cheek like razor blades on a chalkboard. Leaving my skin unmarred beneath the stone sphinx hovering inside me.

"No fucking way," he growled, shaking his head in disgust. "Xin fucking stabbed you."

I shrugged, letting a smile flicker on my lips. "Which I allowed because our queen sat at the table."

"Fucking cheater."

"How's that cheating if I didn't shift?" I smiled wider, keeping my body loose. "Maybe you should go cry about it like a little bitch to the knight."

His eyes narrowed, his mouth opening on a furious roar as he launched at me. "Die, motherfucker!"

Swiping with furious, wild strikes, he raked his claws over my chest, shoulder, and stomach in quick procession. My back. My throat. Circling me. Looking for an opening. A weakness he could utilize against me.

But the General of the All Seeing, Never Sleeping had no weaknesses.

Giving up on claws, Mehen threw himself against me, attacking my throat with his fangs. Or rather he *tried* to rip my throat out, but his fangs couldn't penetrate me either. Not unless I allowed it.

I wrapped one arm around him and jammed my claws up into his side, hooking beneath his bottom rib. While my other hand shot up to wrap around his throat. I jerked his head hard to the side, straining his neck, and sank my canines into his shoulder. Grinding against bone. Hurting him good—without actually dislocating his shoulder. Though I doubted he'd be able to lift the arm for a few hours until it healed.

Bellowing with fury, he kicked at my knee, trying to knock me off balance. When that failed, he threw himself backward, shoving against my chest.

I let him go—because it suited me to get him on his back.

Sailing several feet away, he crashed to the floor and skidded closer to our queen's chair.

Exactly as I intended.

"Do you want me to stuff your mouth or your ass?"

Panting, he glared at me. Bleeding. His arm out of commission.

His cock as rock hard as mine.

"Fuck my ass, motherfucker, so our queen can sit on my fucking face."

SHARA

Holy FUCK.

I loved watching my Blood fuck each other while someone fucked me too. But watching Mehen throw himself so hard at Sekh, with such obvious malevolent intent, had me quivering on the edge of my seat, my nails jammed into Rik's forearms while he nuzzled my throat and licked my pulse. Terrified one of them might get hurt—but so turned on I hurt with need.

My fangs throbbed, my hunger rising at the first drop of blood. Despite Mehen's furious attack, I could only smell his blood. Not Sekh's. Which made me appreciate that he'd let me feed on him even more. I'd never had problems shoving my nails into his chest or my fangs in his throat.

:I couldn't prevent you from feeding if I wanted to, Your Majesty. And let me assure you with the bloodthirsty rage of three-thousand sphinxes—I want your hunger. I want you to feed as often as possible.:

Mehen tipped his head backward, lifting his chin to the ceiling so he could see me. Emerald eyes burning in challenge—and hunger. Licking his lips, he growled, "Bring that pussy to me so I can feast."

Rik lifted my wrist to his mouth and sank his fangs into my skin. He took several deep swallows, which immediately pumped up his muscles and strained the seams of his jeans. Eyes heavy with desire, he released me, leaving the punctures bleeding. "I think they'll both appreciate your blood as lube more than their own."

A shudder rocked Mehen's body, his eyes squeezing shut.

Sekh let out a harsh snarl. "Fuck you, alpha."

Rik laughed. "That's what I thought."

Standing, I untied the robe and allowed the silk to puddle on the floor. My crazy-ass long hair hung up on Rik's foot and tangled around the short leg of the chair we'd been sitting in. Even though we'd tried to corral the thick, long strands into a single braid, tendrils were escaping. Almost like kudzu, spreading with a mind of its own. It was kind of freaky, to be honest.

With my blood dripping from my wrist, power shimmered within me. I thought of a glittering silver net scooping up my hair and pulling it close. Lifting it up off the floor for me so it didn't constantly drag and tug on my head.

Ahhh. So much better. It might be a trivial, frivolous use of my power, but my neck already felt better not carrying so much weight.

As I stepped closer to my downed dragon, Sekh watched me with heavy predator eyes. A lion lying in wait as his prey came closer. I paused near Mehen's head, waiting for my sphinx to glide closer in a loose, slow prowl. Deeply bronzed skin. Sculpted sleek muscle. He wasn't a massive, formidable man like my alpha, but he radiated danger.

Which was exactly why Mehen hated him so much. My dragon liked to be the most dangerous monster in any room.

He reached backward for me, wincing and letting his right arm drop back to the floor. Wrapping his left hand around my ankle, he tugged me closer. His nostrils flared, his eyes burning with thirst.

Like Sekh had done to me, I held my bleeding wrist out to drip on Mehen's face. Thrashing as if I'd thrown acid on him, he groaned and licked his lips. Opening his mouth wider, he silently begged for more. Though he loved it when I teased him too. Not that he'd fucking admit it.

Which was exactly why I took another step closer, standing over his head so he could look up at my bare pussy. Though I didn't give him what he wanted. That'd be too easy.

"Don't waste all that precious blood on his ugly face when you could be bleeding on my cock."

"Shut the fuck up!" Mehen retorted.

Sekh kicked Mehen's feet apart roughly and dropped to his knees between his legs. "Someone's mouth is flapping far too much. Maybe I need to tear your other shoulder apart too. Or maybe I'll just shred this dick with my teeth."

"Be my fucking guest," Mehen snarled. "Do whatever you fucking want to me, as long as she sits on my face. And gives me some more blood."

Casually pumping his dick, Sekh let out an amused chuckle. "That's an awful lot of demands coming from the dragon on his back, exposing his belly."

Smirking, Mehen planted his feet and rolled his hips up off the floor, arching his back and swinging his dick. "I love being on the bottom of a fuck pile, as long as our queen is in the middle."

Silently, Sekh held his hand out, fingers cupped.

But that would be too easy on him too. And I was nothing if not a fair queen to my Blood.

I stretched my arm out toward him, but rather than dripping a steady stream into his palm, I willed my blood to gush out of the small punctures like he'd ripped a hole in my aorta. My blood sprayed all over him, dripping down his face and shoulders. Coating his offered hand in way more blood than he intended.

His fingers curled, clenched into a fist, tendons straining up his forearm and neck. Hunger roared in his bond, louder than his lion. He swiped his tongue around his mouth and chin, shuddering with bliss.

Mehen fucking laughed. "Now that's the perfect fucking pay—"

His words rose to a howl as Sekh seized his dick in his bloody hand, giving him a hard pump and squeeze that made veins bulge in Mehen's neck. "What were you saying, dragon?"

"Fuck you," Mehen forced out, his voice raw.

In their bonds, I felt every drop of my blood burning on their skin. The fierce blaze of my power stirring their hunger. Maddening their beasts to a fevered pitch. Sekh had full control of his sphinx, but Mehen was a king, and he'd been trapped as a dragon for thousands of years. Creamy light green scales popped up out of his stomach as he strained to hold on to his beast.

Without me, he couldn't control Leviathan, king of the depths, and he definitely didn't want to lose in this challenge.

His fingers—claws—dug into my calf, his grip higher on my leg. Trying to pull me down to him—and simply to anchor himself to me.

Still licking his chops, Sekh rubbed my blood onto his own dick. A shudder rocked his shoulders, his breath catching in his throat. "I'm going to keep the rest of our queen's blood—and her desire—for myself unless you start begging."

"Please, Shara, my queen. Fucking drown me in your desire."

I started to drop down to my knees, and Mehen curled his arm around my waist, snagging me down way harder than I'd intended. No hovering for this dragon. Arm locked around me, he hauled me close, smothering himself. His tongue snaked inside me, his head shoving up beneath me. Fucking me, lifting his shoulders off the floor, even though I felt the pain in his shredded joint. It only added to the blistering heat searing through our bonds. Through all of us.

Moaning, I leaned forward, intending to suck my blood off his cock, but Sekh seized my jaw in his hand and locked his mouth to mine.

Filling my mouth with his blood. I didn't even have to bite him.

Mehen's rough groan vibrated through my pussy as Sekh thrust into him with a hard, endless shove, moving all of us on the floor. Nothing hesitant or gentle in this general.

Exactly as we wanted it.

Sekh fucked him like he was trying to break him open and look for candy. Mehen's body heaved and twisted beneath me, absorbing the thrusts as eagerly as he sucked and licked, drinking me down. His teeth dug into my most tender flesh, puncturing the delicate outer lip of my pussy. The sensitive curve of my lower ass. I jerked against their grip, my entire body quivering. Pleasure strained inside me, pushing me higher. The more I struggled against their hold, the harder Sekh slammed into him.

Climax roared through me, a clawing, screaming wave of sphinx and dragon lust. I surged free of Mehen's grip, and Sekh pulled me down to him. So I could take Mehen's cock inside me, riding him while Sekh fucked us both. Every thrust shoving him deeper. Mehen heaving beneath me, straining to take us both to the edge and push us beyond.

"Transfer me," Mehen panted. "Blast me again."

Sekh fisted his hands in my hair, tipping my head back so he could grip my throat in his jaws. *:Fuck you, this is all mine.:*

Hurling himself up to curl against my back, Mehen wrapped his forearm over my face. My mouth. He wanted me to bite him, but he couldn't hold the position while Sekh drilled him. His weight pulled me backward, putting me into a tug-of-war between the two of them.

And Sekh had his canines in my throat again.

I jammed my nails into Sekh's back, clinging to him as he thrust harder. Using both hands to pin myself to him. Then I sank my fangs into Mehen's forearm and *shoved* my bite through all my bonds. Climax ripped through him, his body heaving and bucking like a stormy sea—into Sekh. Multiplying into an off-the-chart hurricane that blasted through all of us. The sphinx roared. The dragon screamed. Flames burst out of Vivian. A crash as Rik's rock troll took out the chair we'd been sitting in.

Even Xin, hundreds of miles away, howled in broad daylight, shuddering as climax rolled through us all.

Fur and scales and feathers, the burn of sunfires and sulfur, the salty depths of the ocean.

I could even feel Thierry laying on his back, his upper body covered in blue feathers the color of my mother's eyes. We didn't have a full bond, but I'd given him more of my blood than any of my other Blood, simply to make his heart beat again and bring him back from the shell of a thrall.

Still pancaked between a massive sphinx laying on top of Leviathan, I opened my eyes but I couldn't see. Not with all this fucking hair everywhere.

Guillaume's hell horse nuzzled me, nibbling on my hair to get it out of my face. *:I guess we all lose.:*

I had to laugh at the smoking black hoof prints etched into the cement.

:Screw you, moron,: Mehen snarled. *:We all fucking won thanks to me.:*

35

EZRA

Something had to suck fucking donkey balls for Daire to seek me out.

I've always been his second choice, though that never stopped me from cleaning up the fucking leftovers. Third choice, now. But I'd take what he gave me and count myself lucky, because Shara fucking Isador more than made up for any lack.

"Hey." His golly-gee shrug didn't fool me one bit. "What're you up to?"

Stretching out my legs before me, I tipped my head back against the bench and closed my eyes. So I didn't have to admire the way the sun glinted on his tawny hair. Let alone the fucking dimples. My fucking weakness. "Getting ready to take a nap before I have guard duty."

He dropped down to sit beside me with a heavy sigh. Even though I didn't fucking invite him. The bench was plenty big enough until he sat next to me, his thigh and shoulder touching mine. His sassy cat scent wound through my mind, tickling my nose. Though thank the fucking goddess he wasn't purring.

He didn't say anything for so long I almost did go to sleep.

The sun felt good on my face, though it didn't have any real heat yet. Concrete and steel and glass all around this little oasis in the backyard of the house made me appreciate the woods back home more.

Home. Our queen's nest, not the mountain of my birth. My lip curled with self-loathing. *I'm turning into a fucking sap.*

I'd never in a million years imagined I'd feel comfortable anyplace other than the forest House Ursula called home in Ukraine. Let alone with my furry ass plopped down as a fucking Blood to a fucking powerful and amazing Triune queen.

"How do you do it?"

I cracked one eye open so I could see him without turning my head. "Do what?"

"Not care if people don't like you."

I snorted. "I don't fucking care about anybody."

But you. And Shara, our queen. Well, and Rik, but only because if something happened to him, she'd be a fucking crying mess, and I couldn't bear to see her cry. The knight. I wouldn't forget how he'd helped me deal with the Skye shit. But not the fucking dragon. He could go drown himself in the deepest corner of the ocean for all I cared, though he was the king of the depths. That had to fucking count for something.

Nevarre wasn't half bad. Or Tlacel. His brother was something else, though. Mad respect for Itztli. I wouldn't fuck around with him any day.

"Well, I care." Daire pouted like only the brattiest brat could. Making my dick stir. Though I honestly didn't think he did it on purpose. "I like being the one who gets along with everybody. Like I don't even have to try, you know? It's my gift." He scowled. "Well, it was."

I knew where this was going but I played dumb. "Who the fuck doesn't like you?"

"Sekh."

I shrugged. "Fucking ignore him. He's too fucking busy

playing wargames with the Templar knight to care about what you do anyway." Though the corner of my lips did curl up at how the sphinx had handled the fucking dragon. I'd pay good money to see that shit again, even if Shara didn't do the fucking transference bullshit again and blast us all.

"I can't just ignore him. It's too important."

"That he like you? Fuck him. Nobody gives a shit as long as you do your job."

His shoulders drooped miserably. "But that's just it. I don't know if I have a job anymore."

"What, because of the fucking sphinx? Fuck that shit. He's too big and bad to play cuddle buddies with Shara. She'll always need you." *So will I.*

"You don't understand."

"Then help me fucking understand."

"What's the most horrible mistake you've ever made?"

My jaw flexed, my face darkening with shame. "Falling for you."

He made a choked, shocked sound of pain, his mouth sagging open. His eyes shimmering with tears.

"Fuck me sideways. I didn't say it right. I meant when we were young. I started to obsess about you. I couldn't fucking sleep if I couldn't see you. Smell you. So I started sleeping under your window, until your mother found out."

His eyes widened. "That was you? You were smashing Mom's roses all that time? She was so pissed."

I let out a harsh, barking laugh. "I know. She got the queen involved, and bam. I found myself sent to fucking Skye."

"Now think about Mister All Seeing High and Mighty calling you out on that mistake. Smirking about it. Rubbing your nose in it. What do you do now?"

"I tell him to fuck off. Who gives a shit? He's nothing to me. As long as our queen isn't pissed at me, I don't give a shit about anything."

He let out another miserable sigh. "But that's just it. She might be... disappointed. In me."

I let out a deep belly chuckle. I couldn't help it. "No fucking way."

"I could let her down," he insisted.

"How?"

"If I have to choose between her and Rik." His shoulders slumped and he leaned forward, burying his face in his hands. "Sekh's right. I'd choose Rik every fucking time. I'm a shitty excuse for a Blood."

I patted him awkwardly on the back. "Look, you're worried about fucking nothing. She isn't that kind of queen and you know it."

"But—"

"She's not," I repeated, louder. "She's done some fucked up shit, sure. The cobra queen scares the bejesus out of me too. That thing with the trees, she and Itztli sacrificing each other. Fucking messed up. Hanging up that poor bastard to drain all the fucking taint out of him. Fucking awful. But she did it because that's how fucking powerful she is, and they sure as fuck aren't complaining. She isn't ever going to point a finger at you and say get the fuck out because you love Rik too much."

"You don't know that."

I rolled my eyes. "By goddess, I know it for a fucking fact. She doesn't fuck around when it comes to love."

Agonized, he turned those kitty cat eyes on me. "How? How do you know? For sure?"

"Because she didn't kick me out for loving you. In fact, me loving you was the reason she decided to give me a fucking chance in the first place."

He sat up enough to drop his head against my shoulder. Naturally my arm came around him. "So what should I do?"

I squeezed him hard enough he grunted. "Tell Sekh to go fuck himself."

He cringed against me. "I can't. He's too powerful and my warcat slinks anytime I'm around him."

"He might be a motherfucking badass but he's not going to fucking touch you."

"Are you sure?"

"Abso-fucking-lutely. He's like the fucking knight. Too much honor in his pinkie finger to mess around and hurt one of our queen's Blood. That's not their style."

"I just..." He swallowed hard, and I felt the guilt weighing on him. Crushing him like the rock troll took a seat in the middle of his chest. "I feel like such a fucking failure."

"Take that shit to Shara."

His head came up, his brow crinkled with doubt. "What shit? Like tattle on Sekh? That's fucking kindergarten bullshit."

I rolled my eyes. "When I felt like a fucking failure after Skye, I moped around like somebody shat in my Cheerios until the knight fucking talked some sense into me. Then I ran straight to her and blubbered like a baby in her arms."

"She's got too much going on right now to deal with me."

"Bullshit. She'll only need five minutes to make you feel better." I tugged on his hair gruffly. "Just mind the mouth and the pouting until you talk to her. That shit gets out of hand real fast when you're feeling desperate and needy."

"Yeah." He dropped his gaze and bit his lip. Fucking hellcat for sure. "Thanks, Ezra. I mean it. Nobody gets me like you do."

I ruffled his hair and tried to lighten my voice. "Because I fucking love you, you little shit."

He leaned in and pressed his mouth to mine. Stilling me in a heartbeat. His kiss gentle, his tongue slipping between my lips to trace the holes in the roof of my mouth. Which fucking did me in.

I fisted my fingers in his hair and twisted his head. Hard. Making him strain his neck. Pulling him in so his lips smashed against mine. Hard enough I tasted his blood on my tongue. His, and Shara's.

Our queen's. Now it was my fucking turn to feel guilty. She'd never said we couldn't show each other affection, but she was the fucking queen. Our blood was hers. Every fucking drop.

I released the fierce grip on his hair, allowing him to lift his head.

His pupils were wide and dark, his bottom lip puffy and red from my beard. "I fucking love you too, Ezra."

I started to bluster and wave him off, but he tugged on my beard, silencing me.

"I love you. I love her. I love Rik. You're my family, and you always will be."

"Family," I said gruffly. "Forever."

36

SHARA

Cleaned up and dressed, I made my way back downstairs rather than go back to bed. I had too much to do to take a fucking nap.

I felt surprisingly good, even though I'd only slept a few hours after seeing my mother. It was amazing what even one extra Blood could do, let alone Sekh who'd filled all my reserves and then blasted us all to queendom come.

:You're fucking welcome,: Mehen said in the bond, taking all the credit once again.

Even though it'd been Sekh's transference gift I used to make sure we all enjoyed the party. The general's lips twitched in what might have been a smile if the dragon hadn't glanced over at him, daring him to say something.

Magnum waited for me at the foot of the stairs, all business with her blonde hair scraped back in a tight bun and black pants suit. I touched Guillaume's bond. :Is she still carrying the gun?:

:She is,: my knight replied approvingly. :And from her stance, I'd say she knows exactly how to use it, too.:

"Good afternoon, Your Majesty," Magnum said. "I've readied the salon for guests and Gina and Queen Carys are waiting."

I'd invited Gwen to come over for an update, and with the library floor torn open, I'd asked Magnum if there was another room where we could meet. "Perfect, thank you. Sorry about the floor in the library."

"Not at all, Your Majesty. We'll get it repaired with a proper access panel to the darkness below so you can open it whenever the need arises."

The darkness below. I liked that. The words pinged in my head, a ripple spreading through a still, deep pool of inky water.

:*Not the Deep Blue, but the Deep Black*,: Okeanos said behind me.

:*I like that even more.*:

"Queen Gwenhwyfar has left the tower and should be here shortly." Magnum gestured to the hallway on my right. "This way, Your Majesty."

"I've never had the chance for a full tour, Magnum. I'd like to see everything after our guests leave."

"Of course, Your Majesty. The house has been shut and quiet for a very long time, waiting for you to come home and throw open the doors once more."

Looking sharp in black jeans and dress shirt, Lew glanced back over his shoulder. "Everything looks exactly like I remember it, Magnum. Thank you for taking such good care of our former queen's domain."

Magnum's cheeks flushed with pleasure. "Of course. I was honored to stay on, though I wasn't sure why the house needed to be ready." She glanced over at me, her eyes shimmering with emotion. "Now I know why, and I'm more honored than I can convey."

"We stayed here more than anywhere else," Lew said. "Though we also shared the London house with Queen Selena when she still had court."

It was strange to think of Mom as a queen. I'd only ever seen her as my human mother.

"Home," Thierry said.

Esetta's home. Softly, I whispered, "She's still here."

Magnum nodded. "I've always felt a presence I couldn't explain, especially in some of the more… private rooms."

I had the feeling she'd almost said sacred instead of private. It'd be interesting to find out how much she understood about the importance of this house to Isis' pyramid.

Lew didn't ask but yearning surged in his bond. The desire to see my mother. One more time. To finally be able to say her name.

:After everyone leaves tonight, I'll ask her to show herself to you.:

Gryphon claws shredded his heart. *:I've been in this house before and haven't seen her.:*

:We'll try,: I promised.

Guillaume and Sekh took up positions on either side of the door as I passed into the salon. A round table, large enough for ten or twelve guests, was centered in a circular room with a doomed, glass ceiling overhead. Though the windows were all covered with retractable blinds. Old fashioned gas lamps burned on the outer walls, illuminating soft sandstone-colored stucco with Egyptian-style columns inset with statues of our goddess. The table was lit with dozens of thick white pillar candles. Woven mats of thick, natural-colored reeds softened the hard sandstone floor underfoot.

Dressed in a flowing black and red dress, Gina stood and curtseyed as soon as she saw me, though Carys didn't even look up from her book. "Your Majesty."

I scowled at her. "Where the fuck did all this formality come from?"

Granted, I'd dressed up a little more than usual too. I hadn't seen Gwen in forever, so I'd asked Nevarre for a dress for this visit instead of my usual jeans and sweater or hoodie. Evidently word had spread without me issuing a single command and everyone had dressed up too.

He'd picked out a simple yet elegant, surprisingly comfortable black maxi dress that hugged my figure without constricting me. We'd re-braided my hair too, though I didn't have much hope it'd stay tidy all evening.

Laughing softly, Gina waited to sit back down until Rik had me settled beside her, directly across from the door. "This room demands formality, my queen."

"Your mother might have called it the salon, but we called it the war room," Lew admitted as he and Thierry circled the table to my left behind Gina and Carys. "She always hosted visiting queens in this room."

Okeanos took position on my right, looking splendid in a shimmery turquoise blue shirt and black pants. His skin looked a little tight and slightly grayish, though anyone but me probably wouldn't notice.

:How much longer can you be away from the grotto or the sea?:

:I'm perfectly fine, my queen. Just a little dry. I'll take a long soak in a tub tonight.:

Muscles flexed across Magnum's cheek. "I vaguely remember moonlit meetings, but I can't seem to remember any faces or names."

Lew nodded. "She preferred to have nighttime meetings with the skylights open, letting the moonlight sparkle off the china."

"Would you like the skylights uncovered, Your Majesty?"

"No, let's keep them covered for now. I prefer the darkness."

Magnum lifted her hand to her ear, touching an earpiece so small I hadn't noticed it. "Queen Gwenhwyfar is arriving. I'll return with your guests shortly, Your Majesty."

"Thank you, Magnum." I reached up and placed my hand over Rik's on my shoulder. "You can sit down with me, you know. All of you are welcome to take a seat with us."

"You know I much prefer to hover at your back so I can glower at anyone who upsets you," Rik said lightly.

"It's a losing argument with Blood," Lew added. "We wouldn't sit with her either."

"Especially when you're holding court," Guillaume said.

"This isn't court. It's simply an early dinner among friends."

"If you're planning to talk Isador business, then you're holding court," Guillaume replied.

"I was actually planning to talk Triune business, which is why I asked you and Sekh to be close."

Gina raised an eyebrow and Carys even set her book aside as if I'd finally said something interesting.

Sekh heaved out a disappointed sigh. "And here I thought we could expect some trouble from your guests. I was looking forward to some *real* hand-to-hand combat."

Of course he had to get another dig into Mehen, even though the dragon was on the roof.

Guillaume flashed a genuine grin of anticipation. He'd traded his usual faded blue jeans for the same all-black look as Lew and Rik, though he'd buckled the Templar sword over his back. Even though we were dining with friends. "Wait until you see who this queen's Blood are."

"I don't know the name Gwenhwyfar but it's not difficult to put two and two together," Sekh replied dryly. "I know full well our queen's sibling at the Tower is the White Enchantress of Camelot. I Saw the red and white dragons battling on Glastonbury Tor when Guinevere was freed at last from the curse her king put upon her royal line."

"Then you've seen her alpha fight," Guillaume said. "They say Sir Lancelot du Lac can't be defeated with a sword."

Which only made my knight's fingers itch to try his hand at defeating the famous knight of the Round Table.

"I have indeed." Sekh nodded. "I've Seen you fight as well, Sir Guillaume."

"And?"

The general's lips quirked. "Let's just say the two of you are too valuable for our queen to lose either of you."

I hadn't really thought of Gwen's Blood that way. They were hers, not mine. But when I'd needed to dump power as Sekh's blood raged through me, her knights had eagerly soaked in everything they could hold. They were my reserves as well as hers. I could tap on Sir Lancelot and—

The hell horse trumpeted a fierce neigh in our bond, though Guillaume didn't say a word. He didn't have to.

:I will never send him anywhere when I have the headless knight at my disposal.:

Mollified, the hell horse's muzzle brushed my cheek.

Magnum tapped on the door, and Gina immediately stood beside me. Though as soon as I laid my hands on the table to also stand, Rik tightened his grip on my shoulders, keeping me in the chair. *:You're the highest queen.:*

:But she's my friend.:

Guillaume added, *:It's your right and our privilege to see you honored by your sibling as appropriate to reflect your power.:*

The door opened and Magnum stepped inside the room to announce my guests. "Her Majesty Gwenhwyfar of House Camelot, with her Blood Sir Lancelot, Bors, and Mordred, as well as Merlinus Caledonesis. Also, Your Majesty, your second consiliarius, Kevin Isador."

Also dressed in all black—though with leather jackets and thick motorcycle boots—Bors and Mordred stepped into the room and shook hands with my two Blood. Sekh introduced himself only by his name, not his rank or lineage.

The two Blood then came closer to the table and saluted me, fist over their hearts as they bowed. "Your Majesty."

"Welcome to House Isador," Gina said.

"Please make yourself comfortable," I added. Not that they would, any more than my Blood would relax and sit down with us.

Lance gave my two Blood a pleasant nod but didn't shake hands with them. Not with his queen on his arm. His hair had grown out some since I'd seen him last, and his face had filled out a little more. With Elaine Shalott removed from this world, his eyes weren't as shadowed. Releasing his arm, Gwen curtsied with practiced elegance I envied.

All her Blood moved with the lean, lethal grace of swordsmen. Except for the one Blood I hadn't met yet, Merlinus, who brought up the rear beside Kevin. The famous wizard of Arthurian legends—though Merlinus looked nothing like the gray haired and bearded wizard in a nondescript robe so often portrayed in movies. He wore elegant black slacks and a long-sleeved old-fashioned silk shirt in brilliant purple. Long silvery lavender hair swept over his shoulders, and his eyes were an even deeper indigo, almost black. He bent in a graceful bow like a courtier. "Your Majesty."

"Our queen, Shara Isador, last daughter of She Who Is and Was and Always Will Be, welcomes you," Gina said. "This is Her Majesty's alpha, Alrik, and her other Blood, Okeanos, Llewellyn, and Thierry, with Queen Carys."

Merlinus' eyes narrowed into dark slits as he looked at Thierry. He didn't say anything, but I could only guess the conversation happening in his queen's bond. I didn't make any excuses or explanations who I brought to my own fucking table in my own fucking house. Thierry deserved to be here more than they did.

Kevin flashed a wide smile and bowed to me, though not with the same flourish as the wizard. "Your Majesty, welcome back to New York City."

"Glad to see you again, Kevin."

He took a seat by Carys, leaving the seat opposite me open for Gwen, who looked absolutely radiant in a white evening gown with slits in the long skirt revealing red velvety material underneath. Her crescent moon necklace glittered in the candlelight but the only other jewelry she wore was a simple ring on her hand. It didn't look like the one Arthur had been wearing, but I'd only glimpsed it briefly when we forced him out of my blood circle. Her mahogany hair was swept to one side, falling in a thick, elegant curl over her shoulder.

"You look like a glamorous movie star," I told her, smiling.

She laughed as Lance seated her, her eyes shining with so much joy and happiness that I felt my own eyes shimmer with unshed tears. "I was going for old-fashioned Hollywood glam. Thank you for giving us a reason to dress up." She reached up and clasped her alpha's hand on her shoulder, mirroring Rik behind me. "Even more, thank you for everything you've done to help us, Your Majesty. We're free of *her* influence for the first time in more than a thousand years. Without your help, I never would have been able to bring Merlin back from Avalon, either."

Merlinus took a seat on his queen's left, but none of the knights sat at the table. Though Mordred did at least step closer. "I would like to voice my personal gratitude for your consiliarius' assistance. Without his help, I may not have survived long enough to be reunited with my queen."

I nodded. "Kevin proves his incredible skills and loyalty in increasingly clever ways every single day. I too am more grateful than I can say that he agreed to become my second consiliarius."

Kevin's cheeks blazed with heat and an embarrassed yet pleased little sound escaped his lips. "My pleasure, Your Majesty. It's an honor to serve in any way I can."

"I'm pleased to report that all of your siblings in Isador Tower are still alive, my queen," Gwen said. "Though I'd love to hear more about what caused you to have such suspicions."

"House Isador is going to war," I said softly, watching her reaction.

She didn't ask against who or why. Instead, she leaned forward with a wide, vicious smile. "House Camelot rides at your side, my queen."

37

SHARA

Before I got into the details, I asked Gwen to tell me about how she'd defeated Arthur while Magnum quietly brought drinks to the table. I wasn't sure what kind of wine she served but it was light and crisp with a hint of honeyed sweetness.

"He said something about fertilizing Tiamat's eggs," Gwen said. "But I don't know how many."

I touched my dragon's bond. *:How many eggs do you think Tiamat had Arthur fertilize?:*

:Dragons rarely lay more than a couple of eggs at a time,: Mehen said in the bond. *:Though She's the Mother of Dragons. She'll hold on to every fucking drop of his semen to fertilize eggs for centuries. She'll have a flight of baby red arthurī in no time.:*

Greeeeeat. "I guess we'll find out. Do you have any other Blood to Call?"

Gwen dropped her gaze to her glass, her fingers lightly tracing the delicate crystal stem. "I'm not sure. At least..." She sighed and lifted her gaze back to mine. Some of the shining light dimmed in her eyes. "I'm afraid Arthur managed to kill most of my former knights, but I'm hopeful some are still in hiding. Though they haven't answered me yet."

"The Knights of the Round Table are notoriously embroiled in quests, my queen," Merlin said, rolling his eyes at Sir Lancelot. "They're probably waiting on you to embark on another epic journey or battle to find them."

She sighed. "Back in the good old days, we'd just have a tournament and invite all the knights to come to me."

"Tournaments and quests for the Holy Grail." Merlin sniffed with disdain. "Ridiculous, in my opinion."

Carys laughed. "Oh, I like him, my queen. Though I admit reading about the grail quest is one of my guilty pleasures."

"Why were you concerned about the queens in the tower?" Gwen asked.

I caught her up on what the Dauphine had done to Mom before I was called to Rome. How worried I've been that the Dauphine might strike against my human family. "And then I found out what she'd done to my mother's former Blood, Thierry."

Thankfully Magnum hadn't started serving food yet. I didn't go into full detail but mentioned the eel-sized leeches and resurrecting my mother's former Blood. And of course, they had eyes and noses. They could smell the whiff of decay around him.

"No." Thierry garbled another word that might have been touch or taint. I honestly wasn't sure.

"We're afraid he might still carry some kind of boobytrap," I admitted. "I've done everything I can for him, but Carys isn't optimistic about the probable outcome."

Carys snorted. "There's a difference between optimism and reality, my queen."

"So you were afraid one of the queens in the tower might actually be the Dauphine? Goddess. You tasted all of them, Shara. If she's already in your blood circle…"

"I know," I replied grimly. "I don't think she could hide that well if I'd already taken her blood as a sibling. If she's as powerful as they say, she'd have already taken over the bond. Right?"

"Nothing is guaranteed," Carys said. "But it's highly unlikely even a lightly forged sibling bond would ever be safe with her."

"I'm a strong healer but I'm sorry, my queen. I don't need to draw my blood to know he's beyond my abilities, if that's why you asked me to come tonight."

"No, that's not what I hoped to talk about. I just wanted you to know what we're dealing with. Xin is tracking back to Thierry's previous location before Christmas, but I'm not hopeful the Dauphine is there. I need to find her before she completely disappears again. And when I do…"

I met Gwen's gaze straight on. "I'm going to kill her. We're here tonight to talk about the ramifications of what that means. I'll remind everyone not to refer to any other Triune queen by her formal name unless she's dead."

Gwen shrugged though her eyes brightened again with anticipation. "You're Triune. Are you worried about fallout from the queen of Rome? I'd think she'd be pleased as punch to have the Dauphine eliminated. She'll have the run of the table."

"Which is a whole other problem," Guillaume said.

I gave him a tug in the bond. Sekh too. Willing them to at least come closer to be an active part of the conversation.

"There's a reason there are three seats at the Triune table, my queen," Guillaume continued, coming to stand at the edge of the table on my right. "A healthy Triune is balanced, each queen checked by the others."

"Are you suggesting the queen of Rome and the Dauphine could have stopped Desideria's reign of terror?" I asked.

He nodded. "In fact, I believe they failed in their sacred duty to our goddesses by *not* checking her actions. Two against one should have been plenty to stop her, but allowing

Desideria to destroy the other courts increased their power too."

"By Triune law, he's right," Gina said. "Much can be accomplished with a quorum of Triune queens, including removing the other queen from her goddess-appointed seat. A quorum is enough to compel the third queen to come to the table for judgment or other Triune business."

"That's why you suspected Skolos might be revolting against each other." Gwen looked confused, so I added, "When I was Calling Sekh, I noticed queens south of us near the Gulf of Mexico. Gina's team was able to confirm two of the Skolos queens are in the area, and Okeanos confirmed his mother is there as well."

Gwen's eyes flared. "A full Triune. Goddess, when was the last time a full Triune even met? What laws require a full Triune to enact?"

"Very good questions I'm afraid I can't answer off the top of my head," Gina admitted. "The only law I'm sure of is the ability to pardon a queen from any guilt or retribution from killing another queen, even a Triune queen."

"Are you saying a full Skolos Triune could pardon me for killing the Dauphine?" Excitement sparked through me. Maybe that's exactly why the three queens had come together, drawn by the Great One…

But Esetta said I'd lose one of my greatest gifts if I was successful, and she hadn't been wrong yet.

"It's possible but not likely, I'm sorry to say," Gina replied. "I wouldn't want you to get your hopes up. Getting three powerful queens to agree on anything would require goddess-level approval. There are also many ritualistic laws governing the Triune, but they're so archaic I don't have any knowledge of them. I doubt many consiliari…"

Her words fell off as Kevin raised his hand, blushing. "Um, actually, Triune-specific law is one of my hyper-focused areas of interest. Though Her Majesty of Rome probably wouldn't be very pleased with Granddad if she knew exactly how much access he'd allowed me during my internship."

I could only laugh. "Kevin's brilliance strikes again."

"I'm not as brilliant as Kevin but I have the benefit of actually seeing a Triune queen seated at the table," Guillaume said.

My Templar knight—who couldn't be killed—shuddered. "Hold on, Kevin. What the fuck was that about, G?"

"When a Triune queen takes her seat at the Mother's table, she's bound to it. I'm sorry, my queen, but it can be... alarming to see. I can't imagine what it must feel like, but it doesn't look pleasant."

"Bound? Like tied up? Caged? I saw the table in Rome and there weren't any chairs. Just a darkened spot where the queens stood."

Though the Triskeles table I'd been called to did have three chairs. When I'd touched my seat, the back had changed into Isis' horned sun-disk crown. If I'd sat down...

"Triune Articles Section 1.1.13," Kevin whispered breathlessly. "Blood flows from the Great Mother of All, through Her daughters to Their queens, and thus a Triune queen is bound to Her table and Her will."

"If you'd agreed to join that Triune, with her present... You would have had a quorum, activating the Great Mother's power. The table changes. It's like it comes... alive, and the queens are inside it. A part of it."

"Have you seen what he's talking about?" I asked Sekh.

He shook his head. "The Great Mother's magic cloaks Her tables. I couldn't even tell you where the tables are in this world, let alone what happens at them."

"I've seen things no other living Blood has seen," G ground out, his voice harsh. His bond ached with a thousand regrets, a million-ton cargo ship sinking to the bottom of the ocean. "No

Blood *should* have seen." He stared down at his hands, his fingers trembling. "Mother, forgive me."

GUILLAUME

THESE HANDS HAD TAKEN HUNDREDS, THOUSANDS, OF LIVES. SOME were honorable deaths, whether in battle or protecting Shara. Like the saleswoman in Kansas City who'd been tainted by Marne Ceresa's blood.

But I would always see the blood of Triskeles on my hands. No matter how many centuries passed since that evil deed.

"Oh, G," Shara whispered softly, her voice breaking as her pure heart cracked open.

"It was me." I dropped to my knees, my shoulders slumped. "I killed Triskeles at Desideria's order."

"But Okeanos said it was the queen of Rome."

"Oh, I'm sure she had something to do with it. Maybe she planted the idea in Desideria's head. She was fucking paranoid to the point of insanity. But I assure you those queens died by my sword. I was there with Desideria. She compelled me."

"What did you hear in Rome?" She asked the kraken.

"There was a meeting between *her* and another queen. They talked at the edge of the koi pond, just like she did with you, my queen." Okeanos paused, his voice softening as if even now he feared the queen of Rome's reach.

"Did she say who the other queen was?"

He hesitated long enough I dragged my gaze up to see his face. He'd dropped to his knees beside Shara's chair, their heads together, her hand clutched in his. "I can hear the soft whisper of music on the breeze, a hint of the name. But then it's gone."

She closed her eyes. "My mother. Goddess. It had to be her."

"The queen of Rome asked her why Desideria had ordered her to Constantinople days before she died. The other queen only laughed, a sound like ringing bells and tinkling chimes, and said she would answer that question if the queen of Rome cared to explain how Desideria knew Triskeles had planned to hold a quorum in Saint Petersburg."

I swallowed the lump of regret choking me. "Desideria and I traveled to the ruins of the fortress once called Nyenskans under cover of her magic. Saint Petersburg is its modern name."

"The queen of Rome denied having anything to do with Triskeles, but the other queen very clearly said, 'Queens who wish to keep their secrets shouldn't accept gifts of mirrors from Rome.'"

"Goddess," Shara let out a shaky breath. "That's exactly what she did to me. Why would a Triskeles quorum have been bad news to Desideria?"

"They were Triune too," I replied. "With three Triune queens present at the table, bound to the Great Mother, they were damned near invincible. I'm sure they intended to compel Desideria to stand for her crimes before the Great Mother, even though she was High Queen of the other Triune."

"If they were invincible..." Gwen said slowly.

I barked out a harsh laugh. "How the fuck did I fucking kill them? It wasn't easy, even for me. First of all, the Triune table itself isn't of this world. It moves to where its queens are. That's why the general can't see them.

"Only someone carrying a Triune queen's blood can even unlock access to the location. When three Triune queens come to the table, they each drop a blood circle around it, making it triple secure. That way, no single Triune queen's Blood can cross the circle to take the other two queens out while they're bound and helpless. No Blood are allowed inside with the queens, either. It's just the three queens in the presence of the Great Mother."

I paused, drawing a deep, steadying breath. "The three queens' Blood waited outside of the ruin, matched up by strength to potentially defeat each other and keep their queen safe. Even centuries ago, the queens didn't fucking trust each other. They should have been more worried about an external attack, rather than an internal coup. Desideria masked our presence and ordered me to find a way inside. Rather than killing them all to raise the alarm, I slit the throats of the weakest Blood, one from each queen. She took enough of their blood to gain access to each queen's blood circle. She brought me through to the innermost sanctum. Where she then ordered me to kill them."

I exhaled a long, controlled breath, allowing the words to flow out of me as my shoulders fell. "I killed the first queen, and the deed was done. Because they were bound to the table, killing one queen killed them all."

The fucking truth.

I didn't try to convey the horror I'd felt. The atrocity. I knew full well I'd sinned against the Great Mother Herself.

Slaughtering three queens doing the Great Mother's will. In Her presence. Her replica stared at me from the table. Watching me raise the sword and strike.

All because one insane queen blinded by her thirst for power commanded it.

Shara's bond flowed through me, trying to soothe away the crippling guilt. *:You had no choice.:*

:There's always a choice,: I replied. *:I could have broken my solemn oath and damned myself from ever carrying another sword with honor for all eternity rather than execute another queen. I chose to honor my oath, even though she used that honor to enslave me.:*

Everyone sat in silence while I slowly climbed to my feet. The Templar sword weighed heavily on my back. A silent judgment. I didn't deserve to carry it. Not after killing for centuries at Desideria's command, but especially executing Triskeles.

"Guillaume," Shara said in a soft, gentle voice that still hammered through me. Compelling me to come the last few steps to her.

I couldn't meet her gaze as I dropped to my knees beside her. Bowing my head, I pressed my forehead to her knees.

And wept.

I wept for the queens who'd died under my sword. The magic this world had lost. The knight who'd first sworn his Templar oaths. Who'd believed in honor and chivalry once upon a time. Ironic the Knights of the Round Table were present as I confessed my most horrific sins to my queen.

Her fingers stroked over my head, soothingly combing through my hair. "If you weren't a knight of your word, then I wouldn't have taken you as my Blood. I would've been too afraid you'd kill Rik."

I lifted my head, swallowing hard at the shining light in her eyes. I didn't deserve her love. "You would have Called other, better Blood, my queen."

"There is no better Blood than you." She gathered my murderous hands in hers. Lifted my damaged fingers to her lips so she could kiss each scar. "I wouldn't have survived long enough to sit in this chair at this table without you by my side. If you want to damn yourself, then damn me along with you."

"Never, my queen. You deserve only the best."

"My mother told me there's always a way around an oath sworn in blood, if you have enough time and are willing to pay the cost." Her eyes flashed with power, her words echoing through the room even though she didn't raise her voice. "But Sir Guillaume de Payne Isador's honor is unbreakable."

Drawn steel whispered in the silence. I didn't draw my sword, but whirled toward the threat, still on my knees, arms spread open, shielding my queen with my body.

Sir Lancelot du Lac held his sword before him in both hands, parallel to his body with the tip pointing toward the floor. The sword glowed with pearly power. Blue runes rippled down its blade and a large crystal on the hilt cast rainbows on the darkened ceiling overhead.

Excalibur. Forged in fae magic beyond the Veil on Tír na nÓg's sparkling shores.

Holding my gaze, he bowed his head, kissed the crystal, and then sheathed the legendary sword once more.

"That is why you live forever, my beloved knight." Shara wrapped her arms around me, her mouth against my ear. "Not because the Great Mother doesn't deem you worthy of redemption—but because She needs you here. I need you here. With me. Forever."

38

SHARA

On my left, Okeanos started to quietly back away. I snagged his hand and kept him down beside me, with my other arm still around Guillaume. Keeping him pressed against me.

My Blood wouldn't sit with me at the table if I was holding court. But they'd gladly go down on their knees for me. Even in front of legendary Knights of the Round Table and the Queen of Camelot.

I turned my attention to the rest of my guests, meeting each person's gaze briefly. "So the question we must ask is why has a full Skolos Triune decided to meet a few hundred miles away. What do they hope to accomplish?"

"That's what I can't get my mind around," Gina said. "They're present—but they're not actually meeting each other. There's been no movement from either House in a week."

"My guess is they're still trying to hash out the particulars before agreeing to meet in person." Guillaume replied. "It's no small thing to come to the table as Triune. In fact, it can be fucking dangerous. The Triskeles queens saw me. They must have known what I was going to do. But they didn't blink an eye or lift a finger to stop me."

Even now with the past act of killing Triskeles laid out between us, he still shuddered at the memory of what he'd seen, just as much as he felt the guilt and horror of the act itself. "If they were united, why didn't they compel Desideria before you could strike?"

He shook his head. "I don't know. They didn't speak a word aloud but perhaps they were talking to themselves. Crying out to the Mother or their Blood to save them. I'm not sure."

"The strongest Triune queen is the Speaker of the Table," Kevin whispered. "Determined by the amount of her goddess' blood she carries and thus the Great Mother's. The queens' blood must be measured before the Speaker can be determined. Triune Articles Section 1.1.15. The Speaker is also known as the High Queen of the Triune, Addendum 8 added in 1503 AD."

"Goddess." Gwen let out a shaky laugh. "How's a queen's blood measured without taking it out of her body?"

"That's exactly what happens," Guillaume replied grimly. "The queen I killed didn't bleed. The table did. All that blood," he whispered, shaking his head. "Wasted. It drained away into the floor and was gone before the bodies were cold."

My stomach quivered. "It would have been fucking great to know all these fun details about the Triune before I agreed to take a seat."

"I'm sorry, my queen." Grimacing, he squeezed my hand. "You were already scared, and rightfully so. Accepting a seat at the Triune table is only for the strongest queens, and not just in power, though of course that helps tremendously."

"I guess that also explains why sibling queens don't sit on the same Triune. It would skew the blood measured for the Speaker position."

"Do you think the Skolos Triune is meeting so they can compel you to come before them?" Gwen asked.

"For what reason, though? To kill me? I haven't done anything to them. Certainly nothing like the queen of Rome or Desideria."

"But they could kill you and then pardon themselves," Gina warned. "Or they could compel you to kill either the Dauphine or the queen of Rome with the promise of a pardon."

"True," I said slowly, letting ideas fire and die out in my mind like sparks from a fire. "Carys, what's the probability Skolos is holding a quorum with the goal of killing me?"

"Thirty-three percent. It's possible—but not their primary goal."

Wait. One third. "What's the probability one of the three queens near Houston wants to kill me?"

Carys made a soft sound of surprise. "Goddess. One hundred percent. I've never seen that before."

"So it's two against one. Maybe that's why they haven't been able to come to an agreement yet. Can you see which one wants me dead?"

Carys shook her head. "It doesn't work like that, unfortunately. Though ask me when I can see their faces."

"Could they have met anywhere? I mean, did they pick a location close to me on purpose?"

"The Speaker determines where and when the Triune meets," Kevin said. "In the case where the table is called without a known Speaker, the blood will be measured first to determine who speaks for the Great Mother. Triune Articles Section 1.1.21."

I looked over at Okeanos. "Your mother is the High Queen of Skolos, right?"

He nodded. "Though I don't know how often the Skolos queens have met or where in the past."

"Who's the Speaker for the other Triune?" I asked.

"No one," G replied. "They haven't met since Desideria was killed. Even long before that, actually."

"Did they ever meet after Triskeles?"

He shook his head again. "Not even before, at least not in my time of service. Desideria never sat at the table with the other two queens after taking my oath."

"I still can't believe they didn't do something to stop her. Especially if it only took the other two queens to remove her from her seat. I have to believe the Great Mother would have immediately supported their decision to remove Desideria from her seat, even if it angered her triple goddesses."

"They were too fucking greedy themselves. As Desideria's reign of terror continued, more and more queens came to Rome for protection. The Dauphine fucked off into obscurity. When Desideria died, it left the queen of Rome without anyone to check her. No one was strong enough—or brave enough—to dare take a seat across from her."

"Damn." I blew out a sigh, my mind racing. "If I'd taken a seat with her that day in Rome, then we could have compelled the Dauphine to join us. I could have removed her then and there."

"Which is exactly why it suits both of them to stay far away from each other and their table, while trying to murder anyone who even thinks about trying to join them," Guillaume replied.

"Do you have a sense of when another queen may be called to join you at Triskeles?" Gwen asked.

I shook my head. "Not at all. Until we have at least a quorum, there's not much I can do alone to protect Triskeles."

Nothing but stay alive.

39

SHARA

Hours later, I hugged Gwen goodbye after enjoying a delicious dinner, and then made my way back upstairs. I'd sent Lew and Thierry up before the food arrived to wait for me in the room of my birth. I loved Thierry and wanted him to be a part of my life while he could, but I didn't think I could stomach eating with the stench of death in my nose.

"Would you like me to wait outside?" Rik asked.

I paused outside the black carved door and shook my head. "No. I need you to come inside, just in case."

He didn't ask why. Perhaps he already sensed what I intended to do, though I hadn't allowed myself to dwell on it over dinner, for fear I might burst into tears.

The door pushed open silently. My two Blood knelt beside the sunken tub, facing the door. I half expected to see Esetta hovering with them, even if they couldn't see her, but evidently she hadn't made an appearance yet. Maybe she couldn't.

Not with the living.

Despite all that Lew had suffered in House Skye, he was definitely still alive.

Rik had died when I'd envenomed him as the cobra queen. Which was why I needed him to stay.

I walked around Lew's side and sat on the low tile wall of the sunken tub behind him. Without needing any instruction, Rik moved closer on my other side, hovering with full attention on Thierry. Ready to stop him if he tried to touch me unexpectedly.

I didn't think he would. Not of his own accord. But the tremors had started again, and his words were getting harder to understand. His body was rotting shockingly fast, and if I needed to heal him again...

I couldn't risk it. Not now.

All my instincts insisted I needed to be ready. Springs coiled inside me, ready to burst free into action. When the time came to strike the Dauphine, I wouldn't have time to stop and feed well and deeply. I needed to be prepared. Not drained.

Before I could say anything, Lew turned toward me, pressing against my legs. "Yes. Please."

My throat tightened but I managed a tremulous smile for him. He'd already taken his shirt off, but he'd kept the rest of his clothes on. Picking up my hands in his, he pressed kisses to my palms and relaxed against me. Stretching out his long legs past Thierry, his head on my shoulder, his body soft and open to me.

Droplets of golden starlight flickered in his eyes. Capturing this moment in his memory bank.

The moment I killed him.

I pressed my lips to his forehead, my left arm curling around his shoulders.

And shoved my right hand into his chest.

His breath exploded out on a long gasp, but he didn't struggle. He tried to make it as easy as possible for me to kill him. Though he was too heavy, too big, for me to hold by myself. Rik shifted closer, supporting my arm with one hand while keeping his other ready to throttle Thierry if needed.

But my mother's former Blood only watched his alpha and friend shudder when I pulled out his spirit in my bloody fist.

Lew's bird was a large golden-brown eagle. Not surprising given his gryphon but far larger than Thierry's white-headed bird. The eagle stretched out its wings and screeched at me, but it didn't try to fly away. It stayed on its back, its talons curling around my arm.

Tears streamed down my face while I watched Lew's body die. The red-gold light in his eyes dimmed to muddy brown with a flat, empty stare. His skin leached of color, as gray as Thierry's. The dead weight of his body cooled against me. On my skirt. My hair. Pinning me in place.

Not that I would have left him anyway, but it was disconcerting just the same.

I waited several long moments, silently crying. I wasn't sure how long he needed to be dead for this to work, but I didn't want to do it again.

"That's enough, Shara," Esetta said.

Rik and Thierry both looked up at the same time as me. They heard her. Saw her. Standing in the same place I'd seen her the night before.

Thierry moaned, a horrible croak. A sob escaped my lips. But he didn't leave his knees beside Lew. Even for her.

Closing my eyes, I focused on the eagle in my grip. Willing his wings tight to his body, a smaller bundle I could shove back inside the cavity of Lew's body. He slid back easily, though my hand made a disgusting pop and squelch as I pulled my fist back out. His body spasmed uncontrollably, his head falling forward against my throat. Instinctively, he bit me. Feeding on me, using my blood and power to more quickly bring his body back to life.

"Llewellyn."

His head jerked up. Eyes wild, roaring with bonfires of

emotion. My blood dripped down his chin. He slowly turned his head to the corner where she stood.

"Esetta." His voice cracked and he said her name again and again. As if he would never stop saying it now that he could. "Esetta!"

I expected him to leap to his feet and run to her. Scoop her up in his arms. But like Thierry, he didn't move from his spot at my feet.

She came to us, dressed in the same white sheath, her hair unbound and flowing around her like a cape, even though she'd also given her hair to me. She cupped Lew's cheek in one hand. Thierry's in the other.

But she leaned down to press her lips to my forehead. "Thank you, daughter of mine."

"You're welcome, Esetta Isador, daughter of the Great One, but not the last."

On their knees, they clung to her. Laughing. Crying. Thierry didn't talk. But he didn't have to. She heard every word. I was sure of it, as I quietly shut the door.

40

SHARA

Perhaps it was all the talk about the Triune tables and what it meant to be Called to the Mother's table. Or more likely it was simply time.

Time for Her to speak to the only queen listening for Triskeles.

I floated in the steamy water of my grotto, though I could taste salt on my lips. Something pulled deep inside me, an insistent fist in my intestines, dragging me down. I allowed the pull to take me, my head sinking beneath the water. Blue-green light rippled through the darkness, beckoning me deeper beneath my heart tree.

The tree I'd died on, giving it every drop of blood in my body.

It could take me anywhere as long as I could hold my intention on the place clearly enough. Beneath its roots, there was another portal. A secret place no one had ever walked but me.

The Great Mother's sacred lair. A dark cave outside of this world connecting me to Her.

I rose out of the water into a circular room. I wasn't even wet. Shadows cloaked the walls, but a ray of soft moonlight shone from above to illuminate the Mother figurine in the center of the room. With a start, I realized it looked like the salon, or war room table, especially with the light shining down from above.

Esetta hadn't been called to the Triune. Yet she might have seen enough to model her dining room table on the Triskeles chamber.

There weren't any chairs or table this time, and the Mother figurine was tall and thick, as tall as me. Her ebony skin gleamed in the moonlight like polished wood. The Triskeles symbol on Her rounded stomach caught the moonlight and amplified it, casting pearly sparkles through the space.

The air weighed heavy with hushed reverence, rich with the scent of warm, living soil and fresh green growth. A living cathedral in an ancient, sacred wood, cloaked in the mists of time.

Dropping to my knees at Her feet, I bowed my head.

The weight of Her hand touched my shoulder, sending an electric spark jolting through me. My entire arm numbed. I sucked in a deep breath, harsh in the silence. She didn't speak out loud, but Her words resounded through my head like a ringing bell.

:DAUGHTER OF MY DAUGHTER, YOU ARE NEEDED. WILL YOU GO?:

"Yes, Great Mother," I replied without hesitation. "Send me where I'm needed."

Her fingers tightened, Her hand so heavy my muscles quivered under the strain. *:THEY NEED YOU, EVEN IF THEY DENY YOU. EVEN WHEN THEY DESPISE YOU. THE COST IS HIGH. BUT IF THEY ARE NOT SAVED, ALL IS LOST.:*

An image filled my mind. Three queens stepping in and out of my sight around a circular table. One of the queens had blue hair flowing like kelp tendrils in the sea. Undina Ketea. Okeanos' mother.

The Skolos Triune.

Then a blur, like a ghost. Seen, but not seen.

The Dauphine.

The Mother leaned harder on me, more than just a hand on my shoulder. It felt like the statue had fallen across my back. I couldn't see. The smell of earth intensified, dark loam and rotting leaves. Death to fertilize new growth.

:THE WORLD TREE DIES. ITS BRANCHES WITHER. ITS TRUNK ROTS FROM WITHIN. ONLY THE ROOTS REMAIN, BUT IF THEY'RE NOT WATERED, EVEN THEY WILL FAIL.:

Crushing weight, ribs smashed. My lungs filled with blood. Dirt clogged my nose. Over my face. A grave.

Buried alive.

Terror washed over me. Trapped in darkness. Far from my Blood.

Bound to the table. To the Mother's will. Even if there weren't any other queens to take their seats.

I had to do this alone.

I've faced the grave before. I can do it again.

:CUT OUT THE ROT. CLEANSE THE DEAD WITH THE FIRE OF YOUR RAGE. THEN WATER THE WORLD TREE, DAUGHTER OF MY DAUGHTER. WATER IT WITH BLOOD.:

I opened my mouth, releasing the blood pooled inside me. The bottomless ocean that Sekh and the legion had given me. All of it. Pouring out of me like the Nile itself.

I couldn't see Her face but I felt it deep in my bones when the Mother smiled.

~

HEART POUNDING, I SAT STRAIGHT UP IN BED.

Rik wrapped his arms around me, offering the security of his body. "What is it, my queen?"

I could still taste blood and dirt in my mouth, and there was dirt under my nails. Like I'd clawed my way out of the grave.

"I need to go."

Nevarre rolled toward the edge of the bed and grabbed my phone off the nightstand. "I'll let Gina know. Do you need the jet?"

I hesitated, letting the dream flow through me. I needed to go, soon, but it wasn't leave in the middle of the night urgent. Yet. "No. At least not yet. What time is it?"

"It's just after 6 AM."

"Let's gather in the salon again, though I don't need Gwen to come back. Oh, text Magnum my apologies that we're up so early. I hate descending on the kitchen like a pack of ravenous wolves."

Nevarre's fingers flew over the screen. "More like ravenous lions and dragons and bears, my queen. But evidently Winston warned her and there's plenty of fresh beef and mutton on hand. I heard Mehen and Ezra talking about a BBQ in the garden space."

Something about his words pinged in my head. "Garden space?"

He looked up from the phone. "I haven't seen it myself. Do you think there's a tree here you can make use of for traveling?"

"It's possible. My mother certainly seemed to have thought of everything. Let's go take a look but ask Magnum to join us if she has time. I still need that tour."

Daire sauntered in looking like the cat who'd swallowed the canary when no one was looking, with an armful of clothes. "I brought you a few things to choose from, my queen."

Outwardly, Nevarre didn't react or say anything, though I felt the surge of irritation in his bond. He usually picked my clothes, allowing his goddess, Morrigan, to influence his selection. Evidently, the Phantom Queen and Goddess of War had impeccable taste and matched my style perfectly, because I was never disappointed in what he selected.

Though Nevarre was also far more mature than my younger warcat. He wasn't blind to the power shifts between the feline Blood, and he was secure enough in himself to allow Daire some grace.

The clothes he'd brought were safe choices for comfort and lying around the house. Which would be fine until I had a plan of attack outlined. Though I had to roll my eyes at the *Twilight* hoodie as I pulled it on. That definitely wasn't something I'd ever pick out for myself.

"Nevarre, be thinking about a wardrobe for a Triune appearance on a beach or near water."

"Hmmm. I believe this week is what humans would call Spring Break." With a careless, effortless toss of his head, he slung his long silky hair back over his shoulder. "I had a vision of you recently that involved water."

"Really? When?"

"When you were healing Thierry."

"Sounds like a plan." Keeping my touch light, I reached for Lew's bond, trying to unobtrusively sense where he was. If he was still in the room with Esetta, I wanted to give them as much time as possible.

He was on the roof, shifted to his gryphon. Watching the sunrise with his friend sitting beside him. Thierry's head was on his chest, Lew's wing wrapped around him.

:*Let them stay on guard on the roof,*: I said to Rik in the bond.

:*Already done, my queen.*:

I gave him a lingering kiss, leaning into his chest. His arms locked around me, one big palm sliding up beneath the hoodie to stroke my back. :*I don't know how it will play out yet but this is it. The battle I've been waiting for. The Dauphine will be at the end of this trip.*:

:*We're ready, my queen.*:

I pierced my wrist, drawing my blood to release enough of my power to corral my hair into the silver net that hung down my back and supported the load. Daire's bottom lip doubled in size but he didn't say a word out loud. "I know you and Nevarre were planning on helping with my hair, but I don't have time to enjoy it this morning."

"Gina's up and headed downstairs now," Nevarre said. "Magnum awaits you in the hallway."

Rik gave a nod to the door and Daire padded over to open it for us, but I didn't immediately follow. Not until I checked Xin's location.

:I have his scent.: The wolf ran flat out, tongue lolling but he didn't feel tired. *:I didn't want to wake you.:*

Chills raced down my arms. *Everything's coming together at the same time.*

:How close are you?:

His bond rolled over me, letting me see and smell through his wolf. We ran down a hill with flatter ground ahead, dotted with trees and pockets of green water. Crickets, buzzing flies, croaking frogs, long-legged birds on the hunt for dinner, softly calling out to each other. The ground felt soft and springy like a sponge beneath his pads, thick and heavy with moisture. The odors of rotting vegetation, mud, and slow-moving water were thick in his nose— but not strong enough to mask the taint of Thierry's footsteps. I could almost see the darkened, dead spots of decay that he'd left behind as he staggered out of the sucking mud.

Xin tipped his nose to the sky and breathed deeply, sorting through all the various scents to identify the sea salt not far away. Maybe two or three hours for his wolf. *:I should find the source soon or run into the gulf.:*

I fisted my fingers in his ruff and breathed in his ear. *:I can't lose you, Xin.:*

Without pausing his run, he snarled in the bond. *:Let her try to take me from you, my queen, and she'll feel my teeth in her throat.:*

:Touch my bond as soon as you find anything. We'll be moving closer to Houston today.:

His wolf's ears pinned back, his teeth bared. *:That's only a few hours away from here.:*

Not a coincidence. Though I wasn't sure what the Dauphine had in common with Skolos. *:Be very wary of any alarm that might notify her we're on her trail.:*

:Understood, my queen.:

I stepped out into the hallway and Magnum curtsied again. Today she wore an all-black suit with her usual chignon and light makeup. Stylish, elegant, and all business, even shortly after dawn. I wasn't sure how she or Gina managed to always be so put together, day or night.

"Good morning, Your Majesty. I thought I could show you a few things upstairs before you go down to eat, though if you're hungry, the tour can wait until a more convenient time."

"No, this is perfect. Thank you, Magnum."

She led me back down the short hallway to the marbled landing. Floor-to-ceiling windows looked out over Central Park with Isador Tower dominating the view. Both stairs and an elevator provided access above and below. Another hallway led to the opposite end of the house.

"We always called this hallway the gallery." Pausing, she gestured to the nearest door but didn't open it. "Queen Carys claimed this room, and the room opposite is Gina's suite. There are larger suites at the opposite end for queens with Blood."

I didn't really care about the rooms themselves—but the artwork in between each bedroom door caught my attention. Various sized oil paintings hung down the hallway, each in heavy ornate black and gold frames. The first one was of a massive white stone house with a faded green slate roof, tall chimneys, and a pair of imposing towers framing the front entrance. It had to be at least ten thousand square feet. "Did my mother paint these?"

"That particular painting was completed by Queen Selena of Isador Hall in London."

This vampire fortune bullshit never ceased to amaze me. "It's a literal palace."

Magnum's lips quirked. "Not quite but you can see Buckingham Palace from the garden, and it's in one of the most prestigious and exclusive areas of London."

"And we live there? I mean, my family?"

"Queen Selena held court in London at that very house until she ended her rule and gave up her power. Her... there was another..." Her face tightened with frustration. "I can't remember the details."

"I understand. I'll ask Lew when he's free later." I moved down to the next painting and my heart clenched so fiercely I couldn't entirely hold back a gasp of pain.

Mom—and my mother, her sister. Two beautiful queens dressed in formal gowns. Mom in her favorite color, lapis lazuli, her eyes shining like magnificent sapphires. Esetta wore blood red, so deeply saturated it was almost black in the shadows. They both wore crowns, Esetta the horned one with the red disk, and Mom's had sweeping wings that hung down on either side of her head, framing her face. Heavy jewels on their ears, around their necks, and on every finger of their hands. Esetta lounged on an antique velvet chaise, and Mom stood behind her.

I recognized her—but she was also a complete stranger. This woman had raised me, changed my diapers, held me when I cried, and taught me how to read. We'd lived a simple, quiet, isolated life in Kansas City. Granted, the house had been nice, but not a palace, and we'd lived in obscurity. She must have been accustomed to a life of servants and imminently gifted and talented "get-it-done" people like Gina and Magnum her entire life. Blood who'd worshiped the ground she walked on. But I'd never seen that side of her life.

I vaguely remembered sitting on the porch steps in the summer, while she and Dad sat in the porch swing. Drinking sweet iced tea or enjoying some ice cream. But that all ended when Dad was killed by the monsters after he took me to the park.

We hardly ever went outside after that, certainly not after dark. I went to school until she decided to keep me home. No family vacations. No sleepovers. No one ever came over. It was just me and her until the monsters got her too.

It didn't dawn on me it wasn't normal to never see any other living person except Mom. We didn't have neighbors to come check on us. Surely Gina must have been stopping by when I was gone, or at least driving by to see if we needed anything, but I'd had no clue this life existed.

"Sister queens," Magnum whispered. "I knew them both, I'm sure, but I can't remember her name. Only Queen Selena's. Though I traveled with her sister back and forth to London quite often."

Even seated, Esetta radiated a quiet, magnetic power, her eyes like sparkling black holes that would pull you under and never let you go. A soft, small smile curved her lips, a smile that said she knew all your secrets—and fully intended to use them against you when it suited her.

Mom—Selena—smiled but it didn't carry the same power or emotion. There was faint tension around her eyes, a tightness in her jaw, that told a different story. The first time I'd gone to Isis' pyramid, Mom said she'd hated being a queen. Having to manage her Blood and power hadn't been enjoyable for her at all. She'd given up all her power for my human father who'd helped her raise me. The first time she'd been truly happy.

Until she took me in. And the monsters started to hunt us. Killing them both.

Selena didn't play the game of queens.

While Esetta reveled in it.

:I did revel in the game,: Esetta admitted in my mind, though I didn't see her. *:But don't be fooled by my sister's role. She played a different game, but it was still very much a part of mine, and ultimately, our goddess' plans for our House.:*

We walked down the hall to the next picture. This one made me smile though tears filled my eyes. Esetta still lounged on the chaise, but Lew stood behind her, his hands gripping the wooden back, his sleeves rolled up to bare the veins and tendons in his forearms. A bite dripped blood down his wrist.

Golden-haired, blue-eyed Thierry knelt beside her. Shirtless. His head tipped back in invitation, leaning toward her. Offering himself to her.

A tiny drop of blood glistened on her lip, so real it looked fresh and wet still on her mouth.

"How many Blood did she have? Do you remember?"

"House Isador had ten Blood," Magnum replied.

My eyes flared and I pulled my gaze away from the painting to look at her face. "They shared their Blood?"

She inclined her head to the opposite wall, leading me over to a similar picture with Queen Selena. A man stood behind her, mirroring Lew's pose. A man I recognized as the man who'd killed her and hunted me mercilessly. Greyson. The same long, silver hair and courtly old-fashioned clothing.

"Queen Selena and her alpha, Lord Harrington Greyson."

I could only laugh and shake my head. "I was just thinking he looked like some kind of lord."

"His family held the earldom of Irgeli. He was hers alone, but the rest of the Isador Blood flowed between the two queens. Primarily... the sister. But the Blood shifted back and forth between them regularly."

Lew said he'd been with both of them. I hadn't known they'd shared the rest of the Blood too. Except Greyson. Maybe that was why he'd come after her for so long. He'd been unable to leave her side.

:The Blood hierarchy is determined by the alpha's relationship with his queen,: Lew said in the bond. *:Because I was mated to House Isador, the rest of the Blood were similarly shared unless the queen wished otherwise.:*

So Mom had wanted Greyson to herself.

I turned as Lew and Thierry joined us, searching my Blood's eyes. Afraid to see any recrimination for what I'd done to him but also desperate to know. If he had regrets—

:Never.: He took my hand and bowed low, kissing the back of my knuckles as formally as Lord Greyson would have done in the palace hundreds of years ago. *:Thank you for being queen enough to give me my heart's desire, while allowing me to still serve you and your mighty house with all the love in this gryphon's heart.:*

41

XIN

Crouched on a large fallen tree slowly disintegrating into thick stagnant water, I whispered in Shara's bond. :*I'm here, my queen.*:

Immediately, she filled me so strongly I could smell the delicate perfume of her skin as if she'd pressed her throat to my muzzle.

Our bond, so deep. So well fed by her blood. She saw through my eyes. A gray-green hump of earth rising out of the surrounding swamp. The stand of cypress trees, branches heavy with Spanish moss. Huge trunks cracked open at the base where they met the ground. Many more stumps rotted and busted open. No structure or house to mark it as a nest or any different from hundreds of other scattered mounds through the miles of swampland.

Only the tingle of a queen's blood circle, prickling my ruff around my neck. A line of fur rising down my spine in silent warning.

She smelled thick, clinging mud and brackish water through my nose. Heard the absolute dead silence in the middle of swamp in broad daylight on a beautiful spring day, where thousands of insects and frogs and birds should be singing their songs of life.

I might have killed dozens of queens for House Wu Tien but never had my queen walked in my body like Shara fucking Isador.

With her focused on our bond, I crept forward along the downed trunk, letting her feel the buzzing blood circle inches away. My gift saw the gleam of red energy pulsing up out of the water with the queen's power. A frequency unique to her, just as Shara's blood circle could only be laid by her. Rich with her unique powers and bloodline from her goddess.

Deep inside my chest, I let out a soundless howl of energy. My fur rose on end, rippling with the waves shifting around me. My bones resonated with each pulse. Higher, changing the frequency closer to the blood circle's. Shifting my own aura to match the enemy queen's energy. Red flickered darker, almost blue. Flashed to searing white. Then gray. Dissipating into nothing.

:*We're invisible to the queen's power now.*: I touched my nose to where the circle of energy still lay, breathing in the queen's scent. Trying to, at least. I knew blood had been spilled, but it was absent of any distinguishing scent. Another factor of how the Dauphine was able to hide so well.

:*Wait,*: Shara whispered in my mind. :*Let me search for any other geas on the circle.*:

I smelled my queen's blood in the bond, even though she was hundreds of miles away. She swelled inside me, her power bulging through my wolf. Her eyes took over, looking through her power at the strange nest. Looking for any pockets of darkness or shadow along the boundary. The Skye geas had looked like a spider to her, but she sensed nothing else on the perimeter. It was incredibly small for a nest. Smaller than a football field.

Her power receded in the bond, and the wolf whimpered at the loss.

:Carefully, Xin.:

:Always, my queen.:

I crept across the blood circle, paws placed carefully without a single splash, nose and tail low, breathing in all the scents. Thierry's footprints sank into the sediment below the brackish water, every step a tainted mark. Leading me to one of the broken cypress trees. The trunk was larger than I could put my arms around, flaring down at the bottom even wider into a wedge of roots. A dark hole gaped in the base. Cracked and splintered wood. Rotted. Torn. Shredded apart as he'd fought his way out. Black sludge oozed out of the trunk onto the ground. Almost like crude oil but thicker and smelling of the same foul rot as Thierry.

Her bond ached with pain, a cutting sharpness like a honed edge, her fury at what her mother's Blood had suffered. *:I wonder how long she kept him trapped in that dark hole.:*

:No way to know for sure, though I don't smell any other scents coming and going from the circle.: Which meant I couldn't track my queen's target back to her den. *:I'd guess years.:*

Just as carefully, I silently glided to the nearest intact tree. Ears flickering back and forth, straining for any sound. Nose wide open. More of the black taint oozed from the tree trunk but it wasn't torn open. Roots split apart, leaving thin cracks like prison bars, covered in some kind of thin membrane.

:Skin?:

I didn't dare touch it. *:It doesn't smell like anything that has been alive. Just the same rotted taint of death.:*

:Another thrall, maybe? Or something else? Fuck. I wish—:

The membrane bulged slightly. Movement inside, deep in the trunk. *:Whatever it is, it's alive.:* Well. As alive as Thierry—a shuffling zombie thrall.

:*Goddess,*: she breathed shakily. :*Check how many more are like this and then get the fuck out.*:

:*At once, my queen.*:

It only took a few moments for me to investigate the remaining trees. :*Three others, my queen.*:

:*We'll have to come back later and make sure those things are dead once I take care of the Dauphine.*:

I slipped out of the blood circle and stood on the same fallen tree as before. Shaking my fur out, trying to clear the stench of taint clinging to me, I waited for her next order. She sat at a table with Gina and Carys, Guillaume and Sekh at hand. Rik, of course. Llewellyn and Thierry. Nevarre too. Not surprising given his heritage.

Who better to help plan battle strategy than the Goddess of War?

:*I'm headed here shortly.*: She showed me a three-dimensional map in her head that flowed to the west, dropping a mental pin on the southern coast of Texas. :*Can you meet me there, or are you too weary after traveling so far?*:

Already running, I sent her a yip of excitement. :*Your wolf is tireless, especially on a hunt.*:

:*I had a dream,*: she whispered, her voice soft with reverence. :*I don't know how Skolos connects to the Dauphine, but our paths will cross there.*:

A full Skolos Triune... and the Dauphine?

I ran harder, my teeth bared. :*Then this wolf flies to you, my queen.*:

~

SHARA

I UPDATED EVERYONE ON WHAT XIN HAD FOUND.

Stiff as a board but shaking, Thierry stood beside Lew near the door. He croaked out several syllables, but I couldn't understand him. Even if he knew who those other trapped souls were, he couldn't tell us.

Black streamed from his eyes, nose, ears, and mouth. I shifted my focus to all the blood I'd poured into him, trying to measure how much of my power remained against the black rot spreading through him. Not much. Enough to keep him upright and moving through the day. At most.

So much pain. Razor blades sliced through him in a constant war as my blood tried to keep him alive. It would have been so much kinder to let him die. To give him eternal peace with my mother.

Though then he wouldn't have had one last time with his two loves at his side.

If I could have Rik and any other of my Blood one last time, I'd endure endless pain too.

I touched Tlacel's bond, standing guard at the door with his brother. :*Could you find Magnum and send her to me, please?*:

:*She's here, my queen.*:

The door immediately opened, and she strode to the table. "Yes, Your Majesty?"

"I'd like you to be a part of this conversation. And Okeanos…" I touched his bond and found him already coming down the hall as if he'd sensed I would need him.

He came to stand between Lew and Nevarre. His skin glistened with droplets of moisture, and his T-shirt clung to his chest.

Relieved, I smiled. "You found water."

"I was going to use a bathtub, but Magnum told me about the pool house in the garden. It's… a very special pool, my queen."

Ah. My smile deepened. "I guess we know how we're getting

to the coast now. Do we have a map pinpointing where the queens are located?"

Gina smiled. "Kevin, why don't you show what we know?"

"Sure thing." He leaped to his feet and moved over to a small wall panel. He hit a few buttons and a large screen descended from the ceiling. "This is a map of the Texas coast. House Gorgos opened their house here on Tiki Island, and House Kijin's mansion is all the way down here on Galveston Island. These are both highly populated areas, especially this month. Galveston is a popular spring break spot, and the beaches are packed."

"Exactly," I said, shaking my head. "So why now? Why that location?"

"Our best guess is Skolos would like to propose some kind of alliance with you," Gina replied. "That's why they chose to be close—without antagonizing you by opening their New York houses, for example. Plus they need to stay close to water for House Ketea. The only other place they could have chosen would be Florida, since both houses also have property in Miami, but they'd have even more college kids and tourists to deal with. House Gorgos doesn't have any property on the west coast."

"Do we have a house in Galveston?"

"We do." Gina tapped the tablet screen, dropping a pin on the Galveston Island beach further down the coast. "Staff opened the house yesterday, quietly of course. But it's ready if you'd like to use it during our visit."

"I guess I'm still hung up on why they haven't met yet. What are they waiting for? Not for me to show up, surely. Or they would have sent an invitation."

"It's no small thing for all three Triune queens to come together," Gina replied. "I think Undina is pushing them to come to the table, but one if not both of the other queens are reluctant. But they also don't want to anger her by refusing outright since she's the most powerful queen on Skolos currently."

I turned to Okeanos. "Can you estimate where she is on the map?"

He closed his eyes, dropping his head to his chest. I didn't hear any sounds with my ears, but the water rippled in the cups on the table. "My best guess is somewhere out in the gulf itself. She's not by the land or islands."

"If I may make a suggestion?" Sekh asked.

I nodded. "Please."

"I haven't Seen a meeting of three queens not already connected by blood in centuries, Your Majesty. Granted, three or more queens would likely try to obscure their meeting, but queens haven't openly met since Triskeles was eliminated. They want to meet but they're afraid. Not only of each other, but they're also afraid of you."

"I met Undina. Her son is my Blood. What does she have to fear from me?"

"You have me," Guillaume said softly. "And they know what happened to the last Triune who met me in person. Plus, I'm sure the queen of Rome hasn't made it easy on them. Their Triune is complete. Hers isn't. That implies their table is more powerful, and that's never a good thing to threaten another queen with. Let alone her."

"So how do I get them to meet without scaring the shit out of them?"

"We could go through formal channels and request an audience," Gina said. "I can contact House Ketea's consiliarius first, or all three of them."

"I think that would scare them off even more. That says I know you're meeting behind my back, and I want to nip it in the bud."

"True," Carys said. "I only see a forty-percent likelihood of a successful meeting with Undina if you reach out to her through formal channels. It drops to under ten percent if you contact all three."

"So I need something unexpected. Would it freak them out if I just showed up at our beach house? But how would they even know I'm there?"

"Carys is the numbers woman, but I think it's unlikely any other House has the same network of affiliated offices like we do, gathering information on all the other queens. That was something your..." Gina blinked, as if she'd completely lost her train of thought.

The network of Talbott offices was something Esetta had done.

"So opening up the house wouldn't be enough," I said. "I need to make an appearance, but nothing formal."

"If the beaches are full of partying college kids, it'll be a zoo," Rik added. "So it can't be vampire shit or you're going to draw unwanted attention."

"Why can't it be vampire shit?" Guillaume asked. "Within reason, at least."

"Do you have something in mind?"

His eyes sparkled with wicked amusement in a way I hadn't seen since he'd told me about what he'd done to Triskeles. "Maybe you should go for a ride on the beach."

My eyebrows rose. "Your hell horse? On the beach? With hundreds—"

"Of thousands," Sekh interjected. "At least two-hundred-thousand humans coming and going throughout the week."

Guillaume shrugged though his lips twitched. "I can't think of anything more spectacular than a galloping warhorse on the beach with a beautiful woman on his back. It'd make the news for sure."

Rik grunted and shook his head. "The rest of us can't get away with that shit, and I don't want her unprotected."

Guillaume barely moved his shoulder, but a knife glinted in

his hand. He casually used the tip of the blade to clean under his fingernails. "She'd be far from unprotected, alpha. In fact, I'd argue the Skolos queens will fear me more than all her other Blood combined. No offense, general. They're not going to know who you are."

"But I don't want to scare them."

"Within reason, you do want them scared. Just not enough to refuse to see you. They need to respect you as the mighty queen you are, and how better could you remind them than openly using the former Triune Executioner as your personal mount?"

"So I just ride up and down the coast a few times and hope they call?"

"Twenty percent," Carys said.

"I can swim," Guillaume said. "And Undina is out in the gulf somewhere. If Okeanos can guide the way, I'll swim you to her. Plus Nevarre and Itztli are relatively normal looking animals, just bigger. They can come along with us. Probably not the bear, though."

Ezra growled in the bond. *:Fuck no. I ain't swimming into the fucking gulf.:*

Sekh laughed. "Put the winged Blood up in the air and fly them out. The rest of us can ride a boat alongside the kraken. Get the attention on you, and then ride off into the waves. That'll definitely cause a stir."

"Ninety-eight percent on making the news." Carys laughed, shaking her head. "Especially if the humans think you're cosplaying or filming a movie."

"And if we get to Undina, what's the probability the other two Skolos queens will agree to come to the table?" I asked.

Carys' head tipped to the side. "Sixty-six percent."

"Two against one again." I blew out a sigh. "And one of those queens wants me dead. Any other ideas we can run by Carys?"

"I hate this plan," Rik said, his voice rumbling with the

weight of an avalanche. "But I agree it's better than sitting around waiting."

"I'd feel better if Xin could also reach us in time." I checked his bond, but he was still hours away from the other queens. "Is there a pool at the Galveston house?"

Typing rapidly on the tablet, Gina raised her head. "Yes."

"Can you show me a picture of what it looks like?"

"Of course. Let's see…" She flipped through several albums on the tablet and then loaded a picture onto the larger screen. "It's not a large pool by any means."

The picture showed a round pool with crystalline blue waters set inside a curved wooden deck. A ring of dark red tiles lined the pool, with an arc of steps in the same tile swirling across one third of the pool. Almost like a yin-yang symbol— only in blue water and red tile.

I touched Xin's bond. *:Head to the coast. When I pass through the portal to Galveston, I'm going to try and pull you through to me.:*

He immediately turned toward the coast, his muzzle tipped up in a howl of pure joy of being reunited with me quicker. No questions. No doubt in my ability to accomplish such a feat.

"Nevarre, how long do you need to get me ready for presentation to Skolos?"

"An hour should be plenty of time, my queen."

Given all this hair, an hour didn't seem like much time but I didn't question him. "Anyone who wants to come to Galveston with House Isador—and doesn't mind going for a swim to get there—meet me at the pool house in an hour."

"Anyone?" Magnum asked.

"Yes. You're welcome to come with us."

She curtsied and rushed to the door. "By your leave, I need to make some arrangements first, but yes. I'd love to accompany you, Your Majesty, so I can personally ensure the Galveston staff is up to your expectations."

"We're going to need a boat," I said.

Gina flipped another picture up to the screen of a gleaming white and red yacht. "Already ordered, my queen."

"Ours? Or a rental?"

She rolled her eyes and zoomed in on the picture to show the name of the boat emblazoned on the stern. *Bloodsport* in a silver raised cursive script, with *House Isador* underneath in a simple black font.

"Do I even want to know how many boats we have?"

Her lips quirked. "That depends on how many major coastal cities you can name, my queen."

42

SHARA

I stared at myself in the full-length mirror and blushed beet red. "Are you sure about this?"

While technically the most pertinent parts of my body were covered, the gown left very little to the imagination since it was made in a light see-through white lace. The halter neckline left my back completely bare except for a tiny bikini string. Not that anyone would be able to tell with my unbound hair flowing around me like a full-length cape. It honestly looked more like a swimsuit coverup than a formal court gown, though it did a horrible job of covering anything.

"Absolutely." Nevarre adjusted the crown deeper into the cascade of my hair, using two narrow braids and pins to help secure it. "The Morrigan loves you in white."

I couldn't help but mutter, "I'm going to be the same as naked."

His lips quirked. "You've got a bikini underneath."

"More like a string and a couple of postage stamps. G's going to be one happy stallion."

:*I'm always happy, my queen. Especially when I can feel your bare pussy on my back.*:

Daire came in with the jewelry I'd inherited from Desideria.
As soon as he saw I was already dressed, he pouted. "Can I at
least help braid your hair?"

"The vision I had in my mind was her hair flowing wild and
free like the river," Nevarre said. "Chaos. Not trapped and tidy."

"For once, I actually like leaving it loose like this. It'll help
cover me up a little." I met his gaze in the mirror. "Would you
mind giving us a few minutes, Nevarre?"

"Of course, my queen." He inclined his head and then turned
to the door, giving his hips a hard enough jerk his kilt fluttered
around his thighs. Enough for me to see that he wasn't wearing
anything underneath.

"You did that on purpose," Daire growled.

Nevarre laughed softly as he shut the door behind him.
"Most definitely."

I turned away from the mirror and stepped closer to Rik. He
sat in a massive armchair, plenty big enough for him though not
as big as the one we used at home. Rather than sitting in front of
him, I climbed onto his lap and draped my arm over his shoulders. Snuggling up against his chest, I breathed deeply, letting
my rising hunger roll through our bonds.

"I'm glad you're here, Daire. I could use a little help."

Daire dropped down to his knees between Rik's legs, though
he didn't purr.

Which told me more than anything exactly how upset my
warcat was.

I slid my other arm around his neck and tugged him closer.
"Rik's big enough for us both."

"That I am, my queen." Rik spread his thighs wider, easily
taking on more of the other man's weight onto his lap, though
Daire didn't come up on top of him all the way. "As long as the
chair holds."

"It will." *I think.* "And I'm queen enough to let you love each
other too."

"My queen." A small, pained gasp escaped Daire's throat and he buried his face against my chest. "I'm so sorry."

I pressed gentle kisses against the top of his head, hugging him. "Don't be sorry. I love being the kind of queen who can look at her Blood and see that they love each other, too."

"But if I had to choose—"

"I'm not asking you to choose," I broke in quickly. "I've never asked you to love me more than you love Rik."

Daire tipped his head back enough to let me see the agony raging in his shimmering eyes. "The general's right, though. If you ever needed me to do something against Rik, I couldn't."

I kept my tone gentle, rubbing my thumb back and forth over his bottom lip. "Am I the kind of queen who'd ever force one of my Blood to hurt anyone? Especially another one of my loves against their will?"

"No, but—"

"Exactly," I broke in, though I kept my voice soft. "Sekh is All Seeing but he's not All Knowing, or he'd know I'm only here because the goddess chose you and Rik to come to me first. I needed to see the way you two loved each other to know it was possible for me to love the same way. I didn't know anything about any of this. Let alone how to love another Aima. You showed me how from the very first moment you found me."

"But if something happens to Rik—"

I pressed my forehead to his. "Then I'm dead too. So I swore to the Mother of the Gods. Rik's my alpha and always will be. Your love is safe with me, Daire. Always. As safe as we both are with Rik."

My alpha pulled Daire up all the way onto his lap, playfully jostling us both against him so we'd be sure to feel how much he enjoyed having us on top of him. "See? I'm big enough to hold you both."

"That's why I need your help, Daire. I need you to bite him

for me, so he doesn't have to change his clothes before we head to Texas."

Of course I could pierce any of my Blood with my nails. Or I could have simply asked Rik to tear his wrist open himself. But Daire had bitten Rik for me when I didn't have fangs. When I'd needed them to show me how to feed.

They'd taken care of me—even when my own pride kept me from asking for any help at all.

The rumbling purr rolled from his chest, and he blinked his naughty, seductive kitty cat eyes that had endeared me to him from the beginning. "Do you think Rik's big enough to feed us both, my queen?"

"I don't know. I guess he'll have to show us."

Rumbling louder, Daire leaned up to drag his tongue up the long column of Rik's throat. Tormenting him, pretending like he couldn't find the big vein pumping just beneath the surface of his skin. Then the other side of his throat by me. Licking and nibbling until Rik shifted beneath us.

A groan of hunger escaped my lips, and Daire immediately sank his fangs into Rik's throat. Lips locked around his punctures, he drank deeply, his throat working. His tawny hair tickled my face as I pressed closer, sliding up beside him. Licking his mouth, coaxing some of Rik's blood onto my tongue.

The jolt of alpha blood made me shudder against them. My fingers tangled in Daire's hair. Dug into Rik's arm, my nails sliding through the long-sleeved white dress shirt he wore to puncture his skin. Giving me even more of his sizzling hot blood. I could taste the burn of his lust in every drop. His urge to jerk his fly open and take Daire right here in the chair while I watched, inches away. Stroking them both.

:Yes,: I growled in the bond.

:You said an hour,: Rik replied. :We don't have time.:

:There's always time for me to watch you fuck.:

Daire lifted his head, letting blood spill down Rik's throat and into my mouth. "Please, alpha. Please fuck me."

Rik fisted one beefy hand around Daire's scruff and lifted him up, letting him dangle in his grip. "Only if our queen's willing to open your pants with her teeth."

~

DAIRE

I WANTED TO CRY AND PURR AND SCREAM AND BEG AND COME SO fucking hard I blacked out. Then cry some more.

My fucking queen. Nuzzling my crotch. Snagging material in her brutal, beautiful teeth and ripping my fucking pants open. Licking my dick while she playfully worked it free.

I couldn't. Begin to thank her. Show her. How much she meant to me. To all of us. So fucking grateful.

She'd let me serve even with all my failings. She'd let me love her alpha, even though that took his attention, blood, and dick away from her.

She was willing to make everyone wait on us.

So I could have this. My alpha. My queen. Together. One more time.

Rising on Rik's other knee, she offered him her throat. No Blood would ever say no to his queen's blood. Even to fuck another Blood. But she didn't allow him to feed very long. A few swallows and then she pulled away.

Dropped to the floor between us. So she could rub her bleeding throat on Rik's dick.

He sucked in a harsh breath, his eyes blazing with lust. Every drop of her blood sizzled on his swollen cock. Fiery flames that he shoved into me. His dick felt like a red-hot sword fresh off his forge. Slicing deep.

Scrambling back up onto Rik's other thigh, she wrapped her

arms around us both and locked her mouth to my original bite. Rik jerked my head back in a hard arc, straining my neck. Pulling me down harder on him, grinding into me. So good. Too good. It'd been ages since he'd fucked me, and I was going to come embarrassingly fast.

Rik tore open my throat in a mean, deep bite that sent a spasm tearing down my spine. His big hand twisted harder in my hair, bringing tears to my eyes. His lips hot coals on my throat, drinking me down. While our queen squeezed my dick and fed on him.

Shuddering, I came so hard I blacked out for a moment. My heart stuttered, my entire body quaking. The scent of blood and cum thick in the air. My queen eagerly lapped the fresh blood on my throat. Then Rik's. Pleased little hungry sounds of enjoyment rolling from her throat. Driving him to hammer me harder. Grunting with each thrust, his big body flexing like one giant muscle bent on crushing me into dust.

He growled deep in his throat and unloaded in me. Still holding us both while our queen continued feeding on us.

But she didn't climax. Rik didn't really even touch her, other than cradling her on his lap.

All this explosive pleasure had been for me—and him—alone.

She held me while I cried and laughed and licked blood from them both.

"We need to get going." She gave my hair a playful tug. "Help me with that foul jewelry so we can head downstairs."

I'd dropped the gold pieces on the bed earlier. My knees still felt rubbery as I got up, and my ass ached in the best way possible. I hadn't taken dick in a while, let alone a man of Rik's size. I'd relish that ache as long as it lasted.

I kissed each of her wrists and then wrapped the bracelets into place. It was freaky watching them disappear against her skin. Rik licked her throat, making sure the bite had closed over. "There's some droplets on your gown, my queen."

"Good."

She shuddered as the gold closed around her neck, and it had nothing to do with the temperature of the metal.

I dropped to my knees and reached under the light lacy skirt to wrap the belt around her waist. Leaning against her, I lightly rubbed my chin against the gold and stared up at her. My lips trembled, my eyes burning with emotion. "Thank you, my queen."

Cupping my cheek, she bent down and kissed me. "Always purr for me, Daire. I need your comforting cuddles more every single day."

43

SHARA

Once the guys got changed—though I had to insist Daire change his pants so his dick didn't fall out at an inopportune time—we headed outside to the garden in the back of the house. It wasn't even noon yet, though it felt like I'd been up for days. The downside to getting up at the crack of dawn for once.

On one side of the garden, a tall stone wall separated us from the neighboring property. The other side was a shorter wing of the main house with a massive garage. The center courtyard was paved in beautiful Moroccan tiles with cushioned chaises and benches around a built-in fire pit. While there were several ornamental trees and shrubs, there weren't any trees large enough to act as a portal connection to my heart tree back home.

The pool house was a low, nondescript building near the rear entrance to the property. Frank stood talking to a pair of guards at the gate, but as soon as he saw us, he joined the rest of the humans and Carys waiting at the door.

Gina curtseyed again, her eyes sparkling. "Oh, Shara, you look fabulous. Nevarre did an amazing job."

"It's not too… risqué?"

Magnum took my hand and bowed low, kissing my knuckles. "Not at all, Your Majesty. Not for a queen of your stature."

Though it still made me blush to walk around in basically nothing, especially with Kevin, Frank, and the other guards watching. Luckily my hair was already doing its chaos thing. Long tendrils hung over my shoulders, covering up my barely concealed nipples.

Everyone planning to go on the boat had dressed in black and white formal wear. Even Carys had exchanged her normal tweed for a spiffy black suit coat with a black leather shoulder pad buckled around her upper body for Winnifred. Nevarre still had on his kilt but nothing else. Itztli, Okeanos, Vivian, Mehen, and Tlacel wore comfortable throwaway sweats and T-shirts they wouldn't mind leaving behind once they shifted.

Guillaume wore a pair of black basketball shorts down to his knees and nothing else. Though he carried a duffel bag and had the Templar sword sheath swung over his shoulder.

I could only stare. Other than in my bed, Guillaume always wore jeans and long-sleeved shirts unless we had to dress up. I'd always assumed that was his preferred clothing because it was easier for him to hide all his blades. I'd certainly never seen him in shorts with his chest bare.

All my Blood had impressive physiques in different ways. Drinking in the way his broad shoulders tapered down to his waist, wrapped in the muscle of a knight who swung a heavy sword for hours, I was reminded of his countless battles. The torture he'd endured. The many times he'd been killed only to rise again. His body was crisscrossed with scars and punctures. Every single one a testament to his warrior honor.

My headless knight, the Dullahan. With an ugly foot-long scar on his chest, where they'd taken out his heart. A thick, jagged scar looped around his neck, where they'd taken his head.

Where I'd taken his head in Heliopolis.

"I guess I'm going to have to wear shorts more often," he drawled. "Especially if you're going to look at me like that."

The sound of ripping material made me jump, dragging my gaze away from Guillaume's chest.

Mehen lopped off the other leg of his sweats and strutted closer in the shredded remnants barely covering his ass cheeks. I couldn't help but laugh, even though he planted his hands on his hips and shot me a murderous glare.

"That's not the reaction I was hoping for."

Ignoring his ire, I stepped closer and leaned against him, playfully batting my eyes up at him. "My, what tiny little shorts you're wearing, my dragon."

"The better for you to fucking eat me up, my queen."

I dragged my nails down the long, bulging muscle of his thigh, not hard enough to feed but enough to make his eyes flare with heat. "When we get home, absolutely."

"I'm holding you to that fucking promise."

I pulled back and looked at each person, letting them see my pride. My love. "Whatever happens, I love you all."

"What happens is Shara fucking Isador kicks their mother-fucking asses," Mehen growled.

"We have to get there first."

Okeanos pulled the door open for me. "I tasted the Deep Blue, my queen, even without your blood unlocking the way."

Inside, the pool house looked more like a sumptuous Roman bathhouse than a casual outbuilding. The walls were the same sandstone finish as the salon, and the floor was paved in the same Moroccan tiles as the patio. Above, the ceiling was painted deep blue darkening to indigo with the first stars gleaming in a night sky. With lapis lazuli tiles surrounding the pool, the water resembled a secret oasis.

"Wow," I breathed out. "This is absolutely gorgeous."

"The throne room is even more impressive," Magnum said.

"We ran out of time today, but I still have several areas of the house to show you, Your Majesty."

"I look forward to returning quickly." I stepped close enough to the pool that the hem of my gown dipped into the water. Lifting my hands, I went to pierce my wrist in my usual spot, but my nail tinged on the gold bracelet. Damn it. I poked the meaty part of my left palm instead and held my hand out over the water.

Closing my eyes, I envisioned the round red and blue pool in Galveston. Waters parting easily, allowing us to pass through without even getting wet. The warm breeze off the gulf. The taste of salt in the air.

Gina gasped softly, and Magnum whispered, "Blessed be."

I opened my eyes. The pool before me remained the same, but at the bottom step, it was like a window appeared to the other round pool's steps.

"Winged Blood not staying with our queen, go first," Rik ordered. "Get airborne and as high as possible to avoid notice."

Mehen leaped into the water, diving beneath the surface without even taking a step. Green scales boiled out of him, and Leviathan shot up out of the pool on the other side, immediately surging into the sky. Vivian and Tlacel went next, steam and water splashing in their wake.

"Daire, Lew, Thierry, Ezra, Sekh you're next. Secure the perimeter."

My throat ached at the sight of Lew gripping Thierry's arm, steadying him on the steps. He didn't have long before I'd have to either drain and heal him again—or put him to rest. Hopefully we'd have some resolution soon. He, of all people, deserved to see the Dauphine brought to justice.

Though thinking about her made tingles burn down my spine. She was still the unknown piece on the board. I could only hope she'd taken notice of the Skolos queens gathering the same as me and was betting on me going to challenge them.

Even more likely, she might have even orchestrated their presence in Texas as the bait to bring me to her trap.

"Humans, you're up," Rik said.

Magnum and Kevin stepped into the pool, followed by Frank and Gina, holding hands.

"Carys and Winnifred."

The owl squawked, hunching down on the queen's shoulder, making herself as small as possible. Carys passed through quickly, and Winnifred's head popped up, turning so I saw the flash of her large golden eyes. Not a single feather was wet.

"Okeanos, Itztli, Guillaume, and Nevarre."

"Shall I go on the boat, my queen?" Okeanos asked. "Or can you send me directly into the gulf?"

I considered my options while the other Blood passed through. "I can probably drop you directly into the gulf when I get Xin. Can you mask your presence from Undina, though? I don't want to give her a heads up that we're close."

"She'd have to be looking for me to find me," Okeanos said with a shrug. "And she's never had a reason to look before."

Which fucking broke my heart. I took his hand and looped my other arm around Rik's waist. "I'll always look for you, my kraken."

As the three of us stepped into the water, I touched Xin's bond. :*I'm going to drop Okeanos into the gulf, and then I'm coming to you.*:

The silver wolf immediately leaped off an embankment into the water below, still a few hours up the coast. Water closed over his head as I sank beneath the surface of the pool.

I released another drop of blood from my hand, willing the pool water to merge with the salty waters of the gulf. Three places at once, hanging suspended in water. Connected only by my blood.

And my will to bring them together.

I released Okeanos' hand and tentacles boiled up out of him

as he swam away. Holding my breath, I turned toward the northeast, stretching out my hand toward Xin. Pulling him toward me. Willing his fur to come to my hand. His scent of wolf and snow. Cold, silent fog.

My fingers closed in his ruff, the weight of his wolf pressing against me. Rik's arms closed around us both, and I shifted my focus to the Galveston pool where the rest of my Blood waited.

Carrying us both, Rik walked up the steps and Xin jumped down, shaking his fur out. He looked skinny and lean from his long run, so I offered him my bleeding hand.

Though his teeth immediately clanged on the golden bracelet.

Grimacing, I pulled my arm back slightly so only my palm was in his mouth. :*Bite my hand for now.*:

I leaned back against Rik while Xin fed. Gina spoke briefly on the phone and then hung up with a smile. "The yacht is anchored, waiting for us. The captain's sending the tender to pick everyone up. They'll be here in five minutes."

Rik didn't say a word, though I felt the surge of his rock troll in the bond. Instant fury at the thought of not having his eyes on me. Of not being able to reach out and snag me up into his arms at the first hint of danger. He hated every moment away from me. But he'd do it.

I leaned a little harder against him, letting my knees sag, even though Xin hadn't fed that long. "I could—"

Before I could even ask, Rik tore open his wrist and pressed his forearm to my mouth. He cradled me against him, his mouth on my hair. Breathing in my scent. Soaking in my power.

Guillaume, Itztli, and Nevarre shifted into their beasts. Kevin picked up Nevarre's kilt, folding it into a tidy square that he slipped into a small backpack I hadn't even noticed against his black suit. Frank picked up Guillaume's duffle bag and started to swing the leather strap holding the sword sheath over his shoulder beside his flamethrower.

"Wait. I want to carry it. If that's alright with you, G?"

The hell horse snorted. *:You're fucking kidding, right? Of course, I would be honored to have my queen carry my sword. Though I must warn you it's extremely heavy.:*

Frank brought the sword to me, and Rik helped move my hair out of the way so the leather strap didn't pull or trap any of the long strands beneath it. The sword weighed a ton, pulling me off balance, but I wasn't going to walk with it. I just needed to ride.

Releasing my hand, Xin sat back on his haunches and looked at me expectantly.

"Are you up for more swimming in the gulf, or would you rather take the boat with Rik?"

:I fucking love the ocean.:

Laughing, I nodded and then turned to Rik. He picked me up, lifting me high in his arms so I could touch his face and press my lips to his.

"If any harm comes to our queen while she's out of my sight, you'll wish you were the general's stone statue so I can't break you into a thousand pieces."

:Understood, alpha,: Itztli said.

Guillaume tossed his head and flicked his tail with irritation, fully confident in his ability to keep me safe.

Nevarre's giant raven let out a raucous caw that sounded more like mocking laughter. Rik arched a brow at him, his alpha instinct sparking with tension. Out of all the Blood, I would have thought Nevarre would be one of the least likely to challenge him in any way.

Behind us, the sound of rushing wings exploded up out of the pool and hundreds of crows poured into the sky.

:She wanted to surprise you,: Nevarre said.

The crow queen landed on my shoulder, her claws tangling in my hair. I reached up to stroke a finger over her shiny black feathers. "Thank you, Nightwing. I can use all the help I can get."

She made several low caws, rustling her feathers closer to my cheek. I didn't need words to understand. My throat ached and I nodded. "Absolutely, you're part of my family. Is Penelope coming too, then?"

In answer, a little furry body paddled up to the surface of the pool and swam over to hop up on the edge. Frank bent down and offered the rat his palm, and she hopped onto his hand without any hesitation. He placed her on my other shoulder, and she immediately burrowed into my hair and disappeared.

G nickered with amusement. *:That gives new meaning to a rat's nest in your hair.:*

I stretched out my hand toward the pool and called my blood back to me, sealing the portal in case anything else tried to come after us. The water shimmered and blurred as the decadent pool house disappeared, leaving only the circular pool.

Sidling closer, Guillaume waited while Rik lifted me onto his back and helped me adjust the long, flowing skirt of my dress. The heavy sword strapped across my back. The wild tangle of my hair.

Then he gripped my thigh, his hand hot and heavy through the thin, lacy skirt. "Ride hell-bent for leather, my queen."

Guillaume arched his neck and pawed the ground with one platter-sized hoof. *:Death rides again.:*

44

GUILLAUME

I 'd ridden into battle countless times, both as a knight and as a warhorse.

But I'd never carried my queen into battle on my back.

Yes, she'd ridden me a few times so I could protect her and keep her off the ground. But this wasn't protection.

This was an open act of war.

And I'd never been more excited for battle in my very long existence.

Her bare legs hugged around my sides. Her hands fisted in my mane. Her magical hair streamed around us like black banners, tumbling over my hindquarters and trailing along the sand. The heat of her pussy seared my back through the tiny bikini. If I allowed myself to dwell on it, a black hole of throbbing need would suck me under a wave of lust.

My hooves thumped on the wooden boardwalk crossing over the low ground from the Isador house to the beach. Our section of coastline was exclusive enough only a handful of humans were present to stare, but stare they did.

:Showtime.:

I arched my neck and shifted to a prancing trot, lifting each hoof high. Gently rocking her on my back without jostling her up against my withers. She didn't have any saddle to protect her delicate flesh or stirrups to help her balance. Nevarre and the crows circled overhead, cawing to draw even more attention as we hit the sand. Itztli bayed like a hell hound on my left, and Xin howled on my right. Even though the humans couldn't see him, it added to the mystery.

Trotting down to the damp sand, I paused, letting her wave to her people boarding the yacht.

:*Lean forward,*: I told her. Then I reared, carefully controlling how far back I tipped so she didn't lose her seat. Her legs squeezed me harder, the gripping sensation exquisite.

Screaming out a challenging neigh, I dropped to all four feet, tossing my head and prancing like I was completely out of control. Though she didn't even jar her teeth together.

In our bond, she showed me the kraken blinking like a radar bleep to the northeast. Snorting and blowing like the mighty dragon, I trotted up the beach, throwing my hooves high and fast. Though not fast enough to keep the sand from melting beneath my smoldering hooves. I had to nicker out a laugh, wondering how the humans would explain the burnt hoof prints and chunks of glass on the news.

The further we went, the more humans we saw. Goddess, I'd never seen so many bodies crammed into a few square feet of sandy beach. Sunshades and umbrellas dotted the coast and people bobbed every foot or so in the water. The hardest part of reaching the kraken might be getting the people out of my way so I didn't injure anyone.

Everybody seemed to have a phone too, snapping pictures and videos as we passed.

"Big bird." A child pointed up at Nevarre's giant bird flapping overhead. "Big bird chase."

:*Big bird my ass. Can I* please *fucking show myself?*: Mehen asked in the bond.

She laughed. :*Absolutely not.*:

Someone else yelled, "Are they filming Lady Godiva?"

Laughing more, she shifted her delectable ass into a deeper seat. Letting go of her fierce grip on my mane, she stretched out her arms wide and let her head fall back. :*I've got an idea.*:

My ears flickered back and forth, listening for her command. Every inch of my hide zinged with awareness, determined to not let her slip an inch. Even if she wasn't holding on with anything but her luscious legs wrapped around me.

Clouds boiled on the horizon and a dark thundercloud swelled over the water. Winds tore at her hair and my mane. The sky took on an eerie green tint, promising bad weather and lots of it. Ozone and the scent of rain filled my nose, so I quickened my pace to a gentle, rolling canter.

:*Small jump,*: I warned her then carefully popped over a sunburned young man passed out or asleep in the sand. She fell forward slightly but caught herself, her hands back in my mane where they belonged.

Lightning crackled across the sky, and people started to shift away from the water, giving me more room to maneuver without trying to dodge them. I didn't want to fight the waves until it was time to swim, and sharp side-to-side movements would make it harder for her to keep her seat.

A particularly foolish man lunged closer, trying to touch her, as we passed. Itztli whirled around and knocked the man down with a hard shove. Snarling and frothing at the mouth like a rabid dog, he stood over the man, one big foot planted on his chest. Teeth bared, hackles rising, his muzzle an inch from the man's face.

"Itztli." She didn't even look back over her shoulder. "Leave it."

The black dog immediately loped after us. :*I love that you called the idiot human an it.*:

:Pretty sure he pissed himself.: Xin laughed. *:He thought you were going to eat his face.:*

We drew even with the kraken. I couldn't see him out in the water, but he was close in the bond.

:Time for one final show.: She reached over her shoulder and wrapped her fingers around the hilt of my sword. *:Fuck, G. How the fuck do you even draw this thing? My arms aren't long enough. I'll have to improvise.:*

Her power shimmered around us, waves of energy helping her pull the long Templar sword free of its sheath and support it despite its weight. I felt a surge in the storm overhead, ozone burning my nostrils. Muscles tensing, I gave her a little hop of warning. Waiting for her to pull the lightning down.

Her knees tightened, and I reared back, pawing the sky, bellowing out a vicious stallion whinny. A perfect gust of wind billowed her hair and the gown like black and white wings. She raised the sword overhead and lightning crackled down in a brilliant blue flash to the tip of the blade. Sparks flew in all directions.

She screamed, "Long live House Isador!" Her words amplified by her power, rolling with thunder.

Then we leaped into the waves with a flock of crows cawing overhead.

~

SHARA

WAVES CRASHED AGAINST G'S CHEST, SPLASHING WARM SALT water in my face. He arched up again, lunging over several waves in a row like a hunter taking fences. As the water deepened, I clung to his mane with my free hand so I didn't slip off.

Before we got too deep, I used my power to lift the Templar sword back over my shoulder and into its sheath.

His back dipped completely underwater, and he started swimming, pulling me along with him. I checked Itztli and Xin to make sure they were faring okay. Itztli's dog grinned at me, easily paddling along beside us. Xin surged ahead slightly, and Itztli fell back to protect our flank while staying clear of the hell horse's giant hooves.

Okeanos reached up one tentacle, guiding the way for Xin while still staying mostly underwater.

:How close are we?: I asked.

:Ten minutes or so at this speed.:

:Can you see her nest?:

:No. It's been hidden from my eyes since she caged me. The only time I saw it again was when you went with me to visit her.:

I kept power humming through my veins, though I didn't want to broadcast my location—or worse, alarm her into thinking she was under attack. This low in the water, I couldn't see anything ahead of us but the waves rolling in. The occasional splash from my swimming Blood. I felt for Rik, and he was moving quickly toward me on the yacht, his grim, formidable alpha focus locked on me. From his higher vantage point, he could see our little group in the water.

:Sharks,: Okeanos said sharply. *:They're Undina's sentinels.:*

:Her Blood?:

:They're only animals though she treats them like pets.:

:Then let's not kill them unless we must.:

A gray fin broke the water just a few feet away, the shark circling us. Another on my right. They didn't attack but I didn't assume they were friendly. They were smart enough to stay out of the reach of the kraken's tentacles.

As if it heard my doubts, one of them sped faster, deliberately bumping into Itztli hard enough his head went under. He snapped at the shark's side as it swept past but missed. Another shark broke the water directly behind us.

Guillaume heaved beneath me, his head dropping lower while his hindquarters bumped up out of the water. One of his hooves thumped the shark directly on its snout. It flew up out of the water, thrashing in a frantic frenzy. Blood dripped from a deep, smoking slash on its nose.

Nevarre swooped down and swiped his talons along another shark's back. Pecking and screaming angry crows swarmed and dive-bombed the sharks until they retreated.

:She knows we're here,: Okeanos said.

A giant wave swelled in front of us, not cresting but lifting us up higher above the rest of the ocean. The air rippled, rivulets of tinkling water running off an invisible surface, casting prisms of iridescent light. Streaming, sparkling curtains parted, revealing an island beach of shining white sand. Palm, banana, and mango trees lined the coast, and the water gleamed a deeper cerulean than the muddy blue gray of the Gulf of Mexico.

Beyond the trees, pink and orange humps rose in graceful curves like waves. Okeanos said the interior of her nest was formed from a living coral reef.

Guillaume's hooves touched ground again. I pulled myself back into position on his back, wriggling around to get upright. The ends of my hair were soaked, dragging even heavier, which made it harder for me to move under its weight.

:Fuuuuck,: he growled in the bond.

:Sorry.: I grinned, not sorry at all.

Xin was already trotting on the sandy beach, nose and ears twitching. *:The blood circle is on the other side of the first row of trees.:*

:Where are you?: Rik's words rumbled like rolling thunder in my head. *:Even Sekh can't see you.:*

:We made it to Undina's island. She must still be masking it from you.:

:There's no island. Only waves and water.:

His misery at not being able to see me made my throat ache. *:I'll speak to her and ask that she allow all of you to at least enter the island.:*

Nevarre dropped down beside us along with the flock of crows. Nightwing rustled her wings, shaking some of my hair away from her talons, but she didn't hop down to join the rest of her family. Closing my eyes, I felt for Penelope in my hair. I didn't want her lost and asleep in the magic, or worse, floating out in the gulf trying to find me.

She scrambled up closer to my ear but stayed hidden beneath my hair, awake and well.

Okeanos hovered in the shallows, his tentacles curled up and his body flattened out, making himself smaller. *:She's coming.:*

I stretched out my hand toward him, and he wrapped one of his smaller tentacles around my hand. Another around my ankle. *:I won't allow her to harm you.:*

His bond still strained with tension. *:That's not my concern, my queen. Please don't allow me to harm her and ruin your plans.:*

Ah. I didn't blame him in the slightest. When I thought about him as a little boy, caged out in the ocean and left alone for years on end, it made me a little crazy. A lot crazy. *:Don't be afraid to show her how mighty you are, my kraken. Especially now that my poison flows in your veins.:*

He unfurled his tentacles, lifting his body so he easily towered over Guillaume. *:My pleasure, my queen.:*

"Greetings, House Isador." The last time I'd seen Undina Ketea, she'd been a mermaid with a brilliant turquoise tail and rows of vicious teeth. Today, she stood above us on the nearest wave of coral in human form, her blue-green hair flowing around her shoulders like a glistening waterfall. Iridescent aqua scales shimmered along her throat, shoulders, and arms. She wore a bright orange shirt, cropped just beneath her breasts, and a hot pink skirt that fluttered around her hips.

"Greetings, House Ketea. I apologize for arriving without notifying you in advance."

Her lips curled away from her teeth, still very shark-like despite her more human appearance. "I see you've brought quite the contingent with you this time, including an entire boat of Blood and humans. Not to mention Leviathan, king of the depths, who nearly murdered his entire Skolos house, and a king kraken who already destroyed my nest once upon a time. As well as Sir Guillaume de Payne, Triune Executioner who slaughtered countless queens in his lifetime including the most powerful queen of all. But yes, Shara Isador, do tell me you're sorry for not having your consiliarius call me first."

G tossed his head and flicked his tail with disgust. *:You're the most powerful queen of all.:*

"*Former* Triune Executioner," I said, stroking his neck. "And I can't help my love for monsters, the same as my mother before me. Nor my ability to do what you could not and help your magnificent son control his beast. My kings are fully mine and won't harm anyone who doesn't threaten me."

She threw her head back and laughed. "Very well. Your Blood may approach my island."

:What was so funny?: I asked Okeanos, bewildered but I already felt a surge of immense relief in Rik's bond, confirming he could see the island.

Okeanos' gills fluttered and deepened from soft pink to match the color of his mother's brilliant skirt. *:You called me magnificent.:*

My eyes narrowed and I fought the urge to retort my opinion about how she'd "cared" for her son. *:That wasn't a joke.:*

:She knows. That's why she's pleased enough to allow her island to

be seen at all. She denied me the sight of these shores for decades, my queen. Not only to protect her people but in her own way, to lessen my suffering by removing from my sight the home I'd lost.:

Mollified somewhat, I waited for the small boat to leave the yacht and bring my people ashore. Rik came first, no surprise, with Sekh, Gina, Kevin, and Carys.

"You may approach for introductions," Undina said.

:I'll wait in the water, my queen,: Okeanos said. *:If she allows you inside the nest, the center is open to the ocean below. I doubt she'll allow me inside the circle, but if you're under attack, swim down through that hole. I'll find you.:*

I stayed on Guillaume's back, though Rik strode beside me with his hand on my thigh. *:Itztli, Nevarre, stay with Okeanos unless our queen or I call you to her side. Vivian, Tlacel, and Mehen, stay in the air. General, with us. Everyone else, await a direct order.:*

:I'm surprised you didn't leave Sekh on the boat to boss everyone.:

:In case anything happens and no other Blood can reach you, you'll have your most deadly Blood within arm's reach, my queen. Ezra took over bossing duties.:

I had to laugh softly. My bear could be a tad belligerent on occasion. *:I bet that's going over well.:*

:Even I'm pissed at him,: Daire retorted in the bond, making me laugh harder.

:Fuck this boss shit. I don't know how you do it, alpha. They're like a bunch of feral, mad tomcats with two peters on a wild goose chase.:

Guillaume snorted and tossed his head. *:You're mixing idioms.:*

:Fuck you and the horse she rode in on,: Ezra retorted.

I was too busy laughing to worry about a formal meeting with the High Queen of the Skolos Triune. Though I managed to quiet myself before Guillaume came to a halt at the edge of Undina's blood circle. Another woman had joined her, wearing a similar short skirt tied around her hips and a loose, cropped vest. Necklaces of shells mixed with gold chain and precious jewels swung between her breasts.

She curtseyed to me. "I'm Aleka, consiliarius for House Ketea. Queen Undina, daughter of Keto, Mother of Sea Monsters, welcomes you to House Ketea."

Gina curtsied back. "I'm Gina, and this is my queen, Shara Isador, last daughter of She Who Is and Was and Always Will Be. Her sibling, Queen Carys Tylluan; her alpha, Alrik Isador; last Templar knight, Sir Guillaume de Payne Isador; Sekh, General of the All Seeing, Never Sleeping legion of She Who Dances in Blood; and second consiliarius, Kevin Isador."

"Sekh Isador," Sekh said, flashing his canines.

Gina's lips quirked. "Forgive me, general. A slip of the tongue."

I flashed a pleased grin at him, and he came closer to lay a hand on my other thigh. *:Thank you for taking my house name.:*

:You honor me, Your Majesty.:

Undina hissed out a word that sounded like a curse in a different language. "You care so little for my son that you don't bring him to see his mother?"

My brows rose in surprise. Carefully, I replied, "He assumed you would bar him from your island entirely and didn't wish to cause any friction between us."

"Are you his queen? Do you hold the kraken as securely as you claim? If so, bring him. Bring the dragon. Show us, if you dare, how well your kings behave."

I kept my face smooth, but my eyes sparked with irritation. *:Okeanos. Leviathan. Bring your glorious beasts to my side.:*

:Be on your best fucking behavior,: Rik growled.

Leviathan dropped from the sky like a meteor and landed behind us hard enough the ground rocked beneath Guillaume's hooves. *:I might be an asshole to any of you, but I'd never fucking embarrass my queen.:*

Okeanos' tentacles slipped around my ankle and waist, draping over Guillaume's withers and hindquarters. Not that my hell horse minded.

"Okeanos Isador and Mehen Leviathan Isador, Your Majesty," Gina said in a frosty tone.

Undina stepped forward and held out her hand past the blood circle. "House Isador may enter my nest."

:We go at the same time,: Rik said. :G—:

:I can do it,: Okeanos offered quickly. :If she wants me to come through, then she can deal with the kraken.:

Leviathan lowered his head over my shoulder, hooking his chin around me to pull me back slightly against him so we were touching.

Rik offered his arm to Gina, and she took Kevin's hand, Carys his. Okeanos stretched out his thickest, meatiest tentacle to his mother, slithering midway up her arm.

My silent, silver wolf had already crept into the nest and crouched near enough to rip out Undina's throat if she tried to harm me.

She backed up, bringing us through the tingle of her magic. Then she twisted her wrist in Okeanos' tentacle, deliberately wrapping more of his limb around her arm. Her broad, toothy smile made my hair float around my head, crackling with power.

"I can't wait to see Basilia's reaction to not only having two unchained kings in my nest, but especially Leviathan."

:Who's that?: I asked in the bond. :And no one's getting chained.:

:Basilia Gorgos,: Daire answered. :Descended from Stheno.:

So one of the other Skolos Triune queens. :A distant relative of yours?: I asked the dragon.

Leviathan's bond sizzled with flames, and he licked his lips in anticipation. After his mother exiled him, he slaughtered all the Gorgons he could find. :My mother's line was Medusa's, her sister goddess.:

The other consiliarius' phone rang. She pulled it out of her vest and her eyes widened. "She's calling, Your Majesty."

Undina let out another hearty laugh, shaking her head. "What the fuck did you do to finally get her to call me?"

I allowed my lips to curve in a secretive smile. "I just took a ride on the beach."

45

SHARA

"You've accomplished more in an hour than I have in a week," Undina grumbled.

We walked side by side down a pale pink pathway of crushed shells around the interior of her nest, with Blood—both mine and hers—walking before and behind us. Well, most of her Blood swam in the inner cove, their heads popping up to glare as we passed. Carys, Gina, and Kevin walked ahead of us with Aleka, the Ketea consiliarius.

Evidently, the other Skolos queen, Nuri Kijin, also called before the first phone call ended. Both queens were on their way to Undina's island, on the move after sitting in their Galveston houses for days.

"I noticed that you were gathered but it didn't seem as though anything was happening."

Undina's head snapped around. "How?"

"I saw three queens nearby, though I wasn't sure who it was. I came to investigate, and only realized you were nearby thanks to Okeanos." A small fib—Gina had figured out who was here before we'd swum out to the island, but I hadn't seen Skolos specifically on the tapestry. I didn't want her to know about our spy network or my dream of the Mother. "Guillaume told me a full Triune hasn't gathered since the fall of Triskeles."

"Indeed. He would know." Undina's breath hissed out softly. "Skolos is only here because I compelled them. Though I couldn't force them to actually come to the Mother's table. Have you learned what a full Triune involves?"

I didn't know Undina well enough to read her cues, but her skin seemed greener than before and she clicked her teeth together. "Somewhat. Though with two empty seats at Triskeles, I haven't experienced a full table yet."

"Even before Triskeles fell, Skolos hadn't met in decades. It's not an easy thing to endure. So many queens set their eyes on the Triune but have no idea what it costs to take the seat. Your mother knew. I thought she was mad for planning to seat you at the table before you were even born."

"How well did you know her?"

"As well as anyone, which is not at all. She was secretive even before..." Her words fell off into silence, as if she'd lost her train of thought. Esetta Isador had that effect on the living.

"How did it come about for you to sell Okeanos to the queen of Rome?"

"Sell? Is that what she told you?" Undina barked out a harsh laugh, sharp as razor blades. "She pushed out a Triune edict that all kings were to be executed before they came to maturity, though she was the only queen who signed it. The Dauphine had fucked off to goddess only knew where, Desideria had mysteriously died, and Triskeles was of course long gone. I couldn't keep Okeanos from shifting. He was too powerful. Even as a child, he completely leveled the nest. But I certainly didn't want him executed. So we hid him."

"You imprisoned him in a cage," I said flatly. "Alone. For years."

"You're young yet so I won't take offense at your words. When you've lived a thousand years as I have, the days and years bleed together far too quickly. For me, it seemed that he was caged for a mere few days, even in Rome."

Rage choked me and I clenched my hands into fists, fighting to keep my face smooth and my mouth shut. She forgot. Her own fucking son. In a cage.

A child. Left alone to starve until he figured out how to feed himself from the ocean without having the freedom to even swim and hunt.

"He was safe, I told myself. It was the best I could do until..."

She stopped and turned to face me. Reluctantly, I turned toward her, not wanting her to see the sheer fury boiling in my veins.

"Was your childhood so much better, Shara? Raised as a human outside of a nest without any access to your power. No one to protect you while the most powerful queens in the world tried to find you so they could eliminate you before you could rise and challenge them. No one to teach you our ways. How long were you lost and alone before your Blood found you?"

My jaw ached from holding back my words. "I wasn't caged."

"Ah, but you were. You were denied all the power in your ancient bloodline. Worse, you were left with humans. I could argue that was a far worse cage. I regret the years of solitude and misery my son endured, but I don't regret hiding him. Saving him. For you."

For me in particular? Or any queen who could finally control the king kraken?

She must have seen the question in my eyes. "Your mother saw a future where kings were free as your Blood. On the off chance she was right, I kept my kraken son hidden. The queen of Rome unfortunately found him before you were born, yet I still hoped your mother had been right. So much, in fact, that I agreed to act as a witness to your birth. The queen of Rome thought she had the upper hand by holding Okeanos hostage, but she didn't know I saw you sworn to all three Triunes. It was a small hope, a fantasy you would even survive long enough, but here you are."

"I'm sick to death of all these schemes and plots that started over a hundred years ago."

Shaking her head, Undina laughed again. "The game of queens is not for the faint of heart, Shara Isador. We play with the kind of power that could destroy the world and all life in it."

"It's not a game to me."

Her head tipped, her eyes flashing in the sunlight. "Then perhaps that's why you play so well."

We started to walk again but I smelled blood. I whirled around so fast that the hell horse's head jerked up, his eyes alert, his ears flickering back and forth searching for danger. He walked beside Rik and seemed fine, but it was Guillaume's blood that I smelled. "You're bleeding. What's wrong?"

He blew out a breath and relaxed enough to bump me with his muzzle. :*It's a small thing, my queen.*:

I sank into his bond and felt pain in his right front hoof. :*Show me.*:

Lipping my hair, he obliged by lifting his front leg, curling it back toward his stomach so I could see the underside. A slash bled in the soft inner part of his hoof.

"I didn't think to warn you," Undina said. "We're on a living coral reef I've fashioned into a floating island over many centuries. The coral can be treacherous."

"Go shift back into my knight." I pressed a kiss to his forehead, laughing as he playfully butted me with his soft, velvety nose. :*I may need your sword more than your hell horse, anyway.*:

:*Kevin has my bag.*:

"Is there a place he can shift in privacy?" I asked Undina, motioning Kevin closer. I touched Xin's bond, checking on his pads.

:*I'm much lighter than the hell horse and not on the sharp path.*:

Her eyes narrowed but she pointed over my shoulder

toward a cave in the opalescent pink hump of coral. "He must be accompanied by my Blood until he returns."

I nodded. "That's fine."

Three of her mermaid Blood surged up out of the water, their tails flowing into legs. Genitalia swinging without a care in the world. I quickly focused on my hell horse. I didn't want other queens looking at my Blood—so it seemed only fair to avoid looking at hers. Not that I wanted to anyway.

"No weapons, Sir Guillaume," Undina said. "I know your reputation all too well."

:Then I can't take my bag.: He snorted, giving his head a toss, making the Templar sheath I'd looped over his neck bump his legs. *:Though I wouldn't need steel to kill them.:*

Not something I cared to say aloud in a potentially enemy queen's nest with two more queens on their way.

:Oh for fuck's sake.: Leviathan dropped down beside us so quickly that Undina recoiled a step and her Blood bared their vicious teeth, dropping to a crouch before her. *:I never thought the king of the depths would be called upon to act as a motherfucking privacy curtain.:*

Laughing, I stepped back, giving the dragon room to lift his mighty wings and hide Guillaume while he shifted and dressed.

:Keep that fucking sword to yourself, knight,: Leviathan growled.

:This sword would cleave you in two, dragon.:

Undina gave me another hard look that I couldn't decipher. "I didn't realize the infamous executioner was so modest."

Damn it. Now my cheeks were heating. "He's not."

Her eyes narrowed, dropping to give me a quick once-over in my scandalous bikini. "You don't appear to be modest either."

My cheeks reddened even more, and I fought the urge to shake my hair forward to cover up. "I'm not. Usually."

She must have said something in her bonds because her Blood grinned and relaxed their defensive poses. One of them made high-pitched barks and squeaks like a dolphin, and the rest laughed even harder.

:*Do I want to know what they said?:* I asked Okeanos.

Even his bond rumbled with laughter. :*Probably not, my queen.:*

Fucking great.

Undina's head turned sharply, drawing my attention in that direction. Two more yachts approached the island. "They're here." Then she whispered softly, "Goddess be with us."

46

RIK

Granite shifted beneath my skin, a monumental landslide ready to slip loose at the first sign of any threat to my queen.

So many fucking Blood disembarked from the two yachts.

So many ways this whole thing could go sideways with a wrong look or a single word from anybody.

Not to mention four of the most powerful living queens staring each other down without a word.

House Kijin had twenty-one tattooed Blood in slick, expensive suits with lots of gold jewelry. They moved like Xin with the easy, graceful promise of a silent, quick death. All except the biggest one, who was shifted into his beast with a bull head and thick curving horns that swept out from his head like a Texas longhorn. Though his bottom half looked more like... a spider? Or an octopus. I couldn't tell.

He didn't move like an alpha despite his size, and he didn't walk close to his queen. When they came closer, I saw why.

The big bull monster's upper body was wrapped in black cloth that bound his arms to his sides. Chains wound tightly around on top of the cloth were attached to a heavy metal collar. His lower face was more human, and his mouth was covered with a tight metal mask, leaving only his nose and red, malevolent eyes uncovered. Four of the Kijin Blood guarded him instead of their queen.

:*He's a king flesh eater,*: Sekh warned in the bond. :*That's why he's gagged and bound. He'll eat anything in his path.*:

:*I can fucking take him,*: Leviathan offered, his hunger pulsing through the bond.

:*Let's see who they bring into the blood circle before we assign targets,*: I replied.

Their queen, Nuri Kijin, was dressed in golden flowing silks with red and gold ornaments in her upswept black hair. A red mask with small black lacquered horns and long white fangs covered her face.

:*Does anyone know her power?*: Shara asked.

:*She's descended from Nure-onna,*: Daire replied. :*Her Blood are different kinds of oni and yokai.*:

:*What's that?*:

:*Japanese demons in folklore, though they're just another flavor of Aima descended from the Great Mother,*: Guillaume added. :*The Skolos courts are known for their darker monsters.*:

:*Nuri can shift into a snake-like sea monster,*: Sekh replied. :*With her power, she could call a tsunami strong enough to flood the entire southeast coast.*:

"House Ketea welcomes Queen Nuri Kijin," Aleka said. "You may select five Blood to accompany you into Her Majesty's blood circle."

Same as us, though we also had Xin. I still didn't like those fucking numbers. At least three to one, depending on how many Blood Undina had.

Leviathan clashed his teeth together in frustration when the bull king remained outside of the blood circle. :*Light the fucker up, Smoak.*:

:*I'll roast his ass,*: Vivian promised.

That still left fifteen other Kijin Blood outside the blood circle with only six Isador Blood.

:*Seven,*: Lew said. :*Thierry says his bite will contaminate them.*:

Undina brought Nuri into her circle and then turned to Gina, who introduced my queen and her Blood. Shara inclined her head politely but didn't touch the other queen. There was no need since it wasn't her blood circle.

It took three tender trips back to the yacht to bring all of House Gorgos ashore. Twenty-nine Blood, some of them almost as big as the bull king. Her alpha was shifted into a giant cyclops. Slightly taller than me but not as thick, and certainly not as big as the rock troll. He moved slowly, too. He stared straight ahead, not even flicking an assessing look at me or the other alphas or kings.

Evidently supremely arrogant.

I wouldn't be so dumb—especially when I had such incredible resources at my disposal. :*Recommendations on how best to deploy our Blood outside the nest?*:

:*Kijin's Blood have katanas hidden in back sheaths beneath their suit coats and hair,*: Guillaume said. :*If Vivian's handling the king, only Itztli has any blade skill. I recommend using Gorgos as shields, forcing them to kill each other to get to our Blood and let Itztli pick them off until they're too close to matter.*:

:*Agreed,*: Sekh said. :*Unless Kijin and Gorgos are willing to work together and pick us off one by one.*:

:*True,*: Guillaume replied. :*Though their body language says they're just as suspicious of each other as us.*:

:*They're Skolos. We're not.*:

:*How about we compromise?*: I suggested. :*If we pair up as much as possible, rather than everyone stick together, we can at least spread the fight out while still having backup.*:

:*That works,*: Guillaume replied approvingly.

I focused on Itztli's bond. :*You're in charge of the battle strategy.*

Use your blade skills to protect our shifters and match up the rest of the Blood into pairs as you see fit.:

:*Understood, alpha. I'll make their empty skins dance.*:

:*What about the legion?:* Guillaume asked.

:*If I bring the entire legion to this plane, the carnage will be immense,:* Sekh replied. :*They must feast to return to their eternal watch. I doubt our queen would be pleased if a few thousand humans disappeared after her publicity stunt on the same beach. Though even ten sphinxes will certainly sway any battle in our favor.:*

:*Can they cross the queen's blood circle?:* I asked.

:*Not until I bring it down. It'll take me a few minutes if it comes to that level of battle.:*

Leviathan let out a disgusted sigh, blowing a plume of smoke around our queen. :*She doesn't smell like a Gorgon. Maybe that's why I missed eliminating her.:*

:*What do we know about Basilia?:* Shara asked.

:*Not much,:* Guillaume admitted. :*General?:*

Sekh's eyes deepened to bronze, and he stared at the approaching queen. Her mahogany hair was plaited and wrapped around her head. She wore a forest green gown to highlight her lighter green eyes, high necked and old fashioned like something from the Elizabethan era with long, wide sleeves down to her knees.

His eyes flashed back to gold. :*Her primary home is on Mykonos. She hasn't demonstrated her power in a long time nor left her island in decades, at least. Though I have Seen her as a hydra centuries ago. She can kill with a stare if she's shifted and breathes poison. She was born after your imprisonment, dragon. Her mother was called to Rome before you went on your rampage and thus was spared.:*

:*Cut off one fucking head and another sprouts,:* Leviathan said. :*Better to eat her fucking heart. I call dibs.:*

"You called this quorum, Undina," Basilia said. "Let's discuss your so-called urgent business so we can all return to our busy lives."

"Oh," Carys said out loud, and then turned beet red. Winnifred flapped her wings and squawked.

:I take it she's the one who wants me dead?: Shara asked in the bond.

"Ironic, Basilia, since you were the one who couldn't be bothered to answer Aleka's calls all week," Undina snapped. "This way."

:Only the second one-hundred percent I've ever seen, my queen.:

:Given our current situation, how likely is she to succeed with her goal?:

Carys paled and swayed, leaning against her as if suddenly ill. *:Goddess, Shara. It doesn't look good at all.:*

Seemingly unbothered, my queen laid her fingers on my arm and started to walk after Undina. *:Then I'll have to be ready to change the game as soon as I have the chance.:*

SHARA

POWER PRICKLED THE FINE HAIRS UP AND DOWN MY ARMS, humming and ready to strike. Though I didn't have a reason, let alone any idea what kind of defenses Basilia might have against me. With three Skolos Triune queens ready and eager to pass judgment, my entire House could be put to the sword if I acted without cause. Even if we fought our way free, Marne Ceresa would be all too eager to back any Skolos execution order.

We'd be hunted—unless I had *cause* to kill another Triune queen. The Mother might have sent me here to save the Skolos

Triune in some way, but I had to assume another queen's death would still be a strike against me.

I kept my blood contained without letting it drip free, grateful for my nails that allowed me to easily pierce my skin without drawing attention from the other queens. Though I had to remember not to touch the bracelets and reveal their presence in front of the other queens. Hopefully they wouldn't be able to smell my blood, either.

Rik walked on my right. Xin padded alongside on my left, invisible to everyone except me. Though as we passed one of Undina's Blood who stood guard on either side of a dark cavern, her nostrils flared and she tipped her head back, her lips peeling away from her vicious teeth. She might smell wolf—but she couldn't see him.

Ignoring her, I stepped into the coral cave. Once my eyes adjusted from the external sunlight, it wasn't dark at all. Everything gleamed like the inside of a shell with soft, pearly light. The pathway sloped downward and wrapped around in a smooth spiraling path like the one circling the open pool in the center. It was wide enough for us to walk side by side, though Leviathan had to tuck his wings and duck his head.

Natural openings in the coral walls showed water on the other side—like windows or peepholes. Brightly colored fish swam outside in gorgeous blue waters. Live plants swayed in the waves like flowers dancing in a gentle breeze. Sharks circled the coral, keeping pace with us as we slowly made our way deeper.

Underwater. Like we were inside a massive aquarium.

:This is amazing,: I whispered to Okeanos.

:When the island's in the Aegean, humans live nearby and fish right outside without seeing the nest at all.:

A sense of weight began to press down on me, my ears filling up with pressure. We had to be deep underwater now, but not a single drop leaked into the pathway. Undina stopped before a large arched door in the center of the cave wall. I expected to see water on the other side, but the opening was dark and solid with a faint oily sheen. She dragged her hand against a protruding spike of coral and then pressed her bleeding palm to the solid surface in the arch.

It shimmered to gray and then lighter, a rippling curtain of water.

"By the blood of Keto, I call upon the Great Mother of All to allow Your daughters and any who carry their blood to come into Your presence."

Undina stepped through the curtain—and disappeared. She'd only brought one Blood down with her, her alpha, I presumed, though she hadn't introduced him. He didn't follow her inside but turned to face the rest of us.

"Blood can pass." Though he clanged his teeth like screeching metal claws on a chalkboard. "If you dare."

Leviathan immediately took a step toward the curtain, but I reached out and laid a hand on his neck, halting him in his tracks. :*Allow the other queens to go first, my dragon. I need you close.*:

We moved deeper into the tunnel past the opening to make room for the others to pass. Head high, Basilia glided toward the opening. Leviathan cracked open his mouth, letting a fresh plume of smoke trickle through his lips in her direction. Then he licked his teeth. Noisily and with enthusiasm. A promise. A silent threat.

Though she didn't even turn her head as she stepped through.

She didn't offer her own blood. She didn't have to, not with Undina's wording, but it still seemed disrespectful to me. Though perhaps Skolos chose to honor the Mother in different ways, because Nuri passed through without offering her blood, either.

I stepped up to the opening and paused, breathing deeply.

Running through everything in my mind. Clear. Calm. Nightwing clucked softly against my neck. She and Penelope both carried my blood, so they should be able to pass. Kevin and Gina too. I reached out to the rest of my Blood outside of the blood circle, letting them feel me in their bonds.

Nevarre flew overhead with the crows, using his eyes to track the other Bloods' locations for Itztli. My bear and warcat stood together, claws and teeth ready. Vivian's flames rippled around her phoenix, but she was on the ground, closer to the largest enemy Blood left outside. Tlacel and Itztli had shifted back to their human forms and stood back-to-back, though they hadn't drawn their blades. Their bare chests glistened in the sun, broad and strong and fearless, but they'd donned basic sweatpants one of the other Blood had brought from the boat.

Lew and Thierry stood together. Alpha gryphon and... My heart squeezed with agony. Thierry's head jerked uncontrollably, his limbs twitching so much he could barely stand. Black rot leaked from his mouth, down his chin to spill across his chest. But he bared his teeth, ready to rend and tear as long as possible.

I reached up and dragged my palm down the coral spike, cutting my hand open. Power surged, making my hair ripple around me like a windstorm gust swept through the tunnel. I sent a wave of power through my bonds. *:I love you.:*

"Shara Isador, last daughter of She Who Was and Is and Always Will Be, freely gives her blood as an offering to the Great Mother from Whom All Life Flows."

Then I stepped through the curtain of rippling water.

47

SHARA

I stepped into the Skolos Triune's chamber.

Circular dark walls and ceiling cast the room into shadow, though the center table glowed with blue biolumines-cence. A darker indigo statue of the Mother stood in the center of the table. Moving. Her lower body flowed like a deep blue jellyfish billowing in the water, trailing long streamers across the table and up into the air.

Rik touched my back, subtly guiding me to step to the side so the rest of my Blood could come through with me. I couldn't drag my eyes from Her. Her center seemed almost transparent, though in the gloom it was hard to tell. The table pulsed with dark blue light, rippling like waves moving across a beach. A darker shadow moved overhead, finally dragging my gaze up as a long, dark tail swept by. Huge. Some kind of whale.

Gulp. The darkness was water. Now that my eyes adjusted, I could see large shapes outside, the flash of tails and fins.

The Skolos Triune chamber was a tiny pocket at the bottom of the sea. A fishbowl—for us.

The other three queens stepped closer to the table in the

center of the room, turned, and faced me. Their Blood remained standing in separate groups against the wall.

Nuri's expression was covered by the mask. Outwardly, Undina seemed calm and unperturbed, but her coloring was oddly green again and her eyes flashed. Though that could be caused by the glowing bioluminescence. Basilia simply looked bored.

"The penitent may approach the Mother's table," Undina said, looking at me.

What the fuck? I wasn't repenting anything. I hadn't *done* anything to repent. Yet.

:*All children should be penitent before the Mother,*: Guillaume said in the bond. :*It's common language for petitioners coming before the Triune.*:

Soft blue light flickered and shifted around the room in a circular motion. I started to feel dizzy. Pressure built in my ears, making my head feel stuffed. I promised Her I would go wherever She sent me. Even here, to the bottom of the ocean.

So I stepped forward to the table.

"You didn't tell me that you had a wolf." Undina's voice rang with displeasure, and she shot me a hard look.

My eyes widened and I turned to look at Xin. He froze a few paces behind me, his ears down, his back low, one foot lifted in midair. Blue light flowed over his silver fur.

Illuminating him like a ghostly wolf.

"Oops." I gave her an apologetic smile. "He's so quiet I sometimes forget his existence."

:*Not true, my wolf. I could never forget you.*:

:*This wolf's heart beats for you alone, my queen.*:

Undina let out a harsh growl. "No Blood are allowed inside the Triune circle. Retreat to your alpha, wolf."

Xin trotted back to Rik and laid down on his stomach, his head on his front paws. The rest of my Blood knelt against the rear wall, honoring the Mother. Though I could hear the faint buzz of their conversation in the bond as they decided who'd kill who if—when—shit hit the fan.

Because it was coming.

The weight of the entire ocean pressed down on me, making it difficult to breathe. My nerves zinged like a million fire ants marched up and down my limbs. I fought the urge to scrub my sweaty palms on the delicate lacy skirt of my gown.

Not sweat. Blood. I'd forgotten to stop the slash on my hand from bleeding.

Good. The Mother needed my blood for whatever She needed to accomplish.

And I'd promised to give Her every drop in my body.

LEVIATHAN

Before my long imprisonment, I'd been called king of the depths.

I'd forgotten why.

I didn't need water like the kraken, but I could make the sea my home if I chose. The salty sea flowed in my bloodline just as much as Gorgon, thanks to my foulest of fathers, Labbu.

I caught myself staring out into the inky depths beyond the transparent walls. Wondering if my scales would glow eerie green as I swam through the darkness. Listening to the echoing calls of whales rolling through the water from miles away. Knowing I could feast as often as I chose.

Or I could curl around my queen and listen to her breathe. Read to her for hours, her hair spread out like black silk across my chest. Now the treacherous magical tendrils would drag me back to her side. To her feet. Where I would beg her to let me love her again.

Something pained me deep inside. Likely a bone stuck in my gullet.

:You'll never have to beg me to love you.: She glided through my bond as easily as the sharks swimming around the nest. *:Though it's ever so much fun when you beg me to sit on your face.:*

:Anytime, my queen. I'll beg you as long as there's still breath in my lungs.:

"Three Skolos queens come before the Mother of All, offering our blood to secure Her circle," Undina said.

My eyes slitted with hatred and draconian alarm when the three queens began to walk blood circles around the table—with my queen inside. First Gorgos, with Kijin and Ketea right behind her. Three powerful Triune queens.

Locking Shara inside with them. Where none of us could fucking reach her.

:I can reach her, dragon,: Sekh said. *:Surely you didn't forget how much fun you had welcoming me inside her blood circle when she Blooded me.:*

:Even three?: I retorted, tucking my wings close to my body. Ready to slither forward before the last droplet fell into place and seize our queen. Drag her out by my teeth. *:They saw the wolf.:*

:I See him too, and yes. Even three. She will not be trapped inside for long. Not with us here to kill them all. Imagine the feast, dragon, and be ready to fill your belly.:

Now that I could get behind.

Ketea closed her circle. Green glistened on her forehead. It took me a moment to realize it was sweat. Her hands trembled as she turned to face the glowing table.

The fucking high queen was scared shitless.

And my queen was trapped inside with her.

48

ITZTLI

The last time I'd gone to the battlefield expecting to die, I'd worn the traditional weapons of my people, the macuahuitl and atlatl. Today, the only weapon I carried was the obsidian blade of Teotihuacan. Yet I was deadlier than any Mexica warrior could have hoped to be.

I carried my queen's power, and she'd blessed me well. Rather than carving out the evil I'd inherited from my sire's line, the Flayed One, she'd embraced every dark urge and honed them to a vicious edge.

Today, I refused to die. My queen loved me so much she'd sworn to die if I fell. So I must find a way to live.

Though the odds were against us. We were outnumbered nearly seven to one.

I watched the other two groups of Blood, assessing their abilities and strengths. The Gorgos Blood had greater size and numbers, but the Kijin Blood carried themselves like warriors. Soldiers used to warfare and battle. I saw long, slightly curved swords in Guillaume's bond, and he played out a few battle scenes from his memories, showing me how they'd fight.

:We need to split up,: I told the other Blood outside the nest. :If

*we spread out, the other Blood should deploy in response. Get a group
of Gorgos between you and the Kijin but don't shift unless a fight
breaks out. We won't draw first blood, but we'll finish it.:*

Vivian and Nevarre circled overhead with a huge flock of
crows, providing an aerial view of the three groups of Blood.
Though the phoenix focused on the biggest Kijin king.

Ezra and Daire immediately strolled off along the beach as if
they were looking at seashells. Llewellyn locked his arm around
Thierry's waist but they didn't walk away.

:He can't walk,: Llewellyn whispered. *:I don't want him to
appear weak before the others.:*

:Understood. Tlacel and I will draw their notice away.:

My brother fell into step beside me, our stride automatically
synchronized as we moved up the beach away from the others.
Sunlight sparkled on the water, and I estimated the sun would
begin to set in another hour. *Let it not be my queen's last day.*

"We haven't made an offering to Coatlicue together since the
day our queen came to House Zaniyah," Itztli said.

Nodding, I halted, casually turning toward him so I could
scan the other groups of Blood. The Gorgos Blood hadn't
moved. They didn't look at us or the other smaller groups of
Blood. They simply… stared. At nothing. They didn't smell like
thralls, and they didn't carry the scent of rot and death like
Thierry. They didn't act like Blood ought, assessing each other.
Preparing to defend their queen to the death.

Unnerved, I shifted my gaze to Tlacel's. "You're right. We
should offer the Mother of the Gods a sacrifice and beg Her
blessing."

He didn't unsheathe the blade he carried. Instead, he held
out his hand. Wanting me to draw his blood.

By the grace of our queen's bond, I could do so without fear.
Because she had looked into the darkest corner of my heart and
embraced what she saw there without hesitation. My loved ones
were safe now. Thanks to her.

I drew the obsidian blade across his palm and then mine. Together, we held our fists out, squeezing our blood through our fingers to splatter on the sand. The Kijin Bloods' heads immediately snapped in our direction, but the Gorgos didn't care about the scent of blood. Even their enemies'.

"Coatlicue, Mother of the Gods, please accept our sacrifice."

"Teteoh Innan, send us a sign," Tlacel said. "Guide our footsteps to victory."

A buzzing sound drew my attention to the left of my brother's shoulder. Hovering in midair, a blue-green hummingbird shimmered in the late sun. Red breast flashing like blood.

"Huitzilopochtli," I breathed out. Hummingbird on the Left.

The hummingbird hung frozen for a moment, his wings stilled, catching the light like delicate stained-glass windows to another dimension. Then the blue-skinned god stood beside us, gazing at the battlefield. Coatlicue's son, patron god of Tenochtitlan, House Zaniyah's former home before it fell to the Spanish. Dressed in his full regalia of long green and red feathers, his famous atlatl, Xiuhcoatl, in his right hand. God of the sun, blood sacrifice, and war.

Also our sister's sire.

Before Shara had gone to kill Ra, she'd resurrected Huitzilopochtli, and then returned his heart stolen by Ra. Returned to his full glory, he'd gone to live forever in Aztlan with his love, our mother, Citla, his star. Though her heart had been nearly destroyed by our sires in House Tocatl before she ever delivered her heir.

"Sons of Zaniyah, our Mother is well pleased with all you've accomplished."

Still gripping the obsidian blade, I pressed it over my heart and bowed to him. "Greetings, Lord of Sun. May you glitter and shine forever."

He held out his hand to me. I wasn't sure why he might want it, but I handed him the obsidian blade.

Lifting the knife up to the sun, he admired the thin, transparent edge. He lowered the blade to his nose, sniffing from the tip to the hilt, as if he could still identify every single drop of blood the knife had ever tasted.

He smiled, nodding to himself. "This blade has been well fed, yet it will always hunger for more."

Yes. I would always carry this monstrous hunger for pain, but it didn't shame me any longer. Not when our queen used me so well.

He touched the blade to Xiuhcoatl's curved tip. "Now itztli is kissed with tletl."

I knew he meant obsidian, the blade, not me. Yet a searing hot flame rippled over my skin, gone before I could even feel a singe or smell burning hair.

Huitzilopochtli handed me back my blade. I bowed low, pressing it over my heart again. "Thank you, Lord of Sun. You honor me."

He turned to Tlacel and smiled. "How may I bless you, precious serpent?"

"May I ask a question regarding blood?"

His eyes flared with interest. He knew all things regarding blood. He should, after reveling in the blood of thousands of sacrifices in his name. The steps of the Templo Mayor had run red with the blood of his offerings. "Always."

Tlacel inclined his head to the group of Gorgos Blood who stared straight ahead, still unmoving. "What's wrong with those Blood?"

Huitzilopochtli stared at the Blood for several long moments. His nostrils flared. Sun glinted around him, bouncing off the golden ornaments around his neck. His upper lip curled with distaste, and he shook his head. "The queen planted a command inside their skulls that controls them. It strips them of their free will."

"Like our Blood bonds with our queen?" Tlacel asked.

"This is violent. Vile, even." Huitzilopochtli shook his head. "They're *forced* to serve. Her command destroys their will without providing any power or sustenance at all. Beware, for it spreads like cuitlacoche, though you won't find it edible. Their blood will not be an honorable sacrifice to anything but the earth from whence it came. Toss their heads into a pyre and don't touch their blood."

Cuitlacoche was a prized, tasty fungus that grew on corn, spreading from a single drop of rain inside the husk. If we couldn't touch their blood... then I had to be the one to dispatch the twenty-four Blood. Me—and the Kijin. The shifters couldn't risk sinking their teeth into something that might spread to them.

Tlacel pressed his fist to his heart and bowed. "Thank you for the assistance, Lord of Sun."

Huitzilopochtli inclined his head sharply to him and then me. "Please convey my eternal gratitude to your lady for protecting the Daughters of Coatlicue. Through my line, Tenochtitlan rises once more. When Shara Isador has need of me, I will answer her Call without fail."

With a loud droning buzz, he disappeared in a flash of green and red feathers.

I touched the other Bloods' bonds. :*Leave the Gorgos Blood to me.*:

:*You can't fucking take on twenty fucking Blood by yourself,*: Ezra retorted.

I bared my teeth in a vicious smile. :*Watch me.*:

49

SHARA

Chills crept down my spine, but I stood still, my shoulders straight but relaxed, my face calm and collected. Hiding a tumult of anxiety crashing like Rik's mighty fists.

Just a few months ago, I'd been completely alone and oblivious to any of this magical vampire shit. Now, I stood inside a blood circle with three ancient, powerful Triune queens, preparing to submit to the Great Mother's will. Whatever that meant.

While my beloved Blood were locked outside.

I knew they'd eventually reach me. We'd find a way.

I didn't have to like it, though.

The last drop of Undina's blood closed the third circle and she turned to face the table. Lifting her hands, palms facing the table, she began to sing. Not in words, but deep, resonating sounds, echoing through the chamber like beautiful whale song. Her voice contained the ebb and flow of the tides. The majesty of an angry, stormy sea. The unfathomable depths sinking into complete darkness.

So deep, the sun never reached this place. Yet this darkness wouldn't respond to me. It wasn't my domain.

An edge of fear sliced through me. Her voice captured the feeling of awe, terror, and magnificence of swimming in deep, dark water where I couldn't see what manner of creature might be lurking below.

"Great Mother of All, Skolos gathers to enact Your will in this world. Long it has been since we came to Your table. It's been a time fraught with danger, but Your Daughters prevail." She looked over at me, the skin around her eyes and mouth tight with strain. "A penitent queen comes before Skolos. Until judgment is passed, Shara Isador, daughter of She Who Is and Was and Always Will Be, is bound to this circle. So decrees the Speaker, Skolos High Queen, Undina Ketea, so let it be."

Bound. No power. Unable to leave.

My eyes flared with shock, and my stomach churned on the bitter acid of betrayal. I'd come to help her. I'd saved her son. She'd witnessed my birth, which had helped me wriggle out of Marne Ceresa's net.

I thought we had some kind of understanding, but evidently I couldn't be more mistaken.

The Mother's words from the dream echoed in my mind. *:THEY NEED YOU, EVEN IF THEY DENY YOU. EVEN WHEN THEY DESPISE YOU.:*

Averting her face, Undina stepped around the table opposite me. Three luminescent blobs pushed up out of the floor, each positioned one third around the table. They glowed with the same soft blue light, gently billowing like breathing creatures, though I didn't see any arms or distinguishing features.

"I willingly take my seat at the Skolos Triune and offer my blood to the Mother."

Her words rang with a sharp edge, and I didn't miss the way she sat hard and quickly onto the gleaming blue blob, as if her knees gave out. She grabbed the edge of the table, and the seat flowed around her, growing larger to cover her entire body.

Even her face. Until she was completely swallowed in blue

jelly-like stuff. I could still see her floating inside the mass, a darker center suspended inside. Her body jolted and red bloomed into the transparent blob.

Blood.

As droplets of blood spread, the blueish blob quickly changed colors. First darker, almost purple, and then gleaming red like molten lava from the center of the earth. Two streams of red flowed down her arms to pour into the table she clutched like a lifeline. Her blood spilled into the surface of the table.

All the blood in her body.

The blob faded back to blue and changed its shape, molding to her mermaid body. Her hands still gripped the table with long, glistening white claws shoved into its surface.

Goddess. Guillaume had tried to describe the process to me, but seeing it actually happen...

I let out a shaky breath. Someday, I'd need to do the same thing with Triskeles. It wouldn't look the same, but the general process would be similar.

Nuri came to stand beside me, facing the table. Voice soft and low, she said, "the kraken is Undina's son, a king, is he not? How do you control him without chains?"

"Love," I replied. "The same way I love Leviathan. My kings serve as Blood because they love me. Not because I force them."

"Fascinating." She glided toward the seat on the left side of the table. "I, Nuri Kijin, willingly take my seat at the Skolos Triune and offer my blood to the Mother."

Gripping the table with both hands, she bowed her head and blew out three deep, hard breaths. Then she dropped into the seat. It flowed around her the same way, draining her blood into the table, until the chair shifted into a sinuous serpent—though it still had her head with long flowing black hair.

My heart thudded heavily, my breathing coming too fast. Once Basilia took her seat, the Triune would be complete.

Though she wasn't in any hurry to join the other two

queens. After seeing with my own eyes what taking a seat at the table meant, I honestly couldn't blame her.

"Skolos has a quorum," she said. "There's no reason for me to take my seat."

"We need to be complete." Undina's voice stretched out in a deep, resonant echo. "Skolos gathers for the first time in nearly four hundred years."

Basilia's eyes seemed to glow eerie green in the bioluminescence. "To pass judgment, you only need a quorum."

"Judgment for what, exactly?" I asked slowly.

She shrugged. "Ask Undina. It's her quorum. She called us to the table."

"I will compel you." Undina's voice rolled with the power of the stormy sea. "The Speaker has the power."

"You can try," Basilia replied with a shrug. "Though I don't think you're strong enough, even united with Kijin."

"Your blood circle is first because you're the weakest," Undina retorted.

"Not any longer." A small smile curved Basilia's lips. "Much can change over the span of decades. For instance, look at how much power Shara's gained, and so very quickly. It's quite impressive. But that's exactly why we're here, is it not?"

After hundreds of years, who knew what new power Basilia may have inherited from a dead queen's legacy? A new Blood?

She certainly had more Blood than the other two queens from what I'd seen. Maybe she'd gained so much power she could claim Undina's place as Speaker. Though that would require Basilia to take her seat first so her blood could be measured.

My head throbbed with pressure, my bones vibrating with urgency. Time was running out.

I need to change the game. Make my play. Before it's too late.

:*Shara,*: Sekh growled, his bond thundering with his sphinx's roar. :*I can break the circles.*:

:Not yet. I have an idea.:

Basilia didn't want to take her seat.

Fine.

Gathering my courage, I took a deep breath, threw myself toward the table.

And dropped into the vacant Skolos seat.

50

SHARA

I couldn't say the words out loud, but I'd already made my offering at the door.

The blob swallowed me whole. It didn't care that I wasn't Skolos. Only that I offered my blood to the table. I didn't feel a prick to draw my blood—but my hand still bled. It felt like slow motion as I pressed my palms to the table, forcing my arms to move through the cold substance around me. It truly did feel like being inside a jellyfish, floating in gelatin.

As soon as my palm pressed to the gleaming surface, I felt a hard, sinking dip in my energy. Like when I'd first given Sekh blood, a massive faucet turned on somewhere, only instead of filling a massive tub, it started to empty.

Out of me.

I reached for my bonds, wanting the comfort of Rik's steady presence. My rock.

But my bonds were gone.

There was only me. Pouring into the Skolos table like a monsoon.

So much blood.

All my blood.

My awareness of my body faded. I didn't feel cold any longer. I couldn't feel the strange, tacky sensation on my skin as the blob shifted around me. But I could feel the other two queens at the table. No, it was more than that.

They were me. I was them.

We are together.

Our blood mingles into one. Blood of the Mother turns the entire table into gleaming red lava. We are complete. We are whole.

Measure the Blood of the Mother.

Shara carries the most, most, most...

Shara is Triskeles. This table is Skolos.

Undina is the Speaker of Skolos.

Our table is complete.

We know everything the others know.

Undina regrets her mistakes. She truly loves her son. She agreed to act as witness for Esetta on the barest hope Shara would someday find a way to free him. Not only from the queen of Rome—but also his beast.

We hear Esetta's name and remember it because Shara remembers it.

Shara screams, "Rik!"

But he can't hear.

Nuri whispers, "We have a king. Can we unchain him?"

But only the Speaker spoke aloud. "The Skolos Triune is complete."

Shock ripples through us. We didn't know a Triune queen could take a seat at another Triune's table.

Though the Mother knows Her blood.

Blood is the key.

We see everything the others see.

We see Shara's alpha surging forward. Granite fists pounding on the blood circles. Rage pouring through him. Through them all. They don't like losing Shara's bond. Not at all.

"Why are we here?" Shara asks. "What must we accomplish?

"The Mother speaks through us," the Speaker said. "Make your claim before Her court."

We had to get Shara here, Undina whispers. *"The lure to bring the three together." Regret flows through us like a drop of ink in the blood. "It wasn't supposed to be like this."*

Basilia stares wide eyed at the table. Her mouth opens. Her eyes change. Darken. Her shock shifts as she makes a cold, mercenary decision. Her face hardens. She has made her choice.

Nothing is guaranteed but Carys saw a one-hundred percent likelihood.

Basilia wants Shara dead.

"Why? Why? Why?" Echoes through us.

She refused to come to the table. She delayed. She wouldn't accept our calls. She wouldn't take her seat. She didn't want us to know.

What?

What does she hide?

Basilia pulls a knife out of her long, tapered sleeve. She steps closer to the table.

Where Shara sits.

Our arms are pinned to the table. We are one. We cannot move. We cannot speak.

Penelope throws her tiny body at Basilia and bites her hand, shaking like a vicious little terrier. Basilia drops the knife with a curse.

"We charge Basilia Gorgos with failing to uphold her duties to the Mother," the Speaker said. "What is Skolos' answer?"

Guilty. Guilty. Guilty.

"The Skolos Triune declares Basilia Gorgos guilty. We expel her from her Skolos seat."

Leaning down to scoop up the knife, Basilia whispers into our ear. "I'm not Skolos."

The knife descends toward our arm. Our wrist. Steel glistens in the red glow of the Mother's blood.

And bounces off the golden snake wrapped around our wrist.

All our Blood surge toward the table. Our alphas. Our best killers. Our kings.

They know our danger now.

Kill one queen seated at the table and kill them all.

Undina's alpha falls. A Gorgos blade in his heart.

We scream, "Iason!"

Shara's Blood bellows a murderous roar. Something pops up inside the circle. A red and green scarab.

We smile.

The first blood circle detonates, an explosion that knocks Blood to the ground and cracks the transparent windows of the chamber. Undina's circle is gone. Outer to inner blood circle in the reverse order in which they were laid. One by one by one.

It takes time.

Time we don't have.

Snarling, the silver wolf crouches at the edge of the remaining two blood circles. Straining to shift the resonance so he can pass through. But two harmonies object to his shift. He cannot unite the resonance to his. He cannot pass. Yet.

"We were careful with the wording as House Isador passed into the nest," the Speaker said.

All Isador Blood may enter our nest. But that won't help them cross the last two blood circles.

We need time. We need our miracle. Say it.

"We need time," the Speaker said. "We need our miracle."

Basilia slashes at our throat. "Die, you fucking bitch."

The knife bounces off the golden collar on our neck.

We feel Shara's Blood coming through our nest. The sky's black with wings. Undina's Blood race down the spiral pathway, leading the way.

We see the Triune Executioner dancing from side to side. Bodies fall. No Gorgos Blood remain inside our nest.

Leviathan blasts flames at the remaining circles. Xin gnaws at the coral floor, tearing his gums. They cannot pass.

Nightwing Starlight flies up out of our hair and stabs her beak into Basilia's eye, her talons ripping at her face.

Basilia screams and slashes at our throat again. Another blow rings like a bell against the golden collar.

"Why won't you fucking die like your mother?"

The gryphon carries a Blood in his front talons. Wings beat frantically as they fly down the spiraled path.

Lew releases Thierry and shoves him toward us.

Another scarab pops up out of the floor.

We smile.

The second blood circle explodes in a wave of heat that rattles the table beneath our palms. Nuri's blood circle is gone. Cracks spider web across the clear surface of the walls but they hold. Barely.

Come in like a lamb. Say it.

"Come in like a lamb," the Speaker said.

Only Basilia's blood circle remains.

She runs around the table toward Undina. No cursed jewelry will protect us all. The Speaker can't be silenced or—

Basilia raises the knife and plunges it into our throat. "Kill one, and they all die."

None of us can speak.

Basilia's words echo in our consciousness. "I'm not Skolos."

Leviathan's words echo. "She doesn't smell like a Gorgon."

Thierry falls across the blood circle. It's still there. Sekh hasn't torn it apart yet. Stumbling. Crawling. To our side. His broken body oozing black taint.

The Dauphine's taint.

Her blood.

He crossed the third blood circle.

We know.

We know who Basilia really is.

Names flicker through our consciousness.

Leonie Delafosse.

Jeanne Viennois.

Dauphiné of Viennois.

The Speaker gurgled, trying to say the name.

Only the Speaker can speak. We are silenced.

Blood pours out of the table like a tidal wave flooding the coral floor. So much blood.

An ocean of blood.

Thierry's fingers close over our wrist. On the bracelet. So careful despite the urgency.

Time. Stops.

Blood stops pouring out of the table. The faucet shuts off.

Our miracle.

We look up. Through the infinite depths of the sea to lighter cerulean. Then baby blue sky. Higher. The air is thin and empty and tasteless.

Here stands the guardian for all time. All Seeing. Never Sleeping.

We will the sphinx's golden eyes to See us.

We look at Basilia Gorgos, bloody knife in hand. Vicious glee glints in her brown eyes. Eyes that aren't Basilia's.

Now See her, mighty sphinx.

See who she really is.

We peel away the mask of Basilia Gorgos. We peel away the mask of Leonie Delafosse.

A blank face stares back at us. At him.

Sekh roared. "The Dauphine!"

51

SEKH

Come in like a fucking lamb, she said. When she was trapped inside with the fucking Dauphine and the Mother's table bled like the foundation of the world had burst open.

Fuck that shit.

At least Thierry had been able to stop time. Everyone was frozen but us—the ones who carried Isador blood.

:It won't last long,: Lew warned. *:In his prime, he could hold time for ten minutes, tops. I don't know how much he has left.:*

A minute longer was all I'd need.

I shoved harder, burrowing the scarab up toward the surface. Crack open the coral. Flood this chamber. Leviathan or Okeanos would be able to get her out. The rest of us…

:If one of us dies, she dies,: Rik ground out. *:You can't risk it.:*

Xin howled, a high-pitched resonance almost beyond my hearing. His fur rippled in the red glow of the table, shifting colors. Red to the eerie blue bioluminescence to a burst of white that seared my eyes and then faded to nothing.

:I'm in.:

Crouching lower, he launched himself, his legs springing his body forward. Flying over our queen. The table. Straight at the queen who stood frozen, arm raised. The bloody knife moved. Her arm jerked.

Thierry's fingers slipped, his failing body shuddering with effort.

:Hold, Thierry,: Lew strained in the bond, as if by will alone he could help his friend. *:Just a little longer. Our queen needs your miracle.:*

Xin's jaws closed around the Dauphine's throat. He slowly fell to the side, pulling her down with him. Her body flopped like a rag doll in his grip. He surged again, leaping toward us. Eyes burning red in the table's glow. Dragging the queen out of her own fucking blood circle.

Thierry's arm slipped to the floor, and he lay face down, unmoving.

The dull roar of blood pouring from the table filled the chamber. The Dauphine's arm slammed the knife into the wolf's flank. Again and again, her scream of rage rose to a shriek that rattled the weakened walls. Glass tinged. Splintering worse.

The wolf crashed to the floor and rolled, flinging the queen toward us.

Leviathan belched flames at her with all the hatred in his black heart. Yet nothing happened to her. Her clothes didn't catch fire. Her skin didn't burn. Even her throat remained unmarked by Xin's teeth.

Rik's rock troll slammed his fists together around her head with all the strength of his giant body. He hadn't been able to damage me much—and she only laughed. Taunting him. Clapping as if we were performing a circus act for her.

The crow and rat had been able to harm her. But not us.

Because we were Blood?

"I've got this." Guillaume de Payne's Templar sword whispered the promise of death as he lifted it before him and kissed the blade. "Find a way to stop the bleeding."

Despite the knight's words, the kraken's tentacles boiled around her. Squeezing her. Trying to crush the life out of her.

But he couldn't make her laughter stop.

Okeanos withdrew but slammed against the blood circle, slinging his longest tentacle toward the table.

Coated with the Dauphine's blood from her cheek and wounded hand—the tentacle passed through the blood circle.

He stretched, straining to reach Undina's throat. His entire body pressed against the shimmering energy of the circle. Even though it hurt. The sizzle and pop of his flesh cooking in the heat of the Dauphine's power.

Roaring in pain, he shoved the tip of the tentacle into his mother's throat.

The circle sheared through the tentacle, severing it from his body. But the twitching limb curled around his mother's neck. Sealing the wound.

Blood stopped pouring from the table. Buying us time.

I could shift into the sphinx—but there wasn't room inside the fragile chamber. Not with the dragon, kraken, and rock troll already shifted. And if they couldn't harm her, what could I do?

"You can't kill me, Executioner." The Dauphine laughed, shaking her head. "My body's wrapped in Eleusinian Mysteries and cannot be penetrated except by creatures of the natural world. Don't you think Desideria would have eliminated me first if it had been within her power to do so?"

Unperturbed, Guillaume causally flicked his sword at her. It wasn't a slash or stab meant to harm or even cut her. His wrist turned the flat of the blade against her wounded cheek.

The Dauphine spread her arms, tipped back her head, and laughed joyously. "I believe you missed, sir knight."

"Did I, though? How does that steel taste, bitch? Because my queen blessed this blade with her very own blood before we left New York City."

Unease flickered over her face, and she slowly lowered her arms. "A mere drop of your precious queen's blood can't stand against me."

The knight smiled. "Desideria said something very similar to me when she first tasted Esetta Isador's venom in my blood. It doesn't take much, though. A mere drop is enough to turn your fucking face as black as your soul, and my queen has feasted on several of her poisoned Blood. Recently, in fact. So the venom should still be nice and strong."

I didn't See any change to her face, but she reached up with trembling fingers to cover the wound.

"She has sibs. Blood. They've tasted her blood and not died."

"True." Guillaume nodded, turning the sword so the blade lay against his other palm. Holding her gaze, he licked the blade close to the hilt, letting his eyes flutter in bliss as if he could still taste Shara. "Though her blood was freely given to us. What do you think her blood will do to the one who turned her mother and former Blood into walking zombies?"

SHARA

THE TENTACLE CURLS AROUND OUR THROAT. STOPPING THE BLOOD *streaming from the table.*

Oh, mighty kraken. How we love you.

So much blood. Waiting to be used.

Call it back. Pull it back to the Mother. Her daughters. We need it.

Deep inside, we pull. The ceaseless tug of the tides. The inescapable gravity of a black hole. This blood is ours. It flows back to the Mother of All.

To us.

The slash in our throat closes in an instant. Our injured Blood rise. The shattered, fragile walls smooth into glistening starlight and clear crystal.

"Now," the Speaker said.

A third scarab pops free of the coral. The sphinx smiles with us.

The boom rolls up from the ocean floor, a rippling wave of energy from the table's epicenter. So much power the water recedes outside of the chamber, swelling waves from thousands of feet deep.

Too much. Human cities won't be able to survive such a tsunami.

Winds rise, a howling wall ahead of the waves. Crashing together, angry seas and dark skies and flashing fins and glistening tentacles. All things of the deep. Catching the waves, absorbing the energy, and dissipating it back to the ocean.

Where it belongs.

An unnatural sound pierces our chamber. A wail of agony.

"Mother, forgive me," the Dauphine screamed. "Take my life and spare me this pain!"

Our venom spreads through her body. A single drop tainting the wellspring of her blood. Cells die. She feels her life draining away.

Nothing can save her. Not her goddess. Not even Her Mysteries.

But it's not enough.

Not after what she's done.

We will never forget.

Thierry's screams as the Dauphine's black leeches slid out of him. His rotted insides spewing from his mouth even as his heart continued to beat. His sweet soul trapped inside dead flesh.

Selena's beautiful spirit shoved inside a decomposing corpse that died five years earlier. A stumbling, mindless zombie forced to find us on foot. A deliberate message to wound and cause as much emotional pain as possible.

Esetta's words echo in our consciousness. "Make her soul rot in the rankest filth for all time."

We take all our pain. All our rage. Thierry's screams. Selena's horror.

We multiply it with the sphinx's power of transference. Making it a million times worse.

And we shove it all into Jeanne Viennois.

52

SHARA

I stood in a shadowed room.

Me, in my body and mind, alone.

I'm Shara Isador. Last daughter of Isis.

I just killed one of the Mother's daughters in as gruesome and painful way as I could imagine. The Dauphine's insides liquified by venom. Her soul wrapped in dead, rotting flesh. Horror upon pain upon poison.

A hard smile curved my lips.

And I'm fucking glad.

"Me too," Esetta said on my left. Her arm wrapped around my waist.

"Me three," Selena said on my right. "Damn her and her entire House for what she did to us."

My mothers.

Then who stood at my back? Because I could feel someone pressed against me. Arms came around me. Polished obsidian. Glittering gold nails. Lapis lazuli and diamonds and gold wrapped around Her wrist.

I smelled blowing sands mixed with precious incense. The white, delicate flowers of night-blooming jasmine. The lush spice of blue lotus. The sensual velvet of roses.

Our goddess's arms enveloped me in Her strength and love. "I build my future—and the Great Mother's—through you."

The gloom lightened enough for me to look around the chamber. Rough, natural stone walls stretched upward into darkness, but the chamber was large enough I couldn't see any ceiling. Roots protruded from the stone and arched around a dark cleft in the rock.

The Mother's words from the dream repeated in my head. :*ONLY THE ROOTS REMAIN.*:

We must be standing beneath the World Tree. Or what was left of it.

A woman strode out of the cleft.

A goddess. Power shimmered around Her but I couldn't see Her face and only the vaguest shape of Her body. She wore a long, heavy cloth over Her head obscuring the rest of Her body. Though the cloth wasn't soft or flowing at all. It seemed stiff and hard, as if carved from cold alabaster.

:*She's known as Despoina.*: Isis' voice rumbled through my head, making my teeth vibrate in my skull. :*Though her true name is known only to those inside the Eleusinian Mysteries.*:

"So this is the woman who murdered my daughter, Jeanne Viennois."

My throat tightened but I didn't flinch. I didn't bow my head with guilt. I wasn't sorry. At all. Maybe that made me a monster. So be it. "Yes."

"I demand recompense. I demand her life."

Isis released a low, rumbling growl of laughter, and the stone shook beneath my feet. "Your daughter tried to kill three queens bound to the Great Mother's table. Without Shara Isador, another Triune would be lost. Her life is too great a price, especially when she was doing the Mother's will." Her voice sharpened like a blade. "When your daughter refused."

A deep, resonating gong rolled from the cleft. :I CALLED

THIS DAUGHTER OF MY DAUGHTER, AND SHE WENT WHERE I POINTED. SHE SAVED WHAT WOULD HAVE BEEN DOOMED.:

Despoina's head bowed, the heavy veil shifting around Her body as if She brought Her hands together in supplication. "She gains too much power, Mother. She already has power over the grave and gained House Modron's legacy through her mother. Now she's to gain mine without any cost to her house or any diminishment of her extreme power? Who's to stand against her?"

I couldn't see Isis' face but I felt Her smile in my bones. "No one."

:THE COST IS HIGH, DAUGHTER OF MY DAUGHTER. SO YOU AGREED.:

"I did, Great Mother." I swallowed hard but tipped my chin up. "Though I beg You not to take any of my loved ones. Please. I can't bear to lose them."

"If she's to gain my Mysteries, then I wish to strip away her power over the grave. Let her carry the fear of death with her that cannot be resurrected."

No. Please. I clenched my jaws, fighting down the words. *I won't beg this goddess for mercy.*

Only the Mother, and She'd already heard my plea.

"I would not be well pleased to welcome Shara Isador home before her appointed time," Isis retorted.

Despoina shrugged. "I could agree to her still being able to resurrect herself. But she should know a fraction of the fear my daughter suffered as she died."

I couldn't imagine the Dauphine fearing anything as much as I feared losing one of my Blood. Someone from my family. I'd already lost both of my mothers. The only father I'd ever known. Must I lose more of the people I loved?

My heart felt bruised and swollen, too large for my chest

cavity. I couldn't breathe through the pain just at the thought of watching any of my Blood die.

No. I won't. I can't.

We all go together. So I promised Coatlicue.

:There's always a way,: Esetta whispered in my mind.

With enough blood. And time.

Silence weighed heavier. Isis' displeasure evident—and mounting by the moment. Her hands closed on my shoulders, Her fingers as unyielding as stone. "So be it."

Something fluttered inside my chest and then was gone. I shivered. My spirit was still seated deep in my body, but I'd felt the loss of… something.

Despoina's head tipped forward in acknowledgement. "I'm satisfied."

:IT IS DONE.:

The room started to fade away, but I noticed a small stream of water trickled from the dark cleft in the rock. Watering the roots of the World Tree.

Arms tightened around me. I clung to them. Breathing in their scents. Soaking in their touch. My mothers. My goddess.

:Fret not, Daughter of Isador,: Isis whispered in my head. *:You still carry many of my gifts, but more importantly, you carry my blood, and thus the Blood of Gaia. Your blood will always be your greatest weapon.:*

53

SHARA

Before I opened my eyes, I knew exactly where I was. In Rik's arms. His heart thudded beneath my ear. His mouth pressed to my hair, waiting for me to come around.

My bonds filled my head, bringing tears to my eyes. I soaked in my Blood. Wallowed in their emotions. Shining rivers winding through my mind, tying us together. Forever.

Penelope's whiskers tickled my cheek, and she slipped back into my hair.

:Thank you, my loves.:

A wet cough nearby made my eyes fly open. I sat up and turned to Thierry.

He lay beside me in a black puddle. I wasn't even sure he could see any longer, not the way his eyes had sunken into his skull. Most of the skin had torn away on his lower jaw, showing gray, pitted bone.

Lew crouched on the other side of him, holding one of his hands in both of his. He met my gaze, his eyes tortured pools of tears. *:It's time to let him go.:*

I closed my eyes for a moment, fighting back a sob. Even if

I'd wanted to try and heal him again, I couldn't this time. I couldn't resurrect him.

I'd never be able to resurrect anyone again—other than myself.

"Miracle," Thierry croaked.

Oh goddess. My heart.

Crying, I opened my eyes and reached for his other hand.

He flopped and jerked away. "Taint. Filth."

"No taint can touch me now." Soothingly, I closed my fingers around his, smearing his hand with my blood. I must have cut my hand deeply on the coral for it to still be bleeding. "You saved me, Thierry. You did what no one else could do."

"Time."

I nodded, my throat aching. "It's time to send you to fly with Esetta now."

His head jerked. I wasn't sure if he meant no, or if it was just his dying nerves. I stroked his hair back off his forehead. His mouth worked, the tendons crackling beneath my palm. "Worth it."

"I love you, Thierry Isador." I switched hands so I could lay my right on his chest. "Give my mother a kiss from me when you reach her."

I wasn't sure I could still pull his spirit out, but I needed to try. I refused to burn him alive, and as long as his soul was trapped inside his corpse, he wouldn't be able to fully die.

I'd lost the power of resurrection. Not death itself. Right?

Closing my eyes, I shoved my fist into his chest as gently as possible. My blood illuminated the way to the small, trapped bird behind where his heart should have been. Most of his internal organs were already dissolved. I wrapped my fingers around his spirit and pulled it free.

My blood melted away the black goo trapping his wings.

I smiled through my tears and lightly stroked my index finger over his white head. "Thank you."

He shook the long red tail feathers and spread his wings partially open but hesitated, his head cocked inquisitively.

"Go. It's time. It's okay."

Nightwing Starlight hopped across the coral floor and sent me an image of many black wings flying away—with a single speck of blue in their midst.

"Yes, please. Show him the way out."

He chirped a long string of high, sweet notes, and then leaped into the air. Nightwing cawed and swept back up the tunnel toward the surface where the rest of her murder waited.

My shoulders slumped and I let myself lean back against Rik. Just for a moment. Soaking in his unfailing, steady strength. Then I closed my eyes and willed my blood to burn.

Flames spread up through the hole in Thierry's chest. Burning hot enough I opened my eyes and let Rik pull me to my feet so we could back up.

Lew came around Thierry's burning body to wrap me in a fierce hug. "Thank you, my queen."

"Thank you for bringing him." I let out a long, shuddering breath. Undina and Nuri both stood waiting for me, listening and watching everything I did and said, so I switched to our bond. :*I'm glad we did what we did in New York City before we came here. I can't resurrect anyone now.*:

Lew's eyes flared.

Rik's arms tightened around me. :*Ever?*:

I still felt a lump of guilt and shame in my throat that had nothing to do with sending Thierry to be at peace, and everything to do with losing one of my goddess' gifts. :*Despoina demanded my gift of resurrection as payment.*:

:*Fuck that bitch,*: Mehen retorted. :*She would have killed all three of you. What the fuck would that have cost her?*:

:*We'll never know.*:

:*Damned straight,*: Guillaume said. :*Because our queen never loses. At least you gained her powers, my queen.*:

:*Oh goody. Now I can turn dead people into zombies and Blood into thralls with disgusting black leeches.*:

I couldn't imagine ever needing, let alone *wanting*, to do such a thing.

I walked closer to my knight and leaned in to kiss his cheek. My dragon. My kraken. I pressed my still bleeding hand to his wounded stump. :*I'm so sorry.*:

One of his other tentacles flitted up to lightly touch my cheek. :*It'll grow back. As Thierry said, it was worth it.*:

I dropped down to my knees before my wolf and ran my hands over his flanks and chest. "I saw her stab you. Did we already heal you?"

:*No mere knife could ever stop me from your target, my queen.*:

I buried my face in his fur and wrapped my arms around his neck. Breathing in his scent. :*I thought I might lose you today.*:

:*Never, my queen.*:

Releasing him, I pushed back to my feet and reluctantly turned to the Dauphine's body. Sekh stood over her, casually guarding her just in case she managed to draw breath again. Though her body was misshapen and lumpy in weird places.

"She swelled up with poison until her skin split open." His lips twitched. "The dragon called dibs on her heart, or I would have taken care of this mess for you already, Your Majesty."

:*I didn't know her heart would fucking melt into a fucking puddle of poisonous slime,*: Mehen retorted.

"I thought dragons enjoyed slime."

:*Shut your fucking mouth.*:

"Or what?" Sekh asked mildly.

:*Our queen looks like she needs to watch another hatefuck.*:

"Enough," I said, shaking my head. Torn between laughing—and shuddering at the thought of Sekh chowing down on the Dauphine's ravaged body—I held my hand out over her corpse and dripped blood from her feet, up her body, to her face.

Still blurred and oddly blank, as if she didn't have cheekbones, chin, or barely even a nose to help me identify her. Even though she was finally dead, I had no idea what her true face looked like.

Not that I fucking cared.

"You were never a fraction of the fucking epic queen my mother was."

Turning away, I willed my blood to light with all the heat of my rage.

Justice. For Mom. For Thierry.

Burn until not even ash remains.

54

SHARA

All I wanted to do was go home and collapse into bed for a fucking week.

But watching the way Gina's eyes widened and her mouth fell open, her phone pressed to her ear, I had a feeling the giant ass stack of folders we'd gone through the last time we sat down to handle Triskeles business was only the tip of the fucking iceberg.

I'd killed the Dauphine, one of the longest living and most powerful—not to mention the most secretive—Aima queens. I had no fucking clue how much shit I'd just inherited with her legacy. Surely there were sibs. Properties. Treaties to figure out. I wasn't sure of the legal complexities. If House Isador absorbed House Viennois, what did that mean for House Valois, Jeanne's daughter?

What about House Gorgos? Where was the real Basilia? Undina and Nuri had both sat at the Skolos table with her hundreds of years ago. Sekh had Seen her. The real queen.

Somewhere, somehow, she'd fallen to the Dauphine. And nobody had noticed a fucking thing.

Had Leonie Delafosse ever been real? Or just a persona the Dauphine created to get close to me?

I needed to go with Xin back to the swamp and see if those… things… had died with the Dauphine or if they still needed to be freed. I'd probably have to go to Mykonos and check there too. See if there were any clues to what had happened to the real Basilia.

Wincing, Gina held the phone away from her ear.

"Is somebody yelling at you?" I asked incredulously.

She nodded and mouthed, "the queen of Rome."

I marched over and took the phone from her hand. "This is Shara Isador. Don't fucking call us back until you can be civil. Good day."

And I hung up.

Kevin's phone started ringing. Eyes wide, he pulled it out of his pocket, glanced at the screen, and looked up at me, his face pale. "It's Granddad."

"Put him on speaker." I held my hand out. He accepted the call and placed the phone in my hand. "This is Shara Isador." Barely, I managed to bite back, *What the fuck do you want?*

"Oh. Since when does the queen answer her consiliarius' phone?"

Byrnes must be rattled to speak so informally. It'd be like Winston slipping up and calling me Shara. "Whenever I want. Was that you or your queen yelling at Gina?"

He harrumphed and cleared his throat. "Her Majesty is… uh… indisposed."

"I see. Maybe she should call back when she feels better."

He lowered his voice, whispering quickly. "Is it true that Jeanne Dauphine is dead?"

"Yes."

"Oh dear. Yes, Her Majesty will call you back at a more suitable time. Unless you… uh… I mean…"

I decided to put the poor man out of his misery. He was

Kevin's grandfather after all. "I have no intention of coming to Rome any time soon."

"Of course, of course. It's just... You see..."

I sighed. "If Marne Ceresa hasn't committed any crimes for which she needs to be penitent, then she has nothing to worry about."

Silence.

That's what I fucking thought. No fucking surprise there.

I made my voice as pleasant as possible. "As I said, Byrnes, I have no *immediate* plans to come to Rome. Now if you'll forgive me, we have a lot of business to discuss here."

Besides, if I really wanted to kill her...

I wouldn't have to go to Rome to do so. Though I didn't admit that to her consiliarius.

I hung up and gave the phone back to Kevin.

"I'm so sorry, Your Majesty."

I gave him a wry smile. "Not your fault at all. If Rome tries to call us again in the next twenty-four hours, our phones aren't working. Agreed?"

"Agreed," Kevin and Gina said at the same time.

The other two Skolos queens stood on the hill overlooking the beach, waiting for me to join them. Our Blood were busy cleaning up the many Gorgos bodies. Without my bonds, I hadn't been able to see what happened outside the nest while we were bound to the table, but Rik had given me a quick rundown. Thanks to Huitzilopochtli, my Blood had known something was seriously wrong with the Gorgos Blood, even though they didn't smell like taint.

Itztli had been fully prepared to take them all on single handedly.

But there hadn't been a fight. At all.

The Dauphine hadn't given a shit about them. She'd left them standing frozen, unable to move. Even after she died, they'd stood frozen like statues, waiting to fall to our blades.

"Evidently, most of them really were Basilia's Blood," Undina said, shaking her head. "Do you know how the Dauphine controlled them?"

I didn't care to explain why the Aztec god of sun and war had given my Blood intel, so I simply said, "When I tried to heal Thierry, I found giant black eel-like things in him." They still made me shudder. "The first thing he asked me was if I'd gotten the leeches out."

"No eel or leech would have done such a thing," Undina replied. "No natural animal wishes to ruin and rot a body like that. Even maggots serve a purpose, but these... things... don't even decompose correctly."

Guillaume used the curved, heavy kukri to hack another head off and tossed it into a burning pile that Frank blasted with his flamethrower. Sure, the dragon or phoenix could have done the job, but he loved having something to do.

Luckily for me, the leech eels the Dauphine had planted in them were still localized in their brains, which was probably why Huitzilopochtli had told Itztli we needed to burn the heads. At least I didn't have to go around pulling stuck spirits out of all the corpses. The thought of this nasty power living inside of me made me want to hurl.

"You could have taken the Speaker position," Undina said without looking at me.

I shrugged. "I'm Triskeles. Skolos is your table. I just helped you complete it."

"We should meet regularly to discuss Triune business. All Triune business."

"I agree." I nodded. "I'd also like to learn more about the Screaming Madness you mentioned once before. None of my Blood know what that is."

"I don't know much more than them, but I'll tell you what I know."

"You don't mind?" Nuri whispered.

Confused, I turned toward her, but with the red mask over her face, I couldn't read her expression for context. "I'm sorry?"

Undina wrapped an arm around her shoulders and gave her a hug. "I told you it wasn't a problem."

Bewildered, I looked from one queen to the other. "You thought I'd be upset about something?"

Nuri reached up to her mask and slowly removed it. Tears shimmered in her jade eyes, and she stared at me for long moments. Waiting. For something.

When I didn't react, she dropped her head to Undina's shoulder.

Okeanos' mother wasn't a warm and fuzzy kind of queen, so any tenderness shocked the hell out of me. But I didn't know what to say. I didn't see any reason for Nuri to wear a mask. She wasn't hiding a deformity or scar, not that either would repulse me anyway. She was beautiful. Her skin glowed with power, and she moved like a graceful, elegant swan.

"I was born male," Nuri finally said. "Few queens see me as an actual queen."

I blinked a couple of times, letting her words filter through my head. "We were bound together to the Mother's table. Our blood mingled into one. Our thoughts merged. And you thought I wouldn't believe you're a queen?"

Her mouth opened. Shut.

"Together, we created a tsunami so powerful it could have leveled every human city on every coast in the world. Who am I to judge you worthy of the gifts your goddess blessed you with?"

Eyes shining, she smiled and reached out to take my hand. "I have someone you need to meet."

I felt Rik behind me, signaling the rest of my Blood I was on the move. Though they already knew. They all hovered close in my mind, as desperate to get home and hold each other as me. *:Let's get everyone to the yacht.:*

:Fuck yeah,: Ezra said. *:Let's blow this fucking joint.:*

:Blow me,: Leviathan growled.

:In your fucking dreams, asswipe.:

:All I dream about is getting another taste of our queen, moth-erfucker.:

Nuri led me to a group of her Blood who stood under a large palm just outside the nest. I turned and gave Undina a wave. She lifted her hand in a casual salute, but her lips moved. *"Thank you."*

"I hope you can help him," Nuri said. "I don't like to see him chained all the time, but we don't have any other way to control him. This is my brother, Vore."

I'd seen the large bull creature when House Kijin approached the nest. Sekh said he was a king flesh eater.

Rik shifted his body ahead of me, not blocking my line of sight but ready to defend me at a moment's notice. Though the king was so heavily bound, he could barely move.

He stood as tall as Rik, his shoulders and neck just as wide, built to carry the immense load of those gleaming black horns. The rest of his upper body wasn't as muscled as my alpha. What I could see of his face was red and mostly human-looking except for his heavy brow, the horns, and the pointed ears of the bull. A heavy shock of black hair hung down over his forehead. A metal mask sealed his mouth and wrapped around his head. Silencing him. Gagging him.

His lower body was spider-like with six jointed black legs with jagged tips that looked as sharp as Itztli's obsidian blade.

"I'm afraid there's not much I can do."

Nuri's smile slowly faded. "But your kings can control their beasts. I thought…"

"Because they're my Blood." I replied gently. "I only take Blood that I love."

Her head tipped to the side. "You can't love him?"

My eyes flared and I had to laugh. "Well, let's see. I usually know pretty quickly…"

I placed my hand on Rik's back, and we stepped closer to Vore. I watched his face, searching his eyes. Mostly red with pupils of inky black. Sparking with emotion.

With hope. Searing, soul-yearning hope.

The kind of hope I would move mountains, drain oceans, and destroy the world to save.

:Fucking hell,: Mehen sighed. :Not another motherfucking king.:

:It'll be like Christmas all the time,: Sekh drawled. :We Three Kings.:

:Shut the fuck up.:

Rik sent an alpha thump through the bond. :Get your asses over here in case we need help wrestling him into submission.:

:Yeah, like the fucking sphinx,: Mehen purred.

:Sounds like someone's ready to whimper and beg again.:

:Anytime, motherfucker. Bring it the fuck on.:

Rolling my eyes, I gestured to the chains. "Let's get these off him, please."

The four Kijin Blood looked uneasily to their queen. At her nod, three of them backed away and drew long, curved swords from underneath their expensive-looking suits. The other Blood pulled a ring of keys from his pocket.

Guillaume suddenly appeared on my other side. Templar sword at the ready. He didn't like anyone near me with steel in their hands.

The dragon and Sekh took up position behind the king. Vore dropped down lower to the ground, making himself as small as possible, but he was still fucking huge. I needed to take his blood first to ensure I had a good hold on him, but his legs looked too sharp to fuck around with too close to my mouth.

:It's my fucking turn to take my queen on a ride.: Mehen shifted his body around the other king, stretching his long neck out toward me. :I can lift you up higher and get you the fuck out if he wants to be a prick.:

I looped my arm around his neck and stepped up on his

shorter foreleg, bracing my body against him as he shifted back on his hindquarters. He clanged his teeth at Vore, smoke puffing from his mouth.

The bull shook his head, brandishing his horns like weapons. But it was one of the sharper spider legs that tapped Leviathan's lighter scales on his stomach. He didn't need to speak to make his threats.

"Oh, I like him," Sekh said approvingly.

:He might gut me but I'll roast his ass first,: Mehen retorted.

Higher up, now, I could see the metal cutting into Vore's cheeks. My jaws tightened with fury, though I couldn't fault Nuri for at least trying to get help for her brother. Most kings were killed before they were ever a threat to their houses.

A loud click sent a shudder through Vore's body. One chain gone.

"I only take Blood that I love," I repeated, watching his eyes. "What this queen takes, she loves, and what she loves, she keeps for all time. Is that—"

He inclined his head, slowly dipping and leaning forward at the same time, carefully moving closer despite the sweeping horns.

I stretched out my hand and lightly touched my palm to his cheek, stroking my fingers over the metal. Sliding behind his head. Searching for the mechanism to free his mouth.

Vore pulled back, giving me a slight shake that didn't jeopardize me with his horns.

"Okay," I breathed out. "Not yet. I do need to take your blood to establish the bond. Are you alright with that?"

He inclined his head again in a nod, but then tipped his chin up, slowly shifting the heavy horns back out of the way.

Throat. Exposed.

And yeah, I wanted to taste his skin. I wanted to breathe in his scent and see what he smelled like. Right now, all I smelled was metal and dragon, chains and smoke.

But if I sank my fangs into him...

I didn't feel right forcing him to climax when he was still chained, bound, and silenced. Especially in front of his former house and sister.

I settled for pushing my nails into his throat.

My eyelids fluttered shut. I still smelled smoke, but it was more fragrant and aromatic than the dragon's sulfur. Sandalwood and sweet resin, sprinkled with herbs and delicate blossoms. His blood flowed into me like a high, cold mountain spring, babbling over polished red and green jade.

I drank long enough I felt his spider legs shriveling. Sinking into his body. But the bull remained. The horns didn't shrink in size.

:*Monster.*: Vore's words rattled in the new bond like clashing swords. :*Always.*:

"I will always be a monster too," I whispered back. "Your monster is safe with me either way. Once you've had my blood—"

:*No blood.*: He threw himself back, stumbling on wobbly, unused human legs. Falling to his knees, he leaned forward until his horns dug into the earth. :*Eater of flesh. Feast. Too dangerous.*:

:*Put me down,*: I told Mehen.

He obeyed, though he wasn't happy about it. All my Blood loved it when they could assist me in some way, and my grumpy dragon was no different. I stayed leaning against him, my left arm looped around his neck. "How much flesh are we talking about here?"

Vore's head snapped up, his heavy brow grooved in a deep scowl. :*Too much.*:

Rik didn't say a word, but his eyes narrowed, his shoulders pumping up with giant stone boulders.

"Sekh, you're a meat eater. So are you, my dragon."

"But we wouldn't eat *you*, Your Majesty." Though Sekh grimaced as soon as he said it.

Because of course Leviathan chuckled, plumes of smoke curling around me. :*I'll eat you any day, my queen.*:

"You know what I meant." Sekh peeled his lips back from his canines. "My teeth are dangerous enough. I already ripped your throat out once. You haven't even seen what his teeth can do."

I shrugged. "I healed it just fine."

"But I didn't eat a fucking piece of flesh out of you," Sekh growled, his eyes glowing brighter. "Your Majesty."

"You thought about it, though."

His eyes bulged and he jerked his head back like I'd slapped him in the face.

But he couldn't deny it.

Because he would never lie to his queen.

55

VORE

Gagged. Bound. Chained. All my life.

Too dangerous.

Too fucking hungry.

The metallic tang on my tongue tormented me. It wasn't steel I wanted to taste, but copper.

But more than taste, I wanted to bite.

I wanted to *swallow*.

I wanted to hold a piece of my queen inside me forever.

The plate over my mouth hadn't come off in three hundred years. The last time I'd been allowed to assist my sister queen in centralizing her power. It'd taken all her Blood to bring me under control once more, even after she gained a broader power base.

I loved my sister. But she didn't hold my bond.

She couldn't hold me like this queen could.

Shara. Isador. I'd heard them whisper her name before we came to House Ketea's island. A curse. A prayer. A hope I didn't dare allow myself to consider.

People talked around me all the time. Over me. Like I wasn't even there.

I knew she had other kings.

But I hadn't quite allowed myself to hope she could take another.

Shara tipped her head toward me. "He's still chained. I want him freed."

Tōno immediately stepped closer and returned to unlocking the chains pinning my arms to my body. The heavy weights fell off me and my shoulders drooped. Relaxed. For the first time in centuries. The strips of material wrapping my arms loosened and slipped off as Tōno unwound the restraints.

My hands flexed. My arms. Blood pumping through my limbs.

My blood belonged to Shara Isador now. I'd seen my sister feed many times. Biting her Blood, sinking her fangs into them.

Shudder. Bliss.

Yes. I wanted her bite. Her teeth. In me. More than anything.

Her lips quirked. Too late, I remembered she could hear my thoughts now. If she was listening.

"I am," she said. "But I must warn you my bite carries an unexpected punch."

:Punch me with anything.:

The dragon snorted another smoky laugh in my face.

I was getting real tired of his bullshit.

"Join the club," one of the other Blood muttered. The dragon gave me a dark glare promising pain and lots of it.

They could all hear me.

Fucking great. I didn't like being an open book. My urges were too dark. Too raw to share widely. I'd have to get better at shutting those emotions down.

"Now take the gag off him," she ordered.

Too many emotions jolted through me for me to suppress them all. But mostly sheer terror.

If I tasted her...

I won't be able to stop.

"Look at me." Her voice was soft but echoed with power to shake the foundations of the world. I met her gaze, and her eyes rolled me under like a riptide. Midnight skies sparkling with a million exploding stars, sucking everything in her path into a black hole. Never to escape.

I didn't want to escape. Not from her. Unless...

Unless I hurt her. Tore her apart. Then I would rather be dead.

"I will stop you. I'm queen enough to allow this."

She stepped closer, even though my arms were free. My hands. Strong enough to break her in half.

Tōno pressed the key into the mask at the base of my skull. I felt the slight pressure. Heard the faint click. The metal band around my face loosened.

One of the bravest, strongest warriors in my sister's Blood, other than her alpha, fled.

Away from me.

They all knew what I was capable of.

How many bodies I'd eaten the last time I'd been freed.

I didn't dare move. Even though every muscle tensed with the urge to spit out the gag. Shake my head and scream to the heavens. Rake the earth with my horns.

Feast. Ravage. And feast again.

"I will stop you," she repeated softly.

Her fingers came up to my face. Both hands, gently prying at the metal embedded into my flesh. Peeling it free, ripping my skin in places. Not that I felt a single thing other than the soft brushes of her skin on mine.

She pulled on the plate and my mouth opened. My entire body heaved. Spitting out the foreign metal that had been a part of me for so long. I worked my aching jaws and licked my shredded lips, tasting my blood.

But it wasn't *my* blood I wanted.

Blood dripped from her bottom lip and roses bloomed in the

air around her. A sound came out of me that horrified me. Shook me.

Hunger.

Like nothing I had ever felt before.

"I'm Shara Isador, last daughter of She Who Is and Was and Always Will Be." Her voice rolled with thunder, rumbling through my bones. "By my blood, I compel you, Vore Kijin Isador. By my love, I bind you. No one gets maimed today. I'm queen enough to hold your bond. I'm queen enough to stop you from harming anyone, especially myself."

Then she lifted her arm up, offering me the delicate skin of her inner elbow. The lower part of her biceps.

"You may take a bite of me."

SHARA

I WASN'T AFRAID. HOW COULD I BE?

I faced Leviathan in his prison and drained him to the point of death. I stood in a storm of locusts and glared down the queen of Rome. I bargained with formidable goddesses to protect my loves.

While bound to the Mother's table, all the blood had drained out of my body and I couldn't even speak. While the Dauphine tried to hack out my throat.

It was no big deal to stand here and allow a Blood to taste me.

My Blood. My king.

Offering Vore a single bite was a minor risk I was more than willing to take.

His teeth were jagged white shards, slicing into me effortlessly. So sharp I barely even felt the pain of it. He didn't put his hands on me, for fear the heat of my skin would push him over the edge.

The taste of my blood exploded on his tongue. The texture of my skin on his lips, his tongue, exquisite. The scent of my flesh. The feel of my skin and muscle in his mouth, his tongue stroking the meat of my arm. Savoring. Tasting.

Eating.

His teeth snapped fully closed, and he swallowed.

My awareness slipped down his throat with the bite of my flesh. I was used to feeling my blood flowing into my Blood when they fed, but this was even more intense. The single bite of my arm slipped through a secret chamber in his stomach, separated from the rest of his digestive system.

He would never dissolve that bite. I would linger inside of him as long as he lived.

Goddess allow it to be a very long time, since he's mine now.

My blood flowed through him like normal. Soaking into his cells. Powering up his gifts. He didn't carry my power along his spine yet, but I had plenty of time to add to my new reserves.

Even better, the rest of his beast folded up and slipped inside him.

He fully shifted back to his human form—for the first time since he'd shifted into the bull-slash-minotaur-slash-spider creature.

Nuzzling the wound on my arm, he licked the blood from my skin. :*Ushi-oni.*:

He shuddered and wrapped his arms around me. Crushing me to him. His tongue pressed over his bite, the hole. In my flesh.

I stroked my hands through his black hair. "Everyone's going to want to take a bite of me, now."

:*Fuck no,*: Ezra growled, at the same time as Mehen and Sekh both said, :*Fuck yeah.*:

Then they glared at each other for agreeing.

"Who's giving me a ride back to Galveston this time?"

"Me," Vivian yelled before anyone else.

Mehen curled around my legs and nudged me with his head. Wanting me to pet him too.

:I'm surprised you didn't argue with her for a turn.:

He worked his head beneath my other arm and gripped my biceps in his jaws. Though he didn't bite me without permission. *:She can fly you all the way back to Eureka Springs if I get to taste you next, my queen.:*

:Take a bite, my dragon. One bite only.:

56

VIVIAN

Flying with my queen over the rolling waves of the Gulf of Mexico, I could pretend we were alone. Here, in this moment, she was wholly mine. Mine to carry. Mine to protect. Mine to love.

She tightened her arms around the phoenix's neck, her face against my chest. :*You're mine to love too.*:

I didn't want to break the illusion we were alone, so I didn't listen to her bonds with her other Blood. Nevarre didn't fly ahead of us with Tlacel. Mehen and Lew didn't fly behind.

Just me. Just her. In the infinite expanse of sky with the sea below.

:*I'm sorry,*: she whispered. :*You should each have more time alone with me. Now that I don't have to worry about the Dauphine sending more zombie thralls into the nest, I hope we can relax for years and years.*:

I kept my eternal flames banked as much as possible to hide our flight through the darkening sky, but sparks popped around us with my laughter. :*I guess I'm too cynical to believe the other queens will ever let you live in peace, my queen.*:

:*I will it to be so. We need peace. Rest. Joy. We deserve it.*:

She deserved everything in this world.

Including the secret Smoak held in our heart.

:*No.*: The single word pulsed with her power, sealing the secret away from her. Even though it could have been hers with the tiniest draw of her will.

:*I owe you everything, my queen. My heart. My life. Certainly my secrets.*:

:*I'm queen enough to allow your secrets, Vivian.*: She rubbed her mouth on my feathers and she might as well have licked my pussy. Flames poured out of me before I could stifle them. :*I love you all the more because of your honor.*:

Though her bond shifted from enjoying my phoenix's flight to something heavier. I wasn't the kind of Blood to hover in her mind all the time, listening to her every private thought. Probably because I wanted my own peace in my head. Apart from Smoak, I hadn't carried any other thoughts or consciousness, not like Blood raised in a nest.

In Heliopolis, it'd been best to remain as invisible and silent as possible. To never give Ra a reason for your name to be on his disgusting lips.

Shara hadn't lived with our kind around her either. Perhaps that's why she was so willing to allow each of us the space to keep to ourselves.

But I didn't like the sense of heaviness in her bond. It tasted like guilt.

:*You have nothing to regret, my queen. I burn with joy every moment I'm allowed to exist with you.*:

:*I was just thinking...*: She hesitated and her bond darkened in my head. Some of her light went out. Some of her spark.

Smoak poured through me, lighting up our bond. Sending molten solar energy to burn away our queen's sadness. Perhaps a tad too enthusiastically because her gown started to smoke.

Rik thumped me so hard we dropped several feet in the air. Close enough I contemplated dropping beneath the surface of water to make sure she wasn't burned. Though her power absorbed the heat and shifted it throughout her body.

Her breath caught and she laughed shakily. :*I'm fine,*: she said down her alpha bond.

So much for the illusion we were alone.

:*We're as alone as I can make it,*: she replied. :*I muted everyone but Rik, and I asked him to back off to allow you this time.*:

:*What made you so sad?*:

:*I wasn't sad. Just wondering how you might feel about the new Blood.*:

Coasting, I slowed our flight, letting my wings catch the breeze to lift us higher. :*I don't understand why you thought new Blood would upset me? They're your Blood, my queen. Call as many as you can. The more the merrier as long as they leave me the fuck alone.*:

She sighed. :*That's what I mean. You're alone.*:

:*I'm never alone. I have Smoak and you.*:

:*But you don't have as much of me as you'd like. Not when I have so many other Blood.*:

:*We'd all love to have more of your time, sure. But I'm happy with you, my queen. Always. I don't have any expectations, other than you feed on me as often as you wish.*:

:*They can spend time together.*:

I still wasn't following. :*I spend time with the other Blood all the time. Rik sends us on duty with the others. Even the fucking dragon can be tolerable on occasion.*:

:*They're all male.*:

:*So? I don't give a fuck...*: My words fell off as it finally dawned on me what she was worried about. :*I could try fucking one of them if that would please you.*:

:*No! Goddess, that's not what I meant at all. I enjoy watching them fuck each other, but you don't have anyone but me. I Called more Blood, but I don't know how many. I certainly don't know if any of them are female.*:

The coastline broke the horizon so our trip back to Galveston was almost over. I dipped a wing, flying parallel to the shore, delaying as long as possible. :*It doesn't matter to me, as long as I have you.*:

:*It matters to me. You should have as many opportunities to love as the men.*:

It honestly didn't matter to me. But it meant the world to me that *she* cared. :*You haven't seen your sweet Mayte in a while. Or is there another sibling queen you'd like me to fuck?*:

:*I'm not close to any of the siblings in New York City except Gwen, and I don't feel that way about her, even if she was interested. Mayte is getting a new sibling for us from Brazil. I don't know if it'll be a romantic relationship for her or not.*:

I couldn't imagine Mayte feeling anything for another queen after she'd had a taste of ours, but I'd been wrong before. :*I have to admit I actually prefer being your only female Blood, my queen.*:

Her bond jolted with surprise. :*Really? Why?*:

:*I get you all to myself when you take me. Smoak doesn't like to share.*:

I couldn't see her face, but I felt the wicked curve of her lips against my chest. :*I haven't had the pleasure of Smoak fucking me yet. Is that something you can manage midair?*:

My heart caught fire and Smoak's flames shimmered to blue. :*Funny you should mention fucking in the air, my queen. Because that's exactly how phoenixes mate.*:

～

SHARA

BURNING MYRRH AND CINNAMON FILLED MY NOSE. FLAMES shimmered around the phoenix. Some hers, her natural gift, but some belonged to the sunfire she carried. Molten sunlight, red-gold flames, searing blue, all melding to white-hot need.

Hot enough to scorch off what remained of my delicate lacy gown.

:*Drop down a little,*: Vivian said. :*We won't let you fall.*:

First, I checked on Penelope to see where she was in my hair. Curled up in a warm little nest, she was sound asleep. Good. Focusing on her, I willed that section of hair to cradle her snugly against my back so she didn't fall.

Loosening my grip on Vivian, I slipped down the curve of her chest. Smoldering feathers rubbed against me, heating my skin. Sweat poured down my forehead and between my breasts, but the flames didn't burn me.

:*Lower,*: she panted. :*Almost there.*:

I locked my fingers around the upper curve of her wings and extended my arms, dangling down her body. Though I didn't want to impede her ability to keep us in the sky.

The freshly healed bites on my lower biceps pulled under the strain of my weight, so I wouldn't be able to hold on long. I didn't realize how much I used my arms—until they hurt.

She flipped her wings up higher over her head, changing the angle of our flight, and molten steel burned between my thighs. I'd seen Smoak's burning hot dick when Mayte came to visit me. I'd even used it once when he'd helped me fuck Nevarre.

But I'd never felt Smoak—Vivian—inside me.

Until now.

Rippling flames caught me, shifting our bodies together. Taking the strain off my arms. She slid into me, and my breath caught on a groan. Heat poured into me. Solid fire without pain, melting my bones. Searing my brain to ash.

Tucking her wings around me, she rolled us in the air. Gliding on her back for a few pumps of her tail feathers, lifting us in the air so each flap made her thrust and glide inside me. Rolling again, harder, whipping her fiery feathers into a corkscrew. I didn't even have to hold on to her any longer, not with our momentum.

Her scent roared hotter, burning spices and feathers. The molten power of the sun. Liquid starlight, compressed into the raging power of a supernova. Exploding. Into me.

I sank my fangs into her, filling my mouth with her smoldering blood. Drinking her down, her flames rippling deep inside me. Searing me from the inside out.

Wings unfurled with a snap, and we shot straight up. Shrieking, the phoenix blazed like a comet. Pouring all her sunfire into me. Higher, through the clouds into thin, crisp air. As if she meant to escape earth's gravity and rejoin the star that had originally birthed the sunfires.

Giving everything to me. Every drop of molten solar energy. Every single flame. Until her blazing fire spluttered out.

Our flight slowed. We hung. Paused. Weightless. Completely alone in the universe.

Our hair billowed around us. Red and black flowing rivers twined together. Her hands cupped my face, her mouth on mine. I breathed her in and wrapped my arms around her waist. Twirling, slowly, our hair flowed around us, wrapping us together, as we began to slowly sink back to earth.

Faster.

Free falling.

Her braids caught fire, rippling through my black hair like shining ruby strands woven through a black tornado. But the spreading firestorm melted into my hair without damaging it, darkening into black flames. A powerful spinning black hole, burning forever in the deepest, darkest corner of space.

I sensed the ocean below, approaching fast. She held her human form as long as possible, her mouth locked to mine. Her tongue stroked the roof of my mouth, probing the holes where my fangs lay. Making me want to bite her again and again.

:Please, anytime, anywhere, my queen.:

At the last possible second, her phoenix exploded out of her. Her wings caught the breeze and swept us along the water, close enough waves splashed us, sizzling in the heat of our wake.

Now, her phoenix burned as black as the night that had fallen around us rather than red-gold fire. Threads of red still flickered through the streaming black shadows of her flames. I thought at first Nevarre had lent us his shadows to hide us from watchful humans on the beach, but this was all Vivian.

Burning myrrh and cinnamon mixed combined with the infinite expanse of space.

Smoak filled our minds with the image of a giant red star. Expanding, swelling, its center darkening, compressing with immense pressure. Burning away the red until the star exploded in a blaze of white light, leaving only the spinning black hole, streaming with flashes of super-charged red energy.

:Home,: Vivian whispered hoarsely, even her mental voice shaking with awe. *:The sunfires' birthplace.:*

:Now you carry your home with you.:

:Our home burns in you, my queen. Forever.:

57

SHARA

"Maybe we should film Lady Godiva," Guillaume said as Vivian landed with me in the backyard of the Galveston house beside the pool.

Both of us stark naked. Though my hair was so bushy and wind tossed I doubted anybody could see much more than a bit of my skin flashing through the heavy tendrils. A quick check confirmed that Penelope was still sound asleep. Though now my hair definitely looked more like a rat's nest.

Rik leveled a hard look at Vivian. "What part of 'fly as safely as possible with our queen' did you fail to understand?"

Tossing her braids back over her shoulder, Vivian tipped her chin up proudly. "Our queen was perfectly safe until someone punched me through the bond so hard I almost dipped her into the ocean."

I leaned against her and gave her a lingering kiss, softening her defensive stance immediately. "Thank you for an incredible ride."

"Anytime, my queen."

Nevarre stepped out of the shadows near the house with what had become one of my favorite items of clothing ever. A robe. Quick to put on—and take off—and it covered enough of me I didn't feel like I was going to make anyone, especially myself, blush if they saw me in it. He helped me pull the silk robe on, lifting the thick mass of hair.

"I'm sorry, Nevarre. I've made quite a mess of my hair."

"No worries at all, my queen," he said cheerfully. "I love a challenge. Besides, this gives me even more time with my hands buried in your glorious locks."

All the jostling woke Penelope up. She peeked out, nose working eagerly, and then clambered down my hair like a rope ladder.

"Where are you going?" I called after her as she ran back toward the beach.

She sent me a picture of a group of rats squeaking and chattering in a circle. Evidently, she had rat business to handle.

:Be back by dawn,: I told her. *:We'll head home before the sun.:*

She gave one last squeak of acknowledgement and disappeared.

I looped my arm through Rik's and let him lead me toward the massive, three-story beachfront house I apparently owned. Party lights were strung around the pool and the two-story deck. One level surrounded the pool, and then another up to a set of French doors. To the right of the entry, an outdoor kitchen had both a huge grill and a smoker.

Daire and Ezra manned the grill, joking about whose sausage was bigger. Even though they were flipping burgers.

Magnum and another woman with dark hair buzzed short on the back and sides, with a thick curly mass on top of her head dyed hot pink, met me at the door. "Your Majesty, I'm pleased to introduce you to Parker Jansen, who handles this house's staff when you're in residence. Jansen, this is our queen, Shara Isador, last daughter of Isis."

Jansen inclined her hand and gave me a short bow. "Your Majesty, it's an honor to meet you. Please forgive the hair. If I'd known you were coming to town, I would have prepared myself properly."

"It's not a problem at all. I actually love it. And please, we barely gave you an hour's notice before a whole ravenous army descended upon you. Whatever you've pulled together with such short notice will be perfectly acceptable."

Jansen's lips quirked with a relieved grin. "Quite the army, Your Majesty. With Magnum and Winston's recommendations, we've appropriately stocked the kitchen. Is there anything I can get you? Tea, wine, something to eat?"

"For now, I'd like to freshen up a little and rest." I gave her a wry smile. "Maybe put on something more appropriate than a robe."

"Of course. The main suite is right this way, and Magnum already unpacked your things if you'd like to bathe or sleep."

I hadn't packed a single bag, and we were only staying one night. So I really had no idea what Magnum might have *unpacked* for me.

:My queen doesn't pack or unpack a single bag,: Rik rumbled. *:She has people to do everything she could possibly need done, and if you have to ask, we've already failed you.:*

We passed into a massive great room with a sectional and dining table large enough to seat ten to twelve people at once. Everything was white and fresh with touches of coastal blue. Pretty, but not really something I would pick out for myself.

Carys, Frank, Gina, and Kevin sat at the table. By the looks of it, I was going to be neck deep in folders before we even got home. I heaved a dramatic sigh, making Gina laugh softly.

She lowered the phone and muted it. "Let's just say the calls are coming in faster than we can keep up. I even put Frank to work on running background checks for us."

Typing madly, Kevin glanced up as we passed, grinning from ear to ear and clearly in his element. "You're not going to believe all the intel we're getting now, Your Majesty. It's going to take months to unravel everything."

The sparkle in his eyes said he couldn't fucking wait.

I punctured my thumb and drew a drop of blood so I could strip off Desideria's jewelry. "Can you add these to the legacy when we get home?"

Gina's mouth hung open with shock, but she nodded. "Of course, my queen."

Upstairs, Itztli and Tlacel stood on either side of another set of French doors, pushing them open for me as we approached. Jansen halted outside. "Please let me know if there's anything we can get for you, Your Majesty."

"Do you prefer Parker or Jansen?" I asked.

"Jansen, Your Majesty."

"Thank you, Jansen."

The bedroom was still mostly white and blue, but a darker indigo with touches of silver. A normal king-sized bed looked small compared to the monstrosity I had at home, but it would be perfectly fine for a few hours.

Even for what I intended.

And because Rik was the best alpha I could ever wish for, my new Blood already waited for me. Of course I didn't have to ask him to make Vore available.

Standing beside a blue-velvet chaise with his hands behind him, he must have jumped in the shower as soon as the boat landed. His black hair was still wet, swept back off his face. Someone had hooked him up with a button-down red shirt and black pants. Nicer than most of the guys wore, so maybe Mehen? Though he preferred three-piece perfectly tailored suits if he was dressing up.

:*There's a wide variety of men's clothing upstairs,*: Nevarre said. :*All types, sizes, and styles. Mehen's still trying on shit and deciding what he's taking home.*:

Esetta must have arranged for all the clothing ages ago. Yet another example of her seeing a hundred steps ahead of everyone else.

"I'm glad you found something comfortable to wear," I said out loud, trying to put Vore at ease. Usually I was the nervous one bringing a new Blood to bed. But his shoulders were tight, his bare feet planted wide, as if he was braced for battle.

He inclined his head but didn't say anything out loud.

Internally, it was a completely different story.

His bond screamed. Shards and razors. A multitude of jumbled thoughts and words. Clamoring, clashing emotions. But most of all, pain.

So much pain it stole my breath. My fingers convulsed on Rik's arm and my knees buckled. He snagged me up in his arms and carried me to the chaise. Dropping to his knees, he settled me on the cushions, holding my hands in his. Pressing kisses to my knuckles and palms. His gentleness despite his massive size always undid me, soothing me like nothing else. Though I couldn't help the tears.

Vore hadn't been able to speak. For hundreds of years. He hadn't been able to walk as a man, let alone pick out something as insignificant as clothing in colors that pleased him. Eat food. Let alone interact with other people.

He'd been silent and chained his entire life.

Worse, he'd been seen as a monster, not a person, even by his own family and house. They'd done their best for him, but they were terrified of him. He'd been terrified of himself.

He still was.

Which was why he gripped his own wrists behind his back. He needed the restraint. The familiar position of having his arms bound to his sides. He didn't trust himself. He certainly didn't trust me to control him, and why should he? He didn't know me, other than the Blood bond I'd given him.

He fully expected to kill and devour every person in the house. Starting with me.

"Tears." His voice cracked, shredding his throat with the effort of communicating beyond the ragged screams inside his head. "You fear me."

I shook my head and held out my right hand, but he stared at my trembling fingers like I offered him one of the Dauphine's revolting leeches.

"I don't fear you at all. I'm crying only because I feel your pain through the bond."

His eyes narrowed slightly, his head shifting back in thought. As if he had no idea what I was talking about.

"What can I do to help you feel more comfortable?"

He slowly shook his head. "Queen."

Which was Blood for *"you're the fucking queen. Why on earth would it matter to you if I'm comfortable?"*

I resisted the urge to sigh or roll my eyes to lighten the mood. He wouldn't understand because he didn't know me well enough to not take offense, or worse, he'd decide I was seriously exasperated with him. My grand plans of taking my newest Blood to bed tonight so he didn't have to wait until we got to my nest were circling the drain. At this point, I didn't even know if Vore would be interested in me that way.

Rik made a soft sound, drawing my gaze to his face. Amusement, by the quirk of his lips. "Do you have any suggestions?"

A pleased glint sparked in his eyes. He fucking loved it when I asked him for help. Especially in matters of the Blood. "Nevarre, our queen's hair needs our attention. In fact, it's so tangled, I think we're going to need several of us to help her fix it."

Nevarre moved toward a door I assumed led to the ensuite bathroom. "How many brushes and combs should I fetch, alpha?"

"Four should do it." In the bond, I felt Rik call Tlacel inside with us.

My gentlest, calmest Blood. Tlacel and Nevarre together

never failed to soothe me. Though I wasn't the one who needed to be assured. Vore didn't think my formidable alpha could stop him from feasting. What would he think of…

My eyes widened when Nevarre came back into the room.

Without his kilt.

Tlacel opened the door and strode toward me. Also naked.

His hair flowed around his shoulders, drawing my gaze across the bronzed planes of his chest. Bright red, green, gold, and black markings were tattooed across his skin. Tonight, the symbols shifted into words I could read. *"Sink your teeth into me, Great One, and I will fly you to Mictlān and back again."*

As if it was the most casual thing in the world to brush my hair buck naked, Nevarre tossed a wooden comb to Tlacel, gave the silver tray to Rik with a couple of brushes on it, and then they dropped down on their knees around me. Carefully picking up one long tendril at a time, combing through the snarled ends, and gradually working their way up.

Without once tugging on my scalp.

Rik set the tray on the floor beside him, picked up one of the brushes, and started to work on the less tangled sections. He didn't command Vore to help. Not even in the bond. In fact, none of them even looked at the new man.

Tlacel lifted his hand to his mouth and breathed in. Deeply. His gaze flickered up to mine. His pupils wide and dark. Hungry.

With need. A very special kind of need.

And I suddenly knew exactly why Rik asked my feathered serpent to join us.

58

TLACEL

Long silken strands of my queen's hair slipped free of my fingers and curled around my throat.

Her eyes flared, as if she hadn't intended for her hair to bind me, but I wasn't surprised at all. I didn't even have to touch her hair to feel the magic flowing in every single strand. Her hair gleamed with the same supernatural glow of her skin, as if the moon itself gleamed inside her, casting rainbows of delicate hues through crystal prisms to flash in every cell.

She smelled like a goddess. Heavy, sultry oil, delicate flowers, sacred incense burning forever on a golden altar. I would gladly worship, on my knees, every moment for the rest of my life. Simply to sink my fingers into her hair once more and feel the goddess' love flowing in her.

Truth be told, she didn't need us to tend to her hair. With a thought, she could command it to braid and curl into the most complex designs or flow about her like a smooth, untangled velvet cape. Though I'd rue the day she came to that realization, because I would grieve the loss of being allowed to serve her. Even in such a small way.

She traced her index finger over my chest, lightly scratching her nail into my skin. "What's Mictlān?"

"It's the Underworld where the dead go."

Her eyes fluttered shut and she leaned closer, pressing her forehead to mine. "Oh, my Blood. How I love you."

"I love you more than life itself, my queen." My breath caught in my throat, and I dared voice the need growing inside me. "Show me, please, my queen. Show me how much you love me."

She cupped my cheek and pressed her lips softly to mine, whispering against my lips. "Yes. I will show you exactly how much you mean to me."

Pulling away, she leaned back onto the chaise, reclining on the cushions. Her hair spilled over the arm and back of the chaise like a silken waterfall, down over her shoulders, trailing across the floor.

Tightening around my throat. A thick, black collar of silken hair.

Nevarre tossed a pile of her hair in my direction. Hitting me in the chest, her hair slipped down over my groin. "This section is all combed out, my queen."

I shuddered at the exquisite sensation. Long tendrils slithered over my cock. Winding around my shaft. Tightening around my balls. Throat and cock bound. For her.

Her lips curved into a wicked, knowing smile. "You're not getting very many tangles out, Tlacel."

"Sorry, my queen." I picked up another thick coiled strand so I could comb it out, but the entire section slithered around my arm. It climbed up around my shoulder. Across my nape. Then down my other arm. Binding my arms together. Pulling tight enough my breath shuddered out.

"Tell me what you want, my Blood." Ever so slowly, she began to reel me in closer. "How do you want me to love you tonight?"

"Take everything, my queen, and make me bleed."

"Would you be okay with—"

I nodded immediately. "Yes. Anything. Use me as you see fit, my queen."

She dragged her gaze away from me, tipping her head to look up at Nevarre. "How do you feel about fucking Tlacel for my enjoyment?"

Nevarre leaned down over the back of the chaise and nibbled lightly at her lips. "I thought you'd never fucking ask, my queen. But first I'd love to unwrap you so your beauty will torment us both."

She let her head drop back over the arm of the chaise, arching her neck and breasts up toward him. Lightly, he stroked his fingertips down her throat to the folded edges of her robe. Followed by his mouth while he slowly untied the belt. He pressed a kiss to the puckered scar over her heart, where the heart tree in the center of her grove had pierced—and killed— her.

Silk whispered against her skin. Opening, baring her body to our gaze.

A rough growl tore through the room, then shut off suddenly.

We all knew it was Vore. But not a single Blood looked in his direction.

We were too busy drinking in our queen's glory. The Dauphine could have resurrected herself and walked into the room, and I wouldn't have been able to pull my gaze away from my queen's beauty.

Even though I'd already worshiped at her feet several times, I had to bite back the same sound of desire. We all did.

The long, elegant curve of her throat. The swell of her breasts. I'd memorized every hollow and line and curve, mapped by my fingers and lips and body. My fingers itched to paint her like this. Her eyes shining and dark, her mouth parted.

The tips of her fangs glistening as her hunger rose. Her tongue moistening her lush lips.

Dipping his head, Nevarre kissed his way down her stomach, letting his own long hair slip and slide to torment her. She planted her foot on the chaise and lifted her hips, opening her thighs for him. An invitation no Blood would ever in a million years refuse.

It wasn't my tongue pressed against her slit. Thrusting inside her. Drinking her desire. Feeling the pounding pulse of her blood in her clit. So close, only feet away, yet so very far. Close enough to breathe in the musky scent of her rising need. Hear the way her breathing caught in her chest. The quickening of her pulse.

She fisted her hands in Nevarre's hair, holding him close.

Even while she pulled me closer with her hair.

Inviting me to join the feast.

VORE

I WANTED.

Taste. Drink. Swallow. Feast.

Like these two Blood.

I wanted to shove them aside and make way for myself between her thighs. Unblock the view of her body laid bare by their shoulders.

A torment unlike anything I'd ever known, and I've known a hell of a lot of pain.

The one she'd bound with her hair leaned over her abdomen, facing the other, so they could both taste her. I didn't understand why she'd done such a thing. When he tore his way free, it would rip her scalp and cause her unbelievable pain.

He lifted his head. His lips glistening with the queen's juices. His pupils blown. His face red. His breathing loud. Strained.

Because she was choking him.

And he fucking loved it.

His eyes. I'd never seen anything like it. As if she'd peeled him open. Flayed him to the bone. Exposing his darkest secrets. Dragging them all out into the open. That should have been a violent thing, but his eyes were soft. Dazed. Even peaceful. As if he'd ascended to some higher plane the rest of us didn't even know existed.

Her bond swelled inside me. A cresting wave that didn't end or recede. Arching up against the other Bloods' mouths, she cried out. Shaking with pleasure. And the wave exploded.

Knocking me to my knees.

I didn't know.

I didn't know a Blood bond would feel like this. I should never have accepted it. Too risky. Too much. Emotion. Eroding away the slight grip of control I'd managed to maintain so far despite the freedom.

So fucking dangerous. Goddess. Please. Don't let me hurt them. Her.

The alpha had been silent while the two lesser Blood touched her, calmly brushing a section of her hair. Clearly, they were no threat to her. Not like me. :*Do you want to taste our queen?*:

My eyes bulged in my head. I would have recoiled backward if I were still on my feet. Had they not seen my teeth? My monster? Had I not bitten a chunk of flesh out of her arm?

Though thinking about that one single bite didn't help. At all.

Because now I felt that piece of her inside my stomach. A sweet, yearning bellyache unlike anything I'd ever known.

My life had only ever been pain of some kind. The pain of hunger. Of being excluded. Feared. Reviled.

Agonized silence. Never allowed to speak or eat or touch another living soul. Unless I was freed for the sole purpose of slaughtering my sister's enemies. Which I had done with great enthusiasm. I deserved the chains. I deserved the fear.

I couldn't touch this queen. I would never be gentle like her other lovers. I would never taste the cream coating her delicate flesh—for fear I would take another bite and maim her for all time.

:*I'm a monster.*:

The alpha flashed a grin at me that made absolutely no sense. :*She fucking loves monsters, and she loves fucking monsters.*:

He, of all the Blood, should know what I was capable of. He should bar me from this room. Chain me in some dark basement corner. Leave me here, never to return. They needed to lock me up and lose the keys. He couldn't risk letting me close enough to touch her. It'd be too late. For her, and for him.

:*You think so? Try me, Vore. Test her bond. See how far you get.*:

I knew exactly what I'd do. I could see it in my head.

I'd surge to my feet faster than the alpha could even blink. Break the two weaker Bloods' necks like brittle sticks. Toss them aside for later. Sink my teeth into the delicate pink flesh still pumped up with blood from her climax. Blood and flesh and cum. Mine.

Her life. Mine.

My muscles twitched, on the verge of moving. Of leaping. Tearing. Feasting.

But I couldn't seem to make—or allow—myself to rise.

Still on my knees.

The other two Blood shifted their attention to each other. The bound one on his knees. Staring up at his queen while the other Blood fucked him hard. The other man's arm locked around his throat, bending him back in a straining arch against him. His genitals wrapped in her hair, tight enough the head of his cock was purple. His dark, wide eyes, flying higher, pulling the other man with him.

The bound one. Pulled the other one. Higher.

I didn't know. Why?

Even the queen. The black silk of her hair loosened on the Blood's cock, and she swung her legs off the chaise. Her thighs wrapped around them. Pulling them both into the embrace of her body. Taking the bound Blood inside her, even while the other fucked him. All without breaking their rhythm.

The white of her fangs glistened for a long, heavy heartbeat, pulsing through her bond. Anticipation surged in the other Blood.

Fisting her hands in the bound Blood's hair, she pulled his neck to the side. Making him wait while the other Blood thrust deeper, harder, a ragged groan escaping his lips. Then she struck.

The cataclysmic blast through the bond leveled me. On my face. Twitching. Shuddering. Beneath the hammering waves of their pleasure.

She's distracted. Incapacitated.

It's the perfect time for the ushi-oni to surge free.

Panting, I waited. Dread. Crushing me.

Another rippling wave of pleasure rocked through the bond. I didn't have to tip my head up to know she must have bitten the other Blood too.

Her bite alone had the power to fuck me.

And I wanted it. More than I wanted to taste her flesh again.

I wanted her teeth in me.

Shining black silk slithered toward me, a rippling vine of her hair. Though it didn't touch me. Breathing hard, I stared at the coil of hair. Inches from my face. Beneath the thick scent of sex in the air, I could smell her scent wafting up from the tendril.

Blowing desert sands, a secret pool shining beneath the full moon, sprinkled with delicate flowers.

I closed my eyes. Remembering the taste of her skin. The searing burn of her blood. So much power. But was it enough to keep me from shifting?

No one had been able to contain the ushi-oni without chains and locks.

No one had even wanted to try.

Until she'd freed me. Her first order had been to unchain me.

My heart thudded heavily as I stretched out my hand and touched her hair.

Immediately, the tendrils curled around my forearm and up my elbow. Tugging me toward her with surprising strength.

Realization dawned on me. I'd missed one very obvious fact. Now that she touched me, I could feel the magic pulsing in every strand. Her hair hummed with her power. No wonder she hadn't feared the other Blood would damage her scalp. Her hair was merely an extension of her power. He might as well have tried to tear apart the chains binding me for centuries with his teeth.

Her hair. Bound in her hair. Her power.

No wonder he flew so high. No wonder he came so hard.

I pushed up to my hands and knees. My gaze locked on hers. Unable to look away now that I saw the infinite galaxies spinning in her eyes. A queen with more power in one strand of her hair than any queen who'd come near me before. Even my sister.

"I want." My voice hurt my own ears, sharp and jagged edges of broken glass and nails and cutting razors. "What you gave him."

And her hair slipped up around my throat.

59

SHARA

I wasn't the kind of queen who liked to see my Blood on their knees, prostrating themselves for me. Vore didn't trust himself—or me—enough to approach with his full strength, and of course, there was a slight problem preventing his walking. His legs were already quivering from his release when I bit my other Blood.

I hadn't blasted him as hard as I could have with Sekh's transference power, but I wanted him to feel something other than pain. I wanted to quiet the noise in his head. The screaming. Goddess, he still screamed internally, and he didn't even realize it.

Tightening my hair around his throat, I watched his eyes for any sign of fear or anger to spark. I couldn't hear anything but endless pain in his bond to know if he was enjoying the bondage or not.

Tlacel cuddled against my side. Nevarre behind him, arms wrapped around him, leaning against the chaise's leg. Rik came around to sit behind me, his body cradling mine. Close, ready to crack skulls if he needed to, but he wasn't concerned about this new Blood. Not like when we'd fucked Mehen the first time.

Vore was very aware of the danger inherent in taking him to my bed. He wanted, as he said, but he feared too. He was terrified of hurting me. Even though he wanted what I offered enough to crawl to me. Shaking with dread, even though his eyes were dark with lust, he settled back on his heels. Hands on his knees, gripping his thighs so hard his shoulders strained beneath the dress shirt.

The reluctance I read on his face gave me pause. Even though I knew why, I didn't like that look on his face. His pulse thundered in his throat, his breathing short and rapid. Sweat trickled down his face, darkening the front of his shirt.

"Take me," he ground out. His jaw flexing, tendons standing out on his neck.

I wrapped another section of hair around his upper body, pinning his arms to his sides. Involuntarily, his muscles swelled and bulged. Resisting the restraint—even though that's what he asked me to do. Straining, he struggled harder. His mouth twisted in a furious grimace, his eyes flashing red. Buttons popped on his shirt. His pants tore.

But he didn't shift. He couldn't.

Because I didn't allow it. I was too strong for him to break free.

He needed to prove it. Not to me, but himself.

I watched the torrent of emotions flickering in his eyes. Rage, shock, lust…

But not fear. Not once.

And then, finally, sweet surrender.

I watched the sharpness fade in his eyes like a misty fog creeping across a meadow. His body softened, his shoulders dropped, and his fierce grip on his thighs eased. Slumped on his knees, he stared at me, still sinking like a stone, searching for the bottom of a well. Only to realize there was no bottom.

"I'm here," I whispered gently, cupping his cheek. "You're not alone."

A tremor rocked through his body. A hot tear splashed on the back of my hand. More tears. Streams of pain that broke my fucking heart. I pressed both of my palms to his face and leaned closer, holding his gaze. Stroking his cheeks softly. "It's alright, Vore. You're safe. You're safe with me. Always."

He tore at his bottom lip with his teeth. Fighting to contain the emotions swelling with him. The rage at what he'd endured. The endless agony of his life. Chained, feared, silenced, with no end in sight. Just like the bottomless well.

A raw, horrible sound came out of his mouth. I fought the urge to flinch because he would immediately assume I was terrified. But the hopeless, broken sound wrecked me.

I'd made the same sound when I watched the monsters kill Mom, and all I could do was stand there and scream through the broken window.

"Scream, Vore. Let it out. I can take it. I can take anything you give me."

"Take. EVERYTHING," he roared.

His eyes blazed red hot. Tendons and muscles strained, his entire body shaking. He sucked in another breath and bellowed again, on and on, and endless roar of pain. Rattling the windows. A car alarm started blaring outside.

I reached for Guillaume's bond. :*Please reassure the humans I'm not killing him.*:

My knight huffed a soft laugh in my head. :*They hear the car alarm and dogs howling outside but not the new Blood.*:

Maybe Esetta had put up some noise canceling paneling between the floors. Or maybe the frequency of Vore's screams didn't register on the human hearing range. Though how they couldn't hear the soul-rending cries, I had no idea.

He screamed until he was hoarse. Until he sagged against me, unable to hold himself upright. His face touched my throat, and he fucking whimpered.

Because he never dared to dream that I would allow him to

touch me. Especially for me to trust him at my vulnerable throat. His mouth so near unprotected skin and flesh. Wrapped in my hair, he finally fell over the edge of the abyss of pain he'd been drowning in.

Straight into my arms. Where I could hold him and keep him safe.

"Please," he whispered, tipping his head back. Letting me see his eyes. Blasted wide open, every barrier down, all chains unlocked, every secret unburied. "Take me. Make me yours."

Braced, I touched his bond, and found only stillness. Silence, finally. Acceptance. Relief. Awe.

Love.

The kind of love he'd never even allowed himself to think about. Let alone hope for.

Desire. To be a part of me forever. To feel my body against his. Any and all bodies. My other Blood. Starved his whole life in all ways, every sensation felt like razors slicing him apart, but he craved it. He wanted more and more, until no part of him remained untouched by a loving hand or body.

This was good pain, and he wanted it all. To make him forget everything else.

Keeping the thicker band of hair around his throat so he didn't lose the sensation of being controlled, I parted the rest of my hair wrapped around him so I could slowly unbutton his shirt. I pushed it off and down his arms, baring his heavy shoulders for my hands. The sculpted muscle of his broad chest, tapering down to his waist.

Fingers on his fly, I watched his eyes. Listening to his bond. His pulse jumped in his throat, and he licked his lips. Flashing the sparkling sharpness of his teeth. He'd climaxed already with Tlacel and Nevarre, but his dick was rock hard again. Chained up as a monster, he'd never had the opportunity to have sex.

"I want to do this right for you."

He blinked rapidly, his gaze flickering to Rik at my back.

My alpha pressed his mouth to my throat and licked a path up to my ear that had me squirming against him in seconds. "Anything you do will be right for him."

"But—"

"Please." Vore's voice roughened with desperation. As if he feared I'd change my mind. "*My* queen."

With extra emphasis on "my."

Usually my alpha squashed any possessiveness from the other Blood with a hard thump, but he didn't react to Vore. :*You're his salvation, my queen. I'm not going to thump him for needing you to save him when no one else can.*:

My throat tightened. :*Have I told you lately how much I love you?*:

:*Every fucking second of every single day.*:

I jerked open Vore's pants. I used my hair to pull him to his feet so I could strip him. Higher, so he dangled off the ground. Just to show him I could. To reassure him of my strength before I took him fully.

His head fell back, his face softened. Peaceful. Sliding into bliss before I even took him inside me.

Rik shifted our bodies so he could lean back against the chaise and hold me, while I held Vore. I pulled him up against me, wrapping my arms and legs around him. Locking my heels around his back. I ran my hands over his body, stroking everywhere I could reach. He glided into me. Not thrusting or straining but simply a part of me. Melting into me.

I sank my fangs into his throat, and his spine bowed. His body jerking on top of me. His soft exhalation of pleasure louder to me than the screams of agony. He poured into me, his blood hot on my tongue despite the crisp, cool mountain spring flowing through my mind.

Closing my mouth over the punctures, I drank him down, pulling on him hard. He needed to feel the depths of my hunger. The rawness of my need. Even with so many Blood already. I drank a long time. Long enough I almost felt... full. For now.

Rik chuckled softly. "A feat indeed, my queen."

Pleasantly buzzed, I licked Vore's throat and released him. Sure that my eyes were just as fuzzy as his now. He lifted his head so he could see my face, his hands braced on either side of me on the chaise. Searching my gaze, he pushed into the bond, surprising me with a hard shove into my mental space.

I could block him out—if I ever wanted or needed to. But I didn't want to keep him out of my mind.

"You're not going to lock me up?"

"No." My eyes narrowed. "I thought I made that abundantly clear."

"You're not going to starve me?"

Now I was starting to get offended. "Absolutely not. I'm not going to silence you either. Or chain you up or toss you in a prison."

"You feed us? And fuck us? All of us?"

I used the tip of my longest nail to prick the soft skin beneath his throat. "Every single one of you."

"Goddess." He smiled, his eyes soft and shining. "I never dreamed it could be like this."

Tears burned my eyes and I pressed another gentle kiss to his mouth. Vicious teeth and all. "Every fucking day."

60

SHARA

I lied. I said I was going to put something else on other than a robe when I first went upstairs. Instead, I was wrapped back up in the heavy silk robe—with Rik's big body wrapped around it. We sat on the sectional which had seemed ginormous. Until fifteen people tried to sit on it at the same time.

Daire chortled, turning the television up. "Human media is fucking wild."

A newswoman stood on the beach with a crowd of people around her. "After the station was flooded with pictures and videos, we came down to the shore ourselves to see the evidence. According to witnesses, a woman rode up the beach from somewhere down past the Holiday Inn Resort on a black horse—"

"Warhorse!" Someone shouted behind her.

"A stallion!" Another person yelled. "It was fucking huge!"

"You should see the size of his fucking sword," Ezra muttered.

"I kept my biggest sword sheathed." Guillaume huffed out a laugh. "You're welcome."

"With a flock of over a hundred crows," the newswoman

said. "No production company is currently licensed to film on the beach, but investigation continues into where this fantastic show might have originated."

"Idiots can't even count," Nevarre grumbled. "Nightwing Starlight brought over a thousand of her kin, and then more locals joined her."

Itztli scowled. "What about the massive black dog running alongside? Surely they didn't miss that."

The newswoman turned to a petite redhead who'd gotten a lot of sun. "Tell us what you saw, Regina."

Regina's eyes were huge with excitement, even though it'd been hours since I rode up the beach. Maybe she was simply excited to be on the news. "She had incredible long black hair and a gorgeous body. The horse didn't even have a saddle or bridle. It was like watching the beach scene in *The Black Stallion*, when the kid goes galloping along the shore."

"Did you see where she went?"

"That's the craziest part. A thunderstorm blew up from nowhere, and lightning struck the sword she was carrying."

"Wait, really? She had a sword? Was she injured?"

"A huge sword."

Guillaume snickered again.

"Blue lightning hit the sword in her hand. The image is seared into my eyeballs forever because it was so incredible. But it didn't hurt her or the horse."

"Did she say anything?"

"She screamed something but the winds were howling, the lightning and thunder were booming. I think she said Isador, but I don't know what that means."

"Like a name?"

Regina nodded. "Then she just galloped out into the water."

"Along the shore?"

"No. Straight out over the waves. I'm too short, and I

couldn't see over the crowd. I don't know if the horse went under or what."

The newswoman looked back to the screen. "We have a compilation of witness videos to play for the viewers at home."

They cut back to the station for a moment and then played a string of bad, jumpy videos. People screamed and yelled as Guillaume galloped by. They'd had to blur out the more suggestive shots of my boobs for television. Thank the goddess.

I leaned over and wrapped my arm around his shoulders. "You do look fucking fantastic, G."

He grinned. "I was prancing for all I was worth, my queen."

Blue flashed on the screen. People screamed, ducking from the violent strike. Giving a clear view of me holding the heavy Templar sword over my head.

"Wow, that's pretty incredible," a male anchor said. "Any chance this was all some kind of deep fake? Maybe generated by AI?"

The newswoman beside him shook her head. "Our analysts say it's real. There're too many witnesses for it to be fake. Police have cordoned off that section of the beach to collect evidence. Evidently there were some blackened hoofprints left on the beach."

Guillaume snorted. "I bet they'll try to get a list of every black horse in a fifty-mile radius and start measuring hooves. Not that they'll find any as big as mine. They don't make warhorses in my size any longer."

"Let alone ones who can burn the sand with hellish hoof-prints," Daire added.

"Well, it's an incredible night for news, folks, because we've got another strange event to report," the male anchor said. "After nightfall, there were reports of a comet or UFO in the sky over Galveston beach as well. Michael, over to you."

Vivian rolled her eyes. "Smoak is most offended. We came from a supermassive black hole, not a fucking alien planet."

A man stood on another section of the beach with a similar group of humans milling around with excitement. "Thanks, Tom. I'm here with college students from University of Nebraska visiting on spring break. Gabriella, describe for our viewers what you saw tonight."

"A fireball came flying toward us."

"Yeah," her friend broke in, obviously drunk and giggling. "It was huge, like a meteor. But it didn't crash into the water."

"Where'd it go?" the newsman asked.

The girls looked up at the sky, the drunk one wobbling and almost falling. "Straight up in a blast of red, gold, and blue light. It was incredible. Then it blinked out."

"Now what's interesting is we checked with astrophysicists at Rice University and there's no record of any known comet or asteroid in the area."

The newswoman back in the station smiled stiffly at the camera and shuffled some papers around in front of her. "What do they think it was, Michael?"

The man on the beach shrugged. "Their best guess is a satellite fell out of orbit, though no one can explain how it went *up* into the air rather than crashing."

"That's very interesting," the woman continued. "In other news, scientists recorded a massive submarine earthquake in the Gulf of Mexico today. Initial reports indicated a magnitude so high it couldn't be recorded. They're running more tests on the instruments but have concluded there must have been some kind of miscalculation. The tsunami from such a massive earthquake would have been astronomical."

The other newsman chuckled uneasily and tugged at his collar. "Is there a solar eclipse or something? Maybe Mercury's in retrograde."

"Or maybe Shara fucking Isador kicked some fucking ass today," Mehen retorted.

"Long live the fucking queen." Rik threaded his fingers

through mine and lifted our hands so he could kiss my knuckles. "Though I have to ask, are your Blood big enough now, my queen?"

I held my other hand out to my newest Blood. Vore stared at it for a moment, like he didn't know what to fucking do. But then he leaned forward and rubbed his face on my palm. His mouth. Lightly pressing his razor-sharp teeth into the meat of my palm.

Though he didn't draw blood. He didn't take a single bite.

I smiled and snuggled into Rik's arms. "I have the biggest, baddest Blood ever."

Though when I closed my eyes, I felt a whisper. A tug somewhere in the night. Too far away for me to tell a direction.

At least one more Blood was still out there somewhere. Waiting for me.

I'm coming, my Blood. I'll find you as soon as I can.

∽

SHARA

IN RIK'S ARMS, I DOSED LIGHTLY AS HE STRODE INTO THE RED AND blue Galveston pool—and up through my grotto.

My strength wasn't taxed. My reserves weren't strained and thin.

Though I was as grumpy as my dragon. I fucking hated early mornings. But I wanted to get home before nosy humans might see something. I didn't want to make the news again.

Plus, my arms were still fucking sore. Even though I'd healed the bites Vore and Mehen gave me, the skin was tender and pulled over the missing chunks of the underlying muscle.

:Dragon bites leave a nasty scar,: Sekh said.

:So do sphinxes, motherfucker,: Mehen retorted.

Though I did feel the ever so slight twinge of guilt in his bond. *:I guess I'm going to have to feed a lot to make sure it heals up properly.:*

:Bet,: all of my Blood swore in our bonds.

All fourteen of them. I think. Though I'd have to count them again when I wasn't so tired.

Rik grumbled. "Very funny." But then he jerked to a halt, jostling me.

I lifted my head, blinking sleepily. "What's wrong?"

"Look up."

I turned my head and looked up into the branches of my heart tree. Branches laden with roses, always fragrant and blooming, dropping petals into the hot spring beneath. Covered in thorns and spikes. Full of my blood.

I died to grow this tree.

So it shouldn't surprise me to see a white-headed blue bird staring back at me with long red tail feathers.

Tears flooded my eyes.

Thierry.

"You were supposed to fly to Esetta," I whispered, lifting my hand.

He dropped off the branch and landed on my palm.

Chirp, chirp, coo.

Love.

No matter the fucking cost.

THANK YOU FOR READING QUEEN'S CRUSADE! IF YOU'D LIKE TO read more about Sekh, Thierry, and Vore before they found Shara, their prequels are available in Queen Takes Blood Volume 2, free to newsletter subscribers. If you missed it, you can also grab the rest of the Blood prequels in Queen Takes Blood Volume 1 (free).

AUTHOR'S NOTE

So much has happened since the last time Shara graced us with her presence. So much has changed.

The ugliness of the last five years is finally behind me. I'm safe and whole and beginning my dream life on the Burkhart farm. My house is finally finished, and I moved in just after Christmas 2023. My beloved sister and father are a five-minute walk away. My adult kids are living their best lives and finding their own way.

I'm living alone for the first time in my entire life. And I love it.

Change is hard, even when it's what you desperately want and need. I have one more major change ahead of me in the next year, but I'm so excited for this new chapter of my life.

Thank you for your patience waiting on Shara to return. She had to lay low until everything was over, and coaxing her back out took longer than I expected. I gave myself extra time to make sure she's as perfect as possible.

I'm not going to set up pre-orders before the book is finished again. While I love the thrill of hitting a tight deadline,

I love my stories more. I never want any of my books to feel rushed or incomplete.

Plus, making myself wait before hitting publish means you got more sex scenes and another 12,000 bonus words I decided to add. Win win, right?

What's next for Shara and Their Vampire Queen?

I'm already working on Shara's next book, tentatively titled *Queen's Alliance*. I said in a Zoom party that the next book would be *Queen's Sacrifice*, but that's not Shara's book. It's Esetta's. She played the queen's sacrifice to put Guillaume on Shara's board.

The catch: I don't think I can finish *Queen's Alliance* without at least Karmen's and Helayna's stories being finished. Possibly also Kora's. I've not been successful writing multiple books at the same time in the past, but I have a feeling I'll be working on all the queens' threads until someone talks the loudest and I can finish it.

Yes, Xochitl and Belladonna will also be important but I think they're still a bit further down the road.

I'll post all the latest news in the Triune, in my newsletter, and on Patreon, where you can follow along with everything I'm working on.

Thank you for going on this journey with me and for taking Shara into your hearts. I know it's frustrating for readers when books are delayed, so I appreciate each and every one of you who stuck with me.

Long live House Isador!

Joely

ABOUT THE AUTHOR

Shop for book merchandise, sign up for Joely's newsletter, and join the Triune for all of Joely's latest book news, fun giveaways, and upcoming projects! If you'd like to read along as she writes, Joely posts regular excerpts on Patreon.